THE BELL WITCHES

THE BELL WITCHES

LINDSEY KELK

MAGPIE

Magpie Books
An imprint of HarperCollins*Publishers* Ltd
1 London Bridge Street
London SE1 9GF

www.harpercollins.co.uk

HarperCollins*Publishers*
Macken House,
39/40 Mayor Street Upper,
Dublin 1
D01 C9W8
Ireland

First published by HarperCollins*Publishers* Ltd 2024

2

ISBN: 978-0-00-860982-5 (HB)
ISBN: 978-0-00-860983-2 (TPB)

Typeset in Sabon by Palimpsest Book Production Ltd, Falkirk, Stirlingshire

Printed and bound in the UK using 100% Renewable Electricity
at CPI Group (UK) Ltd

MIX
Paper | Supporting
responsible forestry
FSC
www.fsc.org
FSC™ C007454

This book contains FSC™ certified paper and other controlled sources
to ensure responsible forest management.

For more information visit: www.harpercollins.co.uk/green

For Willow, Bonnie, Nancy and Samantha,
please accept my offering.

And for you, *wilcuma* . . .

2. WYN'S SUMMER SCHOOL

3. THE BENJAMIN WILSON HOUSE

7. LAFAYETTE SQUARE

1. BELL HOUSE

5. THE OLDE PINK HOUSE

4. LEOPOLD'S ICE CREAM

6. COLONIAL PARK CEMETERY

SAVANNAH RIVER

E. BAY ST

NORTH HISTORIC DISTRICT

E. OGLETHORPE AVE

E. LIBERTY ST

BROAD ST

EAST ST

PRICE ST

BEACH INSTITUTE

GASTON ST

SAVANNAH

Bonaventure Cemetery

Tybee Island

Wormsloe State Historic Site

SAVANNAH
& ITS ENVIRONS

There is always a before and an after, that's what she told me.

Before my father died, before I came to Savannah, before we all learned the truth about who I really was.

Before was easy. After was more complicated.

Before Bell House.

Before Wyn.

Before my grandmother.

After the wolf.

Before I fell in love. After I took a life.

There is *always* a before and an after.

Before

Chapter One

The first thing that hit me was the heat.

My dad always used to say there was nothing like a southern summer. He'd sit on the couch, sipping on a glass of lemonade so sweet just looking at it made my teeth ache, talking about days when the air got so thick you could taste it and the only thing that could chase it away was a good old-fashioned thunderstorm. But no matter how many times he'd warned me, nothing could have prepared me for the real thing.

I shuffled out of the backseat of the car and stepped onto the sidewalk, the heavy humidity pressing down on me, and peeled my already damp hair away from my forehead. Here I was at last: Savannah, Georgia, the town where my dad was born and raised. And now he was dead and buried in a completely different country, three thousand miles away.

'Emily?'

A sweet, sing-song voice called my name from the other side of the car.

'You OK?'

Ashley, the pretty young woman with a long brown braid

I'd met yesterday, examined me with a furrowed brow. I nodded my head even though I was not OK at all. How could I be?

'Here we are, home sweet home,' she said, hitching her purse up onto her shoulder as the driver took my single suitcase from the trunk. 'What do you think?'

Staring up at the building behind her, I felt my mouth fall open.

'This is home?' I said, unable to process the concept. 'You live here?'

'I do,' she replied. 'Don't get excited, it's just a house.'

But calling this place 'just a house' was like calling a Formula One Ferrari 'just a car'. Sure, it had four wheels and an engine but it was not the same thing at all. The elegant white building in front of me was a work of art. It sat apart from its neighbours, as though too grand to be associated with such riffraff, and it was taller than the other buildings, the gentle grey roof reaching higher into the sky and lined with decorative but dangerous-looking spikes. As if a pigeon would dare to land on such grandeur. Each large sparkling window shone in the early evening light, all of them too high up from the street to offer anything other than the most tantalizing tease of what might be inside.

'I think "house" is underselling it,' I told her, pulling the straps of my backpack tight against my shoulders. 'Are you sure this isn't a hotel? Or a museum?'

She chuckled at that.

'Definitely ain't a hotel but it sure does feel like a museum sometimes. There's a lot of history inside those four walls.'

An iron gate swung open on well-oiled hinges, welcoming me into a garden full of fragrant flowers and blossoming trees as I followed slowly up a set of stone steps to a pair of imposing double doors. Dark wood gleaming against the powdery white walls. Between my jetlag and the humid evening air, my vision was soft around the edges. I felt like I was in a dream.

'Welcome to Bell House,' Ashley declared, holding the front door open and ushering me inside. 'Let's go meet your grandmother.'

If at all possible, the inside of the house was even more grand than the outside. I hovered by the door, one foot inside and one foot outside, as my tired eyes took in the glossy floors of the foyer, the imposing curved staircase and each immaculate piece of antique furniture. The walls glowed a soft sage green and when I looked more closely, I saw the silk wallcoverings had been painted with twisting vines that crept up and down, from floor to ceiling. Sleeping Beauty's castle through an Instagram filter.

'It's amazing,' I breathed as I stepped fully inside, hands still welded to my backpack, afraid to touch a thing. 'But I can't imagine anyone actually living here.'

Ashley replied with a half smile that didn't quite reach her eyes. 'And I can't imagine living anyplace else.'

'Why would you ever want to?' asked another voice. 'When we have our own little slice of heaven right here.'

One day earlier, when I opened the front door of our cottage in Wales, and laid eyes on Ashley for the first time, I knew right away that we were related. The dimple my dad hid underneath his beard was on display in her left cheek, her mouth quirked up at one side before she committed to a full grin the same way he did, and most noticeable of all, she and I shared the exact same shade of emerald green eyes. We didn't need all the paperwork she presented to Anwen, the family friend I'd been staying with since Dad's accident. What were stamps and seals and protocols when the family resemblance was as clear as day? And it wasn't just the physical likeness. While Ashley sat in our living room, explaining how she was my aunt, my dad's estranged younger sister I knew nothing about, and that I had a still-living grandmother waiting for me across the ocean, there was a pull in my bones I couldn't explain. Something in me whispered that she was telling the truth. It was the kind of confirmation you could never get from a piece of paper.

And now, as a tall, elegant older woman descended the staircase, the same promise pulsed through my veins. She was my blood, or I was hers. We were the same. Only this time instead of the altered reflection of my dad I'd seen in Ashley, I saw myself smiling back at me. Our hair was different, hers was red where mine was brown, but aside from that, it was as though someone had taken all my awkward facial features – my wide-set eyes and too broad mouth – and reassembled them beautifully, balancing it all out with elegance and grace. Looking at her was like staring into the world's kindest funhouse mirror. Could this really be my grandmother?

'I'm Emily,' I said, fumbling for the right words and finding only the facts. 'Paul's daughter.'

Her arms were around me before I could finish my sentence and unbidden tears filled my eyes at once. She smelled like flowers and herbs and the summer sun, and underneath all that, there was something warm, more familiar. She smelled like my dad.

Eventually she released me, cupping my face in her hands, and I could see she was crying too.

'Any fool could see it,' she whispered, her own emerald-green eyes rimmed red. 'Oh my goodness, my granddaughter. I can't tell you how happy I am to have you home.'

Ashley yawned loudly, breaking the silence as I stared back, mesmerized by this beautiful woman and already missing the warmth of her hug. Dad wasn't much of a hugger, more a solid pat on the shoulder kind of a guy. I had never felt so confused in my life.

'Catherine James Bell, may I present Miss Emily Caroline James,' my aunt said in a ceremonious voice. 'Miss Emily Caroline James, this is Catherine James Bell. My mother and your grandmother.'

'You look too young to be a grandmother,' I blurted out quickly, too tired to mind my manners.

Her skin was porcelain pale and translucent, without a single visible blemish or line, and she wore her long red hair pulled back in a soft French pleat with not one grey strand in sight. There was no way she was old enough to have a sixteen-year-old granddaughter.

Catherine laughed loudly as she wrapped her arm around my shoulders, shepherding me into the parlour.

'Oh, I like you already,' she said, leaning her head against mine. 'Ashley, darling, how was the flight?'

'Awful, thanks for asking.'

My aunt peeled off her cardigan and cast it over the high back of a blue and white chair before rolling up her shirtsleeves. 'How do we feel about tea?'

'Sounds divine, and perhaps a little snack?' Catherine looked down at me kindly, one questioning eyebrow raised. 'Unless you'd like something more substantial? I myself cannot stand to eat a heavy meal when the weather is so ugly but you're still a growing girl. We can't have you going hungry.'

'A snack sounds good,' I mumbled, still struggling to find my voice. 'Thank you again . . . Grandmother?'

The word lingered on the tip of my tongue as I tried it on. Nope, didn't quite fit yet.

'Why don't you call me Catherine for now,' she suggested as Ashley disappeared, leaving the two of us alone in the parlour. 'And no more thank yous, that's an order. There's no need to thank family for being family.'

I bit my dry, chapped lower lip as she guided me to sit on

9

a powder blue loveseat before dropping neatly onto the couch opposite. Catherine was so perfectly put together, I couldn't help but feel like a schlub in my plane-rumpled travel outfit but if she was judging me as harshly as I was judging myself, it didn't show. All I saw on her face was joy, her eyes lit up with delight and staring at me like I was the eighth wonder of the world.

'We'll do a tour of the house when you've had a chance to rest.' She leaned forward and beamed at my hot, pink face. 'Oh, Emily, you really are your father's daughter, aren't you? And I would recognize those eyes anywhere.'

'The same as yours,' I replied. 'And Ashley's.'

Catherine nodded and leaned back against the couch while I shifted around in my seat. Exhausted as I was, I couldn't seem to sit still.

'Scientists might call it a dominant gene,' she said with a wink. 'But as my grandmother would have said, there's simply no denying a Bell.'

Only I wasn't a Bell. Or at least I hadn't known I was until Ashley showed up twenty-four hours earlier. Yesterday, I was Emily Caroline James, sixteen-year-old daughter of Paul and Angelica James, the father who died when his car smashed into a tree during a springtime storm two months ago, and the mother I lost when I was just a baby. Yesterday, I was at home in Wales, an orphan. Now I was in Savannah, gazing into the face of a dead woman.

Chapter Two

'It's hard to know where to begin, isn't it?' Catherine said, reading my mind, or at least the look on my face. 'You must have a lot of questions.'

'A few.'

The silken wallpaper in the parlour was painted, just like the walls in the foyer, but in here, the artist had chosen a gentle blue over sage green with white clouds overhead and willowy trees surrounding us on all four walls. Their branches were full of songbirds and curled carefully around the arched sash windows at the front of the house. I almost expected to look down and see the forest floor beneath my feet instead of polished floorboards, it was so realistic. Above the ornate marble fireplace at the heart of the room was a huge mirror that threatened me with my own tired and sweaty reflection, and two heavy-looking gold candlesticks sat on either end of the mantle. As someone who grew up playing a lot of board games, they made me uneasy. Miss James in the parlour with the candlestick. I'd never been any good at that game.

'When they came to tell me what had happened to your father, my heart was torn in two.'

I looked back at Catherine to see a single tear sliding over her high cheekbone. 'It felt like I would die too. There has never been a pain like it.'

Wedging my hands tightly under my thighs, I tried not to fidget. She looked devastated, truly heartbroken, but if she loved my dad so much, why had he raised me to believe both of his parents were dead?

'You wouldn't believe the hoops they had me jump through to bring you home,' she went on, wiping the tear away only for another to take its place. 'The whole system is a disgrace. Forms on top of forms on top of forms, all of them keeping us apart for far too long. I should have been by your side the moment the accident occurred. I should have been there to bury my son.'

'It's not your fault.'

I thought of all the paperwork I'd seen passed around over the last few weeks, my name, dad's name, doctors, dates, addresses. Who knew death required so much admin? I paused before speaking again, a question she had to know was coming lingering on the tip of my tongue.

'Catherine,' I began, still not sure which words to reach for. 'May I ask you something?'

'Anything,' she replied right away.

I rolled my lips against each other, stalling. It wasn't going to be an easy thing to say and I imagined an even more difficult thing to hear. There was no other way to phrase it but the facts.

'My dad told me you were dead.' I croaked out the words and she winced as though I had struck her. 'Why would he do that?'

Before Catherine could reply, Ashley sailed back into the room, carrying an enormous silver tray.

'OK, who's hungry?' she asked cheerfully, carefully setting

it down on a marble coffee table and unloading the contents; plates groaning with cookies, small sandwiches, fresh fruit and a gleaming pitcher of iced tea. When she said tea, I automatically thought she meant hot tea. It was another reminder that I was really in the south.

'If y'all can manage without me, I'd like to go take a bath,' she said with an exaggerated shiver. 'Wash all that nasty airplane off me.'

She looked to Catherine, who gave an approving nod, and I could almost see the relief roll off her shoulders. She was more anxious to leave than she wanted us to know. Holding the silver tray against her chest like a shield, Ashley slipped out of the room and closed the door behind her with a quiet click.

'When the weather is hot like this, tea is simply all I can tolerate,' Catherine said as she poured two glasses from the pitcher before pushing a silver sugar bowl towards me. I shook my head and watched on as she dumped several heaped teaspoons into her glass, just the way Dad used to take it. 'I must confess, I may not know all that much about climate change and such but I do know the summer is creeping in earlier and earlier. Ninety degrees in May? I don't think so.'

'It sure is hot out there.' I reached for a cookie as my stomach growled menacingly under my shirt. Was she going to answer my question? I didn't know if I had the courage to ask it again. 'It was raining when we left Wales.'

'Look at us, talking about the weather like a couple of real Brits,' she clucked happily. 'Tell me, how did you like living over there?'

Apparently, she was not.

'It was nice. Quiet. We were kind of out in the middle of nowhere. Dad's friend, Anwen, rented us a cottage on her farm so most of our neighbours were sheep.'

'So are mine.' Catherine gave me a quick, small smile before taking a thoughtful sip of her tea. 'I understand you travelled around a lot for your father's research?'

'We did, around Europe mostly. We lived in New Zealand for a while when I was very young but I don't really remember it all that well.'

I reached for another cookie and my stomach growled happily. They were beyond delicious.

'My son, the historian,' she said proudly. 'I should have guessed he'd end up in academia. Paul was always asking questions, always ready to learn. What about you, Emily, are you smart like your daddy? Do you do well in school?'

'Because we travelled so much, I mostly did homeschool but I already took my exams and passed them all,' I replied, an unexpected but vehement need to impress her appearing out of nowhere. 'I took them early.'

'But of course you did!' She pressed her hands to her heart and gasped. 'My granddaughter, as smart as she is beautiful.'

I froze, no idea how to respond. No one had ever called me beautiful before.

Catherine reached across the space between us to hold my warm, clammy hand in her cool dry one.

'Emily,' she said. 'I want the two of us to start off on the right foot, no secrets.'

'No secrets,' I repeated, my mouth suddenly dry. 'I'd like that.'

'Let's start with what you already know.' She clutched my hand in hers and moved closer to me. 'What did your daddy tell you about your family?'

I looked down and touched the toes of my shoes together as I realized this wasn't going to be simple for either of us. Who would feel good about your son pretending you were dead? Sometimes, when I asked about our family, he would ruffle my hair and say I was all the family he needed. More often than not, he avoided the subject altogether. If I pushed too hard, his eyes would glaze over and he'd tell me it was too painful to talk about. Eventually, I stopped asking, resigned to the fact I would never have grandparents or aunts, uncles and cousins like all my friends. It would always be just the two of us.

Until it was just me.

'He said we didn't have any living relatives,' I said, unable to look her in the eye. 'He said he grew up here in Savannah, met my mom in college then moved to New Zealand after she died.' I hesitated and cleared my throat. 'He told me all my grandparents passed away before I was born.'

'All except one,' Catherine said softly. 'He never mentioned Ashley?'

I shook my head. 'I didn't know he'd ever had a sister until yesterday.'

The loving expression on her face faltered and the edges of her smile flickered into something so sad. My dad never lied. He was honest to the point of bluntness, never once lying about what had happened to my missing goldfish and always kindly correcting me when I was wrong. How could he have lied about something so huge for so long? And more to the point, the question I'd been asking myself ever since Ashley showed up on my doorstep – *why* would he lie in the first place?

Catherine let go of my hand and began twisting a large aquamarine ring around and around on the third finger of her left hand, neatly groomed eyebrows creasing together as she processed the information.

'I cannot begin to imagine how you must be feeling right now,' she said, her forefinger still resting on the ring. 'But please don't be mad at your daddy. Everything that happened was my fault. He may have lied to you but he believed he had good reason and back then, once Paul's mind was made up, there was no changing it.'

I tucked my hair behind my ears, a puff of agreement escaping my lips. 'He could be pretty stubborn.'

'Stubborn and impulsive, and that's a difficult mix. I should know, he got it from me,' she replied with a knowing smile. 'The short version of the story is, we had an argument over our differing beliefs, neither of us were prepared to compromise at the time and so he left. I believed he would return home but I was wrong and I have never, ever forgiven myself for losing him over something so foolish. Now he's truly gone forever.'

A sob caught in her throat and before I knew it, I was sitting beside her on the sofa, holding her hand and consoling her as though I'd known her all my life.

'Families fall apart over the most stupid of things,' she said, her voice trembling and fierce at the same time. 'Maybe I can't make things right with your daddy but I can damn well take care of his little girl. I won't make the same mistakes twice, Emily. If you'll let me try, I would like to be a true grandmother to you. We could be a real family.'

A real family. The one thing I'd never had. The one thing I'd always wanted. I gazed into Catherine's eyes and saw all the things I'd dreamt of gazing back. Whatever happened between her and my dad happened a long time ago and it seemed to me that she'd suffered enough. She deserved a second chance. We both did.

'I'd like that,' I told her, falling into another warm hug as exhaustion hit me like a tidal wave.

'Look at me, talking your ear off when you should be resting.' Catherine brushed my hair away from my face, her eyes full of love. 'Emily James, you look worn slap out. We need to get you upstairs to bed.'

'Really, I'm fine,' I protested but when she stood, I struggled to do the same. Five minutes ago, I was so full of energy, I could barely sit still but suddenly, my legs were useless lumps of lead.

With a protective arm around my shoulders, she led me out the parlour and up the grand curving staircase, each step like climbing a mountain. When we finally reached the summit, she turned the brass knob on a white-painted door and bustled me through it.

'Right now, you're going to rest,' she ordered. 'And first thing tomorrow, you are going to tell me everything there is to know about you.'

'That won't take long.' I chased my words with a loud yawn. 'We can probably cover it over a cup of tea.'

'I don't believe that for one second. You look like a girl with a thousand stories to tell and I can't wait to listen to each and every one of them.'

Everything Catherine said sounded like singing. Each word held hands with the last as it slipped out in her sweet, soft southern drawl. I could have listened to her talk forever.

'This will be your room,' she said with tenderness. 'I hope you like it.'

My tired eyes popped open as I took in my new surroundings. The cottage in Wales might have been small and dark but it was still an improvement on most of the university housing we'd lived in over the years. This was something else entirely. There was a four-poster bed in the middle of the room, smothered in blankets and quilts that were surely too heavy for the balmy summer evening, and piled high with so many pillows, I wasn't sure how I was supposed to fit in the bed alongside them. The floorboards were covered in antique rugs and across from where I stood was a real, actual, working fireplace, and the best part of all, four towering bookcases, stretching from the floor to the ceiling. Every shelf was crammed so full with books you couldn't have slid as much as a single piece of paper between them. I scanned the spines, all of them broken and well-loved, and felt the happiness on my face melt away.

'This was my dad's room,' I said, and Catherine nodded. Dad always had a book within arm's reach and never left home without at least two, one for fun and one for work. It was a habit I was happy to have inherited.

'After they were married, your parents took the larger suite upstairs but this is where your daddy grew up. My boy just loved to sit in the window seat and read, gazing out onto the square and dreaming his big dreams. Always had his nose in a book.' She trailed one finger down the broken spines of a bunch of paperbacks, stopping on a beat-up copy of a Stephen King classic before recovering herself. 'There's a new mattress, of course, and all the pillows and linens are new, but everything else is an antique. Some of these pieces have been in our family for more than two hundred years.'

'It's incredible.' I imagined all of the people who might have sat at the desk beside the window, composing their thoughts before me. All of my ancestors.

'Emily?'

'Yes?' I turned back to look at my grandmother as she pulled out the Stephen King book and held it to her chest. There was a look on her face I couldn't quite read, somewhere between happy, sad and afraid, or maybe all three at once.

'Was Paul happy?' she asked, her expression settling on something like hope.

'I think so,' I replied honestly. 'He laughed a lot and he loved his work. The last few months, he was kind of quiet but that's how he got when he was working on a new project, super focused, you know? The only time he seemed sad was when he talked about my mom.'

Catherine slipped the book back in with the others, closing

her eyes and breathing in deeply before she reset herself with a short, sharp clap that made me jump.

'Even in this beastly weather, a cup of hot tea always helps me to relax before bed,' she said brightly, her mood completely changed. 'Let me go boil up some water while you settle in.'

'That sounds nice, thank you.' I offered her a grateful smile as I spotted my pyjamas folded neatly on the bed. Someone had already opened and emptied my suitcase. Only the backpack was untouched, still zipped up and bulging with all my essential items, tucked away down the side of the desk.

'I'll be right back,' she promised as she retreated towards the hallway. 'Holler if you need me.'

My dad used to say the exact same thing.

The door closed behind her and I ran my hand along the silky blue walls, tracing out one of the dozens of hand-painted birds as I drifted across the room, ending up at the window seat. I climbed up and leaned in, my face so close to the glass, I could see the evidence of my every exhalation in front of me. It was almost a relief to know I was still breathing. None of this felt real.

On the other side of the glass was my very own wrought-iron balcony and I wondered if it was safe to stand on. It looked sturdy enough but I wouldn't be taking any chances tonight. Instead, I raised the sash window and poked my head out to breathe in the steamy Savannah evening. Bell House sat on the edge of a square, a little green park, packed with trees and people, a beautiful fountain at its heart. There was bird song and laughter on the air and the happy noises smoothed the edges of my sharper thoughts. Sliding my fingers inside the collar of my T-shirt, I felt for my most precious possession. My mother's gold locket. I never took it off. Wherever I went, the locket came with me, the one remaining constant in my life. I closed my hand around the cool metal, shut my eyes and took what I hoped would be a steadying breath. It didn't help. I still felt like I was living in a fantasy.

When I opened my eyes again, he was the first thing I saw.

Right on the edge of the square, leaning against the trunk of a very tall tree, I saw a boy, hands deep in his pockets, a complicated frown on his face. His hair was wavy like mine but shorter and wilder, a deep dark ash, while his skin was tanned, golden sunshine to my spilt milk. My unruly, jetlagged mind began to wander, imagining what colour his eyes might be, how soft was his skin, how firm were his lips. Then I saw it. Without warning, the room whooshed away from me, as though I'd been yanked backwards, and everything went black. I reached out for something to hold onto as the real world was replaced by a flash of his lips on mine, my hands in his hair, my back against the oak tree and our bodies pressed so close together I could feel the warmth of his skin burning through his clothes. It was quick; just half a heartbeat passed before my eyes snapped open and I was back in my room, but the vision felt so real I had to reach for the window frame to steady myself. Just the thought of touching this stranger was enough to set sparks dancing up and down my skin. Still bracing myself, I swallowed hard and glanced back down into the square. His eyes looked directly into mine, the corners of his mouth lifted into a crooked smile that filled his handsome face and my entire body went up in flames. I pulled away from the window, embarrassed, as though he had somehow seen the same thing I had.

'What was that?' I asked myself, pushing away the image of the two of us entwined underneath the oak tree. In sixteen years and eleven months, I had kissed exactly one person, my friend Gianni, and since he immediately burst into tears and ran away right after it happened, I wasn't sure it counted. All my romantic experience came from my Kindle which meant that, theoretically, I would absolutely know what to do if I ever met a hot orc but had no idea what to do with an actual, real-life human boy. Tensing every muscle in my body, I held my breath and turned back to the window.

He was gone.

While waiting for my heart to skitter into its usual rhythm, I turned back to the vast room, studying every inch, from the shiny floorboards to the decorative patterns that ran around the edge of the ceiling. Everything about the room was extravagant; opulent fabrics, exquisite furniture, it positively reeked of money, and my dad, who never had much of anything, had walked away from it all.

Dragging my backpack over to the bed, I heaved us both onto the mattress and walked my fingertips up the embroidered bedspread, spiralling patterns picked out in gold thread: more leaves, more vines. When I lay down, the bed rose up to hold me, wrapping me in a comforting, secure softness. Bliss. Even the most sensitive princess in the world would have struggled to feel a brick under this mattress, let alone a pea. Sitting up, I opened my backpack and took out the silver photo frame inside, unfolding the three connected apertures and placing it carefully on my bedside table. One side of the frame held a photo of my mom, tall and blonde and beautiful, with an open, laughing smile and enormous blue eyes. On the other side of the frame, I saw my dad, her opposite, dark hair, dark eyes, playful smirk. All our other pictures and mementos were lost years ago in one of our moves, making this all the more important. I used to stare at it for hours, wishing I had blonde hair like hers, wondering where my green eyes came from. Now I knew.

In the centre frame was a close-up picture of the two of them wearing matching black and gold sweaters, standing in front of a tree. My dad's arms were wrapped tightly around my mom and both of them were grinning like they'd solved world peace, won the lottery and scored face-value Taylor Swift tickets all on the same day. Had he come back to this room after that photo was taken? He must have.

Even before the accident that made me an orphan, I'd always felt like an outsider. Life with my dad was exciting and I had loved it, travelling, experiencing different cultures, meeting different people, but there was a downside to living a life so unmoored. I was the perennial new kid, always awkward, never quite fitting in. I had a dozen friends in a dozen countries but no one who really knew me. And no matter how wonderful a parent my dad might have been, it wasn't the same as having a real family. After he died, it was even more apparent. Not quite seventeen and all alone, no one I belonged to and nowhere to go.

I shuffled my backpack under the bed and rolled over on my side to stare at the photos of my parents. Maybe things would be different now. If Catherine meant what she said, I might have a home instead of a bed and a backpack. We could help each other heal, we could be a family.

I might finally have found a place where I belonged.

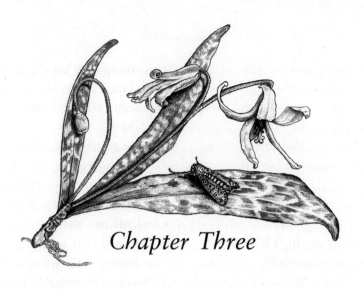

Chapter Three

'Savannah is a city of squares. There were twenty-four origin-ally, twenty-two remain today.' Catherine opened the gate onto the sidewalk early the next morning, the sun already high and blinding in the sky. 'Bell House sits on the east side of Lafayette Square. It was built in 1833 by your ancestors, Emma Bell and her husband, Spencer Paul Gordon, both descended from two of the very first families to settle here in 1733.'

I held a hand over my eyes to get a better look at the building, squinting against the brightness. Did I even own sunglasses? I needed them. Bell House was even more impressive in the morning light, shining and stately, all her windows sparkling and spotlessly clean. I felt like a stray dog Catherine had just picked up from the pound by comparison.

'Today, it is one of the oldest homes in the city to remain a private residence,' my grandmother went on proudly. 'Most others were destroyed one way or another. The rest were turned into restaurants, hotels or museums.'

'Our family has lived in the same house for two hundred years?' I was stunned. 'I've never lived anywhere longer than twelve months.'

Catherine gave me an affectionate nudge as she drew me away from her home.

'That's about to change. Bell House is part of your legacy, she'll belong to you one day.'

That morning, I had woken up fully refreshed after the best night's sleep since Dad's accident. No nightmares, no panic attacks, no staring at the ceiling wondering what would happen to me now he was gone. Just twelve hours of sweet oblivion. Catherine was right, hot tea before bed really did the trick, it knocked me right out and I didn't stir from the moment I closed my eyes until Ashley knocked on my door to check I was still alive. If she hadn't, I might have still been in that deep, dreamless sleep. I'd hoped we would spend the morning together just the two of us, but as soon as Ashley reported I was awake, Catherine had me up, dressed and out the door for a tour of the neighbourhood. My millions of questions would have to wait. But it didn't matter. As long as I was with her, I was happy. We had the rest of our lives to get to know each other.

'Your locket is so pretty,' she remarked, holding up a hand in greeting to a man walking his dog on the other side of the street. Everyone seemed to know her and she seemed to know everyone. 'It is so familiar but I can't quite place it.'

I reached for the necklace, the little gold orb resting against my black T-shirt. 'It belonged to my mom. I love it but the lock is broken, it doesn't open.'

Catherine brightened with recognition.

'That's how I know it. What a lovely heirloom for you to remember her by. Angelica really was the most charming woman, she had impeccable style for someone so young. Your mother had gumption.'

'I'd love to know more about her,' I said, latching on to her every word and storing them safely away. 'Dad hardly ever talked about her.'

We walked slowly, the quiet between us filled with the everyday sounds of people passing through the square. The town really was beautiful: everywhere you looked there was an explosion of red, pink and purple flowers, elegant townhouses and what seemed like a forest full of trees, picked up and planted in the middle of town. It was easy to imagine you were walking through a fairytale. My father never had anything good to say about his hometown, always complaining it was too hot, too small, too close-minded. If I didn't know for a fact I was actually in Savannah, I never would have guessed it from the things he'd told me. I could hardly believe he was talking about the same place.

'When my husband passed, it was very hard on me,' Catherine said eventually, speaking slowly as we crossed a one-way street, leaving Lafayette Square behind. 'He was all I could think of but at the same time, I could not bear to speak his name. Losing your mother was even more difficult for Paul, so young and all alone with a new baby.'

'Then why leave?' I said. 'How could an argument be so bad he packed up and never came back?'

An excited troop of Girl Guides crossed our path, two by two, holding hands and swinging their arms back and forth between them as they went. Catherine glanced down at her delicate gold watch and frowned.

'I wish there was time to explain right now but I'm already late,' she replied, her face etched with regret. 'I don't know about you but I cannot abide lateness. My dear friend, Virginia Powell, hasn't been well and I promised I would call in on her this morning.'

'Yes, totally, I'm so sorry.' Guilt sank in my stomach like a stone. Of course she had other things going on, Catherine's entire world hadn't stopped because I'd appeared on the doorstep. 'I hope she's OK?'

'Oh, she will be. Virginia always was a fragile little thing, her ailments come and go. I sent over an old family remedy yesterday so I'm hopeful she's feeling fully restored today.' Her smile returned and she brightened at the thought. 'You know, her family has been here just as long as ours, Ginny and I have known each other all our lives. The Powells and the Bells are Savannah royalty.'

It was a concept I couldn't even begin to comprehend. Imagine having a friend in your life for decades. Even my longest friendships never lasted more than a couple of years. Dad was firmly against social media and it was hard to convince anyone to keep up an old-fashioned pen-pal relationship, moving around the way we did, people seemed to fade out of my life as quickly as they arrived. Catherine slipped her arm through mine as we strolled on and, just like that, all the good mornings meant for her were also extended to me. I felt a flush of pride and pulled my shoulders back, standing a little taller by her side.

'Now tell me, how do you like Lafayette Square?' she asked, drawing me in closer. 'I know I'm biased but I do believe we live on the most beautiful square in the city. Many people are partial to Monterey but what can really compare with a cathedral? And I much prefer our fountain to the Pulaski monument.'

'Pulaski?' I repeated, not familiar with the name.

'Casimir Pulaski? He was a hero in the revolutionary war.'

I shook my head and she gave a gentle tut.

'A blindspot in your education that we can surely correct,' she replied. 'But nothing to worry about. There are so many monuments around town, it will take some time to learn all of them, and they're almost always those absurd phallic things, as if we didn't know.'

We turned a corner onto another gorgeous square, tall houses, tall trees, lots and lots of people. It was like looping through a movie set, the same but different.

'That's another problem with Monterey Square,' Catherine commented as a group of camera-wielding tourists sprinted in front of us. I watched them race up to a large red-brick house and start snapping away. 'I do not care for all the ghouls who come to ogle at Jim's house.'

'What's so special about Jim's house?'

It was big and grand, pretty enough, but very square and not nearly as elegant or impressive as Bell House.

'The Mercer-Williams house is infamous in Savannah,' she replied, the gleeful promise of gossip in her voice. 'It was quite the scandal. Jim Williams, the owner, shot a boy named Danny Hansford in the study. Killed him. Jim claimed self-defence but most of us believed it was a crime of passion. That's just my opinion of course, the courts had another.'

There were so many people, all straining to get the best selfie outside the murder house, it made my stomach turn. I'd never been a fan of the creepy or macabre. Horror stories were not my thing.

'Did you know him?' I asked, watching someone compare a black and white photo on their phone with the house in front of them.

'Jim? Oh yes.' Catherine nodded readily. 'We were old friends. He threw the best parties in the county. Until they took him away, that is.'

Her tone was so breezy, I wasn't sure I'd heard her right.

'There was a very big court case, someone wrote a book about it naturally. They even made a movie. Filmed it right there in the house if you can believe it, so tasteless.' She sighed and shook her head. 'Jim was acquitted in the end as rich men so often are. But it didn't do him any good, he died of a heart attack just a few months later.'

'I guess karma doesn't care if you're rich or not,' I said, feeling a little queasy. 'It gets you in the end.'

My grandmother smirked in agreement. 'Justice is always served one way or another.'

She pointed towards the downstairs windows on the left side of the house. 'People say if you pass by Mercer House at the stroke of midnight on the first of May, you'll see Danny's ghost enter the house, looking for Jim.'

'Sounds like something they made up to bring in the tourists,' I said as I held my locket tightly in my fist. 'There's no such thing as ghosts.'

'You're in the wrong town if you believe that,' Catherine replied, laughing at my ashen face. 'Savannah is one of the most haunted cities in the world. But you needn't worry, Emily. As long as you're with me, you've nothing to fear from the dead or the living.'

'And if I'm not with you?'

We stopped right in the middle of the street and all the oncoming traffic slowed to a standstill as my grandmother placed her hands on either side of my face, oblivious to the chaos around us.

'Wherever you are and whomever you are with, always remember this,' she said, green eyes boring into my own. 'You are a Bell. Nothing and no one can hurt you now.'

And even though I knew she meant to be reassuring, I couldn't help but think her words sounded like a threat.

Chapter Four

Virginia Powell's home on Madison Square wasn't nearly as big as Bell House but it was still impressive and fancy enough to stun me into silence. A housekeeper answered when we rang the bell, ushering us inside right away. She directed Catherine straight upstairs and sent me to the parlour where I perched on the edge of a hard, high-backed loveseat, keeping my hands to myself. Whoever had designed this room was not concerned with making people feel at home. The walls were painted a stark white, ready to show up any and all fingerprints, and every carefully displayed object in the room just about screamed 'do not touch'. It was all so breakable. The stray dog feeling wandered back into my head and I half wished Catherine had left me tied to the railings outside.

'And what do we have here?'

Standing in the doorway was a girl. She looked like she was about my age with a puff of corkscrew curls that surrounded her like a halo and wide laughing eyes that filled her heart-shaped face. The neon pink of her outfit set off her clear brown skin and I couldn't tell if I was more intimidated or obsessed. Without knowing a single thing about this girl, I was one hundred per cent certain she was one hundred per cent cooler than me.

'As I live and breathe,' she declared, crossing the room with an easy grace I couldn't even dream of. She definitely lived here. 'If it ain't the legendary missing Bell baby.'

'Also known as Emily,' I said, jumping up to my feet. I stuck out my hand, feeling more awkward than ever. 'Most people call me Em. Nice to meet you.'

'Lydia Powell.' She took my hand and shook it firmly, dipping into a low curtsey. Was I supposed to reciprocate? I had no idea. 'Pleased to finally meet you too, it's only taken sixteen years. You know you're the talk of the town, right? How does it feel to be a local celebrity?'

When she let go of my hand, I wrapped my arms around myself to make myself as small as possible.

'Not great?'

Lydia hacked out a laugh and grinned.

'I'm sorry, it must be strange for you,' she said, fluffing out her curls. 'I can't remember a time when I didn't know all about Miss Catherine's long-lost son and his little baby girl. Weird to think of you all grown up, you're always a baby in the stories.'

'It's weird to think anyone would be telling stories about me at all,' I told her, looking away out the window as my face flamed.

Over the top of her neon-pink bike shorts and matching crop top, she wore an oversized white men's shirt that had been embroidered with delicate flowers in blue, silver and gold. Her chunky white sneakers gleamed, box fresh, and both her wrists jangled with stacks of bracelets and bangles. Everything about her looked intentional. Her clothes were put together, her hair had been styled. My clothes were just clothes and my hair was just there, no thought had gone into any of it. It was all I could do not to fall on the floor and beg her to teach me her ways.

'You sure do look like your grandmother,' she said with a low, appraising whistle. 'All except for the hair anyways. Looks like a Bell, talks like a Brit, what a killer combo. You're going to slay out here, Em.'

'Slaying is not on the agenda,' I assured her, sneaking a sideways glance in the mirror mounted on the wall beside the door and silently squirrelling away the comparison with Catherine. Did she really see the resemblance? 'To be honest, I'll be happy if I can get through the next few weeks without melting. Is it always this hot here?'

Flopping on the couch, Lydia patted the seat cushion, inviting me to do the same. 'It will get hotter,' she said as I took the other end of the couch, all tight and tense compared to her loose limbs. 'But don't worry too much about the heat, it's the pop-up thunderstorms you have to watch out for.'

'Summer in Savannah is not the same as summer in Wales.' My face was grim as I pulled the already damp fabric of my black T-shirt away from my skin. 'I'm going to need some new clothes. Almost everything I own was designed to keep me warm.'

'I'll take you shopping,' she offered before I'd even had a chance to ask. 'I just know your grandmother will take you to Neiman's and dress you up like a little debutante doll. In fact, if you even hear her think the word debutante, I want you to run. Call me and I will hide you. I've been dodging the conversation for a year and a half now, I'm an expert.'

I found a smile as she kicked her legs up over the back of the couch, waving her arms around in the air as she talked. Lydia was impossible not to like.

'They still do that kind of thing here?' I asked. 'Debutantes?'

'Oh yeah. And it's every bit as ridiculous as you're imagining.'

31

I tried to picture it, the two of us in fancy white gowns and matching gloves, waltzing around some ballroom with faceless dates in black tuxedos, but just the thought of it made my skin prickle and I looked down to see a red rash flushing on my forearms. Could be hives, could be heatstroke, who could say for sure? All I knew was, I wasn't the debutante ball kind.

'You are joking, right?' I swallowed hard as imaginary me tripped over her own feet at the imaginary ball much to imaginary Catherine's disappointment. 'There's no way I could be a debutante. I haven't done any of the training and I can't dance. I can barely walk in a straight line without falling over.'

'Sorry to be the bearer of bad news but it's tradition, honey, and this town is all about tradition. Especially your family,' Lydia replied ominously. 'Do you really think the missing Bell baby is going to sail back into town and *not* be presented to society? It's the only coming out party our grandmothers are interested in. *Trust me.*'

'If we could stop calling me the missing Bell baby, that would be amazing,' I said, all the blood draining out of my face.

'Lyds, why does our guest look like she's about to bolt out the door and never come back? She's been here less than five minutes and you've scared her already?'

I looked up to see we were no longer alone. A tall, gorgeous boy in a basketball jersey and baggy shorts leaned against the doorframe, grinning, and all the blood that had drained away from my face raced back up at once. His curls were cut close on the sides and looser on top, and the broader planes of his face made more room for his wide eyes and full lips, but there was no way to miss the fact he and Lydia were siblings. Aside from being absurdly good-looking, they both had the same irresistible glint in their eye that promised all kinds of good trouble.

'Em, this is my twin brother, Jackson.' Lydia waved a hand between the two of us and Jackson flashed a grin that made my stomach flutter. 'Don't look directly at him. He's like the sun, one glance and he'll blind you, you'll be ruined forever.'

'Lydia, that's a terrible thing to say about your own brother. Even if it is true,' Jackson said, full of mock outrage before he turned the full force of his charm on me. 'Miss Emily, please forgive my sister, she's the most dreadful host. What can I get y'all to drink?'

'That's me, the worst host in the whole of Georgia,' Lydia declared before hopping up to her feet, hands on her hips. 'You sit, I'll get the drinks. What'll it be? Tea? Lemonade? Arnold Palmer?'

Jackson took his sister's place on the sofa and I felt a warm flush all over that had nothing to do with the weather. I was as bad at dealing with hot guys as I was hot temperatures, maybe even worse.

'That's tea and lemonade together,' he murmured in my ear. 'It's delicious.'

'I know that,' I replied quickly, inching away as he moved closer. 'I've had an Arnold Palmer before, my dad used to make them all the time.'

Definitely worse with hot guys.

'Arnold Palmers it is.' Lydia pointed at her brother with narrowed eyes. 'Jackson, if you could not hit on her for the three minutes I'm gone, that would be amazing.'

He gave her a sharp salute then stretched his arms along the back of the sofa, lowering the force of his flirtation by a few degrees as he turned towards me.

'So, you're the long-lost granddaughter?'

'Apparently,' I confirmed, fussing with the dry ends of my ponytail. A few degrees were not enough. 'Although I only found out myself a couple of days ago.'

His forehead creased with sympathy. 'I heard about what happened to your dad. I'm sorry.'

I silently nodded my thanks.

'He really didn't tell you anything about your family?' Jackson asked. 'Nothing at all?'

'Nope.' I shook my head, my mouth a tight unhappy line. 'Not a thing.'

'And you have no idea why?'

'I wish I did,' I replied, the backs of my eyes prickling with tears as my nose started to burn.

'It must be a lot to take in,' he said, his hand resting lightly on my shoulder. 'You know, if you ever need someone to talk to—'

Lydia came crashing back through the door, three very full glasses in her hands, each of them spilling as she cantered across the parlour.

'Arnold Palmer, Arnold Palmer.' She held them out for us to take, one for me, one for Jackson, the last one for her. 'I put some rosemary in there to gussy it up a little. Let me know if you need it sweeter, I can add a little more sugar.'

'I'm sure it's perfect,' I said, squinting at the woody branch sticking out the glass as I took my first sip. It was the sweetest thing a human being had ever consumed. I could feel my teeth rotting in my head as my blood sugar levels sky-rocketed. Could a human develop diabetes in one day? We were about to find out.

'So great,' I said, struggling to swallow it down. 'Thank you.'

Lydia settled on the floor in front of the couch, stirring her drink with the sprig of rosemary and clashing brilliantly with the antique wool rug. 'What'd I miss?'

'Nothing,' I answered with a quick glance at Jackson. 'I was just asking if the two of you have lived in Savannah your whole lives.'

'Certainly have,' he said with a kind smile and I relaxed a little, knowing he wasn't going to press the subject of my oblivious upbringing. 'Savannahians born and raised but our mom got remarried last year and our stepdad—'

'*Jeremy*,' Lydia interrupted, drawing out every syllable of the name and heaping on disapproval.

'*Jeremy*,' Jackson repeated with the same obvious disdain, 'got a job in Charleston. We stayed back to finish the school year and I guess now we're staying on for the summer while Mom and—'

'*Jeremy*.'

Another gag from Lydia.

'While Mom and *Jeremy* look for a house.'

'They're living in an apartment right now,' Lydia explained. 'No room for us. I kinda think Jeremy likes it better that way.'

'I'd rather stay here anyway,' her brother added. 'Who wants to live in *Charleston?*'

They shared a look that suggested that living in Charleston was almost as terrible a concept as Jeremy himself, and moving there would be second only to relocating to the seventh circle of hell.

'Your parents are divorced?' I guessed, rattling my ice cubes against the glass to help dilute the world's sweetest drink.

'Not quite. Our bio-dad took off before we were born, we never knew him,' Lydia replied with an ease I did not see reflected in her brother's face. 'No one cares now but it was a big disgrace to our grandmother. A Powell daughter hooking up with some travelling artist who disappeared in the night, never to be seen again? Ol' Virginia took to her bed for weeks.' She scowled at her brother when he flashed her a warning look. 'What? Don't look at me like that.'

'TMI?' he replied. 'Emily didn't ask for our entire family history.'

'Whatever, Jackson,' she dismissed before chugging her drink. 'She would've found out eventually.'

'Our grandmother says we're the same age,' he said, turning back to me and ignoring his sister so easily I had to assume he'd had a lot of practice. 'You're sixteen too?'

'Yep,' I confirmed, beyond relieved that he'd asked a question before I had to come up with a response to all of that. I got the feeling Lydia didn't believe in leaving out any details, ever. 'I'll be seventeen in June.'

'We turn seventeen in August,' she said happily. 'Going into junior year in the fall and it better be here. I can't stand the thought of having to start over in—' She paused to shudder. '*Charleston*.'

'With *Jeremy*,' I added.

Lydia rolled onto her back and pointed at me while glaring meaningfully at her brother.

'She gets it. She. Gets. It.'

'What about you?' Jackson asked.

'No idea,' I replied with uncertainty. 'I already took my exams but I honestly don't know what I'll do now. College next year, I guess.'

'And she's a genius,' Lydia declared as I took a deep drink from my glass, trying to knock back as much as possible at once. I felt the granulated sugar grinding against my teeth then something else, something more solid, catching in the back of my throat.

'I've never been more jealous of a living soul,' she added with a dramatic sigh. 'Hey, are you OK?'

I coughed, one hand still holding the glass, the other flat against my chest.

'Something's stuck in my throat,' I choked out as it became harder to breathe.

'Em?' Lydia sounded panicked as I dropped my glass, a woody stick rolling back and forth inside as the liquid seeped into the rug. I dropped to my knees, spluttering for air. It was the rosemary. I was choking on a sprig of rosemary.

My eyes watered then closed as the room went black and again I felt that sudden feeling of being pulled backwards. The next thing I knew everything was quiet. I blinked to find I was still in Virginia Powell's parlour but Lydia and Jackson were gone. In their place I saw my dad, a much, much younger version of him, sitting beside a much, much younger version of Catherine. And right in front of me, just a few inches from my face, was my mother. Blonde, blue-eyed and smiling, just like in the photograph. Except she was really here, breathing, moving, alive. I reached out to touch her but my hand was tiny – small, pudgy fingers that couldn't quite close the short distance.

'She's always trying to grab my locket.' I heard my mother laugh. 'My little magpie.'

'Emily!'

The scene disappeared. I was back in the present, a small sprig of rosemary in front of me on the floor, Jackson kneeling beside me and thumping my back between my shoulder blades. My throat and eyes burned as I sat back on my heels, staring around the room, completely disorientated.

'You're OK,' Lydia exclaimed, slumping down to the floor and crossing herself. 'Thank the Lord. I'm so sorry, I didn't mean to almost unalive you.'

'Do you need some water?' Jackson asked, all his attention on me, his arms around my shoulders, holding me steady. 'Or another Arnold Palmer? *Without* rosemary?'

Whatever I'd seen still hovered at the edge of my vision but when I tried to look directly at it, the whole thing disappeared. This was the same room. The same furniture, the same art on the walls, the same antique rug. It was decorated differently, white now instead of blue, but it was one hundred per cent the same room.

'This isn't the first time I've been in this house,' I said in a scratchy, hoarse voice. 'I've been here before.'

'Probably. When you were a baby.' Jackson put his hand on my back, the spot between my shoulders throbbing from his life-saving strikes. 'You don't look well, Emily, I'm going to get Miss Catherine.'

'No, don't,' I said as fast as I could. I wiped smeared mascara off my cheeks and reached for my locket. Still there. The cool metal soothed my burning hand. My whole body was red hot. 'I'm fine. I'm great. I just need some fresh air.' I rose to my feet and floated out the parlour towards the front door, barely able to feel the floor beneath me. 'I need to be outside.'

'We'll go with you,' Lydia offered, but my hand was already on the doorknob.

'I'm OK,' I insisted, already half out the door. 'Please tell Catherine I'll find my own way home.'

I stumbled down the front steps and out onto Madison Square, leaving the Powell house and my strange vision behind.

Chapter Five

Lafayette Square was teeming with people by the time I realized that's where I was. Bell House had drawn me home like a beacon. I stood on the grass, staring up at my new old home, all proud and majestic, but I wasn't ready to go inside just yet. My mind raced with everything Lydia had told me, everything Jackson said, and whatever it was I'd seen in the strange darkness. Maybe choking on the rosemary had freed a repressed memory. My mother, right there in front of me, speaking and laughing as clear as day, but I couldn't remember something from so long ago, could I? Mom died when I was a few months old, it wasn't possible.

I walked in circles that echoed my thoughts, following a path my feet chose for me. Up and down the diagonal footpaths, weaving in and out of the trees. And there were so many trees. Oaks mostly. I'd seen plenty of those before. What I hadn't seen was the green-grey vines that hung from every branch of every oak, light and feathery and absolutely everywhere. The more I looked, the more I saw, stretching from limb to limb like cobwebs on a chandelier. They swayed above me in a non-existent breeze while the trees held steadfast, not a single leaf flickering. I peered more closely at a low-hanging strand. It looked as though it was made up of millions of tiny feathers. Would it feel so soft to touch? Curious, I reached out and a tendril grazed my skin, making every hair on my arm stand up on end.

Emily . . .

Someone was calling me. My hand flew to my locket as I whirled around to see who was behind me but there was no one I recognized. A few metres away, a couple sitting on a picnic blanket looked up, the woman's brow quirking with mild concern but she met my awkward smile with an irritated eyeroll and quickly turned back to her boyfriend.

Emily Emily Emily . . .

There it was again. I scoured the square for a familiar face, but, even though it was impossible, I knew where the voice was coming from. The vines. Today was a day for impossible things. Holding my breath, I reached for the same tendril, gasping with surprise as it curled around my fingers, wrapping itself around me like a living, breathing, thinking thing. In the same moment, a whole chorus of voices sighed my name, over and over, airy and intangible. It sounded like a radio stuck between two channels that were both playing the same song, one slightly behind the other. Slowly, the static cleared to deliver a message.

Light hides the lies; truth lives in the dark.

The words echoed around the park and as they repeated continuously, the world slowed to a stop. Birds hovered in the air, people froze mid-conversation and I saw a complete rainbow of light frozen inside the droplets of water hanging over the fountain like diamonds. Somewhere between a daze and a trance, I let the vine curl around my wrist and along my arm. My fingers tingled and a warm, powerful sensation built in my bones until . . .

'You know what they say about Spanish moss, right?'

A new voice snapped me out of the in-between space.

Either I let go of the vine or the vine let go of me, I wasn't sure which, and I stumbled forward into the old oak tree.

It was him. The boy I'd seen from my window the night before.

'What do they say about Spanish moss?' I asked, palms pressed against the tree, the vine wafting innocently on the breeze.

One corner of his mouth turned upwards and I felt my already unsteady knees weaken.

'It ain't Spanish and it ain't moss.'

He looked at me and I looked at him and all of Savannah could have gone up in flames without me noticing. There was nothing in this world except for us. The stranger pushed his wavy ash-coloured hair back and his uneven half-smile grew until it took over his whole face. It was his eyes that pinned me to the spot. When his gaze crossed mine, it was like some invisible force held me in place and I never wanted to move again. I'd read about piercing eyes before but I'd never truly seen them until now. Bright, beautiful and intense, fringed with thick golden lashes, his irises were ever-changing, somehow grey and green and brown at the same time. Sparks of something glittered in the air between us and I simply could not speak. Did he recognize me? I backed away from the tree trunk and pulled myself up straight, only vaguely aware of the tiny splinters of bark stabbing into my skin.

'Are you OK?' he asked, those indescribable eyes filled with concern as they flickered down to my hands. 'I didn't mean to make you jump.'

'Don't worry about it.' I rubbed my palms clean against the back of my jeans then held them up so he could see. No harm done. 'Falling over nothing is a gift of mine.'

'Hey, it's an underrated skill. If it was easy, everyone would do it.'

He kept his eyes on me and no matter how hard I tried to fight it, I knew I was blushing. Where Jackson was polished and practised, this boy looked a little more lived in. His blue jeans were soft from wear, with real tears at the threadbare knees rather than carefully placed slashes put there by designers, and his equally well-worn T-shirt was snug around his shoulders and biceps, revealing a sliver of skin at his waist every time he moved.

'I'm Wyn,' he said. 'Wyn Evans.'

'Wyn.' His name rolled effortlessly off my tongue. I took hold of the hand he held out to me – it was warm and strong and I did not want to let go. 'Emily James,' I added when I remembered I was supposed to introduce myself next. 'Or Em. Most people call me Em.'

He held my gaze even when he released my hand. 'All right, Emily or Em. You sure you're doing OK? That was a pretty good spill.'

A single lock of wavy hair slipped over his eyes, dancing tantalizingly back and forth across one high cheekbone, and my mouth was suddenly very dry.

'Totally fine,' I struggled to say, my tongue three times bigger than it had been a moment ago. 'I was just checking the moss, I thought I . . . saw something.'

'In the moss? You gotta be careful, if it's close enough to the ground there could be chiggers in there.' He flicked carelessly at the vines, his T-shirt creeping up even higher. Oh no. There were abs under that shirt. I started to sweat.

'I'll keep my distance. Wait, I thought you said it wasn't moss?'

Wyn twirled one tendril around his finger and it was embarrassing how jealous I was of a plant. 'Looks like moss, acts like moss, not moss. "Bromeliad" doesn't have quite the same romantic ring to it.'

'Not the catchiest name ever,' I agreed. 'I can see how Spanish moss won out at the marketing meeting.' I tucked my hands into my back pockets and searched for something else to say, anything to keep the conversation going, anything that would keep him next to me for even a minute longer. 'You know a lot about . . . plants?'

Better than nothing but only just.

'My grandpa is a nature nut,' he explained, unravelling the moss from around his hand. 'I don't think there's a plant on this planet he doesn't know about and Spanish moss is one of his favourites. Believe it or not, this thing belongs to the same family as pineapples.'

When I pulled a face, he laughed and I almost fell over again. It was a good laugh. Rich and warm and I wanted to hear it always.

'Probably not as tasty as a pineapple,' he admitted. 'But it is kind of amazing. Doesn't have any roots, just floats around on the wind looking for something to hold on to before anchoring itself to a tree like this live oak here.'

Huh. An oddly relatable bromeliad.

I craned my neck backwards to take in the whole tree, draped in moss from the top branch to the bottom. 'So it just wafts around, looking for a tree to hang out with, then they live together forever?'

'Happily ever after,' Wyn said. 'As long as the moss doesn't get too full of itself and I do mean that literally. If the vine grows too big, it can block out the sun which will eventually kill the tree. If it sucks up all the moisture from the air, it gets too heavy for the tree to support it and snaps off branches. It's a delicate balance. Spanish moss sure does love Savannah though. This place has everything it needs to thrive.'

'I've never seen it before,' I said, clasping my hands behind my back as Wyn poked at a dried-out bundle on the ground with the toe of his boot. 'It's pretty.'

'Yeah, it is,' he agreed, his eyes crinkling at the corners. But he wasn't looking at the Spanish moss anymore. 'So you're not from here, Emily James?'

'Kind of but not really,' I said, matching his confusion in my own expression. 'It's a long story. How about you?'

He shook his head and gave me another lopsided grin. 'No, ma'am. I'm from North Carolina. My family live up in the mountains near Asheville but I'm hoping to get into the photography programme at SCAD next year.' He jerked his head backwards in the general direction of the college Catherine had pointed out on the way to the Powells'. 'Savannah School of Art and Design. Figured I'd take some classes over the summer, try to get a head start on my application. It's a tough school to get into.'

Gorgeous, funny and artistic? I never stood a chance.

He patted the tree trunk with the palm of his hand then leaned all his weight against it, stretching his arms up overhead to hold onto the lowest branch. 'You're on vacation? I should have known you weren't a local with that accent.'

'No, sir,' I replied, casually flicking my ponytail over my shoulder and immediately getting a mouthful of hair for my trouble. 'As of yesterday, I am an official resident of the city of Savannah.'

His pupils dilated, huge pools of inky black expanding against the endlessly changing colour of his irises and I was entranced.

'The big house across the square,' Wyn said quietly. 'The one with the grey roof.'

I nodded and pressed my lips together, my heart beating loudly in my ears. He did recognize me.

'I saw you in the window last night. You had the most intense expression on your face.'

'I did,' I said in a whisper. A statement not a question.

'Yes.' He opened his mouth to say something else then hesitated, second guessing himself before he committed. 'You looked exactly how I felt.'

It all came rushing back. The vision of a non-existent kiss that almost knocked me clean off my feet. Whatever he was feeling at the time, I was pretty sure that wasn't it.

'Hey, since you're new here, you're going to need a tour guide,' he declared, his beautiful voice slicing straight through the tension between us. 'I could show you the sights, if you wanted, that is.'

Sights? There were sights? Other than his chameleon eyes and strong forearms and the soft curve of his lower lip that was just begging for someone to lean forward and bite it and . . .

'Or not,' he added when I didn't reply. 'You're probably real busy with your family and—'

'I would love for you to be my tour guide,' I interrupted, talking so fast it was a struggle to separate my words into single syllables. 'If you have time and it's not too much trouble.'

We stood facing each other, less than an arm's length apart and both of us smiling as an invisible thread wound itself around my heart and reached out to his. A new connection that was always meant to be.

'I'll be the best tour guide this town has ever seen.' Wyn pulled an ice-blue iPhone out of his back pocket. 'Can I get your number?'

'You can but it won't do you much good.' I produced my own useless handset and presented it as evidence. 'It's pay as you go and apparently it doesn't work in America.'

'This is your real phone?' he asked before grabbing the tiny plastic flip phone out of my hands. 'Woah, I've never seen one of these in real life before. It really works?'

'Only for calls and messages. I used to travel a lot so I could never get on a real contract,' I explained as he opened and closed it, snapping the two halves of the clamshell together with delight. 'Plus my dad had a no-smartphones-until-I-turned-seventeen rule.'

He looked up, horrified.

'Please tell me that's soon. No one should have to live like this.'

'Next month,' I confirmed, my cheeks turning pink. 'June twenty-first.'

He handed back my sad little phone with something that looked like admiration, the literal opposite expression to anyone else who had ever seen it. 'I think it's kind of cool. We spend way too much time on our phones anyway, right?'

I grimaced as I shoved it back in my pocket. 'Spoken like someone who has never had to watch TikToks on their dad's laptop.'

Wyn laughed again and happiness bubbled up inside me, like my favourite song had started playing on the radio.

'How about we do this the old-fashioned way?' he suggested. 'Pick a time to meet and show up. Tomorrow morning, around eleven?'

I liked the sound of the old-fashioned way.

'That sounds goo—' I started to say but before I could finish, I heard my name again. Only this time, it wasn't a whisper, it was a yell. A very concerned yell.

'Emily? Emily!'

Over Wyn's shoulder, a panic-stricken Catherine stalked towards us at a rapid but dignified pace.

'Emily, honey, there you are,' she said, stepping daintily off the footpath and onto the grass. 'I have been looking everywhere for you. What were you thinking, running out like that? Everyone was so worried.'

'I'm sorry. It was so hot in the Powells' parlour, I needed some fresh air.' I pressed the back of my hand against my clammy forehead to back up my half-truth. 'I didn't mean to worry you.'

She put her own hand against my cheek and pursed her lips. If I hadn't been warm before, I was now, my face burning up. I couldn't talk to her about what had really happened in front of Wyn. I didn't know how I was going to talk to her about it at all.

'Well, there's no fresh air out here. It's the humidity that'll get you,' she replied, seemingly satisfied with my answer before she turned her gaze towards Wyn. 'Now, would you like to introduce me to your friend?'

'Wyn Evans,' he replied with a slight bow. 'Pleased to meet you, ma'am.'

'Wyn was helping me find my way back home,' I added quickly.

'Well, bless your heart,' Catherine said, considering him through narrowed eyes. 'What a little gentleman. Emily, we'd better get you inside before you faint clean away.'

'I feel fine now, maybe I could meet you la—' I caught the look on her face and cut myself off. 'Yes, you're right. We should get home. Thanks for your help, Wyn.'

'Yes,' she agreed, still glaring at him like she recognized him from the FBI Most Wanted list. 'Thank you, Wyn Evans.'

'Any time.'

He touched two fingers to his forehead and, as I dutifully followed my grandmother back onto the footpath, mouthed the words 'see you tomorrow'. I felt the thread around my heart pull tight.

It was going to be a long twenty-four hours.

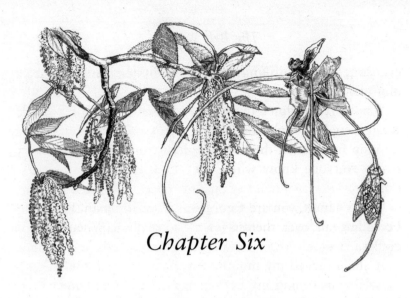

Chapter Six

'Was Ms Powell feeling better?' I asked, sliding my locket back and forth on its chain as we climbed the front steps up to Bell House.

Now Wyn was out of sight, I'd regained control of my senses or at least most of them. Part of me was definitely still underneath the oak tree, staring into his mysterious eyes, and I feared it always would be.

'Virginia?' Catherine replied as though she'd already forgotten about her morning visit. 'Oh, yes, much better, how kind of you to ask. It's a wonder she hasn't lost her mind altogether with those twins under her feet. You know, the three of you were born just a few weeks apart. She and I used to joke about how our grandbabies would grow up to be best friends like us. Or even get married someday.'

She looked at me expectantly, a playful smile on her lips.

'Oh no,' I said with an embarrassed chuckle. 'Neither of them are really my type.'

Not that I'd even had a type until ten minutes ago but now it felt set in stone. Messy hair, crooked smile and, most of all, those strange, beautiful eyes. I flushed a deep shade of crimson, burning up until I was sure my cheeks were practically maroon.

'And I really don't think I'm theirs,' I added. I definitely wasn't cool enough for Lydia and surely super flirtatious Jackson only dated the kind of girls who posted daily videos to let everyone know where they bought every part of their outfit.

'Emily James, you are a gorgeous young woman. People will be falling all over themselves to court you. When the time comes.'

A smile tugged my mouth upwards, even if I couldn't stop myself from rolling my eyes at the same time. I might have been new to this grandmother thing but I was sure telling their grandkids they're cute and smart even if they weren't was part of the job. Not that I was mad at it.

'They mentioned their mom moved to Charleston?' I said as Catherine opened the unlocked door.

She pulled a face and groaned.

'As if poor Ginny hasn't suffered enough.'

Wow, I thought to myself as we went inside. These people really did not care for Charleston.

'Alex always was a selfish little thing, putting herself before anyone else, never thinking how her actions might affect her mother, and it seems to me those children of hers . . . well, let's say the apples haven't fallen too far from the tree.' Catherine set her purse on the table beside the door then turned to face me. 'Now, tell me, sweetheart, who was that young man you were speaking with?'

'Wyn?'

I met her suspicion with feigned confusion but it was all too obvious from the look on her face that she didn't approve, even without knowing whether or not there was anything to approve of.

'I don't really know,' I said, all innocence. 'We only spoke for a minute. He's just some boy, I guess.'

'Perhaps a little old to be considered a boy?'

I grabbed my long brown hair in my hand and wrapped it round on itself in a loose topknot, dressing up my indifferent shrug. 'I would guess we're about the same age. He mentioned something about applying to college next year so that would make him seventeen-ish, right?'

'Seventeen-*ish*. And which college is it he's applying to?'

'SCAD. He wants to study photography. He's from the mountains near Asheville in North Carolina but he's staying in Savannah to take summer school classes.'

Catherine raised one perfect eyebrow and I sucked in my cheeks as I realized my error.

'Well, you certainly managed to find out an awful lot about him in one minute.'

'I'm a good listener,' I muttered, letting my hair back down.

'Honey, I know you're not a child,' she said, her tone gentle but firm. 'You're a smart girl and clearly you've managed quite nicely without me until now but I do have certain rules when it comes to dating.'

'No one's dating,' I replied quickly, suddenly hot again. 'Who said anything about dating?'

'In any case,' she went on, ignoring my panic, 'I do not believe it's appropriate for you to date until you are seventeen. That was the rule for me, it was the rule for Ashley, and I would ask you to abide by it also.'

'Was it the rule for my dad?'

This time she raised both eyebrows.

'Some things are different for boys.'

Wow. It was a long time since I'd heard that one.

'I don't think it's too much to ask.' Catherine peered at herself in the mirror and dabbed at an invisible blemish on her perfect face. 'Your birthday is next month. Is it really too long to wait?'

'Which is why it feels like a weird rule,' I countered, catching sight of my own reflection and wiping away a black smudge. My good old Maybelline mascara was not up to the challenge of this humidity. 'It's not as though I'll be that much more mature than I am now. I mean, how much can a person change in four weeks?'

'A very good question,' Catherine replied, gazing at me with consideration. 'Now, I think this would be the perfect time for a tour of the house, don't you?'

'As good a time as any?'

I was confused. Had I won that one or did we call it a draw? Catherine didn't seem confused at all.

'How wonderful to be in agreement,' she said but I couldn't tell if she was talking about the tour or the dating. She ran her hand lovingly over the wooden banister of the staircase, then gave it a tap. 'Let's begin.'

Bell House was a labyrinth. The tour moved through the foyer and the parlour, before leading us around the staircase to visit the formal dining room, a less formal breakfast room, the study, and finally an enormous kitchen that took up the entire back half of the house with its huge open windows and endless cabinets and cupboards. The windows looked onto a beautiful garden, high walls protecting it from the outside world, and so green and full of life: the only dark spot in the entire yard was Ashley, who glared at us from one of the flowerbeds.

'She doesn't like to be interrupted while she's working. Or any other time,' Catherine explained, giving her daughter a little wave. It was not returned.

'That's the pantry, then there's a second powder room through to the right, and downstairs on the garden level we have three guestrooms and three bathrooms.' My grandmother opened a door off the downstairs hallway to reveal a narrow, dimly lit staircase. 'I keep them closed up. It's been a while since we had guests and it really is a pain to keep the dust out when people are coming and going all the time.'

'Couldn't you use the rooms for something else?' I suggested. 'Like a gym?'

Catherine laughed for a moment, only stopping when she realized I wasn't joking. From the look on her face, you'd have thought I'd suggested we open a slaughter house down there.

'Oh, honey, aren't you just the funniest little thing,' she replied, patting my hand. 'I don't think that would be very fitting for an abode of Bell House's stature. All that sweating and grunting? Besides, you never know when unexpected guests might arrive. It wouldn't do to have nowhere for them to stay, now would it? Before I renovated, these were the servants' quarters.'

'You had live-in servants?'

As someone whose chore had been cleaning the bathroom since the day she was old enough to hold a mop, it was an incomprehensible statement but Catherine didn't seem to find it strange in the slightest.

'My mother did but I couldn't bear the thought of having all those extra bodies under my roof. Ashley manages the house quite well, so a full-time staff isn't necessary. Except for Barnett, my driver? You may not remember but you met him yesterday. His father drove for my parents and my grandparents, and his father drove for us before that. He's practically part of the family.'

'Is he here now?' I asked, peering through all the open doors as though he might pop out to introduce himself at any second.

'Goodness, no,' Catherine laughed. 'He doesn't come into the house. Barnett stays with the car.'

I stared at her, trying to make sense of what she was saying. 'You mean he just sits in the car all day, in case you need to go somewhere?'

'How else would I get around? Drive myself?' She tutted and shook her head. 'Emily, honey, you're just too much.'

Another thought occurred to me as we moved back down the hallway, something I should have realized from the moment Ashley bought two first class tickets on the next available flight when we arrived at the airport without a reservation. The enormous house, the beautiful clothes, the priceless antiques. The Bells really weren't just any old family.

'Catherine.' I started out carefully but there really was only one way to ask the question. 'Are you rich?'

She turned sharply, hands pressed against her chest.

'It's generally considered impolite to discuss financial matters unless that is the agreed upon topic of conversation.' She lowered her voice and checked to make sure there was no one around before adding; 'I would say we're comfortable.'

Which was exactly the kind of thing people said when they were insanely wealthy. I stood, dazed, taking a moment to recover. Catherine was rich. Catherine was my grandmother. Did that make me rich? I couldn't think of a time when I'd wanted for anything but I certainly wasn't spoiled. Dad and I had what we needed and nothing more. Better to travel light, he always said. But I was quickly learning it wasn't what my dad had said so much as what he hadn't that made all the difference now.

'Second floor next?' Catherine suggested.

I nodded and started to follow when a cool gust of wind brushed the back of my neck, making me turn around. There was another door I hadn't noticed before, tucked away across from the powder room and smaller than the others, painted sky blue. It was completely out of step with the rest of the house and I couldn't believe I hadn't seen it earlier.

'That's my craft room.'

Catherine put herself between me and the door as soon as she saw where I was looking.

'Bell House is as much yours as it is mine,' she said, calm but clear. 'Every generation is simply a caretaker of this magical place and I want you to feel completely at home. The only thing I ask is that you don't go in there without me. My craft room is my little sanctuary, the one place I keep for myself.'

'Of course,' I agreed right away and she smiled. Maybe this was the place where she changed into sweatpants, watched *Real Housewives* and ate Flamin' Hot Cheetos. There was no way a person could be that put together all the time. But still, I couldn't stop wondering what was behind that little blue door or how I'd missed it in the first place.

'Obviously it would be wrong to go in Ashley's room without her.' Catherine glanced out the window at the top of the stairs, looking down into the garden. My aunt was still toiling away at a flowerbed in her oversized hat and gardening gloves. 'So we can only take a quick peek, come on.'

She opened the door opposite mine carefully, quietly, to reveal a glimpse of a pretty but basic bedroom. It was much less fussy than my own, dark wood floors and dark green walls but no giant antique bed, no mountains of pillows, no sumptuous silk wallpaper and, to my surprise, I spotted one of those fancy at-home spin bikes tucked away in the corner. Huh. Ashley didn't seem the type.

We left my aunt's room, peeking into all the other guestrooms until we reached the end of the hallway.

'And this is where I rest my head.'

Catherine let me into her room with a showy flourish. It was worth the dramatics. Where the rest of Bell House was dark wood; polished oak, teak and mahogany, everything in Catherine's room was white. White silk walls, white four-poster bed, white loveseat and dresser and plush white rugs on light oak floors. In front of huge arched windows that looked down onto the walled garden was a copper clawfoot rolltop bathtub. I'd never seen a tub outside the bathroom before but now all I wanted to do was fill it to the top and soak under the moonlight.

'You must try it with the lavender bath salts,' Catherine said. 'There's nothing quite like it. Especially under a full moon.'

'You read my mind,' I replied, only very slightly worried that she really had.

'Just your pretty face.' She closed the door and I heard the old catch click. 'I've saved the best for last. Shall we adjourn to the library?'

'I'd really like to see my mom and dad's room,' I said, one hand already on the banister, one foot already on the stairs. 'You said it's on the third floor, right?'

'Yes, but we don't go up there.'

I did hear her but the words didn't register. One foot after the other, I climbed upwards until I lost myself in the darkness of the third floor, leaving my grandmother miles behind. There weren't any windows up here and the light played strangely. I was three steps from the top when I paused and looked up at the ceiling. Leaning against the wall, I tilted my head all the way back to see better. It was painted a deep, dense midnight blue and the paint absorbed all the light like velvet. As my eyes adjusted, a web of delicate patterns came into focus, tiny dots connected by fine lines, and it took me a moment to realize what it was. Orion, Ursa Major and Ursa Minor, Cassiopeia and more I couldn't name. All the constellations of the night sky, picked out in sparkling silver. It felt like I was floating in space and every time I blinked, I was sure I saw a shooting star fly across the sky.

'Emily!'

A strong pair of hands gripped on my shoulders, physically pulling me back down to the second floor and snapping me out of my trance.

'The third floor is structurally unsound,' Catherine said as I came back to earth, the same stern look on her face as I'd seen in the square. 'I believe I mentioned Bell House was built two hundred years ago and a lady of her age requires a little work to look and feel her best. The moment it's safe, I'll take you up there but I'm not going to risk anything happening to you now you're here.'

'I promise I'll be careful,' I said, still irresistibly drawn to the sparkling stars above me.

'You won't need to be careful,' she replied, turning me around and guiding me back the way we came. 'Because you're not going up there.'

Like every other girl raised on Disney movies, I'd occasionally wondered whether or not I would abandon everything I knew in exchange for a beast and a library but it wasn't until I stepped into the library at Bell House that I totally understood what Belle was thinking. I'd never seen so many books in someone's house. I'd hardly ever seen so many books anywhere and as someone who spent most of their childhood hanging out in university libraries, that was saying a lot. Even if I started that very second, there were more words in this room than I could read in one lifetime. Low lamplight glowed, warm and welcoming, and the comforting, familiar smell of paper and glue drew me in.

'There's a ladder,' I said excitedly as though Catherine might not know. And not just any ladder, a wooden ladder attached to a rail with little brass wheels to move it around the room.

'So there is,' she replied. 'And I'm sure you'll be pleased to know we also have our very own computer.'

One hand pushing the ladder back and forth, I turned to

see her hand resting on a dusty beige box that looked older than most of the books. 'I'm afraid we don't have WiFi. This monstrosity connects to the internet through the phone line.'

'Anything is better than nothing,' I lied, approaching the ancient computer with trepidation. She hit the power button and slowly, very slowly, it whirred into life, the grey screen flickering in and out.

'Ashley is the only one who uses it, she'll show you how to get it started.'

She switched it off before it could even get started but I was pretty sure it would be faster to send messages via carrier pigeon.

'Libraries are wonderful, aren't they? Always growing.' Catherine settled behind the desk as I pulled a random leather-bound book from a shelf, half expecting a secret doorway to appear. 'Your great-grandmother used to say there are only two things people could never have enough of, love and knowledge.'

The same words echoed in a different voice in my mind.

'Dad used to say the same thing all the time,' I told her, expecting to see a smile but she didn't quite reciprocate. Instead, she pursed her lips and I slid the book back into place.

'My husband passed when the children were still very young. Ashley was barely out of diapers, but Paul was determined to be man of the house.' She turned her head away from me when I took the seat on the other side of the desk, her profile silhouetted by the warm lamplight, a bittersweet expression on her face. 'In my grief, I let him take on too much and as he got older, he resented me for it. Your father had a fiery temper as a young man, I don't think there's a door in this big old house he didn't try to slam off its hinges at least three times.'

The thought of my dad storming around, slamming doors was unimaginable. He never once raised his voice to me, no matter how hard I pushed. Dad was the kind of person who never got angry, only disappointed, which was somehow way worse.

'What did you fight about?' I asked, still struggling to imagine my dad as a temperamental teen.

'Savannah is an old town and we're one of its oldest families,' Catherine replied. 'My generation was raised to behave a certain way and meet certain expectations, perhaps the last generation that didn't question it. Being a Bell meant honouring our traditions but your father had no interest in any of that and he wasn't afraid to let me know it. Once his mind was made up about something . . .'

'There was no changing it,' I finished.

Now that I could believe.

'Then along came your mother.'

She gave an audible sigh. I held my breath. This was what I'd been waiting for.

'I'm sure you know this already but they met at the Savannah College of Art and Design,' she began with a knowing look. 'The same place your friend is taking his summer school classes. Paul was in his junior year, Angelica was a freshman, and he lost his head and his heart the very moment they met. A rare case of true love at first sight, if you believe in that sort of thing.'

I felt a tug from the invisible string tying me to Wyn. I believed.

'Dad couldn't talk about the past without getting upset so I really don't know much at all,' I said, desperate for more details. When it came to stories about my mom, I'd survived on crumbs for years and Catherine held the promise of a full banquet. 'You're the only other person I've ever met who knew her. What was she like?'

'Angelica was wonderful,' she said decisively and with such

warmth that my heart swelled inside my chest. 'As smart as your father and twice as quick, she had the most infectious laugh, it didn't matter what the joke was, you would always find yourself laughing along with her. And she would do anything for anybody, give you the shirt off her back if you needed it. I liked her very much indeed.'

'She sounds amazing.' My voice was frayed at the edges and I knew tears were near. My grandmother reached across the desk and took my hands in hers.

'Angelica taught your father how to be happy, something I could not do,' Catherine said, her own words crackling with emotion. 'So, naturally, I welcomed her into the family. On one condition.'

'Which was?'

Her eyes were on the desk now instead of me.

'I was very, very young when I was married and still practically a girl when I fell pregnant with Paul,' she explained. 'I wanted them to live at least a little of their lives before they settled down. So I asked him to wait until he and Angelica had both graduated before there was any kind of official engagement.'

'But they got married when they were still in college?' I said with a frown I saw mirrored on my grandmother's face.

'Love is impatient and so was your father. A few months after our conversation, we skipped the engagement altogether and held a wedding here, in the garden.'

'They were too in love to wait?' I guessed hopefully.

'That's one way to look at it. Another is that your mother was three months pregnant with you.'

My dreams of romance were immediately wiped away by the reality of my parents' unstoppable horniness. Another thing I could not and did not want to imagine.

'But it was seventeen years ago not the 1950s,' I said. 'Surely they didn't have to get married right away just because they were pregnant.'

She twisted her aquamarine ring around on her finger as she answered.

'A lot of people still call this place Slow-vannah and not only because we like to take our time. I don't expect you to understand completely but Savannah society doesn't move at the same speed as the rest of the world – certain things are still done a certain way, especially in families like ours.'

Lydia's warning about the debutante circuit loomed over me like a white ballgown-sporting spectre.

'If we could control when we fall in love, life would be a lot easier but we can't, can we?' Catherine went on. 'Regardless, Angelica's pregnancy was a wonderful time for us all and when you arrived, born under a beautiful full moon, well, I don't think there will ever be anyplace filled with as much love as Bell House was on that evening. Those were glorious, happy days. Until things took a turn for the worse.'

'Until my mom died.'

I felt a tremor and gripped the arm of the chair. The walls of the library throbbed like there was a heartbeat trapped behind the bookshelves but Catherine looked unmoved.

'And took your father's heart with her to the grave.'

The eerie pulsing faded away and I let go of the chair when the old wood creaked in protest. None of the books had moved even though I was sure something should've been shaken loose. Unless I'd imagined the whole thing . . .

Catherine opened a drawer on her side of the desk and pulled out a worn Manila folder stuffed with photographs and pieces of paper. With long, slender fingers, she handed me the documents one by one: a wedding certificate; a death certificate; a birth certificate. Paul Spencer James Bell and Angelica Caroline Smith, married in Savannah, Georgia, 24 December 2006.

Angelica Caroline Bell, died in Savannah, Georgia, 24 November 2007. And Emma Catherine James Bell, born in Savannah, Georgia, 21 June 2007.

My birthday but not my name.

'I wanted to raise you the same way I had been raised, according to our family's traditions,' Catherine said. 'Your father did not. After we lost your mother, he became even more resistant to the idea. That's why he left, to protect you from something he thought was wrong.'

'But my name is Emily Caroline,' I said, staring at the birth certificate and only half-listening. 'Not Emma Catherine.'

She shook her head and passed me a stack of photographs.

'You were named for me, just as I was named for my grand-mother and she was named for hers. My grandmother went by Emma so I go by my middle name, Catherine. You were meant to be an Emma. Paul changed your name after you left town.'

The first photo in my shaking hands was of Catherine and even though she was clearly younger than she was now, the harsh look in her eyes aged her by decades. Her gentle smile was a burgundy slash and there was no colour in her cheeks at all, just a sickly pale complexion against violently red hair. The next photo was in black and white but the similarity undeniable. Another Emma Catherine Bell, her grandmother, and even with the sepia tones, I could tell she was another redhead. I leafed through the stack of long-gone relatives until I reached painted miniatures and pencil-drawn portraits, even-tually left with just one.

'She was the first of us,' my grandmother said, so much reverence in her voice I could have sworn I saw the lamplight flicker out of respect. 'She arrived here in 1733 and ever since that day, there has always been an Emma Catherine Bell in Savannah.'

The portrait was so old, the facial features of the woman

had mostly faded away but my imagination filled in the blanks. Catherine's hair, Ashley's eyes, Dad's lips, my nose. The first Emma Catherine Bell. And I was the latest.

'My name isn't my name,' I said, the first Emma Catherine's eyes following me as I laid her down on top of her descendants.

'Emily, your daddy had what he believed were good reasons for his behaviour. You are who you are – who you've always been.' Catherine collected up everything laid out on the desk and slipped my history back inside the folder, returning it to its place in the desk drawer. 'We could call you Ulysses S. Grant and it wouldn't change a thing. You know what they say, a rose by any other name.'

It didn't make sense but this lie felt bigger than the others, or maybe it was a culmination of everything I'd discovered over the last couple of days and this was the final straw. My father took away my family, he took away my home, he even took away my name, and he wasn't even here to explain himself. I wasn't sure which part I was the most upset about.

'Tell me what else did he lie about?' I demanded. 'Are there any other surprises waiting for me?'

'I'm parched,' Catherine said calmly as she locked the drawer with a quiet click. 'It's time for tea.'

'I don't want tea!' I exclaimed. 'I want to know why my dad lied!'

'And I want you to calm down.'

The steady patience on her face took on a hint of displeasure as she sharpened the edges of her words. 'This is a very difficult time for both of us and confusing for you, I know. We're both grieving our loss, Emily, and right now, I would ask you to give your daddy some grace. With that in mind, would you prefer hot or sweet tea?'

'I need to use the restroom,' I said, curling my hands into tight fists. I didn't care if she was right, it all hurt too much and just the thought of drinking tea, my dad's answer to everything, made my stomach curdle.

She nodded and I stood up too quickly, my head spinning as I barrelled out of the library and pinballed down the hall to the powder room. How could he have done this? It was such a betrayal. Worse, it was a violation. My father had taken something away from me and as far as I could tell, he'd had no intention of ever giving it back.

The creak of footsteps on floorboards stopped me in my tracks as I reached the powder room but when I turned to see who was behind me, there was no one there. Instead, I watched as the door to Catherine's craft room inched itself open, daring me to come inside.

'Hello?' I called out. 'Ashley, is that you?'

No response.

The pale green wallpaper that covered the hallway walls seemed to shimmer as I moved closer to the open door, a trick of the light on the hand-painted fabric, and icy gusts of air blasted down on me even though the AC vents were a ways down the hall. I was right on the threshold of Catherine's craft room, fingertips grazing the sky-blue painted wood, when I heard footsteps again, this time coming from the opposite direction. I pulled the door closed and scrunched my eyes shut. Toddler logic. If I couldn't see them, they couldn't see me. Pressing myself against the wall, I waited for whoever it was to pass me but they didn't make it that far. Halfway down the hall, the footsteps stopped. Right in front of the library.

'Ashley, honey. Perfect timing. Could you be a sweetheart and bring us some tea?' I heard Catherine call, and in response, Ashley laughed.

'What is it that's so funny?' my grandmother asked. Holding my breath, I peered around the corner just in time to see Ashley disappear into the library.

'I was about to ask what your last servant died of. What do you think, too soon?'

There was a pause and I slid silently around the corner, keeping close to the walls.

'Did you tell her?' Ashley asked, her voice lowered. 'Does she know?'

'No and we're not discussing this now,' Catherine replied airily as though the question didn't dignify a response. 'Besides, I can't be sure she has it.'

'Really? Because I'm sure. Don't tell me you don't feel it.'

A loud tut.

'Regardless of your expert opinion, I say it's not the right time. She's been through a lot already, any more would be too much.'

The frigid air blasted down, chilling me to the bone, but the walls of Bell House were oddly warm to the touch. Right time for what?

'There's no such thing as the right time,' Ashley countered. She sounded frustrated. 'You should tell her tonight, I'm sick of lying.'

A harsh laugh split the air.

'I find that hard to believe,' Catherine replied. 'You're so good at it.'

I moved down the hallway until I could see through the crack between the wall and the door. Ashley loomed over the desk from where Catherine returned her attention with a dark glare.

'Emily has suffered too much to be burdened with this right away,' my grandmother said, pushing back her chair with a decisive screech. 'The truth would kill her.'

'If she doesn't kill us first.'

I bit my lip to keep myself silent, the heat of the walls burning up through my clothes while the cold air froze in my lungs.

'No one is going to die,' Catherine declared as my legs

wobbled underneath me and my vision blurred. 'I will find a way to save her. To save all of us.'

It was the last thing I heard before the darkness took over and I crumpled into a heap on the floor.

Chapter Seven

'How do you feel now?'

'Like I'm being choked to death?'

I pulled at the seatbelt, high and tight around my neck, only for it to snap right back into place, cutting into the flesh at my throat.

'I'll take that to mean you're doing better.'

Catherine relaxed against the backseat, seatbelt-less, as Barnett, the Bell family's third-generation driver, chauffeured us away from the house.

'You gave us quite a scare, fainting clean away like that,' she said, lightly combing a strand of red hair out of her face.

'It's never happened to me before,' I replied. 'I feel fine now.'

According to my grandmother, I'd passed out in the hallway on the way back from the powder room and she and Ashley had carried me up to my room where I slept the whole afternoon away. I couldn't remember a thing. One minute we were in the library, Catherine casually breaking the news that my name wasn't actually my name and the next, I was out. I didn't even remember getting up to leave the library, let alone making it into the hallway.

'Must be the jetlag,' she suggested. 'Or the heat.'

Or maybe my brain had just decided enough was enough and opted to take a couple of hours off, I did not say out loud.

The last rays of the late afternoon sun lit up Catherine's face, bouncing off the silver leaf-shaped pin she wore at the collar of her white shirt and making her eyes sparkle. It looked like an antique, with delicate strands of precious metal woven around one another in an intricate filigree design and a milky white stone set in the centre that hinted at rainbows within, when the light hit it right.

'As long as you're feeling better,' she said with a perfunctory pat of the hand. 'Tonight should be a fun time.'

Neither of us had mentioned the argument. I was still upset, still confused, but the sting had gone out of my anger and there was no point in picking a fight with Catherine over choices my dad had made. Catherine and Ashley were the only family I had, the last thing I wanted was for my brand-new grandmother to decide I was more trouble than I was worth and send me away, all alone with nothing and no one.

'Where are we going?' I enquired politely.

Catherine glanced over at me and smiled.

'We're going to meet the rest of the family.'

Or at least I thought they were the only family I had.

'We have more relatives?' I sat bolt upright and my seatbelt yanked me back. 'Here in Savannah?'

'We sure do,' she confirmed, eyes sparkling. 'They're not a very chatty bunch but I just know they're going to love you.'

The drive only took about ten minutes. Our sleek black car slowed down at a four-way stop, a small stone-clad church on the left and a larger red-brick building on our right. Ahead were two tall stone columns, each topped with a sad-looking figure, their solemn heads bowed.

'Bonaventure Cemetery,' I read aloud as we drove slowly through the gates. '*This* is where we're meeting the rest of the family?'

'Where else would they be, honey?' Catherine gave me a questioning glance. 'It's not as though your ancestors can come to you.'

Visiting a bunch of dead people was not my idea of a good time but she was positively gleeful as the car crawled along the narrow concrete road, moving even slower than we might on foot and leaving plenty of time for me to shudder at the graves as we passed. This wasn't like any other cemetery I'd ever seen. Instead of stark, evenly spaced rows and regulation headstones, driving through Bonaventure felt more like travelling through time and ending up in a fairytale woodland. The statues and monuments seemed to be part of the natural way of things, like they had grown up out of the ground alongside the trees and plants and ferns, all of them different shapes and sizes. Some were sparkling marble and sharp corners, as though they'd been installed yesterday, and others had been softened by lichen and moss, all the edges worn away as the earth reclaimed them for itself. The air held a powdery scent and the fading light cast a muddled, soft green glow over all the grey stone and white marble and, just like downtown Savannah, everything was draped in Spanish moss. It poured over the gnarled branches of the oaks, tickling the tops of crypts and wrapping itself around the necks of angels like long, soft scarves.

Or a noose.

'Bonaventure has been here as long as we have, it's part of our heritage,' Catherine said, staring dreamily out the window. 'It's quite beautiful, don't you think?'

'I think it's a cemetery,' I replied, goosebumps prickling up and down my arms. How could a patch of land full of dead bodies be beautiful? 'I'm not really a big fan.'

'We treat death a little differently here,' she conceded as we passed a large parcel of land full of identical small white slabs. 'People who have passed over are still part of our family. Years ago, we Savannahians treated Bonaventure more like a public park than a regular place of rest. Families would picnic here, spend time with their departed loved ones, even court their beloved on these grounds. Would you believe it's still to this day one of the most popular places for proposals in the whole state of Georgia?'

'I'm starting to think I'd believe anything about this city,' I murmured as we drove on. 'They really let people drive around it? Isn't that disrespectful?'

'Only if disrespect is your intention.'

She straightened the folded-back cuffs of her shirt as the car slowed to a stop. 'To answer your other question, visitors are welcome to drive around the cemetery during daytime hours but our commitment to the preservation of Bonaventure has always been appreciated. As such, our family is afforded special privileges. Thank you, Barnett, we'll walk the rest of the way. You can circle back and wait for us at the entrance.'

I gave Barnett a polite nod when my car door opened but all I really wanted to do was slam it shut and beg him to drive right back to Bell House as fast as he could. Catherine might have other ideas but cemeteries left me cold. Even though Dad didn't leave a will, he'd always made it clear he didn't want to be buried and left alone in a place like this so I'd scattered his ashes over Llyn Y Fan Fach, one of his favourite lakes in the Brecon Beacons. It was beautiful, somewhere I knew he'd be happy to spend eternity, and not trapped in a box in the cold, hard ground.

'It's so peaceful,' Catherine murmured as Barnett drove away, leaving us stranded. 'So calm.'

'That's because everyone here is dead.'

She laughed loudly, too loudly for a cemetery.

'Aren't you just your father's daughter?' she chuckled before setting off down the path with a distinct skip in her step. 'This way, little spitfire. I want to introduce you before the sun sets.'

My grandmother, Savannah's leading cemetery enthusiast, took a leisurely approach to her tour, giving me a history lesson as we walked. Bonaventure sat at the edge of the Wilmington River and covered more than one hundred acres. Hundreds of residents rested here and Catherine lovingly pointed out her favourites as we strolled by. Every so often, a violent burst of colour would appear, blood red or hot pink flowers hiding around a muted grey corner, waiting to stun you when you least expected.

'Even though they say Bonaventure is one of the most haunted spots in all the world, I've never encountered a ghost here,' she said, pausing to admire a marble statue of a young girl. 'You'd think the place would be crawling with spirits but not for me, not one single sighting in all these years.'

I pulled the sleeves of my sweatshirt down over my fingers, reluctantly glancing at the statue. She looked too real, in her pretty party dress and neat shoes.

'You sound disappointed.'

'Darn near devastated,' Catherine replied and I couldn't tell whether or not she was joking. 'Maybe you'll have more luck than me.'

It was enough to send an icy shiver down my spine.

We continued on, the pale outline of a rising full moon appearing above us in the dusky sky as we stopped at a huge slab of granite with the name Vogel inscribed in big block letters. At the side of the monument was a small green dome, popping up out of the ground like a copper mushroom that had been left out in the rain.

'See that little old thing?' she asked, pointing to the Vogel grave. 'It's a bell. Do you know why it's there?'

'In case Mr Vogel gets hungry and wants to order a sandwich?'

'Close. Sometimes, not often but sometimes, people were accidentally buried alive. That bell would have been attached to the resident's foot inside his casket. Should he happen to wake from a particularly deep sleep all he had to do was wiggle his toes and help would come running.'

'What if no one was around?' I asked, horrified at the thought.

'Oh, someone always was,' Catherine replied as she moseyed along. 'Where'd you think the phrase "graveyard shift" comes from?'

I stared at the bell until I was almost certain I saw it move. A whisper of wind blew through the branches of the nearest tree, a soft tinkling sound on the air as a strand of moss fell across my face.

'Wait up!' I yelled, swatting it from off my skin and running to catch up to my bemused grandmother.

'Here we are. The Bell family monument.'

I wasn't sure what I was expecting after our long stroll through the cemetery, but this fenced-in, sombre block of solid grey stone wasn't it. There were so many more elaborate crypts, memorials and tombs, and I'd assumed the esteemed Bell family with their two-hundred-year-old home, entire floor of unused guest suites and on-staff driver would have chosen something a little fancier for their eternal resting place. The only interesting thing about the monument was a statue, a beautiful angel that sat on top of the six-feet of stone, its face tilted down to watch over the Bells, living and dead.

'Should I say hello?' I asked as Catherine opened a low metal gate and stepped onto the plot. With great reluctance, I followed.

'Be my guest,' she replied. 'Or rather, their guest. No need to be shy, you're among family.'

When I said I'd always wanted a family, this wasn't exactly what I was thinking. I scanned the plot, so bare compared to some of the others, no plants or trees or flowers, just the solid grey monument, the angel statue, and a slab of concrete on the floor. Engraved into the stone was one name. Emma Catherine Bell.

'Not at all creepy seeing your own name on a grave,' I said, a queasy feeling in my stomach. 'Even if I did only just find out it is my name.'

'Would it help to know it isn't technically a grave?'

Catherine produced a shiny silver flask from the pocket of her neatly tailored pants and raised it first to the ancestors then to me and my look of confusion. 'It's a grotto chapel.'

'Sorry, a what now?'

'A grotto chapel,' she repeated. 'This concrete is only a few inches deep, underneath it are boards covering the entrance to the chapel below.'

Above, the moon grew brighter as I stared down, imagining exactly what was below.

'There's a whole chapel down there?' I shuffled back until I felt the metal fence against the backs of my legs. 'Like an entire little church?'

Catherine unscrewed the cap from the flask and took a sip.

'In the early days of the cemetery, it was quite common for wealthier families to build their own underground chapel. I believe there are a dozen or so here at Bonaventure. After regular services at the church, the preacher would perform a private service for the families. You know, spend a little extra money, get a little extra salvation. It's quite lovely, not at all what you're picturing, I'm sure.'

'You've been inside,' I realized as she drank again. 'You've been down there.'

'For my grandmother's funeral. It has everything you might expect: pews, a pulpit, some even had electricity and running water although ours used oil lamps. More reliable.'

'That is so creepy.' I forced myself to relax and moved a little closer to the monument. Yes, I was extremely freaked out but also undeniably curious. If I was a cat, I'd be down to my eighth life for sure. 'I'm glad they filled it in.'

'It's not filled in, just sealed,' Catherine corrected me. 'The city doesn't allow them to stay open the way they used to but we can still unseal it to inter a body. Every Emma Catherine Bell who ever lived in Savannah has the honour of spending eternity here. There are still several seats inside.'

An involuntary shudder shook every bone in my body. Seats for every Emma Catherine Bell. Seats for my grandmother and seats for me.

'I sure wish your daddy could have been buried here. Not in this exact chapel, naturally, but we have another plot across the way for our relatives. He should have been laid to rest where we could be close to him.'

She looked so sad and the reality of it all hit me again. I wasn't the only one whose life had been turned upside down by the accident. I'd lost my dad but Catherine had lost her son, a son she hadn't seen in years, and been forced to take in a teenage granddaughter she didn't even know. I made a silent vow not to make things any more difficult for her. I wouldn't get mad at her for my dad's actions and, just for the time being, I wouldn't tell her about the strange things I'd experienced at the Powell house or in the square. The further removed they were, the less real they felt. Catherine was probably right when she said the jetlag and Georgia heat were getting to me.

'Is that where my mom's ashes were scattered?' I asked as she replaced the cap of her flask. 'Dad told me she was cremated.'

Embarrassment and regret coloured her beautiful face as she slid it back into her pocket.

'I don't know,' she confessed. 'Your father scattered her ashes someplace special to the two of them and refused to tell anyone, even Ashley and me. I guess I should have realized our relationship wasn't in the best shape back then but it all happened so fast with poor Angelica, I was still reeling with grief.'

'He said she got sick after I was born and her health went downhill very quickly,' I told her, trying to remember the story exactly, word for word. It was so long since we'd last spoken about it, the details were fuzzy. If I'd known I was going to lose him, I'd have asked again and again until I had it all memorized. It was a hard lesson learned.

'All of that is true.' Catherine rested one hand against the angel's cold marble foot. 'But the whole story is a little more complicated. All through her pregnancy, Angelica lit up like she was carrying the sun itself but after you were born, there was a dark shadow over her. She was never quite the same woman. If I'm to be completely truthful, we were all so obsessed with you, none of us noticed how sick she was until it was too late.'

What felt like a rusty nail scraped all the way down my spine, digging into every knot and stabbing at every nerve.

'She wasn't sleeping well so your daddy would get up to feed you in the night to let her rest but one time, when he came back to bed, something was wrong. She was awake, her eyes were open, but she simply wasn't there. I wanted to help her at home but Paul insisted on taking her to the hospital and right away the doctors there moved her to Atlanta for specialist treatment. I never saw her again.'

There it was. A fear I'd always had but never dared say out loud.

'So it was my fault,' I replied, my mouth dry as a bone. 'Something went wrong after she had me. My mom died because of me.'

Catherine took my hands and held them to her heart, her eyes soft and pleading as I stared blankly at my future grave.

'Don't you ever think that,' she admonished gently. 'Angelica lived because of you. Your mama thought the sun came up just to see you smile. You were everything to her, the very reason she was put on this earth, she was sure of it.'

'But if she hadn't had me, she wouldn't have gotten sick,' I protested, too many feelings rushing up inside of me at once, feelings I'd been fighting to keep bottled up ever since I set foot in Savannah. 'She and my dad would've stayed here and he wouldn't have been in Wales so he wouldn't have had the accident. They would both still be alive.'

'Emily, no, you can't torture yourself.' Catherine pulled me, sobbing, into her arms. 'We can play the "what if" game until the cows come home. What if I'd paid more attention? What if I'd realized Angelica was sick sooner? What if I'd insisted your father keep her at home instead of taking her to the hospital? Destiny is destiny, fate is fate. We can make anything our fault if we want to but what's meant to be will be and not one of us has any say in the matter.'

'There's so much I don't know about my own family,' I mumbled as she wiped my tears away. 'There's so much I don't even know about myself.'

She lifted my chin to look into her green, green eyes.

'All you need to know is this. You are my granddaughter and you are exactly where you're meant to be. Here with me.'

The wind whistled a soothing song and high in the sky, the light of the moon shone down on her like a spotlight. Catherine's expression was so certain, so without doubt, I couldn't help but believe her. Behind the Bell monument, I watched as a long, delicate tendril of Spanish moss slipped over the branch of a nearby oak tree and caught the breeze, wending its way down towards us almost as if it knew what it was doing. Familiar whispers began to fill the air and I raised my hand to greet it as Catherine's breath caught in her chest.

'Emily,' she said, her soft embrace shifting into a steel vice. 'Do not move one muscle. Stay exactly where you are and do not turn around.'

Immediately, I turned around.

The strand of moss fell away as I staggered backwards. There was something on the other side of the gate. In the shadowy half-light of the cemetery, I saw the dim outline of an animal, large and grey, saliva dripping from open jaws as it tore up the footpath with sharp, ugly claws, shredding the concrete like it was tissue paper.

It was a wolf.

And its golden eyes were set on me.

Chapter Eight

The wolf stopped moving when I did, holding just as still but looking far less afraid. If anything, it seemed eager, like it had been looking forward to this. But then, who didn't enjoy going out for dinner? We weren't much of a challenge, two defence-less women alone in a cemetery at night, but perhaps the idea of the hunter who lived for the hunt was a myth. Work smarter, not harder, that's what people said. Maybe this wolf was a genius.

'Catherine.' I edged closer to my grandmother. 'What do we do?'

'We don't do anything,' she replied. Her voice was low and clear as she stepped in front of me. 'And everyone walks away in one piece.'

She moved around me, positioning her body between me and the wolf. I noticed on her, fear looked an awful lot like excitement.

Oh good, I thought, back pressed against the Bell monument. My grandmother is certifiably insane. We were alone with a salivating wolf, and I had no phone and no idea how to get back to the car while she swayed from side to side with a feverish light in her eyes. Like a child about to open her Christmas presents.

The wolf raised one front paw, clawing at the air and the open gate as though something substantive was holding it back.

'Do not cross that line,' Catherine ordered. 'Turn around and leave while you can.'

'Maybe we shouldn't be threatening it?' I suggested as calmly as I could. 'Given that we have literally no way of defending ourselves?'

Shaking her head, she stood her ground, torso angled slightly forward, legs braced against whatever was to come.

'Emily,' she replied. 'There is always a way.'

What came next happened very quickly. I once read that the reason it feels like time slows down when we're in danger is because our brain speeds up to process everything that's happening, giving us more time to react. So when the wolf crossed through the invisible barrier and set its first paw onto the Bell plot, every single second split into a million more. I had a choice. Stay or go. Climb over the fence and run as fast and as far as I could. But running meant leaving Catherine behind, and even though I had very real concerns about her mental state and decision-making skills, I couldn't do it. Besides, I couldn't run fast enough to catch an ice cream truck, how could I outrun a wolf? There was no decision to be made, not really. I would stay. I would stand beside her. And I would fight. An unexpected charge shot up from the earth itself and surged through my whole body, urging me on until I found myself standing shoulder to shoulder with my smiling grand-mother.

'Oh, the mistake you have made,' she said softly.

But she wasn't speaking to me.

With a soul-splitting howl, the wolf reared back on its hind legs and launched itself through the gate, a blur of fangs and claws and matted fur. It didn't take kindly to threats. Without warning, Catherine pushed me out of the way, replying with her own battle cry, screaming as they collided, both bodies stumbling backwards into the monument. Her carefully styled hair came loose, swirling all around the two of them as they crashed to the ground as one.

Too much was happening all at once. Ears ringing, I pressed a hand to my forehead and saw blood on my fingers. Was it mine? Ignoring the shooting pain in my head, I rolled over to see the flash of the wolf's jaws and my grandmother's arms up in front of her face, its massive body pinning her small, fragile form in place. She was reaching for something, one hand scrabbling in the dirt beside her as the other fought off a mouth full of daggers. Her silver leaf-shaped pin. It glinted in the moonlight and before I knew what I was doing, I was on my hands and knees crawling towards it. The earth trembled and the steady beat of my pulse thudded in my ears, pushing me on. I grabbed for the pin but the wolf's hind leg shot out in my direction, slicing the flesh on my forearm and kicking it out of reach.

The branch, a voice commanded as I stared at the blood pulsing down my arm. *Pick up the branch.*

Then everything went quiet.

Catherine and the wolf continued to brawl, its teeth gnashing at her throat as she fended it off, but my focus was elsewhere. I knew what to do. All instinct, I stood slowly, grabbed a large, heavy branch that had fallen next to the Bell monument, and with strength I didn't know I had, raised it above my head and slammed it down as hard as I could. There was a crack and a whimper and the wolf rolled off Catherine's prone body, scampering away, staying low and close to the ground.

'Can you stand?' I asked Catherine, brandishing the branch as the wolf began to pace back and forth. 'We need to go.'

'There's no time to run.' Her breath came in short, jagged gasps as she pressed her hand flat against her collarbone. 'My pin, where is my pin? We need it.'

Obeying without understanding, I dropped my weapon and took three stilted sidesteps to the right where the pin lay nestled in the dirt. Never taking my eyes off the wolf, I stooped to pick it up, blood now pouring from my arm. Almost as much as I saw pumping out of the gash I'd left on the wolf's head. It streamed down its face, a sticky streak of crimson against its grey fur.

'I have it,' I told her, back by Catherine's side as we all considered our next moves. 'What now?'

'Just keep hold of it,' she instructed. 'Do you trust me?'

'Yes,' I replied without hesitation.

'Good. Because you're not going to like this.'

With a primal scream, Catherine stood and charged at the beast.

As it reared back for another attack, I seized the tree branch and swung at it again but this time I missed. The wolf wasn't coming for me. It charged straight at Catherine and she screamed as it lunged but I knew I could be faster, I knew I could save her. Diving into the fray, I hurled my body over hers, my eyes closed and her silver pin tucked into the hand I held out to protect us both.

When I opened my eyes, I was looking directly into the wolf's. Sickly yellow, streaked with violent red, the black pupils expanding then contracting until it was nothing more than a pinprick. The silver brooch was cool in my hand but everything else was hot and sticky, and when I looked down, blood was pouring out from its throat, painting all three of us a deep and vivid crimson. With a final tragic attempt at a howl and one last desperate snap of its jaws, the wolf slumped down on top of me.

'Emily, you brilliant girl,' Catherine panted as I pushed the motionless body off me, my own breath coming back in uncontrollable gasps that couldn't quite fill my lungs no matter how quickly I gulped down the air. 'You did it, you saved my life. You saved both our lives.'

But I couldn't hear her. All I knew were the matted clumps of bloody fur and handfuls of dirt that smothered all my senses. Whatever adrenaline rush had given me the strength to fight dissolved into nothingness and the ground rushed up towards me, promising blissful oblivion.

'Emily? Emily!'

Somewhere deep inside, I registered a sharp palm striking my numb face and I came back at once. Catherine's eyes bored into mine as she dragged me up to my feet.

'That's right, stay with me,' she said soothingly. 'The worst is over now.'

'It's dead,' I choked, looking past her to the pool of blood that was spreading out around the wolf. Too much blood to have come from a puncture made by one silver pin. The gravestones spun around me and I was certain I was going to be sick. 'I killed it.'

'It was him or us,' Catherine replied, her fingertips digging sharply into my shoulders. 'Which would you rather?'

She was right, I knew that, but it didn't make the ugly truth any easier. I watched her as she turned the body over and extracted the silver pin from its throat. Carefully, she wiped it with the hem of her silk shirt, once an elegant ivory, now a horrifying collage of all the colours of war.

'This came over from England with the first Emma Catherine Bell,' she said, pressing it into my hand, the central stone sparkling through a muted red smear. 'Now it's yours.'

81

'We need to go to the hospital,' I mumbled, clinging to the things people say in an emergency as I shoved it into my pocket. I didn't even want to look at it. 'We need a tetanus shot, we have to call animal control, we have to call the police.'

Catherine stared at me for a moment, her ashen face streaked with blood – mine, hers, and the wolf's – and then she laughed. A short, sharp howl that shocked me back into the present moment.

'And tell them what?'

With a look of foul disdain, she poked the corpse with her foot and its head lolled over to the other side, my stomach turning with it.

'What we need to do is move the body,' she said. 'We cannot have the custodian finding this scene on our family plot when he makes his morning rounds. Do you want this in the news-papers, on the internet? Do you want to have to relive it over and over while you justify and explain?'

'No but—'

'Do you want to be known as the girl who killed the wolf in Bonaventure for the rest of your life?'

I'd always worn unwelcome labels. The American who had never been to America, the girl whose mom died when she was a baby, the orphan whose dad was killed in that accident, and now I was back in Savannah, I'd already been christened the famous missing Bell baby. Did I really need another dark story following me around? I shook my head at Catherine.

'No,' I said. 'I don't.'

'Then help me.'

Catherine ordered and I obeyed. Together, we pushed the wolf's body, still warm and supple with a seemingly endless stream of blood pouring from its throat, along the ground. I lifted my head to look past it, focusing on the trees in the middle distance. Whether it was coming for me or not, I killed this thing and guilt pulled me down like a pair of concrete boots. I couldn't swat a fly without feeling guilty about it.

Eventually, we heaved the carcass through a small cluster of palmetto trees and onto the bank of the dark, wide river as tears streamed freely down my filthy face. Falling backwards onto my heels, I closed my eyes and drifted away, thinking back to the day we'd scattered my dad's ashes in the lake in Wales. It was so peaceful, so full of love. It was not this. I heard a loud splash and when I opened my eyes, the wolf was gone. Waves, ripples, and then nothing.

Catherine pulled a wad of moss from the trunk of a nearby tree and pressed it to my arm to staunch the flow of blood still pouring from my wound. I sucked the air in through my teeth at the sting.

'Hold that there and you'll be fine tomorrow,' she promised, pulling me up to my feet.

'Are you sure?' I blanched when I saw my flesh through the damp green of the moss. 'It looks deep.'

'It may look ugly now but you won't need stitches. That thing's bark was worse than its bite.'

Now that I simply did not believe.

We leaned against each other, turning away from the river to stumble back through the cemetery, and as we passed the Bell monument, I searched the ground for traces of blood. But there was nothing to see, just a single fallen branch in front of the gate and nothing more. Bonaventure had already drawn the evidence deep into the earth, making a silent promise to keep our secret.

'I was going to suggest we step out for supper,' Catherine said, an attempt at lightening the mood as we picked our way carefully through the darkness. 'But perhaps that was quite enough excitement for this evening.'

'Can't say I have much of an appetite,' I replied with a dry croak. 'Besides, we're not really dressed for it.'

She pressed her lips together into a thin, grim line that turned up very slightly at the edges. 'You saved my life tonight, my brave, bold girl. Your father would be so very proud of you.'

'Do you think so?' I wanted so desperately to believe her. 'I'm not sure, he was pretty anti-hunting.'

That earned a smile. Not the bright grin I'd seen on the way into Bonaventure but something more tempered and hard earned.

'Anti-hunting but pro-keeping you alive. He would be proud.'

We reached a fork in the path. The right side in total darkness while the bright, silvery moonlight shone off to the left, beckoning Catherine and I on. We followed dutifully, the full moon guiding us through the trees and moments later, in the distance, I saw two blinding white lights. Barnett. The car.

'I think it would be best if we didn't tell anyone about this, not even Ashley,' Catherine said, slowing down as we got closer. I looked over at her, waiting for the punchline of this strange joke, and saw she was entirely serious.

'You don't think she's going to ask what happened?' I waved a hand at my torn clothes, my blood-covered body. 'I think Barnett might notice too.'

'Ashley will be in her room when we return and Barnett is very discreet.'

'Your car has white leather upholstery,' I reminded her.

'We'll put down blankets.'

'But Catherine—'

'It would be for the best,' she repeated more forcefully. 'I must ask you to trust me and say nothing.'

The discussion was over. This was not up for debate.

Somewhere in the undergrowth, I heard a rustling sound, turning just in time to see a large, long-legged bird swoop out of the trees and soar off into the night.

'Wolves hunt in packs,' I whispered, relieved not to see

another pair of golden eyes staring at me from the darkness. 'What if there's another one out there somewhere?'

'There's always another out there somewhere,' Catherine said with a weary sigh. 'But next time, you'll be ready.'

Next time?

'You're sure there's no one we should tell?' I asked. I was shaking again, my limbs trembling at her casual certainty. 'No authorities or anyone?'

'Trust me, Emily,' Catherine replied as we crossed through the gates of the cemetery, officially leaving Bonaventure grounds. 'No one mourns a wolf.'

Chapter Nine

When I opened my eyes the next morning, it could have been any other day until I rolled over and saw a long, silvery scar on the inside of my forearm.

Bonaventure, the underground chapel, the wolf.

How had the wound healed already? I touched it gingerly with the tip of one finger. No pain, just cool, smooth skin. Even with the sun beating through my bedroom windows, I was suddenly freezing cold, yanking the sheets up to my chin as I shivered uncontrollably. There was a china teacup on the nightstand, empty except for a few leaves in the bottom, and I fished through a hazy memory of drinking it before collapsing into bed, exhausted. Catherine sat by my side until I fell asleep. Next to it was a shining leaf-shaped pin.

'It's a moonstone set in pure silver,' she had explained as I drifted off. 'Keep it close and it will protect you.'

After that, I didn't remember anything. I didn't even dream.

'Emily? Are you awake?'

The sound of Ashley's voice and her disembodied head appeared around my bedroom door. Instinctively, I opened the drawer in my nightstand, pushed the piece of antique jewellery-slash-murder weapon into the drawer and slammed it shut, sealing the pin inside.

'We're having a lazy day today, I see.'

'Catherine's tea knocked me out,' I said as she strolled into my room. 'What time is it?'

'Time you were out of bed. Almost ten.'

Cautiously, I pushed back the covers to examine my arms and legs for telltale evidence that might give our secret away but there was nothing other than the mark on my arm: no cuts or bruises, not even any dried blood under my fingernails. If it weren't for the almost invisible scar and the pin in my nightstand, I might have written off the whole thing as a bad dream. A very, very bad dream.

'Is Catherine downstairs?' I asked, climbing out of bed and into my slippers, pulling a sweater over my pyjamas. 'I need to talk to her.'

Ashley shook her head as she placed a fresh cup of steaming hot tea on my nightstand, next to last night's empty one, and gave my thick wool sweater a confused look.

'She left for a meeting hours ago. Like I said, it's late.'

Without asking if it was OK, she took herself off on a self-guided tour of my room, inspecting my possessions one by one and turning up her nose at everything I owned. 'She was wearing her big sunglasses. Y'all must have had some fun last night.'

Without her mother around, my aunt's demeanour changed. She seemed younger and more ready to speak her mind but also much less eager to please. There was a definite vibe of reluctant babysitter as she picked through my things. The two of us had barely been alone together since I arrived and as she took a dismissive inventory of my minor additions to the room, I decided I would be happier if it stayed that way.

'Do you know when she'll be back?'

Ashley replied with an indifferent shrug. 'Who knows? She's rarely around in the mornings. The venerable Catherine Bell has a lot of responsibilities. She's on the board of a bunch of charities and non-profits, then there's all her "business inter-ests". Her life ain't all strolling around the neighbourhood and taking trips to Bonaventure. You have a lot to learn about Catherine.'

'Right,' I replied, biting my tongue to stop myself from volleying the same accusation right back. She might not be so blasé if she knew we'd been attacked less than twelve hours earlier by a bloodthirsty monster roughly the same size of her Peloton.

'But she did leave orders for you to drink that,' Ashley said. 'Said you weren't feeling so great. Again.'

Pointing to the fresh cup of tea, she watched expectantly as I gave it a cautionary sniff. The strong herbal smell stung the inside of my nose.

'I didn't ask you to smell it, I told you to drink it.'

'It's intense,' I replied as diplomatically as possible given I was literally choking on the fumes. 'What's in it?'

'My own blend. Chamomile, arnica, a few other herbs. I grow everything myself in the garden. I'm not leaving until I've seen you drink so I would be eternally grateful if you could hurry the heck up.'

I raised the delicate cup to my mouth, fully intending to fake a sip, but when the warm liquid touched my lips, I couldn't stop myself from gulping it down.

'There you go,' Ashley said with a self-satisfied smirk. 'Don't you feel better?'

'Actually I do,' I admitted with surprise. Whatever it was, her offering tasted better than it smelled and before I knew it, the tea was gone. The tight knot in my stomach unravelled itself and the vivid, ugly memory of the wolf with its bloodshot yellow eyes faded into black and white. Maybe it hadn't been as bad as I remembered. Was the wolf really that big? Did it scratch that deep? Things always seemed worse in the dark and nothing was as scary in the light of day.

'You should sell this stuff,' I told her, tipping back the cup to get the very last drop. 'It's delicious.'

'It's an old family recipe. Can't have our secrets falling into the wrong hands, now can we?'

She laughed and I smiled back but I couldn't quite fight the feeling that she was laughing more at me than with me.

'I have things to do in the garden,' Ashley declared as she grabbed both empty cups, the fine bone china protesting as they clattered together. 'Catherine told me to keep an eye on you. Do you want to come outside with me?'

Confirmed reluctant babysitter vibes. Even my stuffed bear could tell she didn't really want me around. I glanced at the clock and suddenly remembered my plans for the day. Wyn. I was meeting Wyn at eleven.

'Honestly, I feel great, a thousand times better,' I insisted, desperate to get her out of my room so I could get ready. With no way of contacting him, I couldn't risk showing up late. 'And, I thought I might go for a walk. You know, start figuring out the town, get some fresh air. I heard that's the best thing for jetlag.'

Ashley studied me for a moment and I fixed a too big, I'm-totally-OK grin on my face, willing her to leave without a fight.

'Whatever,' she said eventually, sauntering out of my room and off down the hallway, leaving my door wide open. 'Don't wander too far. We wouldn't want you getting into any trouble now.'

'I'll do my best,' I called as I leapt out of bed, closing the door and turning the lock. I would be just fine. As long as I didn't run into any more giant wolves.

Chapter Ten

'It's not a date so I'm not doing anything wrong,' I reminded myself as I walked quickly across Lafayette Square. 'It's a casual hangout with a stupid handsome human who has, for reasons best known to himself, taken pity on you. Probably some kind of community service. If he even shows up. But it definitely isn't a date.'

But no matter how many times I told myself the same thing, my heart still pounded so hard I worried I might break a rib, and when I saw Wyn waiting for me underneath our tree, I was sure I heard one crack.

'Oh,' I whispered, stumbling up the kerb. There he was, looking even more beautiful than I remembered.

'Don't say anything weird,' I warned my brain when he waved me over. 'Don't tell him about the wolf, don't show him how you can turn your eyelids inside out and don't tell him about the time you got so sick you puked spaghetti through your nose.' If I could manage all of that, this would be easy.

'Well, hello, Miss Emily,' he said with a small bow, wavy hair falling into his face as he looked up at me.

'Hi.'

Suddenly I didn't have to worry about saying the wrong thing because it was almost impossible to say anything at all. He really was the most stunning person I'd ever seen. The dark ash tones of his hair, the moss-coloured eyes that shifted with the sunlight and the inviting broad slope of his shoulders that seemed made for me to rest my head against. Wyn looked strong and tanned in a way that casually suggested he spent a lot of time outside throwing tree trunks around rather than sculpting his muscles in a gym, and his loose jeans and snug shirt fit his body in a flawlessly unstudied fashion. Every aspect of him was perfect and I wasn't the only one who thought so. Dozens of pairs of eyes peered out from behind books and sunglasses, and a lot of his admirers were a good few years older than me. Despite the fierce sting of jealousy that stabbed at my heart I couldn't really blame them – once you'd set eyes on Wyn Evans, it was almost impossible to look away.

Only he wasn't there with them, he was there with me.

But it wasn't a date.

'Glad you could make it,' he said, completely oblivious to the thirsty looks he'd garnered from every corner of the square.

'Same,' I squeaked, trying to block out my competition.

He flashed a smile that almost knocked me off my feet. 'Can't think of a single thing on this earth that could have kept me away.'

Someone hadn't spent his evening tangling with an enormous wolf and it showed.

'I hope I didn't get you into trouble with your grandmother,' he said, rubbing the back of his neck as he cast a glance back at Bell House. 'I know how strict grandparents can be and she didn't look too pleased to make my acquaintance.'

'It's fine.'

Complex sentences were too much of a risk, better to stick

to single syllable answers until I could look directly at him without being completely dazzled.

'Great, because I've been thinking about our tour.' Wyn stuck his hands deep into his pockets and ground the toe of his boot into the ground. 'Savannah is a great town and there's a lot of cool stuff to see but I think it's important to start someplace good. An historical landmark of the utmost significance.'

'Sounds good to me,' I managed to say. 'Where are we going?'

'It's a surprise,' he replied. 'I think surprises are always more fun, don't you?'

'Sometimes,' I murmured, flashing back to the night before. 'Not always.'

'This one will be worth it.'

He held out his arm and after a split-second of hesitation, I slid my hand through the crook of his elbow. It fit like two parts of the same puzzle and I knew I would follow him off a cliff if it meant prolonged physical contact.

'Never in my life will I doubt a word you say,' I declared just twenty minutes later. 'Historically significant doesn't even start to cover it. This is life changing stuff.'

Wyn touched his huge, double-scoop waffle cone ice cream to mine in a dairy-based toast before taking a rapturous lick.

'Sure, the Telfair academy has some cool art,' he replied in his best official tour guide voice as we escaped the din of the jam-packed Leopold's Ice Cream Parlor. 'But did they invent tutti-frutti ice cream? I think not.'

'Put it on the historical register, give it a blue plaque, make it a UNESCO site, whatever it takes,' I said with great solemnity. 'This place must be protected.'

Finally I had found the solution to the unbearably humid weather. Ice cream. My double scoop of chocolate chip and butter pecan wobbled ominously atop the waffle cone but I wasn't about to lose even a mouthful. It was so delicious, I could have cried.

'We used to come down to Savannah sometimes when I was a little kid,' Wyn said, wandering happily down the street. 'I always got the lemon custard, Gramps always got the strawberry.'

My eyes widened as I attacked my cone with surgical precision.

'Wait, I didn't see lemon custard. That's it, as soon as we finish these, we're going back.'

'Leopold's is over one hundred years old, it's not going anywhere,' he said laughing at my serious expression. 'We'll get it next time.'

Next time. I felt my whole body light up with joy. He was already thinking about next time.

Soon the main street was far behind us. Wyn led the way, strolling into another leafy green square shaded by a dense canopy of oaks, and right away the temperature seemed to drop by ten degrees. Everything felt better when he was around, even the weather.

'You said you just moved here, right?' He slowed his pace, giving me a chance to enjoy the momentary break in the heat. 'Where did you live before? I'm guessing it wasn't in the US.'

'I was born here in Savannah,' I replied as I ploughed through the chocolate chip and into the butter pecan. Every bite was worth the brain freeze. 'But I've lived in a bunch of different places which explains my weird accent. Before I came here, I lived in Wales.'

'Wales? Really?' He looked pleased when I nodded. 'That's where my family is from. Originally, I mean, generations back. I've never been.'

'You should go if you can, it's beautiful there,' I told him, equally as delighted by the connection. 'The weather isn't always all that great and we lived in a pretty remote part of the country – lots of sheep, not a lot of people – but I really did love it.'

'Sounds good to me. And for what it's worth, your accent isn't weird. I think it's kind of pretty.'

I took another chomp out of my ice cream to hide the size of my smile.

'If you loved Wales, what brought you back to Savannah?' he asked and just like that, my smile was gone. 'You don't have to answer if that's a difficult question,' he added when he saw my discomfort. 'If you're an alien or a super spy, do not tell me. I do not hold up well under questioning, I would give you up right away.'

'My dad passed away,' I said simply. Better to get it out the way now. 'It was just me and him, my mom died when I was a baby, so I came here to live with my grandmother.'

Wyn faltered for a second before falling back into step beside me. 'I'm sorry. We don't have to talk about it if you don't want to.'

'Most of the time when people say that, it means they really don't want to talk about it.' I laughed lightly even though it wasn't really funny, but it was true. 'I know it's not exactly something people like to think about.'

'Well, if you do want to talk about it, I'm a good listener.' His face was warm and open as he popped the last bite of his cone into his mouth and something in the air shifted between us, pulling a little tighter, binding us closer together. I did want to talk about it. I wanted to talk about it with him.

'Whenever I would get upset about my mom, Dad would say death is only sad for the people left behind,' I began, the words coming more easily than I thought they would. 'He always told me wherever she was, she wouldn't want us to be sad forever, so that's what I keep telling myself. Either his energy is out

95

there somewhere, floating around in the universe, or he's some-place else with my mom. Whichever one it is, I have to keep reminding myself he wouldn't want me to be sad forever either.'

We reached a busy main road and stopped at the crosswalk, waiting for the light to change.

'That's a good way to look at things,' Wyn said. 'Kind of beautiful.'

I was so lost, staring into his green-grey eyes, the sensation of his hand covering mine took me by surprise. I looked down as our fingers wove themselves together, then back up at him and the smile on his face knocked the air out my lungs. A beeping sound sliced through my wonder, the walk sign turned white, and with one quick squeeze of my hand, he led me across the street and safely to the other side.

'That's how I feel today,' I admitted, struggling to focus on the subject at hand. My palm was hot and sweaty against his and walking in a straight line became a complex manoeuvre. 'For the first couple of weeks I was a total zombie, just stayed in bed, staring at the wall. Then it started to get, not better, but bearable. Like, I could get through a day without losing it *completely* but who knows? Tomorrow I might want to cry for three hours straight or punch a wall, it's hard to say.'

'Definitely don't punch a wall,' he advised with what sounded like earned wisdom. 'It looks cooler than it feels.'

'I think that's more of a guy thing,' I replied, laughing. 'And let's be honest, it doesn't look *that* cool. You should call a meeting, let the menfolk know they're not impressing anyone with that stuff.'

Our arms swung easily between us, like holding his hand was the most natural thing in the world and I wasn't testing the limits of my twenty-four-hour antiperspirant with every step. I'd never met anyone so easy to talk to. It felt as though we'd known each other forever.

'I can't imagine growing up in such a small family.' Wyn squinted against the midday sun and grinned. 'No siblings, no cousins, nothing. Wow.'

'You have siblings?'

Surely there couldn't be more than one like him.

'One brother and four girl cousins,' he said with comically bulging eyes. 'I grew up with the cousins, they're practically my sisters.'

'I can't imagine growing up in such a big family,' I replied truthfully. 'What was it like?'

'We aren't that close these days, everyone is busy all the time.' He sounded a little regretful but not really sad. 'The girls are all older than me. Jennifer and Susie, the twins, they both moved out last year. Susie got married in the spring. Lena is the middle kid, she moved to Canada with her girlfriend a couple of months ago and Sara, the youngest, still lives at home but she's in college all day and works evening shifts at a bar in Asheville so I never see her anymore. Her mom, my Aunt Rue, she's cool. She runs an art gallery in town. Sometimes I hang out with her there. My gramps lives with us too but he's getting older. Mostly he just reads and sleeps.'

It sounded like the dream to me.

'What about your parents?' I asked.

He shrugged as I swallowed the last bite of my ice cream cone.

'Busy, busy, busy. Mom is an artist, she paints mostly, practically lives at her studio. Dad is the one I see the most but that's only because he's the art teacher at my high school. He's way more popular than I am.'

I didn't believe him for a second.

'So many artists in one family,' I remarked. 'What about your brother, is he an artist too?'

'Cole is whatever Cole feels like being on the day.'

He let go of my hand to push his hair out of his face, a

gloomy look turning down the corners of his mouth. Cole, I suspected, was not his favourite family member.

'Still, it must have been cool growing up with so many siblings,' I suggested, looking for a positive. 'I always wanted a big brother or sister. Must be nice to have someone who gets you, someone who sees the world the same way you do.'

'I'm not sure any of them see the world the same way I do,' he replied, his smile back but bittersweet. 'But I definitely learned a lot from my cousins. Don't know a thing about sports but you can ask me anything about the Twilight movies. And I was always getting dragged into dance routines and rituals.'

'Rituals?'

'Lena and Sara are big on astrology,' he clarified. 'You can always count on me to know when Mercury is in retrograde, which is a big deal if you need to buy electronics or sign some kind of contract. Or so they say.'

Soft wefts of clouds covered the blazing sun when I blinked upwards, as though I might see the planet rushing backwards across the sky.

'I do need a new phone,' I said. 'Is it in retrograde now?'

'No, you're good. Time to go nuts at the Apple store.'

High on sunshine and ice cream, I reached for his hand and took it in mine. The sizzle of the sun on my skin was nothing compared to the heat that radiated through my body when he squeezed it again, warming the coldest, darkest parts of me, lighting me up from the inside out. I couldn't speak, I could barely breathe.

And I never, ever wanted to lose this feeling.

Chapter Eleven

'Stop it! That's disgusting!' Wyn yelled.

'You said you wanted to see it!' I protested as I popped my eyelids back the right way around. 'I had to look at your creepy double-jointed elbow, it's only fair.'

We'd been walking around Savannah for what felt like hours and so far, I'd seen nothing of the city. Wyn's sightseeing tour involved lots of interesting historical facts and figures but the only fact I had registered was just how much I was starting to like him.

'It's gross enough to make me puke pasta through my nose,' he said, grinning as he took a slurp of his Starbucks.

I also had some minor regrets.

'I knew I shouldn't have told you that,' I groaned. 'OK, my turn to ask you a question. What's your favourite book?'

As we strolled up and down the Savannah streets, Wyn had suggested a game, quick-fire questions with immediate answers, no thinking. So far I had found out his favourite colour was blue, his birthday was in May, he loved old movies as much as I did, and his favourite pizza topping was pepperoni. None of it was groundbreaking but each crumb of information we shared felt like the key to understanding the universe.

Slowing to a stop, he grabbed hold of the iron railings behind him and swung from side to side. The sleeves of his T-shirt stretched over the tense muscles in his arms and I quickly looked away before he could catch me staring. Again.

'I don't think I can choose just one,' he said. 'Different days need different books.'

'Agreed,' I said, honestly relieved he hadn't said he didn't read at all. There was nothing less attractive than someone who didn't read. 'How about . . . city or country? Which is your favourite?'

'You know I'm a mountain man.' He puffed out his chest and planted his fists on his hips. 'Give me a wide-open space any day. Savannah is as close as I want to get to city living, couldn't stand the thought of all those skyscrapers boxing me in. What about you?'

'I really like cities.' I answered according to the rules, without thinking. 'I always figured I'd go to college somewhere like London or New York but I like the quiet of the countryside too and I love being by the ocean but Dad hated the beach so we hardly ever saw the sea.' I shook my head and laughed. 'I guess what I'm trying to say is I don't know.'

'You'd love it where I'm from. Asheville is a really cool town and the mountains are real peaceful. Unless my cousins are around anyways.'

Wyn was so grounded. He knew who he was and where he was from, he had so many relatives, he could barely remember all their names. He had a favourite pizza place and local sports teams and the same school friends he'd known all his life. He had all the things I'd always wanted.

'OK, what's next? Cats or dogs, which do you prefer?' I asked, changing the subject before I started fantasizing about visiting the North Carolina mountains with a boy I'd only just met.

'Dogs, I guess. I love cats but they never like me.'

He swirled the ice in his plastic cup and looked at me intently.

'What?' I swiped at my mouth with the back of my hand. 'Do I have something on my face?'

Instead of answering, he carefully hooked a long strand of my hair with his forefinger and held it out between us.

'When the light hits your hair just right, it turns this real pretty shade of red.'

I tried to respond but none of my muscles felt much like moving, even the ones I needed to breathe. It was only when Wyn let my hair fall through his fingers that I was able to exhale again.

'Must be the sun,' I mumbled before taking a noisy slurp through the straw of my giant iced latte. 'Oh hey, what's this?'

Without waiting for a reply, I pushed past him and through an open gate to what looked like a park, but as soon as I stepped inside, I knew it was not a park at all.

'It's a cemetery,' Wyn said, right beside me as I scanned the crumbling headstones and randomly placed monuments. 'Colonial Park, one of the oldest in the country. If I'm remembering correctly, it dates all the way back to the 1700s and there's at least one guy in here who signed the Declaration of Independence, over that way, I think.'

He pointed off to the left but something pulled me to the right, a nagging feeling that gnawed away at me like I'd forgotten something but couldn't remember what. This place was so different to Bonaventure, much, much smaller and more open and bright.

'That tree over there doesn't have any Spanish moss,' I said, wandering off the path towards the middle of the lawn. 'Do you know what kind it is?'

'It's a magnolia tree and as far as I know, it should. There's only one explanation I can think of.'

The shade provided by the thick, glossy leaves was cool and welcoming, and the fragrant white flowers that bloomed on the enormous tree filled the air with a light, sweet scent. Without even needing to ask each other first, we both sat down on prickly grass, appreciative of the magnolia's generous shadow.

'In Florida, they call Spanish moss Old Man's Beard because of an old story of how it supposedly came to be.' Wyn stretched out his long legs and the white rubber toecaps of his shoes almost touched the trunk of the tree. 'Legend has it Gorez Goz, a villain with a long grey beard, bought an Indian maiden for a yard of braid and a bar of soap, but she was so afraid of him, she climbed up into the trees to escape. He tried to follow her but his beard got all tangled up in the branches and the maiden dove into the river to escape.'

'Was she OK?' I asked, pinching my toes through my shoes.

'Sure was. She got away but Goz and his beard were trapped up there for all eternity.'

'Good, the girl hardly ever gets away in those old stories. That doesn't explain why there's no moss on this tree though.'

'That's the other part of the story,' he replied in a spooky voice, eyebrows arched over playful eyes. 'They say Spanish moss cannot grow where innocent blood has been spilled.'

I looked around, checking all the trees in the cemetery. Every single one of them dripping with moss, all except for this one. 'Well, that's super reassuring.'

'I'm just the tour guide.' Wyn shrugged, a mischievous sparkle in his eyes. 'There's no way of telling everything that happened right here on this very spot over the last three hundred years.'

'Her outfit looks extremely vintage, maybe she knows.' I

nodded at a tall woman with extremely pale blonde hair trailing down the back of a floor-length ivory dress. She looked so washed out compared to the green grass and red brick of the wall beyond her, as though she'd been run through a black and white filter when the rest of the world was in vivid Technicolor. She held my gaze with watery eyes as she moved slowly through the headstones.

Wyn frowned as he followed my gaze. 'Maybe who knows?'

I turned to point her out but she was already gone.

'There will be some boring reason,' he said, rolling onto his back and cradling his head in his hands. I leaned backwards, trying to see where she might have vanished to but there was no trace of her. 'Pesticides or pH levels or something.'

'Probably,' I agreed, ignoring the uncomfortable feeling in my gut that wasn't quite so sure. 'Hey, I have another question.'

'Shoot.'

'What do you want to do?' I asked. 'After you graduate, I mean.'

He made a long humming sound and tapped one foot against the other while he thought about his answer. 'You got me,' he said after a good long while. 'I don't know for sure.'

'Something with your camera?' I suggested.

'Maybe,' he replied. 'I would love to travel the world, taking pictures of everything I see. What about you?'

'I'm not sure either,' I admitted. 'I only had plans set in stone as far as my seventeenth birthday. Dad's travel schedule was so unpredictable but we had a deal. I went with him wherever he needed to go until I turned seventeen, after that, I got to make my own choices.'

'What kind of choices?'

'College first, one school where I could stay and study for four whole years. After that, I'm not sure. Maybe teaching or something to do with books.'

'Better stick to the books,' Wyn said with a grin. 'If you were my teacher I would never graduate.'

His smile was infectious. I lay back on the ground beside him and beamed up at the sky.

We stayed in the cemetery for what felt like hours, laughing and joking and sharing stories about our lives. Wyn talked about growing up in the Blue Ridge mountains and I told him stories about my life in Wales. He was easy to talk to and listening to him was even easier. His voice was deep and warm with an inviting, lilting accent, and every time I made him laugh, I felt like I'd won a prize.

Under the shade of the magnolia tree, even though the grass was dry, the earth was almost cold to the touch, damp and soft as I pressed my fingertips flat against it. Then I heard it again.

Emma Catherine Bell . . .

My name, my *real* name, whispered like a rustling in the leaves.

Light hides the lies; truth lives in the dark.

'Do you hear that?' I asked, standing up too quickly and spinning in a dizzy circle. There was no one else in the cemetery but us.

'Hear what?' Wyn hopped up and held his hand above his eyes to scan the grounds. 'Was it thunder? I heard it might storm today.'

I didn't answer. The voices faded away again and the ground rushed towards me.

'Emily!'

He caught me as my legs buckled and I fell to my knees with stars in front of my eyes.

'Are you OK?' he asked, holding my hand tightly.

'Just tired, I think, or maybe it's jetlag,' I replied, echoing Catherine. My mind was a swirling mess of whispers and wolves and everything else that had happened in the last forty-eight hours. 'I'm not usually this clumsy. I mean, I'm clumsy but not usually this bad, I swear.'

'You did warn me falling over nothing was your special skill,' he replied with a wry smile. 'Maybe we should look into getting you some kneepads and a helmet.'

'No way, I do not look good in hats,' I said, managing to return his expression as the confusion faded. 'I haven't been sleeping super well and I was out with my grandmother last night and we were attacked by a—'

I looked up into his startled eyes and Catherine's warning came back to me. Don't tell anyone. Don't be the girl who killed the wolf.

'A dog,' I lied quickly. 'A small dog. Small but like, super loud. It came right for us.'

'Oh yeah, the small, loud dogs are the ones you have to watch out for,' he replied as I slowly rose back to my feet. 'Em, you look really pale. I think I should take you home.'

As much as I didn't want our afternoon to end, I didn't protest when he led me out from under the magnolia tree and along the footpath. Things still weren't quite right in my head. A stone statue of an eagle sat above the main gates of the cemetery, its majestic wings outspread, and as we passed underneath it, I thought I saw its feathers flutter.

We walked slowly and quietly down the street. Wyn kept throwing concerned looks my way, as though he was waiting for me to faint away like some corset-wearing Jane Austen character. I felt so foolish. What must he be thinking? Wasting his day with a blundering weirdo who couldn't even stand up on her own two feet. I'd ruined everything.

'This isn't really how I was hoping the day would end,' he said with a rueful glance. 'Savannah has heaps of other cool things besides ice cream and cemeteries, I swear. You can say it, this was the worst tour ever.'

I looked past him at a row of beautiful old townhouses with their wooden shutters and Juliet balconies, manicured bushes loaded with vivid pink flowers out front, and the ever-present oak trees lined up along the footpath, their long, winding branches reaching out to create a canopy over the street. It was just about the prettiest street I'd ever seen. Jetlag and heat stroke aside, Savannah had already found a place in my heart. Besides, anywhere Wyn was, I wanted to be.

'It was the best tour ever,' I insisted. 'Even if we'd only gone to Leopold's, it would have been the greatest tour of all time. Everything else was icing on the cake. Ice cream on the cake, even.'

'You're only being polite,' he smiled. 'I do believe your southern manners are coming back, Miss Emily.'

When we reached the edge of Lafayette Square, Bell House just around the corner but thankfully still out of sight, I came to a reluctant stop.

'I should probably walk myself the rest of the way,' I said. 'Unless you want to answer a lot of awkward questions from my grandmother.'

Not that Catherine could be upset with me or Wyn. I wasn't doing anything wrong, no one had ever called this a date. He looked down, his unruly hair covering his perfect face.

'OK,' he replied, shifting from foot to foot and staring at the ground. Why didn't he want to look at me? Unless . . . he was trying to work out how to let me down gently. My stomach dropped at the thought of never seeing him again, something that suddenly seemed all too possible.

'This is the awkward part,' he said after what felt like forever.

I reached for the railings beside me and clung on tight as he raked his hair away from his face and looked up.

'Where I ask if you want to hang out again sometime,' he finished his sentence with bright pink cheeks. 'And hopefully you say yes then I say I'll call you and I go home happier than a guy with unlimited Leopold's for life.'

'But you can't,' I replied, flustered when panic flashed across his features. 'Call me, I mean. Because I don't have a phone. But I would really, really like to hang out again.'

He blew out a breath I didn't know he was holding in and the tension in his face turned into joy.

'How about Sunday morning, nine thirty?' he suggested. 'I've been thinking about it and I reckon I know a place you're going to love.'

'Sunday morning is great.' I folded my arms across my chest to stop myself from throwing them up in the air to celebrate. 'Where should I meet you?'

It was my incredibly unsubtle way of letting him know he still shouldn't come calling at the house.

'Sunday, nine thirty a.m., Lafayette Square,' he said, chameleon eyes shining. 'Until then, Emily James.'

We stayed right where we were, smiling at each other without saying another word until Wyn shoved his hands in his pockets and took a couple of backwards steps away from me as if struggling to break out of my orbit. But it didn't matter where he went, Wyn Evans was the sun, everything revolved around him now. I waved as he went, leaning against the railings and watching until he disappeared. It might have been the worst tour of Savannah anyone had ever given but it was, without a doubt, the greatest non-date in the history of the world.

Sunday couldn't come soon enough.

Chapter Twelve

'Here she is, just in time for supper.'

Catherine was sitting at the dining room table when I waltzed through the door and floated down the hallway, barely registering the ground beneath my feet as I followed her voice. She looked so elegant, I felt as though I'd walked in wearing a garbage bag.

'Are you going out?' I asked, my magical time with Wyn melting away and memories of the night before rushing back to take his place.

There was no evidence of our epic battle anywhere on my grandmother. I could hardly believe this was the same woman I'd stood beside less than twenty-four hours ago, fighting for our lives. Her glossy hair was pulled back from her face in an elaborate knot and she wore huge emeralds in her ears, almost as big and bright as her eyes, and the exact same colour as her fancy silk dress. I couldn't see a scratch on her. To her left, Ashley looked neat and tidy in a not quite so fancy but still very pretty blue dress. Her long chestnut braid fell down her back and she wore a typically uninterested expression on her face.

Catherine shook her head and smiled. 'I like to dress for

supper. It's an old-fashioned idea, I know, but why not bring a sense of occasion to the everyday and mundane?'

I checked my watch, shocked to see it was already six p.m., Wyn and I had whiled away seven hours together. Across the table, I saw Ashley attempting to hide a smirk.

'I'll go change,' I said, one hand already on the door handle, even though I had no idea what I was planning to change into. All I'd brought with me were blue jeans, black T-shirts, a couple of my dad's old white button-ups, a handful of useless, warm wool sweaters and one plain black dress I'd worn once and once only. I had no desire even to see that dress again.

'I think we can make an exception for tonight.'

Catherine fussed with my hair as I sat, attempting to straighten the one weirdly wavy bit at the front that required far more than sheer force of will to tame. 'You and I should plan a little shopping trip. There's a boutique down on Barnard that has the cutest little sundress in the window. It would look just heavenly on you.'

This time, Ashley didn't even try to disguise her amusement.

'Yeah, they have this cool new concept there,' she added, saccharine sweet. 'It's called "colour". Have you heard of it?'

'Ashley, darling, would you be an angel and go check on the soup?' Catherine said lightly. 'It might need a scooch more seasoning.'

Ashley gave her a thunderous look.

'It was perfect when I tried it five minutes ago.'

'How strange,' her mother replied as she fanned out her napkin with a flourish. 'I found it to be a little tasteless.'

Pushing back her chair, the legs screeching along the wooden floor, Ashley stalked through the door that led to the kitchen, muttering something ugly under her breath.

'Catherine?' I said hesitantly, waiting until the swinging door came to a complete stop.

'I need to talk to you about last night.'

My voice dropped to an urgent whisper even though there was far too much banging around in the kitchen for anyone else to overhear. 'Are you OK?'

'Perfectly fine,' she replied. 'And so, it would seem, are you, so there's no need to discuss any further.'

'But the way we were fighting, I should have more cuts and bruises.' I pulled up the arms of my long-sleeved T-shirt to reveal the suggestion of a scar that marred my forearm. 'And look how fast this healed. There was so much blood, it can't have all come from . . . it.'

I didn't need to say the word, she knew what I meant.

'Emily, honey, if you must dwell on it, and I really would rather you didn't,' Catherine said, her words hushed, sharp and straight to the point, 'please remember what happened. That thing was going to kill us both. You saved my life. You are the hero of this story.'

'But what if there's another?' I pressed. 'Are you sure we shouldn't tell anyone?'

'Trust me.'

She raised a glass of white wine in my direction. 'Anyone who needs to know, knows.'

And I knew when I was beaten. Catherine didn't want to talk about it and who could blame her? I sat back in my seat as the sound of breaking dishes and curse words coming from the kitchen filled the air.

'Now, I would just love to hear about your day,' she said as her daughter pushed through the door, silver serving tray in hand. 'Ashley says you took yourself on a tour of the town? Tell me everything. Even after all these years, I believe there is always something new to discover in Savannah.'

'Sure.' Ashley grunted as she dumped a bowl of soup in front of me. 'Like tourists and overflowing trashcans.'

'And daughters who don't sass their mothers at mealtimes,' Catherine added sharply.

'This is the best soup,' I said, caught off guard by an unexpected pang of sympathy for my scowling aunt as I took my first taste. 'Is it homemade?'

'It is,' she muttered, refusing to meet my eye and accept the compliment.

'Speaking of homemade, I thought perhaps I could tell you a little more about your ancestors tonight.' Catherine picked up her spoon and skimmed the surface of the thick orange liquid for the tiniest possible mouthful. 'We could start with our namesake, the first Emma Catherine Bell.'

'I'd love that,' I replied as I shovelled the soup into my mouth. Everything that came out of Ashley's kitchen was delicious. So good, my worries about the wolf were forced to the back of my mind again and all I felt was a safe, cosy buzz as the warm liquid settled in my stomach.

'It only makes sense to begin at the beginning,' Catherine said, resting her spoon on the plate next to her barely touched bowl. 'Emma Catherine Bell was born in England in 1715. Her husband, John Stevens, decided the newly married couple would brave the perilous eight-week voyage across the Atlantic Ocean rather than pay off his debts and made that decision without asking his wife, but Emma Catherine quickly warmed to the idea and they boarded the good ship *Anne* in 1732. The British wanted to establish colonies in the American south to fend off the Spanish who had settled in Florida, and a great many promises were made to those who agreed to travel to the New World. Sadly, promises were not enough to ensure everyone survived the two months they spent on board the *Anne* and John Stevens was one of many who didn't live to see Savannah. By the time Emma Catherine set foot on American soil, she was a widow at the age of eighteen.'

'That's only just older than I am now,' I replied with wonder as my spoon scraped the bottom of my soup bowl.

Catherine nodded.

'And I for one am very relieved your voyage across the ocean was far less treacherous, and that you came to us without a husband. Dead or alive,' she said with a wink. 'Emma Catherine wasn't the only one to lose her husband in such a way and many women, too many, disappeared from the history books once they arrived in the New World without a man to keep them safe. But our Emma Catherine was resourceful. She made herself useful, helping to take care of the children and tending to the sick as they travelled to the settlement that would become Savannah. By the time the group arrived here, she was considered invaluable and even though she was already with child from her first husband, another man quickly made her his wife.'

'What do you mean, "made her"?' I asked. 'She didn't have a choice?'

'When it comes to marriage, choice is a relatively new idea. This man was a general in the army and he was powerful. Perhaps not the man she would have selected for herself, but he did afford a certain protection and status, meaning she could help even more people as the city grew around them.'

Ashley's head popped up, suddenly interested in the conversation. 'Help them how?'

'She was an experienced herbalist and a dedicated student of nature,' Catherine replied. 'There were very few doctors back then and fewer still who would help those who had little to offer in return. Emma Catherine was able to provide assistance to those in need. People who were sick and couldn't afford a doctor, people suffering from new diseases they could not yet treat. Most commonly, she helped women who wished to control the size of their families.'

'Ohhh,' I replied slowly as I realized what she meant.

'There have always been women who will help other women in that regard, and there always will be,' she added. 'No matter how hard men might try to take away their power.'

'What happened next?' My gaze caught on a painting of Bell House's back garden behind her. It was so verdant and blooming, so perfectly captured by the artist, it was as though I could see the flower petals being ruffled by the wind. Catherine's voice drifted away and I pictured myself standing in that garden, watching her tell the story through a window.

'Emma's second husband was not a kind or a good man,' she said with disappointment in her voice and on her face. 'In the early days, Savannah was a very different place to the city you see today. It was decreed there would be no rum, no lawyers, no Catholics, in order to lessen the threat of the Spanish settlement to the south, and no enslaved people, but as we all know, when you tell someone they cannot have something, it only makes them want it more. It is rightly impossible to tell someone how to worship so the no Catholics law fell quickly. In a feat of great irony, a lawyer sued to reverse the no lawyer ruling and won, and the rum flowed into town even more quickly than the lawyers. Sadly, it did not take long for the dark and greedy hearts to change their mind about enslaved people also, and according to surviving records, Emma Catherine's second husband had one of the darkest and greediest hearts of them all.'

The warmth of the dining room disappeared and I felt a chill on my skin. When I looked down at the floor, I saw flowers sprouting up between the cracks in the floorboards and brushing against my legs. On the walls, painted vines twisted into life, curling around painted trees while tiny living illustrations of birds hopped from branch to branch, singing silently above us.

'But Emma Catherine had not survived all she endured only to be brought down by a man,' Catherine said in a faraway voice. 'She waited and she planned and before too long, she was a widow again.'

I watched, wide-eyed and wordless, as a roughly sketched woman appeared among the trees, followed by a tall and menacing man. They circled the room until she stopped to pick a flower and pressed it into his hand. The moment he raised it to his face, a single blood-red tear slid down his cheek, followed by another then another, until a river of scarlet flowed over his face. The woman, with her long red hair, stood by motionless as he fell to his knees, convulsing with terrifying violence. When he was finally still, the vines rose up around him and dragged his body deep into the earth, every trace of his existence extinguished.

'Emma Catherine Bell protected the city,' Catherine said. 'And in return, the city protected her.'

The sound of Ashley's spoon clattering against the table broke the spell and when I turned away from the deathly scene, I was back in the dining room. No flowers coming through the floorboards, no ancestors strolling through the wallpaper. I stared hard at the painting and heard myself gasp. There was a red-headed woman in the corner who I was sure had not been there before.

'The Bell name still commands a certain respect in Savannah but what she and the rest of our ancestors did for this city has been long forgotten.' My grandmother shook her head bitterly. I held on to the edge of the wooden dining table with white knuckles, fighting off what felt like a landlocked case of seasickness. 'Still, we remain and continue her work. We don't make demands, we have no expectations. Emma Catherine Bell gave everything and asked for nothing in return.'

She reached across the table to pull sticky strands of hair

away from my damp forehead and pressed her cool palm on my hot cheek. I didn't realize I was crying until she wiped away my tears.

'And now we do the same.'

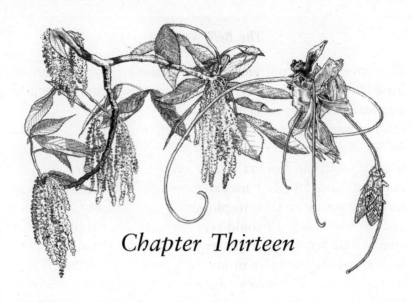

Chapter Thirteen

It was early when I woke the next morning. Instead of the hot coffee and fresh pastries I'd found the day before, there was only a note waiting for me on the kitchen table. Catherine would be out all day and breakfast was in the refrigerator. My hands were shaking as I opened the fridge to find a glass of orange juice, some Greek yoghurt with honey and a bowl of freshly cut fruit.

Something was wrong with me, I was sure of that now, and it wasn't the heat, the humidity or the jetlag. I remembered sitting down for dinner and my grandmother telling me the story of how the first Emma Catherine came to Savannah but what my memory insisted happened next didn't make any sense. I couldn't even remember how I got to bed, everything after dinner was a blur.

I sipped the juice and grabbed a banana from the fruit bowl, leaving the rest of it behind. My stomach felt as uncertain as I did. There was one theory that kept coming back. Wolves were wild animals, wild animals carried diseases, and no matter how many times Catherine told me it was all OK, I couldn't stop thinking about all that blood.

*

The library was cool and calm and completely silent or at least it was until the click and whir of the ancient computer bounced off the bookshelves. It was like a clap of thunder in the peace and quiet and I winced at the endless leatherbound spines in apology. Everyone always told me how smart I was, how capable, but I didn't feel too smart at the moment, only confused and afraid. I needed answers and I needed them now, there was no time to plough through all of Catherine's ancient books when I could type my symptoms into a search engine and get results right away. Upstairs, I had my dad's laptop squirrelled away in my backpack but without Wi-Fi, it was no use. The screen of the desktop computer came to life slowly, one bar of green blinking against a grey progress bar as the dial-up connection screeched its way down the phone line.

'Come on,' I muttered, the progress bar flickering for a second then starting all over again.

'Don't get too excited, it never connects.'

Ashley stood in the doorway, holding two cups in one hand, a plate of cookies in the other.

'You scared me,' I said, my heart pounding with surprise.

'And I wasn't even trying,' she replied.

She sauntered into the library, closing the door behind her and placing the plate of cookies and one of the mugs down on the desk. Great, I was trapped. But at least I was trapped with hot tea and cookies.

'I had the phone company out to see if we could get fibre optic broadband but they would have had to drill all through the house and run cables down from the street and Catherine wouldn't allow it.'

'There's literally no way to connect a computer to the internet in this entire house? You only have your cell phone?' I asked, clicking the mouse again and again just in case.

117

'I don't have a cell phone.' Ashley shrugged off my look of disbelief as she settled on an old leather couch, cradling the other mug of tea. 'They say the less time people spend online, the happier they are. You should try it.'

'It's not like I'm constantly online,' I replied, still shaken by her revelation. 'But the internet is useful for a million reasons, phones are useful for a million reasons. What if there's an emergency or you really need to find the nearest Starbucks?'

She glared at me, unimpressed.

'Something tells me our definition of an emergency might be very different.'

'I didn't say finding Starbucks was an emergency,' I muttered, even though sometimes it definitely was. 'There are other import- ant reasons to have a phone, like keeping in touch with people. Like Anwen. I really should let her know I'm OK.'

'The woman you were staying with in Wales?' Ashley gave a slight scoff. 'You don't need to speak to her. Catherine took care of her.'

It was news to me.

'She did? When? What did she say?'

'I don't know, I don't take notes on her private conversations. Catherine is not the kind of woman who will run things by you before she does them so don't waste your time thinking that she might.'

She pointed towards the cup and the plate she'd placed on my desk. 'And you're welcome, by the way.'

'Thank you. Did you make them?'

She nodded as I picked up one of the cookies and broke it in two, half expecting to find a razorblade baked inside, but there was nothing but chocolate chips. Still suspicious, I took a tiny bite. As far as peace offerings went, it was a good one. Crunchy on the outside, soft and warm on the inside, the perfect ratio of chocolate chips, sea salt, cinnamon, and something almost herbal I couldn't quite put my finger on. Even though I was useless in the kitchen, when it came to cookie recipes I was an expert. But I couldn't quite figure this one out. Just like Ashley.

'Can I ask you something?' I said, covering my mouth while I chewed.

'What?'

'How come you call Catherine "Catherine" and not "Mom"?'

She shucked off her shoes and stretched her legs out along the couch, head propped up on a pillow like she was preparing for a therapy session.

'Can't really say,' she replied before taking a sip from her cup. '"Mom" never felt right and I find people who call their mother "Mother" to their face are almost always straight-up strange, so I started calling her Catherine like everybody else. There wasn't ever any kind of rush to correct me. Could be it makes her feel younger. She sure won't be begging you to start calling her Grandmother any time soon, believe me.'

'She does look good for her age,' I admitted as I caught the outline of my reflection in the computer monitor. 'I hope I inherited those genes.'

A bitter chuckle escaped Ashley's lips. 'I'd bet my bottom dollar on it, although I can't say you're looking your best today.'

'Then I look as good as I feel.'

'What's that supposed to mean?'

Her expression shifted to something more curious, a glimmer of interest in her eyes, and I pressed my top teeth into my bottom lip. How much did I want to tell her?

'I'm not sure how to explain it,' I said, not ready to share with her, not yet. 'Just feeling off, I guess.'

She grunted as she lay back down, almost like she was disappointed. 'Drink your tea, it'll fix almost anything.'

'Must be magic tea then.' Maybe if she knew I'd been playing blood brothers with a potentially rabid animal, she might've shown more concern.

'Better?' she asked as I sipped from the cup.

'Yes.' The silky liquid slipped down my throat to soothe my frayed nerves, sweet and comforting.

'Swell,' Ashley remarked. 'Like you said, must be magic.'

I picked up another cookie and closed my eyes to savour the taste. It was hard not to inhale the entire plate, they were so incredibly good. She might not be the world's best conversationalist but my aunt definitely had a future as a cook. Everything she touched was delicious.

'I have another question,' I said.

'Sure you do,' she replied.

'I don't mean to be rude . . .'

'. . . Which means you're about to be incredibly rude. What is it you want to know?'

'What do you do?' I asked. The colour rose in my cheeks as the words left my mouth. She was right, it was rude. 'For work, I mean. Do you have a job?'

Her green eyes glowed in the dim light of the library, her long brown braid coiled over her shoulder like a pet snake.

'I'm a caretaker.'

'A caretaker?' I repeated. 'Taking care of what?'

'Whatever needs taking care of.'

She stood abruptly, her movements startlingly fast and fluid as she walked over to one of the bookshelves. I stayed perfectly still as she casually pulled out a book at random, read the front and back covers then put it back on a completely different shelf, spine in, pages out. The chaos of it would've given my dad a panic attack. No wonder this library didn't make any sense.

'I know everything must be real strange for you right now,'

she said, reshelving another undeserving book in the wrong place. 'But look at it from my perspective. A complete stranger just moved into my house and changed everything I've ever known. Catherine might be all excited to have you here but don't expect me to roll out the red carpet.'

'I don't expect anything—' I started to say but she cut me off before I could even try.

'No one cared about me until Paul disappeared. I was the spare, second to the golden child, until you were born. After that, I could have dissolved into dust and no one would have noticed. Then Paul vanishes and it's all eyes on Ashley. One second I'm invisible, the next I couldn't even sneeze without Catherine wanting a full written report on how, why, when, and where.'

'I'm sorry,' I said quietly. 'I didn't know.'

She turned quickly, spinning on the heel of her pointed shoe.

'You didn't know because your precious daddy was a selfish asshole.'

A sharp, sudden burning sensation sprang to life in my chest. Anger. I was angry. It wasn't a feeling I was used to.

'How can you say that?' The rage in my voice rattled my bones and echoed off the walls of the library. 'My dad was an incredible man.'

Ashley's lips twisted into something ugly. 'You're going to defend him when he dragged you all over the world, when you could've grown up here, with all of this? When he lied to you about everything? Me, Catherine, Bell House. Even your own name?'

'He had his reasons,' I replied, my fury simmering down to a confused frustration. 'You didn't even know him.'

'He was my brother before he was your father,' she reminded me. 'Paul never wanted anything to do with me when I was a kid. Did you know, when he was supposed to be babysitting, your incredible dad would lock me in my room so he could hang out with his friends instead?'

'He was a teenager,' I said, defensive but chastened. 'Teenagers do dumb things.'

'No, dumb people do dumb things,' Ashley snapped. 'He wasn't a teenager when he stole you away, when he left me behind without a second thought.'

If looks could kill, I'd have struck her down on sight. I looked away, just in case, and stuffed another cookie into my mouth to stop myself from saying anything I might regret. I was angry because she was right. He did lie. He did leave her behind. I couldn't defend what my dad had done and now he'd never be able to give us his side of the story.

'Paul was a selfish, uncaring, wicked man and I'm not sorry he's dead,' Ashley pronounced. 'As far as I can tell, there's only one downside to his accident and I'm looking at it.'

Stunned, I swallowed and opened my mouth to speak but as I tried to inhale, a chunk of cookie got stuck in my throat. I coughed, trying to clear it, but instead of moving down, the blockage seemed to grow, stabbing at the soft tissue and closing my airways, just as at the Powell house. I clutched at my throat and doubled over in my chair, beginning to panic as my lungs burned, but Ashley stayed where she was, fingers twitching at her sides, watching. She wasn't going to help me.

This time it all happened more quickly. The edges of my vision turned grey and fuzzy as I was drawn backwards, then, all of a sudden, I could breathe just fine. I was still in the library but Ashley was gone and in her place, I saw my dad and, when I turned towards the door, my mother.

'I didn't want to wake you,' he said, the warmth of his love filling the room. 'How do you feel?'

She came inside and closed the door quietly, her eyes never

leaving my face. She was beautiful, even more beautiful than she looked in the only photographs I had. A perfect heart-shaped face and a wide, angelic smile, but that smile didn't last long. When she turned her attention to my dad, her gentle expression transformed into something uneasy.

'Fine now but something's wrong. I've never blacked out before and last night makes it three times in one week. I'm serious, Paul, I think we need to get away from Savannah. Just for a little while, just until I'm myself again. Think of it as a vacation.'

Her voice again, the same sweet tones I'd heard the day before but roughened with an edge of exhaustion. She looked tired with dark circles under her bloodshot eyes. Tears poured down my cheeks but when I tried to call her name, all that came out was a cry.

'Looks like Emma agrees with you,' Dad replied, picking me up and cradling me in his arms. 'OK, let's go. I'll talk to my mom tonight.'

The scene clouded over and everything faded to black before bringing me right back to the present. The blockage in my throat gave way and I reached for what was left of my tea but it did nothing to soothe the raw burning sensation in my throat. On the plate, in among the crumbs, I saw a sharp splinter of something woody sticking out of one of the cookies. The sort of thing that could easily get stuck in someone's throat.

'What the hell?' I croaked, staring at my aunt in shock.

'That will teach you not to speak with your mouth full,' she replied. 'It's bad manners. Or did your perfect daddy not teach you that?'

With something like a triumphant smile, she sailed out of the library, leaving me with watering eyes and shaking hands. I might not be any closer to working out what was happening to me but at least now I knew how Ashley really felt about my arrival.

It wasn't only wolves, blackouts and hallucinations I had to worry about.

Chapter Fourteen

Nerves shot and throat raw, I sat on my bed, sipping water and counting the seconds until Catherine came home. Hours had passed since the incident in the library and there was still no sign of her. Not that I had no idea what I was planning to say. 'Hey, Catherine, hope you had a good day, by the way, Ashley baked me some really great cookies but I almost choked on one while she stood and watched, oh and I think I might have rabies and also, should I dress for supper this evening?'

Reaching across the bed to put down my empty water glass, I felt a warm pulse in my palm as it hovered over the antique nightstand. Slowly, I opened the drawer and the silver pin that saved my life in Bonaventure winked at me in the darkness. The pulse became a throb and all I wanted to do was touch the pin. I needed to feel the cool silver against my skin, run my fingers over the filigree and the centre stone, but before I could reach it, two sharp taps sounded against my window and I slammed the drawer shut.

Someone was clinging to the trunk of the tree that grew all the way up to my balcony. A magnolia tree, I noted, as I cautiously crossed my room to get a better look, but their face was obscured by its enormous white blossoms. Thankfully, their canary yellow tank dress and bright blue sneakers were perfectly visible as were the handful of little round stones that sat on the balcony.

'Hi neighbour!' a voice exclaimed as I lifted the sash window.

'Lydia,' I replied, leaning outside. 'What are you doing?'

Lydia Powell sighed with relief and pocketed her remaining pebbles. 'I'm so glad you're home. I'm almost out of ammo.'

'And you almost broke the window.'

On the other side of the fence that separated Bell House from the street, I saw Jackson leaning against a No Parking sign, as though he had absolutely nothing to do with his sister's shenanigans.

'We are here to deliver a very formal invitation to hang out with us,' Lydia said brightly as if climbing a tree to hurl pebbles at a window was the most normal thing in the world. 'It's hot as balls out here, we have no money and no plan, but you should definitely leave your beautiful air-conditioned house to walk around town with us.'

'As tempting as that sounds,' I replied, pressing my hand to my forehead to check for a fever, 'I haven't been feeling so good.' My voice was still raspy from choking and it hurt to talk.

'That's because you need to acclimatize,' she insisted. 'Get out here, girl, you'll feel better, I promise.'

Unless I started foaming at the mouth, bit the both of them and we all died of rabies.

'At least come and save me from my sister,' Jackson called. 'I promise I'll catch you if you start to swoon.'

He didn't realize how much that promise meant.

'Why didn't you come to the front door?' I asked as Lydia began her descent.

'Because I'm scared of your aunt.'

I looked over at the chair wedged underneath my door handle. She wasn't the only one.

'I'll be down in two minutes,' I said as she climbed down the tree, taking several huge flowers with her. 'Don't go anywhere.'

'No phone and no internet,' Lydia uttered as we strolled down Abercorn Street. 'It would be like losing a limb.'

'I do have a laptop but the battery is flat,' I told her, wrangling my hair into a topknot to get it off the back of my neck. Every single strand that touched my skin felt like too much; the humidity was even more oppressive than before. 'It's from the UK so the charger doesn't work with the outlets here.'

'If I took Lydia's phone away, she would cease to exist.' Jackson held up his empty hand in front of his face and posed like he was taking a selfie. 'The bones in her wrist are deformed from holding it all the time.'

'Evolved,' his sister corrected. 'I post, therefore I am. And don't act like you don't spend half your life on TikTok. I see you, big brother, I see you.'

'Big brother by twelve blissful minutes,' he explained when he saw the look on my face. 'After nine months with no escape, it was the least I deserved. She hasn't left me alone that long ever since.'

'He loves me really,' Lydia said, bounding off to the end of the block to grab hold of a lamp post and twirling around it, her pink belt bag spinning around her body like she had her own moon. She was a blur, always in motion. Jackson was much more calm and considered but they both moved through the city with total confidence. It was so obvious that they belonged here and I wondered if I would ever feel that way.

'What kind of laptop do you have? We have a bunch of chargers and cables lying around. Lydia breaks everything.'

Jackson hit me with the full force of his big brown eyes and even in the unbearable heat, my body found a way to make me blush.

'It – it's a MacBook, not sure what kind but I can check,' I stammered, caught off guard by his undeniable good looks. That kind of charm really was dangerous. 'It was my dad's computer. All his research is on there and I'd hate to think his work had disappeared forever.'

He shrugged like it was no big deal and I looked down at the ground, waiting for my face to return to its normal colour. Any and all interactions I'd had with guys my own age were extremely limited but I couldn't say any of them had gone well. Even if we spoke the same language, and that was rare since we moved to a different country every couple of years, just holding a perfectly normal conversation felt like an impossible task to me. I couldn't get out of my own head, too obsessed with what they were thinking, trying to guess what they might say back before they'd said it and so busy working out what I was supposed to say after that, I hardly ever got past the first 'Hello'. Wyn was the first guy I'd ever met who didn't make me feel like our conversations were a game of chess no one could win.

'How are you liking your new home?' Jackson asked as we walked on, the fierce afternoon sun boiling me alive in my jeans. 'Gotten up to anything fun?'

'I don't know about fun,' I replied, mentally going over the events of the last few days. 'But I am getting used to the place.'

'There's nowhere like Savannah.' He smiled at the city and it truly felt as though the city smiled back, his adoration reciprocated. 'Since we never really got through proper introductions, what else do we need to know about you, Emily James Bell?'

'Emily James Bell,' I repeated. 'That's going to take some getting used to.'

He shot another irresistible grin my way but this time I was too preoccupied with the addition to my name to react. It was so strange to hear out loud but it also felt unbelievably good to be openly claimed as part of the family.

'You already know way more about me than I know about you,' I pointed out. 'There isn't much else.'

'Sure there is,' he insisted. 'Do you have any hobbies, what are you into? What do you love?'

'Books,' I replied readily, remembering the similar conversation I'd shared with Wyn. 'I love books. Wherever you are in the world, a book can take you back to your favourite place.'

Jackson screwed up his face then laughed. 'Wish I could say I have the same passion. I've never had enough of a concentration span to last more than a few pages at a time.'

'Maybe you're reading the wrong books,' I suggested, a little disappointed in my new friend. There was nothing less attractive than someone who didn't read. Not that I was attracted to him, but he was, objectively speaking, gorgeous.

'He's not reading *any* books,' Lydia said as I tried to unravel the hole I'd fallen down in my head. 'Believe me, Em, I've tried but he's allergic to fiction. The last book he read by choice was *The Cat in the Hat*.'

'And Lydia reads a lot of fantasy,' Jackson countered, dry as a bone. 'Because Lydia thinks life *is* a fantasy.'

I grinned, pausing to check for traffic before we crossed the road. The twins didn't bother, confident they could stop traffic without trying. 'Aside from hating Charleston, do you two have *anything* in common? You don't seem very alike for twins.'

'You hear that, Lyds?' Jackson called as his sister pulled out her phone to take pictures of an old, creepy-looking house. 'Em doesn't think we're very alike.'

129

'That's because Em is smart,' she replied without looking back. 'And she's smart because she reads.'

'Please. I could give you a penny for your thoughts and still get change.'

'And you're not the dumbest person in the world but you'd better hope that person doesn't die—'

'Do you know the people who live in this house?' I asked, diverting the conversation before an actual fight broke out.

'No.' Lydia shook her head and put on a dramatic voice, still snapping photos. 'But everyone knows about the people who *used* to live here.'

'Lydia, cut it out.'

There was a mild warning in Jackson's voice which only made me more curious. In the top-floor bay window, I saw a little girl's face pressed up against the glass. She gave me a wave before dashing away out of sight.

'This is one of the oldest houses in Savannah,' Lydia said, ignoring her brother completely. 'The Benjamin Wilson house. It was built in 1870 and it was the most expensive house in Savannah at the time. Then the city built the first free public school right across the square and like most richie-rich men, Mr Wilson was an asshole—'

'An alleged asshole,' Jackson corrected.

'What's he going to do, sue me? The dude is dead.' She fluffed her hair before continuing with her story. 'As I was saying, he was an asshole, and when he found out one of his beloved daughters was playing with the kids from the free school, he tied her to a chair in the attic and made her sit in the window to watch them play without her.'

'Sounds like a charmer,' I muttered, even the Savannah sun not enough to stop a shiver from prickling my skin.

'That's not the worst of it,' Lydia replied. 'Georgia was in the middle of a heatwave and he left his daughter all alone for two whole days. When he finally went back to let her out, she was dead. She died of heat exhaustion.'

'That's awful,' I replied, thinking of the little girl I'd seen in the window. 'Imagine having to live in a house with such a miserable history. Do you think the people who live there now know the story?'

'No one lives here now,' Jackson said. 'It's been empty for years.'

I looked back up at the window.

'Empty? But I just saw someone in the attic.'

Lydia zoomed in on her picture and turned the screen around to show me. Not a single soul in any of the windows. I was sure the girl was waving at me when she took it.

'They say his daughter still haunts the house,' she whispered. 'Some people say she's appeared in their photographs or that she messes with your camera so the pictures come out all blurry but that's never happened to me.'

'That's because the whole story is untrue,' Jackson replied as I pinched the image outwards until it was a bunch of meaningless pixels. 'The house was built in 1868, not 1870, and there are marriage licences and death certificates for both of Wilson's daughters, filed years after your story was supposed to have taken place.'

'Like rich people aren't still out here falsifying records today.'

Lydia tutted and deleted the whole group of photos. 'Jackson thinks he's a history professor because he spends hours on Wikipedia and got a special badge at school one time.'

His nostrils flared and he pursed his lips. 'It wasn't a badge, it was a trophy, and I don't think it's so peculiar to be interested in the place where you live. Savannah is one of the oldest cities in the whole United States, we're lucky to have so much history around us.'

'My dad was a historian, wild to think he never told me any of these stories,' I said, struggling to keep the tremor out of my voice, my eyes glued back on the attic window. 'Are you sure no one lives here anymore?'

'That's about the only thing she got right,' Jackson confirmed. 'I sometimes work with one of the historic walking tours on weekends and they reckon the guy who lived there got sick of people gawking. He's super wealthy, does something in finance I think. He still owns the house, I heard he uses it for storage, but he moved someplace else.'

'Probably Charleston,' Lydia said with a scowl.

Jackson laughed, nodded in agreement and the twins walked on, their fragile truce restored. But I didn't follow. I was far too busy watching the little girl in the white frilly dress and ringlets press her nose up against the glass of the top-floor window and wave again before slowly but surely fading away.

'Welcome to Forsyth Park,' Lydia said before spinning around in a huge circle with her arms outstretched. 'My favourite place in all Savannah.'

The park was beautiful, lots of people and wide open footpaths, the sound of happy voices in the air. It was just what I needed to shake off Lydia's ghost stories. The twins were both wrong, I decided, after prising myself away from the Benjamin Wilson House. Someone had to be living there. Just because they hadn't seen the girl in the window, didn't mean she didn't exist.

Like the rest of the city, Forsyth Park had more than its fair share of trees and the trees had more than their fair share of Spanish moss, but it was less hemmed in than the carefully planned-out squares, sprawling on and on and on. In front of us was an enormous fountain with cool streams of water arcing out from the sides. If it weren't for all the people lined up to pose in front of it for photos, I'd have been tempted to jump in. There were so many people in the park, seniors taking a stroll, teenagers moving in packs or sunbathing on blankets, and harried-looking parents chasing after little kids, high on the thrill of being outdoors. A little girl with her hair in pigtails ran past us and I felt an involuntary shudder, thinking of Benjamin Wilson's daughter.

'The buildings around the park are some of the best examples of Savannah's classic architecture,' Jackson said, pointing across to a large building with a lot of windows and what looked like even more columns. 'That was Savannah's first hospital. It's part of SCAD now.'

Was that where my parents had met? Or where Wyn was taking his classes? I hadn't mentioned him to the twins. I could tell Lydia maybe but not Jackson. I was still building up my immunity to his charisma.

'But the best thing about Forsyth Park,' Lydia said, 'is our grandmothers don't come to Forsyth Park.'

'Why not?'

Lydia answered first. 'They don't leave the historical district.'

'NOGS,' Jackson added. 'They are strictly North of Gaston Street only and they're the last of a dying breed. I swear, they'd both be happier if they could turn back time and live in the nineteen hundreds. Our grandmother gets worse every day, last week she asked me if I was courting anyone.'

'I'm surprised she hasn't gone full Scarlett O'Hara and made me a gown out of the drapes,' Lydia mimed a swoon, hand pressed to her head. 'It's the twenty-first century and she still looks like she's going to faint clean away every time she sees me in jeans. At least Catherine dresses pretty cool. For an old person.'

'I'm pretty sure Catherine's only in her late fifties,' I replied.

'Ancient.' Lydia paused and reached for a strand of my hair. 'Hey, did you get streaks?'

'No?' I replied, checking the same strand myself. She wasn't wrong, there was definitely a red tint. 'Must be the sun.'

Jackson led us across the grass and safely out of the way of a runaway toddler on a tricycle. 'It suits you. Like that accent of yours. Half the time you sound like you're Savannah born and raised and the rest of the time it's full-on Downton Abbey. So cute.'

'What? No, it's not cute,' I rambled, quickly falling back into old, awkward habits at the first sign of a compliment. 'My dad never lost his southern accent but I picked up bits and pieces everywhere I went. You two have the best accents, mine is a mess.'

'You like my accent?' he asked, hitting me with another sleepy-eyed smile.

'Jackson Charles David Powell, we have talked about this.' Lydia swatted at the back of her brother's head then slid her arm protectively through mine. 'You do not have permission to make a move on my new friend.'

'She's my new friend too,' he said, trying to smother a guilty chuckle. 'I can't help it. Supposedly, I get the rizz from our bio-dad.'

It was tough for me, knowing I had two parents who were both gone but I couldn't imagine how it must feel to know your father was out there somewhere, still alive, but not part of your life.

'Have you ever tried to find him?' I asked.

Jackson shook his head. 'Why would we? He never came back to look in on our mom.'

'Hit it and quit it,' Lydia confirmed. 'I don't need that kind of energy in my life.'

'All we know is he was a charming Black artist who came

through Savannah seventeen years ago,' her brother added. 'We don't know his date of birth, he lied about his name and the number he gave Mom was for a burner. Even if we did want to find him, we don't have anything to go on.'

'I'm sorry,' I said. 'I didn't mean to pry.'

'Don't be, I'm happy with what I have.' He looked over at his sister and rolled his eyes as she flipped effortlessly into a handstand and walked across the grass on her hands. 'Most of the time.'

'This is the best part of the park,' Lydia announced as we passed a noisy playground and approached a quieter, white-walled structure. Behind tall plaster columns and wrought-iron railings was a park within a park. The same looping footpath in miniature and dozens of different flowers and plants. There was even a tiny fountain in the middle.

'It's a fragrance garden,' she said, running her hand over the railings. 'The people who take care of the park planted all these cool flowers that smell good and have interesting textures, and all the signs are in braille so everyone can enjoy it.'

'I don't know if enjoy is the right word,' I said, almost choking on the overpoweringly sweet scent of the garden. It was like walking into the perfume department of ten different department stores at once. 'It's a little intense.'

'Really?' she replied. 'I can barely smell a thing. Must be allergies.'

She went to open the gate but when she tried to flip the latch, it was locked.

'What the heck?'

'We're too late,' Jackson said, scanning a sign posted on the wall as she rattled the lock. 'They closed early for maintenance.'

With my eyes closed, I held on to the bars and breathed in.

It was such a heady perfume, a dense, overwhelming combination, but at the heart of it was something familiar. Jasmine? My dad loved jasmine-scented anything. Once he told me it reminded him of my mom and I'd held on to that memory forever.

'These gates have a history all their own.' Jackson grasped the railings too, his hand right above mine, not quite touching. 'They're from Union Station, the railway station they knocked down in the Sixties to build the interstate. It's cool how they were able to repurpose them here.'

'My brother the history buff,' Lydia said, this time with admiration. 'And what's even cooler is that before this was a fragrance garden, it was a poison garden.'

'Really?' I searched the flowerbeds for evidence.

'Lydia, quit it,' Jackson groaned. 'No, not really. They didn't even build this place until the nineteen-sixties. Seriously, you cannot believe a word my sister says.'

'It's a good job you're pretty, Jackson Powell,' she replied before grabbing my arm and marching me back the way we came. 'Because you have no imagination.'

In the distance, I heard a low and foreboding rumble. It sounded like a big truck driving by but from the matching looks on the twins' faces, I suspected it was not.

'Thunder.' Jackson grimaced as the blue sky clouded over with unbelievable speed. 'We should move.'

'Why didn't I bring a jacket?' Lydia wailed, letting go of my hand and taking off in a sprint. 'I don't want to get my hair wet, I just washed it.'

I hated surprise storms. A surprise storm took my dad from me and I had no desire to get caught in this one, but there was no outrunning it. With only that one warning, the heavens opened and down it came. Living in Wales, I was used to rain, but this was something else. Huge, heavy raindrops that hit so hard they almost blinded me as I ran side by side with Lydia. I felt my feet slapping against the footpath but all I could hear was the driving rain. The packed park was suddenly completely empty, everyone had run for shelter.

'Wait up!' Jackson yelled, his voice lagging somewhere behind us. 'Shit! I think I twisted my ankle.'

We slowed to a stop and turned back to see him limping, his white shirt transparent and glued to his body. I swiped my waterlogged hair out of my face as Lydia rushed to her brother's aid, understandably less distracted by his suddenly visible abs.

'Can you put any weight on it at all?' she asked, ducking underneath his arm and forcing him to lean on her for support.

'It's not that bad,' he claimed, sucking the air in through his teeth every time he touched his foot to the floor. It certainly looked that bad. 'Y'all go on without me, I'll be just fine.'

'Oh, sure. It's not that bad.'

With a pointed look, Lydia bent over and poked his ankle with her forefinger. He let out an unholy howling sound.

'He broke it last summer playing ball and it never did heal right,' she explained while her brother cursed her out loudly and creatively. 'Catherine gave him something to help heal it up but I just knew he didn't use it. Your grandmother's remedies always work.'

'I did too use it,' he muttered in response but from the sullen set of his jaw and shifty look in his eyes, I was pretty sure he was lying. 'Give me one minute to catch my breath and I'll be fine. Go on.'

'One minute and we'll all be drowned,' Lydia argued. 'Em, you run on home, you're soaked to the bone. If you catch a cold and die, your grandmother will kill me too. No point everyone dying.'

'People don't die from summer colds,' I assured her, catching

Jackson's eye before he could look away. Suddenly I was too aware of the clinginess of my own shirt and folded my arms across my body. 'Besides, I don't know that I could even find my way home in this.'

'OK then,' she sighed with acceptance. 'Let's at least get out of the rain.'

Lydia and I helped Jackson hobble over to the closest oak tree. The ground underneath its dense canopy of leaves was relatively dry compared to the rest of the park and we lowered Jackson carefully to the ground, his ankle already swelling up inside his sneaker. Carved into the sturdy trunk of the tree, I spotted a heart about the same size as my palm, with an arrow shooting through it. Inside were two initials but they'd been worn away by time and the weather.

'And I thought the heat was bad,' I said, the rain still hammering down as though it might never stop. 'Does this happen a lot?'

'Usually later in the summer but the weather has been all over the place this year,' Lydia replied. 'Once things really heat up, we might get a storm like this every day. You don't get much of a warning.'

'I wouldn't say exactly like this.' Jackson winced as he tried to flex his foot as the rain thrashed down.

'No,' she admitted. 'This is a doozy.'

From underneath the tree, it looked like a solid wall, pummelling all the plants and flowers into submission and closing in on us until I couldn't even see the footpath anymore. Another roar of thunder echoed through the park and the Spanish moss above me trembled.

'You know what's strange?' Lydia said, peering up at the sky. 'When there's thunder there's usually—'

The words weren't even out of her mouth before a streak of electric white light shot out of a cloud and stabbed the ground in front of us, scarring the park with a smouldering scorch mark.

'That's not great,' Jackson said as the earth sizzled.

'We're not safe here,' I said, combing through my memory banks for weather safety tips. 'The tree is too tall, we're basic-ally sitting under a lightning rod.'

'You want to walk out into the storm instead?' Lydia asked. 'Are you crazy?'

'She's right,' Jackson said with grim resignation. 'We're toast if we stay here and the lightning gets any closer. Literally.'

'Then you'd better butter me up because we can't do much else but sit,' she replied. 'You can't even walk, let alone run, and this storm ain't fixing to clear up any time soon.'

Another rumble of thunder shook the sky, much closer on this occasion, and I knew we were running out of time.

'We have to move him,' I told an unhappy Lydia, who dropped her head backwards and growled. 'I know it's horrible out there but we're not safe here. I've got a really bad feeling in my gut.'

Jackson did his best to bite back his moans as we hoisted him to his feet but I could see tears in his eyes once he was finally upright.

'Your gut better be so smart,' Lydia grumbled. 'I'm talking early acceptance to MIT followed by a Nobel prize smart, because if I get struck by lightning I am going to be so mad at you.'

'You won't be mad because you'll be dead,' her brother corrected through gritted teeth.

'Awesome positive thinking,' she grunted as he curled his arms around our shoulders. 'Y'all are ready?'

Getting out from under the tree was the right decision but one we didn't make soon enough. The moment we made our move, another flash of lightning pierced the clouds directly above my head. Lydia screamed and shoved Jackson out of its path but there was no way to avoid the inevitable. It was going to hit us.

For a split second, everything turned a blinding white and when the world came back into focus, the three of us were untouched, but something had changed. Everything was moving at a fraction of its usual speed. Lydia and Jackson were still falling but in slow motion, suspended above the dirt like puppets on a string. I could see every molecule of every raindrop and as I stepped out of its path, I watched the lightning bolt strike one of the lowest limbs of the oak tree instead of me. But we were still too late, the severed limb was going to hit us.

Then I saw her.

The fair-haired woman from the cemetery was standing right in front of me, her hands touching mine.

'Breathe in,' she commanded.

And I did.

'Now breathe out. Slowly.'

I controlled my breath as best I could, air passing over my pursed lips as I exhaled. The tips of my fingers tingled, sparks flickering underneath my skin, and I watched in shock as the Spanish moss that hung from the oak tree began to bind itself together into thick ropes. They wrapped around the tree and the falling branch, tensed like steel cables on a suspension bridge, pulling tight to hold it fast but even as it stretched, I could see the fibres tearing apart. It wouldn't hold for long.

'Now, run.'

I blinked as rainwater ran into my eyes. She was gone.

'Move!' I screamed at my friends as time caught up with itself and thunder rolled out over the city. 'We have to move!'

Jackson was already on the ground, Lydia having pushed him out of harm's way, but if she didn't run, she would be crushed. I reached for her arm and yanked, stronger than I knew I could be, and pulled her clear of the tree as the moss ropes gave way. The falling limb crashed to the ground, landing so close to us, I felt a sharp scratch against my cheek. When I touched my fingers to my face, they came away bloody. Too afraid to move, I stayed exactly where I was, staring up at the sky and willing the storm to pass. It did, ending as quickly as it had begun. The lightning-severed branch smouldered harmlessly beside me, the clouds blew away, grey skies turned to blue and the world was bright and sunny once more.

'Em.' I heard Lydia gasp my name. 'You saved our lives.'

'You saved Jackson,' I replied weakly. 'You pushed him out of the way.'

'Should've let it hit me,' Jackson joked as he pushed himself upright, cringing at his swollen ankle. 'I'll never hear the end of this now.'

But Lydia wasn't listening, she was too busy gazing at me with big, open, awestruck eyes.

'If it weren't for you, I'd be dead right now.'

She scrambled across the wet grass, already steaming as the sun came back with a vengeance, and covered my body with hers, smothering my face in noisy kisses. 'You're amazing and I love you and I will do anything for you forever.'

'Better think about what you're saying before you make that promise,' I replied, trying to laugh along with the twins.

Two lives saved in three days. It was an impressive record, especially given that until I moved to Savannah, I hadn't had to save a single life in the last sixteen years. I was just as happy as Lydia and Jackson that we'd survived but for whatever reason, I couldn't shake the growing suspicion that if it weren't for me, they would never have been in danger in the first place.

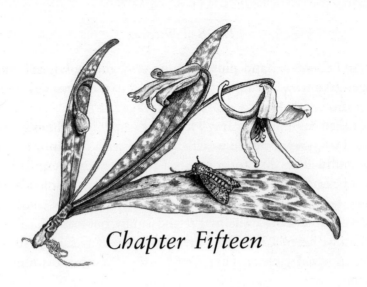

Chapter Fifteen

'Emily, honey, you're home. We were so worried.'

Catherine was on me the second I walked through the door. She pulled me into a hug, my wet clothes soaking her through, and all I wanted to do was pretend nothing was wrong and stay right where I was. But I couldn't. We had to figure out what was happening to me before someone got really hurt. I pushed her away so she could see the determined look on my face.

'I need to talk to you. Something is really wrong.'

Ashley stood behind Catherine, dutifully waiting with a fluffy white towel in her hands. The moment we made eye contact, she scowled.

'Alone,' I added.

'Let me look at you first,' my grandmother muttered, gripping my upper arms tightly, checking me over for any visible injuries. 'That storm came in so fast and lit up all creation, there's not a dry thread on you—'

'Catherine, stop!'

The sound of my voice reverberated off the silken walls of the foyer and all three of us looked equally surprised.

'Something is happening to me,' I said, suddenly tearful and so, so frightened. 'I need your help before something really bad happens.'

She held me out at arm's length, two anxious lines carved into her flawless porcelain skin, bracketing her unhappy mouth.

'Emily, you need to go to bed and rest,' she said, words wrapped in barbed wire, sharp and pointed. 'Ashley, make some tea. I'll bring it up when it's ready.'

'Rest isn't going to help.' I refused, standing firm. 'Can't you see something is wrong? I'm blacking out, falling over, I'm hearing voices, seeing people who aren't there. I keep having flashbacks to things I couldn't possibly remember, and whatever just happened in the park, I can't even begin to explain it. At first I thought I'd caught something from the wolf but that doesn't even make sense anymore. Nothing makes sense. Catherine, I'm frightened.'

Ashley flinched when I mentioned the wolf, her eyes flicking over to Catherine, who gave a slight nod, and I watched as my aunt scurried away. The foyer filled with a strange sense of peace, waves of soothing energy smothering my panic but not erasing it completely. I propped myself up against the wall as my legs trembled underneath me and the house seemed to sigh contentedly at my touch.

'Very well,' Catherine said at last. 'Come with me.'

She pulled me away from the wall and led me into the parlour, directing me to the loveseat where I sat obediently. The water seeped out of my sodden clothes and into the light-coloured silk but she didn't seem to care.

'Before we begin, please remember this; you're home, you're safe and nothing can hurt you inside Bell House,' Catherine said, perched on the edge of the coffee table in front of me. 'Now, tell me exactly what happened in the park.'

'I was with Lydia and Jackson when the storm hit,' I began,

trembling as I searched for the right words to paint the picture. 'We were in Forsyth Park. The rain was coming down so hard, we tried to shelter under a tree but it was struck by lightning.'

'My goodness,' she replied, interested but not as shocked as I thought she would be. 'Then what happened?'

'The lightning severed this huge branch,' I said, reliving every moment. 'It should have crushed us, all three of us. We should be dead.'

It was too fresh in my mind, not far enough away to be safely called a memory. Catherine rested her hand on my arm, holding me in place as though I might otherwise float away.

'And why is it do you think, that you're not?'

I closed my eyes, willing myself to speak. It was time to tell her everything.

'You're going to think I'm losing my mind,' I whispered. 'Because it doesn't make sense.'

'You keep saying that,' she replied, head tilted to one side. 'How about you let me be the judge of what makes sense and what doesn't?'

Breathing in deeply, I filled my lungs until I thought they would burst then pushed all the air out in one loud exhalation.

'The branch didn't crush us because the Spanish moss caught it.' I shook my head at the improbability of my own words. 'It held it up long enough for me to move and push Lydia out the way.'

'That's all?'

'No. There was a woman who appeared out of nowhere to tell me what to do then disappeared when we were safe.'

'I see. Did Lydia or Jackson speak to this woman?'

I shook my head. There was no one to back up my version of events. I pressed my hand against the scratch on my cheek, relieved to find it was still there, evidence at least that I wasn't gaslighting myself. Wiping a mixture of rainwater and tears from my face, I heard a sob catch in my throat as more shattered fragments came back to me. Might as well throw all the fuel on the fire at once.

'Also, it felt like time slowed down,' I said, searching for any sign that she believed me but my grandmother's perfectly balanced features were inscrutable. 'Or maybe I was moving super fast, I'm not sure, but it's happened before. Once in Lafayette Square and again when the wolf attacked you. This time it lasted longer.'

'Is that right?' Catherine said calmly. 'How very interesting.'

'It's not interesting, it's terrifying,' I replied, running out of patience. 'What's happening? Am I losing my mind?'

She moved to sit beside me on the loveseat and pulled my hand away from my face, the scratch stinging sharply when she pressed one careful finger against it.

'Emily, I told you on your first day in Savannah, no harm will come to you here. I meant that.'

'You were wrong,' I replied. 'This feels like harm.'

'No,' she said. 'This feels like an awakening.'

She straightened her shoulders, looking as regal as ever but the impassive expression on her face had turned into something else. Pride burned in her emerald eyes, and she smiled, lips curling with admiration.

'What does that mean?' I asked, twin tides of panic and confusion rising in me, threatening to roll in and wash me away. 'Nothing like this has ever happened to me before, I swear, I'm normal.'

Catherine clucked with distaste. 'Normal, indeed. What a terrible thing to say about yourself. You, Emily James Bell are anything but.'

Her chin dipped expectantly and my heart skipped several beats ahead of itself. The whispers in the moss, the appearing-and-disappearing woman, the little girl in the window, the tree branch. I closed my eyes, squeezing them until I saw stars, and released all the other things my mind had hidden away from me until I was ready. Catherine and Ashley talking in the library, the painting of the garden, the living wallpaper. The first Emma Catherine Bell. Everything came rushing back and when I opened my eyes, the trees and vines that decorated the parlour walls twisted and turned, growing and flourishing as they snaked along the floor towards me.

Catherine was right, this wasn't normal. I wasn't normal.

'What about the blackouts?' I gazed down, transfixed as the vines wended their way over the polished floorboards. 'And why do I feel so strong one minute but the next I can barely stay up on my feet?'

'Your body is overwhelmed. Your strength is growing. It's a lot for you to cope with all at once.'

'The hallucinations?'

'Visions. Of the past and, I suspect, the future.'

'How do you explain the blonde woman? And the little girl I saw in the window of the Benjamin Wilson House?'

This time, her answer rode on a sigh. 'Oh, Emily, you already know the answer. What else could they be?'

My mouth made the shape of a word but no sound came out.

'Ghosts,' I managed to breathe. 'I can see ghosts.'

'Honey, you can do much more than that.'

I reached out to meet the encroaching vines as they surged forward, rising upwards when I raised my hand and lowering down when I did the same. This couldn't be happening, it simply couldn't.

'Ghosts aren't real. They're just stories made up to scare people. Fairytales. It's not real history,' I murmured, a slender trail of ivy wrapping itself lovingly around my ankle.

'History is written by the victors,' Catherine said. 'That's the saying, isn't it? But it's not entirely true. Your so-called "real history" is made up of the stories men wanted people to believe. Sometimes the past lives within us, not written or recorded, but handed down from one generation to the next. Our history is alive.'

The room hummed as she turned delicate circles with her wrist, sending the vines into retreat, back across the floor and up into the wallpaper.

'Tell me, does it feel like a fairytale now?' she asked.

'No,' I replied, so timid I was barely able to hear myself. 'It feels very real.'

My grandmother directed the vines up the walls like she was leading an orchestra. Clouds crashed with thunder and every bough of every painted tree trembled.

'And what do we call a woman whose abilities exceed natural expectations?' she asked, sweeping the clouds away and summoning the sun. 'A woman who sees things others cannot. Can perform acts others might consider impossible. What name is she given, Emily?'

'When you said my dad left because he didn't agree with your beliefs . . .' I murmured.

It suddenly was all so obvious. Power and strength rolled off her and somehow, into me, an unexpected pulse of something rushing through my veins and stealing my words away.

'Go on, you can say it,' she encouraged when I faltered. 'You'll feel better when you do.'

'You're a witch,' I said.

'Yes, I am,' Catherine replied. 'And so are you.'

Chapter Sixteen

'I must say, it's a relief.'

With impossible grace, Catherine moved from the loveseat to her preferred armchair, her posture noticeably looser than usual. 'Doesn't it feel good to have everything out in the open at last?'

'I haven't made it to "good" just yet,' I replied, still reeling as all the puzzle pieces my mind had stored in different pockets, slotted themselves into place to form a very clear picture.

'Take all the time you need,' she said. 'I wanted to tell you everything the moment we met but I had to be sure the blessing was alive in you. That's what we call our magic, what it has always been called. The blessing had to develop in its own time and now we know for sure. Emily, you're one of us.'

'I'm a witch,' I said, trying out the impossible statement for the first time.

'That's right.' She laughed lightly as though I'd just declared myself a Libra or a Swiftie or any other normal thing.

'And you're a witch too?'

'Surely am.'

'Is that where you go in the mornings? To hang out with your coven?'

This time her laughter was much louder.

'Oh, honey, I wish. Most days I'm out there arguing with tedious little men over tedious little things. There is no coven, it's just us. Things are not as they used to be but I do believe that's all about to change.'

Before I could ask one of the thousands of follow-up questions that were tripping off my tongue, the door flew open and Ashley entered carrying her usual tray, her usual iced tea.

'Are you a witch?' I asked bluntly when she set the tray down on the coffee table. My aunt looked up at me, her green eyes as hard as flint.

'No, I'm not a witch. I already told you, I'm a caretaker.'

The silver sugar bowl clattered onto the marble top of the table and without waiting for a response from me or Catherine, she strode out the room, slamming the door behind her.

'The blessing passes from grandmother to granddaughter,' Catherine explained, the glasses on the table still rattling with the force of Ashley's exit. 'This demands a great sacrifice from the middle generation. The sons and daughters of witches, their mothers and the fathers, are not blessed with magic. Their sacred calling is the duty to nurture and care for we Bell witches.'

I'm a caretaker.

No wonder she hadn't exactly rolled out the welcome wagon. Catherine was a witch, I was a witch, Ashley made the tea. Not exactly a good deal.

'This morning, in the library,' I said, eyeing a plate of cookies beside the tea. 'I almost choked and Ashley just watched, she didn't try to help or anything. That's her idea of taking care of me?'

'Your aunt was quite keen to discover whether or not our magic was with you,' Catherine replied with a disappointed eyeroll. 'I suspect that may have been her way of hurrying things along. Moments of crisis can expedite access to our abilities.'

'Like in the park. And the cemetery.'

'Precisely.' She poured my tea and passed the glass across the table.

'You said it passes from grandmother to granddaughter?' I asked, grasping for solid facts, things I could learn and hold on to. 'What about people who aren't assigned female at birth?'

She gave me a sour look over the rim of her glass. 'Emily, magic comes from nature. Do you think it is concerned with something as vulgar as flesh? Man invented this idea of male and female and like most things created by mankind, it means very little as far as nature is concerned.'

The cold, sweaty glass of tea felt good against my hot skin and I wrapped my hands around it, breathing in the herbal scent before taking a sip.

'Your abilities will show themselves more quickly now. If you'd been raised here, they would have expressed themselves slowly, over time, but your being oceans away from your family line limited the both of us. Not anymore.'

I swirled the tea around in my glass, listening to the ice cubes clink against each other. Did I feel different? It was so hard to tell, I already couldn't remember what normal felt like.

'My abilities,' I repeated. 'You mean my magical powers?'

Catherine raised her hand, the internationally accepted sign for 'hold up'.

'The first and most important thing you need to learn: the concept of power is corrosive. It simply screams world domination, don't you think? People who desire power seek to control and that's a mistake. We work with the world, not against. At its heart, the blessing is simply the ability to see things others miss.'

'Like little girls who died decades ago and platinum blondes who disappear after saving your life.'

'People fear what they can't explain,' she said. 'Much like witches, ghosts are just another natural part of our world with an undeservedly nasty reputation. I have to tell you, I'm quite envious. The ability to communicate with those who have passed over is very rare.'

'If I could regift it to you, I would,' I replied. Then another thought occurred to me. 'Unless there's a way to summon a particular ghost?'

'I think I know what you're going to say next. You won't be able to speak to your father. Spirits can't cross moving water.'

'What about my mom?' I asked, knocked down but not defeated.

'As I understand it, when one opens a door to the dead, there is no way of knowing who will walk through it,' Catherine replied, the warning in her voice loud and clear. 'I don't think that's a risk we're ready to take right now, do you?'

The deep ache of grief returned, stronger than ever, the brief flicker of possibility snuffed out. I put down my glass and looked at the backs of my hands then turned them over to inspect the palms. No evidence of magic here. Just a girl who could speak to random ghosts but not her dead mom and dad.

'Is it a secret?' I asked, eyeing my grandmother with curiosity.

She lounged back in her armchair, waving one hand around as though she might pick the right answer out of mid-air.

'It's *not* a secret. But I would think very, very carefully before you choose to share the truth with anyone.'

Like I was about to get a T-shirt printed that said 'I'm a witch, ask me how'.

'I can't believe this is something that's been in me since I was born,' I said, flexing my fingers as though laser beams might shoot out from the tips at any moment. 'What if I'd never come here? What would have happened then?'

'Your abilities would have withered on the vine after your seventeenth birthday,' Catherine said in a soft voice. 'And taken mine along with them.'

My hands curled into two fists, holding tight to something I didn't even know I might've lost. Whatever this was, it had only been mine for moments but already the thought of losing it was like losing a limb. No one should be allowed to make that kind of decision on behalf of someone else. No one should have the power to fundamentally change who you really are.

'That's why my dad took me away,' I said, so very sure of the fact. 'To stop this from happening.'

Catherine looked as though she was struggling to answer my question, biting on her bottom lip and twisting her aquamarine ring as she sought the correct response.

'There is a difference between knowing something and understanding it. He thought he was making your life easier. Paul didn't want you to grow up to be different.'

She leaned forward to caress the petals of a live orchid in the centre of the coffee table. It trembled at her touch and when she moved her hand away, a tiny pink bud appeared on the stem.

'Think of yourself like this flower,' she said. 'The blessing is like any other living thing. In order to flourish, it must be nurtured and protected. The Bell family has always taken care of their line. Magic is something you are born with but still something that must be cultivated, otherwise . . .'

As she spoke, the bud began to pulse, blooming right in front of me and blossoming into a magnificent flower. It was beautiful. But it wasn't done. Even after every petal had unfurled, the flower carried on growing until it was so big, the supporting stem snapped in two and sent the plant crashing onto the floor.

'When nature is allowed to run wild, things can go wrong.'

Catherine scooped up what had fallen and laid it all back on the table.

'Can we fix it?' I asked, staring at the sad, broken orchid. 'Can *I* fix it?'

'Let's find out.' She knelt down on the floor, nodding for me to do the same. I slid off the loveseat in my still-damp jeans and sat across from her, cross-legged.

'Hold your hands out over the stem,' she instructed. 'Now, just like before, I want you to breathe.'

It shouldn't have been a difficult request but as soon as she told me to breathe, I was lost, overthinking everything, like I'd forgotten how and was afraid I'd get it wrong.

'In then out,' she chided with tenderness. 'I'm not trying to trick you.'

A quiet, nervous laugh stuck in my throat as I settled myself, searching for the same sense of stillness I'd found in the park but it was impossible. I could hold an incredibly heavy tree branch up in the air in the middle of a torrential downpour but I couldn't mend a broken plant stem in the safety of my own home?

'Don't be disheartened,' she said when I huffed out a sigh of frustration. 'Your mind and your body need to be in harmony. That probably isn't the case right now.'

'Not so much,' I agreed.

There wasn't an ounce of peace inside me, only too many questions and not enough answers. Catherine reached across the table, looking more bemused than anything else, and covered my hands with hers.

153

'I wonder, what might we be able to do if we work together.'

She held out her hands the same way the blonde woman had in the park and when I pressed my palms against hers, a warm, tingling sensation passed over my skin. At first, nothing changed. The orchid lay on the coffee table, just one or two fibres left unbroken in the stem, one petal falling to the floor like a crumpled-up piece of paper.

'Stop trying to force it,' Catherine said. 'Nature can't be bullied, only asked and encouraged.'

Simple instructions that were impossible to follow. I focused hard, pursing my lips and forcing my eyebrows together, but the orchid stayed exactly as it was.

'It's not working,' I said, slapping my hands against my thighs.

'Because you're doubting yourself. Clear your mind and believe that the orchid will be whole again. Stop trying and know it is done. See it, feel it.'

Clearing my mind was not a top-tier skill of mine. Ever since my dad's accident it was always racing, always overanalysing, searching for the safest, quickest, most efficient option. The only time I'd been off high alert in the last two months, was when I was with Wyn. The warm tingle in my skin spread all over my body as my mind wandered away from the orchid, filled instead with all the colours of his eyes, the soft grey, the vivid green, the warm golden brown. I pictured the freckles on the bridge of his nose, imagining myself leaning in closer and closer until . . .

'Emily, open your eyes.'

I hadn't even realized they were closed.

The stem of the orchid glistened, bright green threads knitting themselves together, binding into strong, thicker fibres until it was complete again, and the blossoms that had wilted away entirely were lush and healthy. I pulled my hand away from my grandmother's to stroke one of the unfurling petals and felt a rush of joy as if we were still connected; me, Catherine and the plant.

'Oh,' I whispered, stifling a laugh of happy surprise. 'We did it.'

'You did it,' my grandmother said tenderly. 'When you have faith in yourself, you can accomplish anything.'

'Anything?' I replied.

'Anything within reason.' She smiled as the orchid bloomed more beautifully than ever. 'You will have so much strength, Emily. All you have to do now is learn to control it. You must show discipline.'

I heard her, somewhere in the back of my mind, but I wasn't really listening, too busy staring at the thriving plant in front of me.

'I can't believe it,' I marvelled, still speaking so softly, afraid to make any loud noises in case it spooked the newly revived flower. 'We brought it back to life.'

Catherine had no such concern.

'No, we didn't,' she said, speaking sharply. 'That's not how our magic works. We cannot bring anything back once it has passed.'

This time I was the one who knew what was coming next.

'Or anyone,' I added.

'The blessing works hand in hand with nature and there is nothing more natural than life coming to an end,' she replied with tenderness, confirming my assumption. 'We can speed things up and slow them down, but we cannot and should not interfere with the natural order of things. That would be very dark indeed.'

'If we're good witches, does that mean there are bad ones?'

'Good and bad are subjective concepts.' She took my hand, ran it over the orchid's brand new blossom once more. 'Nature requires a balance of light and dark and the blessing exists to uphold that balance.'

One by one, the petals floated down to the coffee table and rocked back and forth on the marble before they shrivelled up to nothing.

'There is always a before and an after,' Catherine said softly. 'That is all we know for certain. Dawn and dusk, fire and ashes, life and death. We treat both sides with respect, neither one is good or bad. When it comes to the light and the dark, they both have the power to blind you.'

Chapter Seventeen

'And where are we going this morning, little witch?'

I had one foot out the front door when I heard Ashley's voice and froze. She'd been invisible ever since I'd asked about her abilities the day before, even choosing to eat alone in her room when dinner time rolled around. Not that I'd missed her, my evening was consumed with questions about this so-called blessing and by the time Catherine finally convinced me to go to bed, my head was spinning. But here she was, Sunday morning, lurking behind the staircase, waiting to pounce.

'I'm going to meet Lydia.'

It was a lie. Could she tell?

'Does Catherine know?' Ashley asked, prowling around me.

'I think I mentioned it.'

Even under the arctic blast of the air conditioning, I was starting to sweat.

'She's out, isn't she?' I added, knowing full well that she was. She told me she had business to attend to this morning and I'd watched her leave twenty minutes earlier, peeping out of my bedroom window as Barnett drove her off.

'That doesn't mean you should be running around town,'

my aunt replied. 'Not right now. Who knows what kind of trouble you'll get yourself in, especially with that Lydia Powell.'

'You don't like Lydia?'

'No, I don't like Lydia. She's loud and impertinent and I don't know how her grandmother stands her.'

I had to duck my head to hide my smile. Ashley probably didn't need to know the feeling was mutual.

'Well, I can't just not show up. I don't have the number for her cell and she's probably already on her way to meet me.'

It was mostly the truth, only it wasn't Lydia I was supposed to meet.

'I don't know.' Ashley slipped her hands into the pockets of her skirt. 'Catherine might not like it.'

'Catherine wouldn't want me to be rude,' I countered. 'I won't be gone all that long anyway. She'll never know.'

I held up my hand in a Girl Guide salute, about the only thing I remembered from the two meetings I'd convinced my dad to let me attend years ago, right before we moved again.

'Before you go, how do you feel?' she asked and if I didn't know better, I might have said she sounded worried about me.

'Tired,' I replied. 'Very tired.'

It was the easiest honest answer I could give her. Sleep did not come easily, and even with the help of my favourite hot tea, I'd tossed and turned for hours. Catherine was right when she said people were afraid of the unknown. I was people. I was afraid. But underneath the layers of anxiety and trepidation, all the what ifs and the why me, something else had burrowed its way under my skin and into my bones. Excitement. Curiosity. *Magic.* The tingling I felt when Catherine and I repaired the orchid had never fully left me, instead it covered me like a warm blanket, protective and strangely familiar.

'And what are you planning to do if there's another incident?'

'There won't be,' I replied, even though I didn't feel as certain as I sounded.

Ashley raised an eyebrow. 'You're sure about that?'

I wanted to say yes but I couldn't. I'd told too many lies already.

'Just go,' she said, stepping out of my way. 'But try not to end the world if you can help it.'

'Thanks for the vote of confidence,' I said as I raced through the door, already too late to second guess myself. 'I think that's a bit beyond my abilities.'

'Let's hope so,' she replied, closing it loudly behind me.

I saw Wyn before Wyn saw me. He was waiting, just like he said he would be, leaning against the same old oak tree, sleepy-eyed and smiling. My heart lurched at the sight of him. So much had changed in the last two days. Part of me knew I should be at home, safe in Bell House, waiting for Catherine to return to teach me more about my newly discovered legacy. But there was another, even more powerful part of me that was desperate to see Wyn. A longing so overwhelming, it was almost as frightening as finding out I was a witch.

I had already decided I wasn't going to tell him, not yet. Sure, he said he knew a little about astrology but knowing your rising sign was a long way from believing witches were real and, oh, by the way, I am one. All I had to do was keep a lid on my magic, avoid storms, dangerous trees and unexpected ghosts, and we'd be completely OK. Simple.

'I'd offer you a penny for your thoughts but I reckon they'd be worth a whole dollar,' he said, interrupting my train of thought. 'What's on your mind?'

'I was just thinking about, um, what was I thinking about?'

Don't say kissing you, don't say kissing you, don't say kissing you.

159

I gulped and turned away, searching the park for an alternative answer. A golden retriever bounded towards the fountain, dragging its owner behind it.

'Dogs. I was thinking about dogs.'

His crooked smile stretched so wide he couldn't rein it in.

'You were thinking what about dogs?'

In fairness, I wouldn't have believed me either.

'How come there are cat cafés but not dog cafés?' I replied, fighting off an overwhelming internal cringe. 'People like dogs just as much as they like cats, why don't they have their own cafés?'

For what felt like a very long moment, he stared at me as if trying to figure out the joke. I smiled back too big. Why couldn't I behave like a normal human being? What was I supposed to do with my hands? Why did my feet suddenly feel too big for my shoes?

'Personally, I think it's a million dollar idea but I think your question just answered itself.'

Wyn pointed at the same golden retriever as it hurled itself into the fountain, splashing its owner and anyone else within a five metre radius. 'Would you trust him around an espresso machine?'

'Oh, yeah,' I agreed, wondering if the dog would consider dragging me into the fountain and leaving me there. 'Probably a little too unpredictable.'

He smiled again and my heart skipped several beats.

'Unpredictable can be good. Speaking of, how do you feel about a field trip?'

The owner of the dog wrangled it out of the fountain, and it wagged its tail until it was a blur. As soon as it was out, it leapt right back in, racing around in a circle and soaking the owner through. Unpredictable wasn't good. Unpredictable was risky. What if I saw another ghost? What if I had another vision? Travelling too far away from Bell House was a bad idea. The sensible thing would be to stay right here in the square.

Wyn reached out and took hold of my hand and all my fears fluttered away on the breeze.

'There's that look again,' he said. 'What is on your mind, Em?'

'Absolutely nothing,' I replied, closing my hand around his. 'Let's go.'

Sensible thing be damned.

Tybee Island was only a twenty-minute drive from downtown but when Wyn's vintage cherry-red pickup truck pulled off the road and into the parking lot, I felt like we were a million miles away. The change of scenery was extreme, Savannah's careful squares, with their centuries-old townhouses and towering oaks, gave way to beach houses, cute shops and restaurants, and as we drove into Tybee, Wyn pointed out the kind of lighthouse that looked like it should be in a movie.

It didn't take long to find a quiet spot on the beach even though it was a scorching hot Sunday. It was still early by Savannah standards, no one ever seemed to be in a rush around here. I turned my face up to the sun and soaked it all in while Wyn opened a striped beach umbrella, his biceps straining against his sleeves as he drove it into the ground.

'Welcome to Tybee Island,' he said, grinning down at me while I attempted to lay out a matching blanket without kicking sand all over it.

'It's gorgeous,' I replied, kicking sand all over it. 'I can't believe we're so close to town.'

'You said you didn't get to visit the beach all that often before. Now it's right on your doorstep, you can come any time you like.'

Sitting back on my heels, I shielded my face from the sun. 'You remembered that?'

Wyn pinched his shoulders into a casual shrug that was completely betrayed by the way his cheeks shone bright red. Digging around in a massive backpack, he produced a pair of red, retro plastic sunglasses and a tube of sunscreen.

'Can't have you burning to a crisp,' he said, handing them both over. 'The lady in the pharmacy said this was the best brand for redheads.'

'But my hair is brown,' I protested until he gently grasped the end of my messy braid and held it between us. 'Except in this light where it definitely has an auburn tint.'

'Reminds me of the way the sky looks at sunset,' he said, still holding my hair in his hand. 'Right after the sun goes down.'

A million tiny jolts of electricity burst through me as he carefully laid my braid back over my shoulder and reached for the tube of sunscreen, pretending I didn't feel the tingling sensation building in my fingertips.

'Let me look at this,' I said, popping the cap. 'SPF 50, nice. How about I do you, then you do me?'

Wyn let out a howl of laughter as I turned into the human embodiment of cringe.

'Whatever you need,' he replied, a playful grin lighting up his eyes. 'Always happy to help.'

'Appreciate it.' I squeezed a glob of thick white lotion into my hand and slapped it against my face, rubbing ferociously as I pressed my lips together to seal them shut, hopefully forever.

Tybee was heaven. A cool breeze blew in off the water, transforming the sticky city heat into perfect beach weather, and the vibes were undeniably high. Wyn, in his T-shirt and swim shorts, was already perfectly golden while my limbs gleamed a conspicuous white, peeking out from my loose cotton shirt and new denim shorts that were formerly old jeans. We sat side by side on the beach blanket, not quite touching but close enough for me to be intensely aware of his body. I silently catalogued the parts I hadn't noticed before: the worn leather strap of the watch on his left wrist, the freckles on the backs of his hands, the long indent of a scar on his left shin.

'That looks rough,' I said, pointing to his leg. 'Get into a fight over the last scoop at Leopold's?'

'It was lemon custard and it was totally worth it.'

He traced the mark all the way up from ankle to knee. 'Truth is, I don't know how I got it. Happened when I was six. According to my folks, they left me playing outside with Cole then my grandpa found me with this crazy gash on my leg. I don't remember a thing. Only that my dad took us out for McDonald's afterwards which was a big deal because my dad does *not* approve of fast food.'

'Did you get a Happy Meal?' I asked, still staring at the scar.

'Complete with SpongeBob SquarePants on a skateboard. And yes, it's still on my nightstand.'

'Can't go wrong with SpongeBob,' I smiled. 'You don't have any theories about what happened? Whatever it was must have been sharp.'

'And clean too, it healed up right away. Guess my brain decided I was better off not knowing. I heard that kind of thing can happen when you go into shock, you know?'

I nodded, I did know.

'And your brother didn't see what happened?'

'Not exactly a surprise. Cole isn't that observant,' Wyn replied flatly before nodding to the scar on my arm, the one from Bonaventure. 'While we're comparing war wounds, how'd you get that one?'

163

'Oh, boring story.' I rolled my sleeve all the way down to the wrist. 'It happened a long time ago. I fell. Off a scooter. In Italy.'

'Doesn't sound boring to me but I've never fallen off a scooter in Italy.' He stretched out his legs and leaned back on his elbows. 'I really want to travel after I graduate. Get out and see the world, maybe backpack around Europe for a year. Maybe you can give me some pointers.'

My stomach turned at the thought of him getting on a plane and disappearing from my life, strolling through European cities with girls falling all over him.

'What about SCAD?' I asked, keeping my jealous thoughts inside and out of my voice.

'Oh, yeah. SCAD.' He rubbed the underneath of his chin with the back of his hand and frowned. 'Maybe I could travel for the summer before the fall semester, hit up a few hotspots.'

'Funny how you want to leave America when I was always desperate to get here,' I said. 'Dad used to call us part-time Americans.'

'How come you never came back before?' He turned and reached into his bag, pulling out a small, soft-sided cooler full of sodas and seltzer waters. 'Y'all didn't want to visit family? Or did they travel to Europe? I guess that's what I would do if I had the chance.'

I popped the tab on a can of Diet Coke. Wyn had put so much thought into our day.

'Our family is complicated,' I replied with a scrunched up face. 'To say the least.'

'I'll toast to that.' He raised a lemon seltzer in my direction and we tapped the two cans together. 'At least you got to live in some cool places, probably met some cool people.'

'Meeting people was easy but making friends was more

difficult,' I explained before flashing back to all my awkward first days in new places. 'My dad was kind of strict about curfews, hanging out without an adult present, things like that. He didn't even like me going on the internet if he wasn't there.'

'I have seen your cell phone,' Wyn replied. 'I believe you.'

'Exactly. No messaging, no social media. It's tricky to stay in touch with people when you can't send them a DM or like their posts. Parents love to hate on phones but they're the easiest way for people to stay connected.'

With sparkling eyes, he twisted the bottom of his seltzer into the sand and reached back into his bag, the tip of his tongue sticking out of his mouth as he dug around inside.

'Well, that's about to change. This is for you.'

Triumphantly, he pulled out his ice-blue iPhone and presented it to me with both hands.

'What is this?' I asked as I took it from him.

'We full-time Americans call it a cell phone,' he replied, enunciating carefully. 'You use it to call people, send them photographs of cool dogs you see on the street, that kind of thing.'

'Oh, OK,' I laughed. 'It's like that now, is it?'

One tap brought the screen to life. On it was a picture of an oak tree. Our oak tree.

'The guy at the store said he could put in a pre-pay SIM, so, I did. If you want it, it's yours.' He swiped through to the contacts list where there was only one name listed. Wyn Evans. 'I put my number in already. Like I said, in case you need to send me a photograph of a really cool dog.'

My top teeth cut into my bottom lip as I stared at the phone, not sure what to say.

'It's really not that big of a deal,' he rambled, filling the awkward silence. 'I was due for an upgrade anyway and I figured this was a good way to recycle the phone and—'

'It is a big deal,' I interrupted. 'It's one of the nicest things anyone has ever done for me. Thank you so much.'

'We should take a selfie.' He took the phone back, leaning in close to me until I could smell his fresh deodorant and under that, the soft, woody warmth of his skin. Suddenly, I was looking back at the two of us side by side on the phone screen. I pulled a face and Wyn laughed.

'Delete it, please,' I begged, covering my eyes with my hands. 'That's a terrible angle.'

He deleted the picture, then went back to the camera setting, his arm raised a little higher.

'Let's try again,' he said.

I leaned into him, daring to rest my head against his, red-brown hair against dark ash. His chest rose and his shoulders lifted, both of us holding our breath as he took the picture.

'Now that's a good one,' he declared, handing the phone back to me. 'Can you send me that?'

'Yes,' I said happily. 'I literally can.'

The photo left my new phone with a swoosh and a quiet ping inside his bag confirmed delivery.

'Seriously, thank you,' I said. 'It's so generous.'

'Don't even mention it,' Wyn replied with a self-effacing grin. 'I walked by your place last night and I wanted to call in but I get the feeling your grandmother might not love unexpected evening visitors. Now I'll be able to text first, give you some warning.'

'Last night would not have been a good time to come calling,' I confirmed, endlessly grateful he'd kept on walking. Hi, Wyn, how are you? What's that? Why is the wallpaper alive? Well, that's a very good question. Perhaps my grandmother, the witch, can answer.

'Probably best you didn't see me anyway,' he added with a

chuckle. 'I got caught out in that crazy afternoon storm. I looked like a wet labradoodle.'

A brief flash of him in a sopping wet T-shirt was quickly replaced with the memory of what almost happened in Forsyth Park, followed swiftly by a sharp stab of guilt.

Jackson.

I should have called on him first thing, made sure he was OK. There wouldn't be much point having a phone to keep in touch with friends if I didn't have any friends to keep in touch with.

'What did you do yesterday?' Wyn asked.

Almost choked to death while my aunt watched, went for a walk in the park and nearly died, saw a couple of ghosts, found out I'm also a witch.

'Not much.' I flicked the tab on my soda can backwards and forwards until it snapped off in my hand. 'What were you doing out in the rain, school stuff?'

'School stuff?'

He looked perplexed.

'SCAD stuff,' I clarified. 'Jackson showed me some of the campus buildings. It's a pretty school.'

To my shameful delight, something that looked a lot like jealousy took over his face and tightened his features.

'Who's Jackson?' he enquired all too casually.

'A friend. His grandmother is besties with my grandmother,' I said, smiling as his tension eased. 'We knew each other when we were babies but obviously I don't remember that. We really just met.'

'That's great. Can't have too many friends.'

He rested his hand on the blanket between us, right next to my leg.

'Yep,' I agreed lightly. 'Friends are important.'

Slowly, so slowly, he slid his hand towards me until we were touching. The lightest possible connection, skin barely brushing skin, but the quake it sent through my body was seismic.

When I looked up into his eyes, I saw all of my emotions reflected back and of all the impossible things that had happened since I arrived in Savannah, this felt like the most impossible of all. Something even more rare than magic. Looking at Wyn was like looking into a mirror. Hope, anxiety, and longing, it was all there. His pupils dilated as he leaned in towards me, coming closer until my vision blurred, his lips parted and my eyes closed. I took one last breath, both of us drawing in the same air, but instead of the soft promise of his lips on mine, I felt something grab the scruff of my neck and yank me backwards, hard.

'Em?' he said, his eyes snapping open.

I jumped up, searching for whoever had grabbed me, but there wasn't anyone close enough to have laid a hand on me.

'Are you OK?' Wyn asked, rising to his own feet, one hand awkwardly cupping the back of his own neck. 'What are you looking for?'

'I don't know,' I admitted, unexpected anxiety gnawing at my edges. 'Something.'

'Something like that?' he breathed with disbelief.

I looked up to see a cloud of colourful butterflies surging out of the fronds of a palmetto tree, dancing in the air right above us before fluttering away towards the water.

'Emily, look!' he exclaimed as more and more butterflies appeared. We watched them go, their delicate wings carrying them too far, too fast. 'Are you seeing this?'

'Can't really miss it,' I replied weakly. This wasn't right. This wasn't *normal*.

'I don't think I've ever seen butterflies at the beach,' he said, observing them with a look of wonder. 'Heck, I don't think I've ever seen this many butterflies anywhere.'

People were on their feet with their phones in their hands, snapping pictures of my butterflies and the tingling in my hands scorched with unwelcome fire. I didn't know how exactly but this was my doing. They moved as one, a kaleidoscope of colour in the sky, swirling up and down, onwards, onwards, onwards, out over the ocean. Beyond beautiful, and shimmering with all the colours of the rainbow and every shade in between. The rest of the world began to fade away. All I could see were the butterflies.

'Is the water warm?' I asked Wyn, my attention drawn away from the colourful cloud and to the ocean beyond.

'Should be,' he replied. 'You want to swim?'

I nodded, drifting forward, passing blindly between towels and loungers, folding chairs and sandcastles. I needed to be in the water.

'Watch out,' Wyn called when I reached the firm wet sand at the ocean's edge. 'There's a tidal shelf, it drops fast.'

But his voice was a million miles away, nowhere near me or my butterflies or my ocean. The water was perfect. It swirled between my toes as I sailed straight in, rising around my ankles then up to my knees, the ripped hem of my shorts already damp and darkening. Somewhere in another life, Wyn was yelling my name but I was too busy listening to the waves. I saw him rushing past worried onlookers as they lined up along the sand but I couldn't work out why they were so worried. Couldn't they see I was exactly where I needed to be? Beyond the swarm of people was another familiar face. A tall, pale-haired woman in a long white dress. She gazed out at me, worry written all over her face as she moved, invisible, through the crowd.

Emma Catherine Bell, she sighed, words for only me to hear. *Return to me.*

But I didn't want to go back.

The water was up to my waist and the butterflies just out of reach. One more step and I'd be able to touch them . . .

'Emily!'

A hard slap struck me, a massive wave taking my legs out from under me and dragging me down beneath the surface. I snapped back to myself and panic set in right away, my arms and legs kicking in every direction, but instead of driving me up, I seemed to sink deeper. The water coiled itself around my limbs, no longer liquid but solid, sentient. It wanted me for itself. Just as the light above began to narrow into a long dark tunnel, something else grabbed me around the waist, pulling me up and out with determination.

Seawater burned in my eyes as Wyn dragged me into shallower waters and I swiped at them with useless, salty hands. Overhead, the butterflies disappeared, replaced by sudden storm clouds, threatening the sunny day.

'You're OK, you're OK,' Wyn repeated over and over when we were back on the sand, well away from the waves. 'Can you hear me? Can you say something?'

He knelt down at my side as I struggled upright, spluttering out a mouthful of water in response. The crowd melted away, returning to their friends and families without anything too exciting to report, and as they dispersed, I searched the beach for the woman in white. Just like the butterflies, she was gone.

With one hand, Wyn peeled wet hair away from my face, and held on to my wrist with the other, as if he was afraid I might hurl myself back under if he looked away for so much as a second.

'I'm sorry,' I croaked as the menacing clouds faded back into fluffy white cotton wool. 'It must have been the tidal shelf, like you said.'

'The waves went crazy,' he murmured, fingers still combing through my hair. 'Didn't you see the storm coming in? I thought

170

we were going to get another like yesterday and you don't want to be in the water when the lightning hits.'

A harsh worry line that had embedded itself deep between his eyebrows smoothed out as his hand curled around my cheek. I tried to concentrate but the way his thumb caressed my face left me ragged and breathless.

'What would I do if something happened to you?' he asked himself so quietly I had to strain to hear him. 'I can't imagine the world without you, Em, I don't want to. Even if this is the last thing I expected to find in Savannah.'

'None of this is what I expected,' I whispered back. 'But I'm so happy I found you.'

'I think we found each other. I think we were meant to.'

He gazed at my lips and slid his thumb down the side of my face, tracing my cheekbone, my jaw, finally resting underneath my chin. Was this it? Was it finally going to happen? His eyes darkened with desire and locked on mine, until something else caught his attention.

'Em,' he said softly, turning his face to the sky. 'Look up.'

I was afraid to, terrified I would see another cloud of inexplicable butterflies, but when I made myself look, I gasped. It was so much better and so much worse. A bold and brilliant rainbow, unbroken from end to end, shimmered in the air, stretching from one end of the beach to the other. Everyone was back on their feet, mouths hanging open, awestruck.

'I didn't even feel it rain,' Wyn said. 'Did you?'

'No,' I replied. 'I didn't.'

We hadn't felt it rain because there wasn't any rain. This rainbow had nothing to do with sunlight refracted by water in the air and everything to do with the way I felt about Wyn. All eyes were on the rainbow, shining even brighter against the bright blue sky, but I was too busy staring at a miracle of my own.

'It's beautiful,' he said, squeezing my hand so tightly it sent a rush of golden sparks up my arm and straight to my heart. 'I wish it could last forever.'

'Me too,' I replied, squeezing back just as hard. 'Me too.'

Chapter Eighteen

'You really have to be home so soon?'

Wyn pulled over into an empty space on Macon Street, put his truck in park then turned off the rumbling antique engine. 'They're showing *Jaws* at the theatre down on Reynolds Square. Did you ever see it? Could be fun.'

'I would love that but I can't,' I said with genuine regret. Old movies were my kryptonite. 'My grandmother is expecting me home and—'

'No need to explain. Protective grandparent, I get it,' he said. 'What if I come by and introduce myself? Last summer, I worked at the restaurant in this fancy hotel and I did real well with the afternoon tea crowd. Grandmother charming was my specialty, I swear.'

I didn't doubt him for a second.

'It's not you,' I replied.

'The thing is, Catherine doesn't want me to date anyone. At all. At least not until after my birthday.'

There it was again, the brilliant grin.

'On June twenty-first,' he said.

'That's right,' I smiled. Another thing he remembered.

'Then there's no problem because we're not dating,' he declared, stopping my heart with three words. 'We're just two people who like hanging out and eating ice cream and occasionally holding hands and maybe don't hold hands with other people.'

My heart resumed business as usual.

'Can they eat ice cream with other people?' I enquired with forced earnestness.

He wrinkled up his nose as he considered the question.

'Can't say I'm crazy about the idea but sure.'

'OK then,' I agreed, laughing. 'She might fall for that. But I still think we should hold off on the introductions for now.'

'Whatever you say,' Wyn replied. 'Would you maybe want to date me again? Like, tomorrow?'

I had no plans but even if I did, they would have been instantly cancelled.

'I'll text you,' I promised, thrilled by the fact I actually could. 'But I think that'll work.'

He looked over at Bell House and shook his head. From here, it looked more imposing than elegant, a solid grey block designed to keep people out rather than invite them in. Even the decorative finials on the roof glinted sharp in the sun. Unwelcoming and uncompromising.

'Still can't believe you live in a mansion like that,' he said. 'I would get lost looking for the bathroom.'

'Thankfully I have my own or I'd be in trouble too,' I replied, steering his gaze with my finger. 'That's my room. Second floor, far left. Three big windows with the balcony.'

'That's where to imagine you later.' His words became a promise I hoped he would keep. 'Out on your balcony, staring at the sunset.'

'And where should I imagine you?' I asked, combing out my

snarled up braid and hoping he would picture me with less seaweed in my hair.

'In my apartment. In bed.'

Neither of us said another word. There were too many swirling around in my head to choose just one and I didn't trust any of them.

'Guess you'd better get going,' Wyn said as I pushed the image of him tangled up in bedsheets out of my mind. 'I really don't want to get you in trouble with your grandmother.'

'Thank you for this.' I waved my new icy blue phone in the air. 'And for the sunscreen, because I would definitely have burned without it. And the sodas and the sunglasses. And for pulling me out the ocean.'

He reached for the sunglasses that were perched on top of my head and flipped them down over my eyes.

'It's all part of the service. Any time you need me to save your life, just let me know.'

'Same,' I replied. 'Any time.'

Hopefully neither of us would need saving again for a while.

There was no AC without the engine running and the inside of the truck was suffocating. A bead of sweat ran down the side of Wyn's face, gliding over his jaw, down his neck and disappearing under the collar of his T-shirt. I squirmed against my seatbelt as I turned molten and when he reached across me to unclip it, the belt snapped back but his hand stayed where it was, right beside my sun-warmed thigh. Across the square, the cathedral bells chimed the hour, an unwelcome reminder of where I was supposed to be.

'I'd better head in,' I said, flipping the handle on the truck and all but falling out onto the street. 'I'll text you later.'

'I'll be waiting.'

Wyn raised a hand in a goodbye and as I stumbled away, I

could feel his eyes burning into my back, the connection between us stronger than ever.

The front door of Bell House swung silently on its hinges as I slipped inside. Easing off my shoes, I tiptoed up the wooden staircase, somehow managing to avoid every creaking floorboard. It almost felt as though Bell House was complicit in my sneaking around. Not only that, it approved.

Gritty with sand and smelling of sunscreen, I floated across my room to hide my new phone and the charging cable that came with it in my nightstand, alongside Catherine's silver pin. Keeping secrets wasn't something that came naturally to me but neither was having an aunt or a grandmother or finding out I was a witch. All I wanted was one thing that was just mine. That thing was Wyn. I wasn't ready to share him just yet.

On my desk, my parents smiled at me from the folding silver picture frame but I could only find a frown to return. So many things might have been easier if my dad had told the truth. His version of our world was the only one I'd ever known and I'd trusted him completely. But now here I was in his old bedroom, asking myself if I'd ever truly known him at all.

'I wish you were here,' I told the smiling photograph. 'I wish you could make this stuff make sense.'

My whole life, I'd studied the pictures of my mother so closely they felt more like memories than photographs, as though I'd somehow gone back in time and taken them myself. But today, for the first time, I noticed something new. My parents were posing under a tree, Dad facing the camera, Mom resting her head on his shoulder, arms wrapped around his waist and both of them wearing their matching black and gold sweatshirts. But there was something else. Above my mom's tilted head, an arrow shot through a freshly carved heart, containing the letters P + A.

Just like the heart I'd seen on the tree in Forsyth Park.

'Aren't you just precious.'

I turned quickly to see Ashley standing beside my bed.

'I didn't hear you come in,' I said as I folded up the silver frame, laying it face down. She didn't get to look at it.

'Jinx,' she replied. 'You said you wouldn't be gone long. Catherine is going to flip when she finds out you disappeared all day.'

'I told you, I was with Lydia,' I lied. The muscles in my legs twitched, ready to run. 'We lost track of time.'

The door closed slowly behind her, protesting all the way with a long, complaining creak as she hopped up onto my bed and lay back against the legion of pillows I removed every night and replaced every morning.

'So,' Ashley said, staring through me like an X-ray machine. 'How's it feel to be a witch?'

'OK,' I answered. 'How does it feel not being a witch?'

Even though it wasn't my intention, that made her laugh.

'Well, I'll be. Do you know, you're the first person ever to ask me that?' She crossed her legs at the ankles and I noticed her muddy shoes shedding a trail of dirt across my comforter. 'For a long time, I was real mad about it. Can you imagine growing up around women capable of incredible things and knowing your only destiny is to be a glorified babysitter?'

She picked out a soft round cushion from my pile and held it to her chest, cuddling it like a stuffed animal. 'The generations before me, they were honoured. Even when I was too young to understand, my grandmother would try to convince me this was another kind of sacred gift, a blessing of our very own.'

'But you don't see it like that,' I guessed.

'All I saw was a blank space where my life should have been.'

I kept one eye on the door, sympathetic but still on edge.

'Things got worse after Paul left,' she said, picking at a feather that poked out of the cushion. 'Catherine was terrified I might try to run away so she kept me on a short leash. No dating, no college, no parties, no friends.'

'No friends?' I repeated. 'How could she stop you having friends?'

'It's pretty difficult to make friends if you never leave the house.' Her eyes flickered towards the closed door. 'No one ever cared about me. Except for Ellie. But that didn't last long.'

'She must've been a special friend if you still think about her,' I remarked and from the look on her face, I was fairly sure Ellie was more than just a friend.

'I saw her on the street,' Ashley said, an almost smile warming up her features. 'She was painting Bell House, painting a picture of it, I mean. She was such a talented artist. After that, she came by every day for a week and we just sat on the porch talking each other's ears off. I could talk to her for hours and never run out of things to say.'

'Why aren't you friends with her now?'

She looked up and met my genuine curiosity with fiery resentment.

'Because she had a whole life to live and I have to waste mine here, taking care of the extraordinary Bell witches.'

The weight of her resentment pinned me to my chair. I'd never felt so guilty about something I had no control over. Even though I couldn't possibly have done anything to change things, her unhappiness was due to me.

'I'm so sorry,' I offered, but my contrition wasn't nearly enough for my aunt. 'You know I didn't choose any of this. If we could swap, I'd hand it all over in a heartbeat.'

'You really think I'd want it?' Ashley asked. Her furious expression turned into one of surprise and the corner of her mouth flickered bitterly. She looked away and shook her head. 'I know it's not your fault. Hating you won't help me any, but if your dad hadn't run away, if he had stayed and I had left, things would have been very different for all of us.'

'Catherine says he left because he wanted me to have an easier life,' I said cautiously, tiptoeing around our uneasy truce. 'What do you think?'

She pulled at a loose thread on my comforter, pulling it taut and wrapping it around her finger.

'Men don't do so well with the reality of our situation,' she replied. 'Historically speaking, there haven't been many sons in the Bell line. But when Catherine fell pregnant with Paul, she failed to take the proper precautions to ensure the baby was a girl. She won't admit it but I reckon Daddy wanted a boy first, a good old-fashioned southern son and heir. As if that means anything in this family.'

'Is that something we can do?' I asked, unable to hide my surprise. 'Choose the sex of a baby, I mean?'

Ashley looked at me like I'd just asked if the sky was blue.

'Sure. It's just a matter of giving nature a push in the desired direction.'

She twisted the thread tightly around her forefinger, the thin cotton digging sharply into her flesh. Then she flicked her wrist and snapped the thread in two.

'Can't change the past,' she said as she tossed it away onto the floor. 'Your magic is all that matters now. The blessing comes first, everything else is a liability.'

'Things change,' I replied as she climbed down from the bed, tracking more dirt behind her on her way out. 'You could still meet someone else.'

She stared at me from the doorway, head tilted to one side as though considering my suggestion and whether or not I might be right.

'Not while there's a Bell witch living in this house,' she decided before slipping away into the darkness of the hallway. 'There's nothing for me in this whole world while you and Catherine are alive.'

Chapter Nineteen

I found Catherine in the sunken back garden of Bell House. High walls, camouflaged by flowers and vines, kept us in and the rest of the world out. The flowerbeds were so full they looked like a patchwork quilt and every inch of available space was filled with dozens, if not hundreds, of different plants, from seedlings in tiny thimbles to towering trees in wooden boxes more than half my height. Birds sang in the trees and bees buzzed around my grandmother as they flitted from one flower to the next, happy and pollen-drunk. Ashley's thinly veiled threats had sent me spiralling but when Catherine smiled at me I couldn't help but smile back.

'There's my little witch.' She tipped her chin towards the empty seat across from her and I sat. 'I see someone caught the sun today, wherever have you been?'

She plucked a glossy leaf from a spiky plant and snapped it in two, handing half to me. A cool, clear gel oozed out over my fingers.

'It's aloe, it'll soothe the burn,' she said as I cautiously dabbed it on the bridge of my nose. 'There, doesn't that feel better?'

'It does,' I replied, tapping the gel into the tight skin on my cheeks. 'I went out to Tybee Island but I guess I didn't wear enough sunscreen. It's gorgeous out there.'

Catherine's eyebrows drew together and her mouth tightened.

'It most certainly is but I wish you hadn't gone alone,' she said. 'The ocean can have a strange effect on our magic, especially when everything is in flux as it surely is for you. Did anything peculiar happen?'

If I told her about the pull of the ocean, she would only worry and maybe even try to keep me in the house. Not that my aunt was the most reliable source but it sounded as though Catherine had grounded Ashley for an entire decade and I couldn't take that risk. I couldn't lose Wyn the way Ashley had lost Ellie.

'No,' I said. 'Not that I can think of.'

'The tides can have an unpredictable impact on our magic,' she replied as I turned the chunk of aloe over in my hands, thick and shiny and edged with sharp spikes. Helpful and dangerous at the same time. 'Sometimes they amplify our abilities, sometimes they take them away. Or they can simply confuse matters, the way a magnet can confuse a compass. Witches and water do not play well together.'

'Is it the same for rivers?' I asked, thinking back to all those times my dad had made excuses not to take me to the beach.

'Just the opposite. Rivers represent a positive flow of energy, they refresh and revive our magic. That's one of the reasons our family thrived in Savannah. But the ocean is truly unpredictable. Until we have a better understanding of your abilities, it would be best to stay away from the beach.'

She took her half of the aloe leaf and sank it back into the ground, patting down the soil around it.

'Is that magic?' I asked as she picked up a little red watering can.

'No,' she replied. 'It's gardening.'

Everything around us was full of life, vibrant and promising. Even the woodshed looked like it was part of the garden, aged by the sun with honeysuckle vines climbing up one side. I tried to imagine what life might have been like if I'd grown up here, Dad pushing me on the swing that hung from a tall beech tree, picking strawberries with my mom, watching the fish in the koi pond with Catherine. Would Ashley like me more if I'd always been here? Through the kitchen window, I saw her bustling around, wearing her usual miserable expression. At least she might not wish I was dead.

'At least one of us had a good day,' Catherine declared. 'Mine was thoroughly wasted by the fools at the Savannah Historical Society.'

'Sounds thrilling,' I said, turning my back on Ashley when she saw me watching her and flipped me off.

'Then I'm overselling it. Since we began debating whether or not to rebuild the two lost squares, at least ten babies have been born, gone off to college and come back to join the committee and start the debate all over again. It never ends.' She pressed her fingers into her temples and massaged in gentle circles. 'This is what you and I are up against, Emily. No one has any respect for the history of this city. To this day I can hardly believe they tore down the original city market *and* Ellis Square to put up a parking lot. All in the name of progress.'

'And that's bad?' I guessed. 'I thought progress was usually a good thing.'

'Not when the people in charge can't see past the end of their own noses,' Catherine said. 'They destroyed an important historical site because they needed more parking. Now there are too many cars and the traffic is damaging the city.

183

When the original plans were proposed, my own grandmother spoke against them for that very reason, but did they listen to her?'

'I'm going to say no.'

She confirmed it with a sigh. 'I've seen it too many times. Build it up, knock it down, build it again, knock it back down. Men simply cannot help themselves; they light the world on fire just to watch it burn. Protecting this city, its past and future, is part of your heritage as a Bell witch.'

'Speaking of witches,' I replied, still stumbling over the word. 'I was thinking. Surely there are more of us. There have to be other families with the same abilities we have, right?'

Catherine didn't respond right away. Instead she pushed back her chair, stood up and walked across the garden to a wooden tray full of plants and herbs in small clay pots, examining their leaves and flower buds before bringing it back to the table.

'Yes and no,' she answered. 'Once upon a time there were a great number of witches here in Savannah and the Bell name was well known to our sisters all across the world but that was before my time. Today, it's just us.'

It wasn't the answer I'd been hoping for.

'So there's no secret society of witches?' I pressed. 'No meetings under a full moon? Not even a secret handshake?'

My grandmother laughed as she rearranged the plants on the tray.

'You seem to be confusing witches with Freemasons. And I could tell you some stories about them that would make your hair curl. But we do use the full moon and, if it helps, you and I could create our own secret handshake.'

I poked a despondent finger in the soil of the plant pot closest to me, damp and dark and dank. I'd been more into the idea of a secret coven than I wanted to admit.

'The Powells were like us once. Lydia and Virginia's ancestors were witches.'

'They were?' I looked up in surprise. 'But not anymore?'

'As I explained last night, magic must be cultivated and tended to,' she replied. 'Virginia's ancestors lost track of the line and the blessing fell dormant.'

'Does Lydia know?' I asked.

Catherine shook her head as she moved the plants around, lining them up in what seemed to be a specific order.

'No and I don't think it would be helpful to tell her.' Focusing on the plant closest to her, a woody-looking shrub, she picked up a pair of clippers and delicately trimmed away some of the tired leaves. 'Losing the connection to the blessing is almost too easy. All it takes is one generation that doesn't follow the rituals and . . .'

She sliced through the stem with a decisive snip. The top half of the plant fell sideways onto the table.

'Life is very fragile. We might be witches but we're still human.'

I thought back to the beach, to the thunderstorm, to the wolf and silently agreed.

'I think it's time we learned more about your magic, don't you?' Catherine said, shifting effortlessly back to her happier sunshine self. 'Our magic expresses itself in different ways, the blessing acts like an antenna. Each of us picks up a different signal and that signal comes through with varying degrees of strength.'

'So my magic might be different to yours,' I replied. 'We could have different abilities?'

She nodded. 'That's right. There will be some talents that we share but a witch's strongest connection to the blessing is almost always hers and hers alone.'

I shuffled my chair closer to the table as Catherine pushed

the first pot in her line-up towards me. 'Tell me, what do you know about this herb?'

'Nothing.' Without a store receipt or a plastic name tab in the dirt, I was completely at a loss. 'Can't say I've ever had much of a green thumb. I even killed my Chia Pet.'

'You're doing it again,' she chastised. 'Stop doubting yourself. Listen to the plant and tell me what it says.'

Even after everything that had happened, I still felt faintly ridiculous as I wrapped my hands around the mystery herb, running my fingers lightly over the feathery leaves and clusters of tiny white flowers, waiting patiently for it to politely introduce itself. It was all pointless, there was no way—

'Yarrow,' I exclaimed with alarming certainty. I picked off one of the flowerheads and rolled it in between my fingers, breathing in its gentle scent. 'It enhances courage and self-belief and removes fear.'

'Anything else?'

'You can use it to dress wounds,' I said slowly, as though turning a page in my head. 'To improve focus and enhance restful sleep. It's also used in love potions but you'd need to combine it with other ingredients for that to work.'

The fragrance of the yarrow flower fired up my neural pathways, my anxieties fading away and leaving nothing but a razor-sharp sense of clarity. When I looked over at my grandmother she was smiling.

'That's correct.'

'As soon as it touched my skin, I just knew,' I told her, my words bubbling over with excitement as I explained, as much to myself as to Catherine. 'Like, sure, it's yarrow, how could I not know?'

'Because you were born knowing,' she said, her face so full of love. 'My wonderful girl.'

Catherine didn't look as much like my dad as Ashley

did, I figured they both took after their father, but when she looked at me with pride in her eyes, I could see him smiling back at me. Pushing the heavier emotions away, I reached for the next plant. It was similar to the yarrow, leafy and small, only its flowers were yellow instead of white.

'This one is rue,' I said, stroking a leaf as it told me its story. 'Used for protection, to ward off harm that might come to us, but also to attract good people, people who are meant to be in our lives.'

'And one of the herbs the first Emma Catherine Bell held dearest.' Catherine plucked a single petal from the plant and pressed it firmly between her thumb and forefinger, a delicate fragrance filling the air. 'Prepared correctly, it can help with a number of digestive problems. It can also be of assistance with many women's health issues.'

'What happens if it's prepared incorrectly?'

Her eyes flashed, sharp and bright.

'A knife can be a tool or a weapon. Never forget that.'

It was exhilarating, unlocking all this information, and I felt renewed, like someone had changed my batteries when I didn't know they were running out. I ran my hands lightly over the leaves and flowers of the other plants, all of their names and properties dancing around inside my head. Bay leaves for prophetic dreams, sage for healing, rosemary . . .

'. . . for remembrance,' I finished out loud, hovering over the unassuming herb. 'Rosemary helps you remember forgotten things.'

'It can,' Catherine agreed absently, her attention focused on collecting more plants to add to the tray. 'If prepared correctly and ingested.'

Or when used as decoration in an Arnold Palmer or added to a freshly baked chocolate chip cookie. The visions of my parents flashed in front of me; visiting in the Powells' parlour, talking together in the library.

'What can you tell me about the others?' Catherine asked. 'Which herbs are you drawn to?'

'Um, let me look,' I muttered, reluctantly pushing the past out of my mind to concentrate on the present. Belladonna, basil, verbena, henbane, lady's mantle . . .

'Aconite,' I sputtered, yanking my hand back from a beautiful blue flower. 'This is poisonous.'

'Not to you or me.'

My grandmother lovingly caressed the petals, her fingers flushing red then fading back to a calm, unblemished pink.

'You're a natural apothecary,' she said. 'Just like the first Emma Catherine Bell. I have studied for years just to attain a fraction of the knowledge that is instinctive to you. Ashley and I follow the recipes handed down through the generations but a natural herbalist like you will be able to work miracles with what we have here. Emily, it's such a wonderful gift.'

Recipes handed down through generations . . . I scoured my new knowledge, pairing the ingredients to everything I'd consumed at Bell House. At least half the herbs in the garden had found their way into my food and drink, yarrow to help me sleep, chamomile to calm me down, valerian to soothe my nerves and ease my grief. I felt like Alice down the rabbit hole, nibbling on mushrooms and drinking from unknown bottles. Only Alice knew what she was doing. Alice made her own choices.

'All the tea, all the food, everything Ashley makes,' I spoke slowly, not wanting it to be true. 'It's all drugged.'

'Drugged?' Catherine echoed with a derisive chuckle. 'Emily, all your meals have been carefully prepared to help you rest and recover. Ashley only uses natural and organic ingredients and what we grow here is a darn sight cheaper than it would be from that fancy health food place off the parkway.'

It wasn't exactly a denial but I didn't believe she was trying to hurt me. Ashley on the other hand . . .

'If I'm an apothecary,' I said, fingering the rosemary bush and breathing in its powerful scent, 'what kind of witch are you?'

'It's probably easier if I show you.'

Rolling up the sleeves of her silk shirt, she reached down to retrieve the discarded branch of the woody shrub she'd chopped in half. Catherine snapped her fingers and the branch burst into flames.

'My abilities express themselves through the elements,' she said as I reared back in my chair. The fire burned fast and fierce, white at the centre, black around the edges until there was nothing left but a pile of ash. Suddenly my ability to name random plants didn't seem quite so cool.

'Water, air, earth, and fire. That's my specialty.'

'But I can see ghosts as well as understand plants,' I said, watching the ashes of the shrub slip through the decorative ironwork of the table and disappear back into the earth. 'And then there are the other things, the visions, the Spanish moss. How do those things connect to me being an apothecary?'

'The blessing adapts to our needs,' Catherine replied, her demeanour still calm but perhaps not quite as certain as before. 'My grandmother came into her magic during World War Two. She was a conduit, her abilities allowed her to move through people's dreams and communicate with those who had passed which was a great help to the war effort and a comfort to those searching for closure. Her grandmother was a healer who saved hundreds of lives during the 1918 Spanish flu pandemic.'

'Did either of them have more than one ability?' I asked, lightly tracing a finger along my itchy, sunburned skin.

'Not that I know of,' she answered. 'But perhaps you are in need of greater strength for what lies ahead.'

I froze, my finger pressed against the tip of my nose.

'Well, that doesn't sound terrifying.'

Catherine pulled my hand away from my face and stroked another dot of aloe into my skin.

'Our family's story may begin with Emma Catherine Bell but the history of the blessing goes back much further. The origins of it all, why each of us has different abilities, it's lost to the ages. All we know is that our blessing is protective, it expresses itself differently in every witch, serving whatever need is most dire at that time. Also, we know it is bound by the natural order of things, but you'd be surprised at what nature and the human body can do when necessary, at what a person is capable of when they have no choice.'

'I don't want to find out what I can do when I have no choice,' I replied, extremely alarmed. 'Having a choice is my favourite thing in the entire world.'

Dusting a sprinkle of ash from her lap, Catherine stood and picked up the tray, carrying it over to a bright little sunspot by the fishpond.

'Don't worry so much,' she said with sweetness. 'Everything will be clearer after your Becoming.'

'My *what*?'

I stared at her from my seat, barely even noticing as all the flowers and leaves I'd picked from the herbs regrew right in front of me.

'There's no need for that reaction, it's just a name. Our ancestors had a tendency towards the dramatic.' She picked up the watering can to drench the herbs as they bloomed. 'The Becoming is simply a brief ceremony, a sort of initiation ritual, performed on the full moon closest to a witch's seven-teenth birthday as she comes into the fullest expression of her magic.'

'Sounds completely chill,' I replied. 'Totally normal and not weird at all.'

'How lucky I am to be raising the first Bell witch in existence to call the Becoming "chill",' Catherine said drily. 'My Becoming was one of the best days of my life and yours will be even more beautiful. Did you know you were born under a full moon?'

I shook my head, I did not.

'And it just so happens, the full moon falls on June twenty-first again this year. Your Becoming ceremony will take place on your birthday.'

'Is that good?' I asked, gulping down a nervous breath.

'It's very good.'

Catherine had left one plant on the table. The aconite. Its blue flowers trembled in the sun then exploded, a storm of indigo carpeting the whole garden. One of the petals landed on my arm, leaving a bell-shaped mark.

'Such a fascinating plant,' Catherine said, watching the red welt fade away. 'What do you know about it?'

I blew out a steady breath and carefully picked a single leaf from the plant.

'It first grew from the saliva of Cerberus, the three-headed hound of Hades,' I recited. 'It's one of the most toxic plants on the whole planet, if ingested incorrectly, it can make the heart stop.'

'And what is its most common name? What do we witches call it and why?'

'Wolfsbane,' I said, quiet, disbelieving.

'And why do we call it that?'

My answer came out in a whisper.

191

'Because it's poisonous to werewolves.'

'A knife can be a tool or a weapon,' Catherine said again, her green eyes burning into mine. 'And so can you.'

Chapter Twenty

As the clock chimed a soft midnight, an untouched cup of tea sat cooling on my nightstand. Chamomile, valerian, yarrow and lavender. Grown in the garden at Bell House, dried in the pantry, blended by Catherine, prepared by Ashley, and drank by me every night to induce a deep and dreamless sleep.

But not tonight.

Tossing and turning, I kicked off the single sheet that was draped over my body, too hot and sweaty for even the feel of cotton on my skin. Even the air conditioning couldn't compete with the dense, sultry warmth that filled my room, smothering my limbs and dampening my hair but now I knew what was in the tea, I couldn't bring myself to drink it. Rolling over, I pressed my face into my pillow and searched for my happy place, imagining myself back in Wyn's truck, driving with the window open and the smell of salt in the air. I pictured the strong lines of his profile, the way his brow furrowed every time we approached a light or a stop sign, how hard he concentrated on reversing into the parking space, one arm thrown over the back of his seat so he could see better through the small cabin window.

My imagination and my memories melted together, transforming the suffocating heat of my room into the bold sunshine of the beach. I was no longer alone in bed, instead I found myself walking behind Wyn on the narrow boardwalk that led down to the sand, the striped umbrella over one of his shoulders, backpack over the other, and hands outstretched to touch the feathery grass that grew tall on either side. Then we were on the beach blanket, an easy, honest smile on his face and my heart stuttering in my chest when our hands met. Floating on the current of our connection, I rolled back over and touched my fingers to my lips, wishing he was here with me now.

Bell House played a sympathetic soundtrack, sighing and groaning like it understood, as though it was too hot for her as well. Everything was too much effort, the fan whirring above my head, water running through the copper pipes, floorboards and furniture creaking as they expanded against their will.

Then something else.

My ears prickled at the sound of something striking the window.

'Lydia?' I muttered, checking the clock again. Five minutes past midnight. Too late to be throwing stones from magnolia trees.

I heaved my heavy limbs out of bed, praying I reached her before she woke Catherine or Ashley. I didn't know what kind of security system we had here but I was extremely worried it might be a little more excessive than regular cameras and silent alarms. I carefully opened one wooden slat of my shutters, just to make sure it was definitely Lydia visiting and not a good old-fashioned break-in.

But it wasn't Lydia or a burglar.

Standing on my balcony, was Wyn.

194

The night air whooshed into my room as I opened the window. The loud chirp of the cicadas kept time with my pulse and the moon, sliced in half overhead, etched his features in silver.

'I was just thinking about you,' I said in disbelief, reaching out to touch him and make sure he was real. 'How are you here?'

'Because I was just thinking about you,' he replied with shining eyes. 'It's too hot to sleep in my place, so I took a walk. Turns out it's pretty easy to climb the magnolia tree out front up to your balcony.'

'Weirdly, you're not the first person to tell me that. But you are the first person to try it after midnight.'

His eyes flicked past me into my room, skimming over the rumpled bed covers before settling back on me. In my dresser, there were dozens of cute outfits I could've chosen to sleep in, cotton pyjamas with my initials embroidered on the pocket, soft nightgowns with delicate straps, things Catherine had bought for me before I even got here, but of course, this was the night I fell into bed in my underwear and an oversized baseball shirt, full of holes from where it had been washed at least a thousand times.

'Braves fan?' Wyn asked.

'It was my dad's,' I said, turning the same colour as the team's logo. 'I stole it from him years ago.'

'They're having a pretty good season.'

'I'll have to take your word for it.'

I pulled the hem of the shirt as far as it would go over my thighs but it covered nothing.

It felt dangerous, seeing him at night. Without the sun to chaperone, there was no telling what we might do. My eyes skimmed his body, his broad shoulders, that full lower lip, all of it too tempting.

195

'I'd invite you in but I don't think it's a very good idea,' I made myself say, glancing over my shoulder at my room. My bed. 'My grandmother would kill us both if she found out.'

Or at least put some kind of curse on you, I did not add.

'Not the right time for a tour,' he agreed. 'You won't believe me but I don't even know how I got here. I was planning to walk down to the river but the next thing I knew, I was outside your house and I couldn't stop myself. Something took over.' He leaned against the window, his arm framing his face. 'Were you really thinking about me?'

'Yes.' I sat down on the edge of the window seat, holding one of the little plush pillows in my lap. 'And now here you are.'

'Maybe my heart heard you,' he whispered. 'And maybe yours heard mine.'

Spanish moss swayed in the branches of Lafayette Square's oak trees and a light breeze picked up, cutting through the humid night. Wyn's eyes glowed, moss green and slate grey with flashes of bronze and rich, deep brown. Even if I had a hundred years, I wouldn't be able to put a name to every single colour in his eyes but I would be very happy to try.

'I've never seen green eyes like yours before,' he said, stealing my thoughts and my heart. 'They're beautiful.'

'You took the words right out of my mouth,' I replied. 'Can you read my mind, Wyn Evans?'

With grace I could only dream of, he crouched down, balancing on his toes to bring us face to face and stared at me the exact same way I was staring at him. Everything fell silent and still. Even the cicadas quieted themselves for us.

'My life is very complicated right now,' Wyn said, shaking his head as though he couldn't believe what he was saying.

'There are so many things I should be doing but you're all I can think about. I can't concentrate on anything else.'

'I don't want to get in the way of your studies,' I said, totally half-hearted. I wanted to get in the way of his everything. His hand slipped over the threshold of the window and rested on my knee.

'You're not in my way. You are my way.'

A shooting star streaked across the black velvet night as his hand moved up my leg, grazing my thigh, the hem of my shirt. I held my breath as he found my hand and covered it with his, stilling a tremble I couldn't control on my own. He was so close. It would take less than nothing to pull him in to me, run my hands over his body and feel it respond in the ways I'd already dreamed of. An undeniable urge to make him mine surged through me but this wasn't the right time, we both knew it. I held my breath, waiting for the moment to pass but it lingered and I wondered if this yearning would ever truly leave.

'Hey, look.' Wyn raised our joined hands up to the sky. 'A shooting star.'

'There's another one?' I craned my neck to better see out the window. Sure enough, there was. Quickly followed by another. And another.

'It's a meteor shower,' he said, quietly delighted. 'I've never seen one so bright before, even in the mountains.'

He rocked back on his heels as the sky put on its sparkling show just for us. I handed him a pillow and we lay down side-by-side, Wyn on the balcony, me on the window seat, his little finger curled around mine. The breeze caught single strands of my hair and made them dance around my face.

'Stay for a while?'

A question and a command, one he accepted willingly.

'Forever,' he vowed.

And in the sky above, we watched ancient meteors soar through the night, burning too brightly before melting away into nothing at all.

Chapter Twenty-One

I woke up on the window seat, my window still raised but the balcony empty. Wyn was gone. When I sat up, a piece of paper fluttered to the floor.

Didn't want to wake you. Meet me by our tree at two xo

Down in the square, commuters rushed by on their way to work, sweltering in their shirts and ties, and dog walkers strode down the footpaths with purpose, little green baggies dangling from their fanny packs while their four-legged friends galloped over the grass. Even though the breeze had vanished and the weather was as hot and muggy as ever, they all wore smiles as they slowed under the shelter of the shade of our oak tree or lingered by the fountain. It was a perfect morning. Who could be anything other than happy on a day like this?

Four agonizingly slow hours had passed since breakfast, when I'd devoured so much food, Ashley asked if I'd developed a tapeworm overnight, and it was still only midday. I'd spent my morning in the garden, meeting more herbs and flowers and learning how to blend them together to achieve different results. It wasn't just the combination, Catherine explained before disappearing on another mysterious errand, it was the intention behind it. Anyone could make a lavender tea but the way it was prepared, on what day of the lunar cycle, using which tools – all those things made a difference.

'Emily?' I heard Ashley yell from inside the house. 'You have a visitor.'

I leapt to my feet and ran back inside. Was it him? Was he feeling just as impatient? But this time, instead of expecting Lydia and finding Wyn, I expected Wyn and found Lydia, a scowl on her face, arms wrapped around her chest, one toe tapping the floor like a cornered animal. It looked as though the only thing she disliked more than the city of Charleston was Ashley Bell.

'Hi!' I called happily, Ashley glowering menacingly at the pair of us. 'Why don't we go up to my room?'

'Gladly.' Lydia sidestepped my aunt and followed me up the curved staircase. She paused, her face pressed close to the wallpaper. 'Huh. When you walk by, it kinda looks like the vines are growing.'

'Optical illusion,' I replied, pulling her up the last couple of steps and into my bedroom.

'This house is wild,' she declared, a statement, not a judgement. 'It's like a living museum. Miss Catherine ought to let them film movies here or something.'

'I wouldn't count on that happening any time soon,' I told her as I set two glasses of freshly made lemonade on my desk.

Strolling over to the window, floral tank dress clashing with literally everything in my room, Lydia climbed up on the window seat where I'd slept.

'Oh my god, I think I'm in love,' she said with a swoon. 'Check out that girl by the fountain. My window looks out on the dumb garden, the most exciting thing I see is the gardener's ass crack every Thursday morning. You must see the craziest things up here.'

'You're welcome to come over and watch Lafayette Square TV any time,' I offered, joining her at the window. The girl by the fountain really was cute. 'But please know this is the only TV I *can* watch because the only other television in this entire house is in Ashley's room and I am definitely not welcome in there.'

'Then I couldn't have come at a better time.' Lydia delved deep into the well-worn tote bag she carried on her shoulder. 'Wanna see if any of these work?'

She pulled out a ball of thick grey-white cables and I gasped as though she'd presented me with the crown jewels.

'Chargers for Dad's laptop,' I exclaimed. 'Lydia Powell, you are amazing.'

'It's true,' she agreed with a toss of her hair. 'But I try not to let it go to my head.'

I practically dove under my bed, retrieving the laptop from my backpack before joining her on the other end of the window seat, my hands shaking with excitement. I'd more or less resigned myself to never getting into the laptop again and the thought of actually getting it to work, of accessing all of dad's writing, it was too much.

'One of these has to work,' she said, weaving a grubby rubber plug through the tangle of cords and wires. There were at least four different chargers all coiled around each other and as she yanked at different parts of the puzzle, loosening one end but tightening the other, I could feel myself getting impatient. Rather than sit by and watch, I hurled myself at the floor, crawling around on the hunt for the closest outlet. Old houses never had enough outlets.

'Got it!' Lydia yelped triumphantly as she freed the first charger. 'Try that while I deal with the rest.'

The first cable we tried was the right brand but the wrong model, the second plug fitted the socket but had a loose connection and the third was for a completely different kind of computer. With her fingers crossed, Lydia tossed me the fourth and final one. The three prongs of the grounded plug clunked into place and I heard a familiar start-up chime.

'I don't believe it,' I breathed. 'It works.'

'Well, don't I feel like Cinderella.' She held up her hand for a high five and I gladly obliged. 'You said this was your dad's laptop, right?'

'Yup.'

'Any idea what's on here?'

'His work,' I said, watching the empty battery icon appear on the black screen. 'He was pretty deep into the research for a new book and he'd been digitizing his archive for a few months, all his notes and journals, that should be on here too.'

'What if it's full of porn?'

The look I gave her could have scorched the sun.

'OK, fine,' she replied, holding up her hands in surrender. 'I'm just saying. Single man, passed away unexpectedly, no one to wipe his search history? Don't be upset if you see something you're not prepared for.'

'Thanks,' I muttered. 'Now I don't even know if I want to open it. What if he *was* looking at something weird?'

'Babygirl, he was definitely looking at something weird. There is not a doubt in my mind that you will definitely find something random, like when we found out all guys are obsessed with the Roman Empire. In my experience, the more normal the person, the freakier the search history. You just need to be prepared, is all.'

'In your experience?' I replied with a quizzical eyebrow.

'Limited as it may be,' she admitted. 'But there have been

times when I borrowed Jackson's laptop and let me tell you, I have seen some things I was not prepared for.'

I knew I'd regret it but the words were out of my mouth before I could stop myself.

'Like what?'

Lydia shook her head. 'I literally cannot talk about it or my brain will explode but know that it was *not* the Roman Empire. Besides, I don't think he'd want me talking to you about that stuff. My brother totally has a crush on you.'

'He does not.'

'Uh, yes, he does.'

She swung her legs back and forth on the window seat, each of her toenails painted a different colour, while I made an incredibly unattractive spluttering sound in the back of my throat.

'He talks about you all the time, he hasn't mentioned a single other girl since we met, and one of the creepy things I saw in his search history was your name, so don't freak out or anything but you definitely have an admirer. Not a stalker though. He's still laid up thanks to his busted leg.'

'Someone like Jackson would never go for someone like me,' I reasoned, curling my legs behind me to hide my unpedicured feet.

'Someone like Jackson?'

'You know what I mean,' I said, wishing she hadn't said anything. 'He's so smooth and cool.'

'Never let him hear you say that,' she scoffed. 'If only you had known him in junior high.'

'Exactly!' I replied. 'I don't know him, just like he doesn't really know me. I'm just a novelty.'

Lydia gave me a big cheesy grin.

'He knows enough. And it doesn't hurt that you're totally cute. Jackson has always been a sucker for a green-eyed gal and that's before you throw in the whole "our moms used to talk about us getting married when we were grown up" stuff. A cute-ass girl *and* a love that was destined to be? He's got a Libra moon in his eleventh house, he's destined to be a hopeless romantic.'

'Does everyone know more astrology than me?'

I groaned as I lay down, stretched out on the wooden floor. This was not a problem I was used to dealing with. The astrology or the boys.

'I said don't freak out.' Lydia hopped down from the window to lie beside me. 'All you have to do is let him down gentle, lie, tell him you already met someone. He'll mope around for six months or so but he'll get over it eventually.'

'Actually,' I started nervously, tapping my fingers against the floorboards, 'I think I have met someone.'

'Aww, that's cute but you're not my type,' she laughed. 'Hold up, you're serious? For real, you met someone in Savannah?'

Nodding, I covered my face with my hands as she started snapping her fingers.

'Emily! When were you going to tell me?' she shrieked. 'I need every last little detail. Name, age, hair colour, rising sign, what they were wearing the first time you saw them, plus any distinguishing features in case I ever have to give a description to the cops.'

I turned my head to look at her. 'Wow, you are full of positivity today.'

'I'm only joking,' she replied, before turning deadly serious. 'I would never go to the cops.'

Rolling over onto my side, I gave her the most stern look I could muster and she shook herself down before returning my solemn expression.

'If I tell you, you have to promise not to say anything to

anyone. Not Jackson, not your grandmother, and definitely not my grandmother.'

'Because Miss Catherine Bell and I are always sitting down for tea and sharing secrets?'

'His name is Wyn Evans,' I said, shooting her a warning glare when she squealed. 'He's seventeen, he's taking photography classes at SCAD and the first time I saw him, he was wearing the perfect jeans and a T-shirt that was kind of too small—'

'Officially the sluttiest thing a man can wear,' she interrupted before running an invisible zip across her mouth. 'Sorry, I love it, go on.'

'He's tall, maybe six two, his hair is like a dark, ashy colour and his eyes are incredible. Astrology TBD but he was born in May.'

'The police would never be able to find him with that description,' she tutted. 'I love a Taurus for you. A Gemini we could work with but a Taurus is better. How much DNA has been exchanged so far?'

'We've held hands,' I replied. 'Does that work for you?'

'Not really.'

'Apologies. He's amazing and I really like him but it's a bit complicated.'

Lydia propped up her chin in her hands. 'Complicated how?'

'Catherine doesn't want me to date until I'm seventeen.'

No need to fill her in on any other potential, magical roadblocks in our future.

'Plus she's probably interviewing a shortlist of appropriate boys from good families to escort you to all the upcoming social events of the season,' she replied, chuckling as she blew a springy curl out of her face.

'This is twenty-first century Savannah, not Bridgerton,' I reminded her, tapping my foot against her. 'Speaking of which,

I wonder if I still have the last season downloaded on Dad's laptop.'

'Don't change the subject,' she said, kicking me back. 'You don't get it. Your grandmother and my grandmother? They are beyond old school. Both our families are deep into their history and Jackson always laughs at me but I'm completely-totally-positively sure we're both descended from witches.'

As quick as I could, I wiped the horrified expression off my face.

'What makes you say that?' I asked, my voice ultra-high pitched.

'Stories my grandmother used to tell us,' she replied, far too casual for her own good. 'And stuff Jackson found when he started researching our ancestry a few years ago. Between us, I think he was looking for our dad but he couldn't find anything on that side. The Powell side though? So much.'

I stared at her, trying to work out if she knew more than she was letting on. What if this was a test? What if she wanted to tell me but didn't know if I knew? Catherine wasn't the oracle, Lydia might have stumbled into her family's real history without getting my grandmother's approval first.

'What kind of stories?'

'They didn't burn anyone at the stake or anything but there was a lot of weird stuff going on with the Powell and Bell families,' she replied in an eager whisper. 'People getting sick then being mysteriously healed, women surviving fires that killed hundreds of other people, that sort of thing.'

'Doesn't sound that strange to me.' I was starting to sweat. Did she know? 'There are weird stories about every family if you dig deep enough. And there's no such thing as witches, right?'

Her mouth twisted with disappointment.

'Maybe I just want it to be true,' she said with a shrug. 'I wouldn't mind having the power to turn people into toads.'

'People like Jeremy?'

'*Exactly.*'

I managed a weak smile as she rolled over. She didn't know. I was all alone in my secret again.

'But less about Jeremy and more about Wyn,' Lydia said, grabbing hold of my hand. 'Crazy question but as the queen of the unrequited crush, I have to ask. Does he feel the same way?'

'I think so,' I replied, instinctively turning towards the window seat and picturing him there. 'I've only known him for a few days and I don't know how to explain properly. It's intense.'

'Intense how?'

It was impossible to describe my feelings with something as limited as words. There wasn't a single sentence that could do justice to the way I felt when I was with Wyn.

'Well, there's a lot going on right now—'

'Moving to a new country, meeting your family, finding a bunch of porn on this laptop probably.'

'Thank you,' I said and Lydia bowed her head as though I had given her a compliment. 'But when I'm with Wyn, it's like we're the only two people on the planet. He makes me feel completely seen and heard, like every word that comes out of my mouth is the most important thing anyone has ever said.'

She sniffed. 'Not what I expected you to say but I can see how that might be nice.'

'There's also the fact he's incredibly hot,' I added to her delight. 'When he held my hand, all of Savannah could have set on fire and I wouldn't have noticed.'

'Maybe that's how the city managed to burn to the ground twice in thirty years,' Lydia mused. 'Everyone was too busy holding hands with their sweeties to notice.'

'Savannah burned down?' I replied. 'When?'

'Oh, a million years ago.' She waved a hand as though the complete decimation of a city wasn't that important. 'Seventeen something something. Ask Jackson, he'll know. Or don't ask Jackson because he's totally in love with you and you're totally in love with this Wyn dude and oof, this has the potential to get messy.'

'I didn't say I was in love with him,' I replied too quickly.

'No, you said when he touches you the world stops spinning, your heart pounds, your hands shake and everything else ceases to exist,' Lydia's eyes rolling so far back in her head I wondered if she could see her brain. 'Em, I've seen all the movies and I've read all the books, and you're blushing hard enough to start the next great fire of Savannah all by yourself. Get your face away from the floorboards. You are in love.'

'What am I going to do?' I muttered, pressing my cold hands against my hot cheeks. 'He's just so amazing. I could listen to him talk forever.'

Lydia made a bemused clucking sound. 'Bestie, if all you want to do is talk to this stud then I don't think Miss Catherine is going to have a problem with your relationship.'

'It's not like I haven't thought about things that aren't talking,' I admitted. 'But my experience is non-existent. What if he's done more than me?'

'Then he'll be patient and respectful of your boundaries, or he'll get his ass kicked.'

She held up her hand for a high five and I hit it without missing a beat.

'And what if I want something more than hand-holding?'

'Then you'll be patient and respectful of his boundaries, and should you ever need someone to cover for you while you explore those boundaries, I'm your girl. Just remember this when I need an alibi, OK? I swear it won't be for anything illegal. If I can help it.'

I smiled at my new friend and she smiled back.

'It's wild to think we knew each other when we were babies,' Lydia said, wiggling her multi-coloured toes. 'I know the circumstances suck but Emily Bell, I for one am glad you came back to Savannah.'

'Me too,' I agreed. 'And more than anything else, I'm glad you didn't move to Charleston.'

Before she could let out the torrent of abuse I knew was on the tip of her tongue, the home screen of my dad's laptop flashed into life and Lydia nudged the trackpad to bring the cursor into view.

'Touch ID or enter password,' she read from the screen. 'What's the password?'

'I don't know.'

I was crushed. All I had left of my dad was right in front of me and I couldn't even open it.

'Hey, we don't give up before we've even started,' Lydia said, her Pollyanna optimism out in full force. 'It's probably his birthday or your birthday or a family pet or something. Dads aren't known for their ultra-cryptic passwords. Or at least that's what I hear.'

She fished around in her tote bag, pulling out a notebook and pen and an even brighter smile. 'You'll never find out if you don't try.'

'You're right,' I said, sniffing back tears that hadn't fallen yet.

'Almost always am. We'll figure it out together,' she replied as she opened her notebook and pushed the laptop towards me. 'That's what friends are for.'

'Thank you,' I told her, fingers hovering over the keyboard. 'It's nice to have a friend.'

And it really was.

Chapter Twenty-Two

'Huh.'

Lydia stood in front of Catherine's craft room, her head cocked all the way to one side. 'I wouldn't have thought your grandmother would be into that kind of stuff.'

'What kind of stuff?'

'The door, it's Haint blue, right?' she said. 'We use it to ward away spirits. It's supposed to represent water or something, Gullah legend says spirits can't cross running water.'

'I have no idea,' I admitted. 'Who are the Gullah?'

'Hello, girls.'

We both jumped at the sound of Catherine's voice. Lydia managed to land in a perfect curtsey while I managed to slip on the freshly polished floor and skid face first into the wall. My grandmother calmly placed her handbag on the console table and removed her sunglasses, to make sure we both appreciated the full weight of her glare.

'Good afternoon, Miss Catherine,' Lydia sang. 'Emily was giving me a tour of your beautiful home. I do believe Bell House is the most gorgeous abode in all of Georgia.'

'Good afternoon to you, Lydia,' Catherine replied. 'Thank

you for your most gracious compliment. You laid it on a little too thick but still, I appreciate it.'

Lydia clicked her tongue and shot her with double-finger guns and from the look on Catherine's face, I was worried the gesture was just as likely to kill her as a real gun.

'We're going out for a while,' I said, ducking my head to hide the mini makeover Lydia had insisted I didn't need but 'wouldn't be the worst thing in the world' but there was no way to hide the fact we'd swapped outfits. Sometimes you had to be cruel to be kind, said Lydia, after pronouncing each and every thing in my closet 'mid at best'.

'If that's all right with you,' Lydia added, digging her hands into the pockets of my denim shorts while I yanked up the straps of her dress. 'Ma'am.'

The smallest muscles around Catherine's eyes contracted as though she was trying to read the fine print.

'I thought perhaps you might join me while I catch up on my correspondence this afternoon,' she said. 'And I've made a reservation at The Olde Pink House for supper.'

A dismissive snort escaped the back of Lydia's throat, quickly turning into a cough.

'Love that place,' she said when Catherine gave her a death stare. 'So trad-core.'

'That sounds really . . . fun?' I replied, panicking at the idea of missing my meeting with Wyn. 'But I already promised Lydia that I would . . .'

My words faded away and I stared at my friend. What had I promised her? Thankfully, at least one of us was prepared.

'This is all my fault,' Lydia said, drowning every word in sincerity. 'I was so hoping to introduce Emily to some of my friends in the Junior League. Do you think I might be able to steal her away for just an hour or so?'

'You aren't old enough to be a member of the Junior League,' Catherine countered and Lydia gave a loud, disappointed sigh.

'Not yet, gosh darn it. But I still try to help out with their projects when I can. You're never too young to take an interest in your community, isn't that right, Em?'

'Oh, yes,' I agreed, nodding so hard I was surprised my head didn't snap off my shoulders. 'It's something I'm very passionate about. Community.'

The lies rolled off Lydia's tongue like water off a duck's back but I couldn't have looked guiltier if I'd tried. Catherine zeroed in on me, hooking one arm of her sunglasses over her bottom lip as she focused her gaze.

'Very well,' she said and I almost passed out from the shock. 'Emily, I shall expect you home and ready for supper by six p.m. sharp. I would very much like to discuss everything that will *be coming* up in the next few weeks.'

'Oh. *Oh*,' I replied, realizing what she meant right as Lydia bundled me out the door. 'Yes, sure, totally. I'll be ready.'

'And if it's at all possible,' Catherine called as we sprinted through the front garden and hurtled out the gate, 'it would be wonderful to see you wearing your own clothes.'

'Two questions,' I panted as we looped around the block then back across Lafayette Square to meet Wyn. 'What is a Junior League and what is The Olde Pink House?'

'The Junior League is a delightful organization for delightful young ladies who volunteer to do delightful things for the community,' Lydia replied before forcing herself to gag. 'And The Olde Pink House is a restaurant. It's old, it's pink, grand-mothers love it. Personally, I think it's a total tourist trap but don't sleep on the jalapeño poppers. Also, just so Miss Catherine knows, that is one of my coolest outfits. This dress is vintage, it's almost as old as her.'

'I thought you said it was from Target,' I said, pulling the tiny tank down over my hips.

'*Vintage* Target. And Em, don't worry about your dad's password. We'll figure it out eventually.'

I wished I could be as certain as she was. We'd tried a million different things, only giving up the search when we had to leave or be late. At least my dad had the presence of mind not to put a limit on the number of password attempts, but I suspected that had more to do with him regularly forgetting it himself than the vague possibility of me, lying on his old bedroom floor in Savannah, trying to hack into the computer myself.

But when it came to my list of things to worry about, my dad's laptop wasn't even in the top five. Right now, my priority was very clear. Across the street, I saw Wyn and Wyn saw me, and I had to hold my breath just to stop another rainbow from flashing across the sky.

'Wow, that's him?' Lydia whistled as we crossed into the square. 'No wonder you're in love. Is he even human?'

'God, I hope so,' I murmured. He really was almost too beautiful. Without warning, Lydia marched straight up to him and punched him hard in the shoulder.

'Hi, I'm Lydia Powell, Emily's friend,' she said with a killer smile. 'Nice to meet you. If you hurt my girl, I'll ruin your life in ways you can't even imagine. Break her heart and they'll never find your body.'

'Hi,' Wyn replied, looking from me to Lydia and back again with genuine and completely justified fear in his eyes. 'I want to say it's nice to meet you because I was raised right but to tell you the truth, that was terrifying.'

She gave the pair of us a thumbs-up. 'Correct response. Stay scared, my friend. Now y'all have fun. Em, I'll talk to you later?'

'She's only joking,' I told him as she jogged off across the

214

square, definitely not on her way to volunteer with the Junior League and definitely not joking.

'As threats go, it felt legit,' Wyn replied. 'But she doesn't have anything to worry about.' He held out his hand, I took it in mine and the branches of our oak tree shimmied with happiness. 'What's the plan for today?'

I gave him a look of disappointment. 'Do you even need to ask?'

'No, but I was being polite,' he answered with a grin. 'Leopold's it is.'

'I can't believe I spilled on Lydia's dress,' I groaned as we raced through the city streets, trying to outrun a chocolate ice cream stain. 'She's going to kill me.'

'No, she's going to kill me,' Wyn corrected. 'I know it'll be my fault somehow. What I can't believe is how you managed to completely miss your mouth.'

'It *is* your fault,' I exclaimed. 'You made me laugh! If you hadn't pointed out that dog, we would still be sat by the river enjoying our ice cream.'

'Was I supposed to let you go through life without seeing a dog in a tuxedo?' he replied with an incredulous look. 'I could never be so cruel.'

'That's true.' I slowed to a jog, pressing my hand into a burgeoning stitch. I was not a runner. More of a slow walk followed by a long sit down kind of a girl. 'Where do you think he was going? He was very formal for a Monday afternoon?'

'If you hadn't spilled your ice cream, maybe we could have asked. Good job I have a washer drier at my place.'

My heart did a somersault in my chest. Did I want to clean Lydia's dress? Yes. Did I want to see Wyn's apartment? Yes. Very much. But was I *ready* to see his place? That was a different question altogether. In the back of my mind, I saw Lydia lying on my bedroom floor with her notebook, crossing out what felt like our millionth password attempt.

You'll never find out if you don't try.

'OK. Wow.'

I audibly gasped as we stepped inside a two-storey carriage house and Wyn unlocked the door to the first ground-floor apartment.

'Really?' he laughed, closing the door behind us and hanging the keys on a hook. 'What were you expecting?'

'I don't know but not this.'

I hadn't given much thought to what Wyn's place might be like but if I'd had to guess, I would've said something closer to 'dorm room' than *Architectural Digest*. Low ceilings gave the open plan space a close but cosy feeling, the walls were whitewashed, the floors wide wooden planks, and the light that streamed in through the windows was cool and inviting. At the other end of the room was a pair of French doors that revealed a tiny private courtyard. Next to the double doors was a desk covered in pens, pencils, and sketchbooks, his camera off to one side, and right next to the desk was his bed.

'It's not usually this much of a mess,' he said, scooping up a hoodie and a pair of sweatpants from the sofa and draping them awkwardly over the back of his desk chair.

'This is not a mess,' I replied, turning in disbelieving circles. 'Believe me, I'm familiar with mess and this is not it.'

'Thanks. I'm doing my best not to live like a total pig in case my folks decide to drop by,' he chuckled. 'They own the building. My grandpa bought it back in the Seventies when regular people could still do things like that.'

When he told me he grew up in the mountains with a family full of artists, it didn't even occur to me that they might have money. If they owned the whole building, his family were definitely not a bunch of starving artists.

'The washing machine is in the bathroom.' With one hand anxiously gripping the back of his neck, Wyn pointed at my dress. 'You wanna . . .?'

'Yes, I do,' I replied, tugging at the chocolatey fabric. 'Um, do you have something I could borrow?'

He grabbed the hoodie again and held it up for approval.

'Perfect.'

He held it out towards me, stretching his arm as far as it would go and I did the same, plucking it from his grasp without making contact. Five minutes ago, I'd wanted to be as close to him as physically possible but now we were here, alone in his place, my stomach was full of butterflies and not the magical kind. Outside in the world, we had some control over how people saw us, but this unplanned visit to his apartment left him laid bare. Wyn couldn't control my perception of him and I knew if our roles were reversed, I would feel vulnerable. It was beyond intimate, being this close to his clothes, his camera, the place where he slept. The whole apartment felt like an extension of him.

'Em, I need to tell you something,' Wyn called as I slid into the bathroom. Thankfully, it was as impressively clean as the rest of his home, facewash, toothpaste and sunscreen on a shelf by the sink, shower gel and shampoo beside the bath. 'Something I should have told you already.'

'Tell me what?' I called back as I shucked off Lydia's dress, soaking the stain with laundry detergent before putting it in the machine. 'That you're secretly the heir to the Leopold's fortune?'

'Not quite.'

His hoodie drowned me, the arms flopped over my hands like a pair of glove puppets. The hood hung halfway down my back as I left the bathroom, the washing machine whirring into life behind the closed door. Wyn met me outside. The afternoon light shone brightly behind him, blacking out his features.

'I'm not in Savannah for summer school,' he said. 'I'm not even in summer school.'

'What do you mean, you're not in summer school?' I replied, my fingers curling around the overlong sleeves. 'Wyn, what are you talking about?'

'I'm here looking for my brother. He's missing.'

Even though it was still very warm, the atmosphere turned frosty.

'You should sit down.' He pointed in the general direction of the sofa, his eyes downcast. 'I'll get you some water.'

'I don't want any water,' I told him as I reached for the marble kitchen counter and held on tight to the sharp edge, something cold, something real. Something true. 'I want you to tell me what's going on right now. You lied to me?'

Outside, the sun shifted and the light found his face, the tight, tense set of his jaw etched with gold and grim disappointment in his eyes. He sank, defeated, onto the end of his bed.

'I'm not supposed to tell anyone,' he said, weaving his hands together and tightening his grip until his knuckles turned white. 'If they find out, we'll both be in so much trouble.'

'Find out what? Who's they?' I demanded, still clinging to the marble countertop. 'What could be so bad it's got you this freaked out?'

The minimalist apartment seemed to grow smaller by the second, suddenly stark and bare. There were no plants anywhere. It was the first time I hadn't been able to see something green since arriving in Savannah and it felt wrong, like I couldn't breathe properly. On the bed, Wyn pushed his hair back, away from his face.

'Cole came to town a couple of months ago,' he began, his downcast eyes on the floor. 'He works for my mom, she sent him here on some project, something to do with the rental unit upstairs, I think, I don't know all the details. A couple of weeks ago, he stopped answering his phone, so Mom sent me down to check up on him. This is his place but when I got here, it was untouched. Like no one had set foot inside since the last tenants left, bed not slept in, no food in the refrigerator, nothing.'

'Not a great sign,' I admitted. The solid marble counter creaked ominously in my hand. I loosened my grip before I accidentally snapped it in two. 'Why did they send you? Why didn't your parents come looking for him?'

'Dad doesn't get around so well, he busted his hip in a car accident a couple of years ago, and Mom . . .' He rubbed the palms of his hands down his thighs and exhaled heavily. 'Mom is not big on answering questions. If she tells you to do something, you do it.'

He looked up at me, clearly upset. His face was red and blotchy, and his voice was strained, like he was having to force out every word.

'Aside from the school stuff, everything else is true,' he insisted. 'Mom didn't want anyone asking me difficult questions about why I was here so she said it was better to have an easy story to share. I wanted to tell you the truth but I couldn't.'

'But you're telling me now,' I said. I wanted to trust him. I wanted to believe him, I needed to. But I couldn't, not just yet.

'Just couldn't lie to you anymore. You're too important to me.' He shrugged and gave me a thin smile. 'You're the only thing that makes sense when nothing else does. This should've been a simple errand, drive down here, kick Cole's ass for not calling our mom then hang out in Savannah for a few days. Cole's not great at keeping in touch, I figured he'd lost his

219

phone again or met someone and gotten distracted—' He paused to shake his head at the irony of that statement. 'But there's no trace of him, Em. I've been searching for two whole weeks, no one's seen him, no one remembers him, he's not on the security cameras. It's like he was never here in the first place.'

'Are you sure he was?' I replied. 'If he's that unreliable, maybe he bailed on his job altogether.'

'Not even Cole would go against our mother.'

His eyes slowly worked their way up my body, lingering on my lips for a second, before finally meeting mine. 'Something's wrong. Mom and Dad are freaking out, my grandpa is calling me around the clock, and I don't know what to do.'

A cloud passed over the sun and the whole apartment fell into shadow, white walls turning grey. So Wyn had a family secret he felt he couldn't share. That was hardly something I could hold against him.

'I still don't understand why you didn't tell me,' I said. 'Don't you trust me?'

'I would trust you with my life,' he answered, standing abruptly. 'But what if you'd told someone else, your grand-mother or Lydia, and they went to the cops?'

'Because that would be bad?'

'Very bad. Cole has a record.' Wyn's words were flat and devoid of emotion. 'And a violent temper.'

'Then why did your mom send him here alone in the first place?' I asked, my heartbeat quickening in my chest.

'Because Cole has a record and a violent temper,' he answered. 'Whatever she sent him here to do, she thought that might be helpful.'

'When you said your mom was an artist, are you sure you didn't mean mob boss?' I took another look around the apart-ment, searching for clues to the truth about his family. No horses heads or machine guns lying around but that didn't mean his parents weren't into something he knew nothing about. Parents, it turned out, were good at keeping secrets.

'Em, I'm sorry,' he said, his voice low and husky. 'I told you my family was complicated.'

He moved towards me slowly, digging one hand into his dark ash waves, and my toes curled inside my shoes as I watched and waited. 'I would understand if you didn't want to see me again. I don't want to get you into any trouble.'

'Believe me, I'm entirely capable of getting myself into trouble without your help,' I replied, shaking. 'And you know there's nothing in the world you could say that would make me not want to see you again.'

When the caps of Wyn's boots touched the tips of my shoes, he stopped and waited for permission to cross the invisible barrier I'd put up between us. I placed my hand on his chest. Permission granted.

'Every family has its secrets,' I whispered as he rested his forehead against mine. 'There are things I haven't told you yet.'

'But we're not our families, right?' he replied. 'We shouldn't have to carry their burdens.'

'We're not our families,' I agreed. His breath was warm on my lips and I felt a tingle of magic begin to spark under my skin. 'We're just us, we belong to ourselves.'

'And to each other,' Wyn murmured against my lips. 'I'm yours, Emily. Forever.'

Any doubt in my mind disappeared the moment I kissed him. Tipping my head back, I pulled him down to me, hands lost in his hair, his mouth hot and firm against mine. My feet skidded out from under me as he pressed my body against the kitchen counter, but I didn't fall. Wyn held me so tight in his arms, I couldn't tell if I was standing or floating and I didn't care either way. It could've been raining fire outside for all I knew. The only real thing in this world was his kiss.

My whole body trembled with the force of my desire, a secret I'd kept even from myself. Wyn was mine and I was his and nothing made more sense than to stay here with him until the end of time. I was silent as his lips drew a line along my jawbone and down to the hollow of my throat, testing and tasting, until I heard myself moan and guided his mouth back to mine. It was uncontrollable, inevitable, and I liked it. Slowly at first then all at once, the apartment filled with light lavender smoke, hazy and beautiful. Wyn's eyes were closed, blissfully oblivious to the white flames that began to flicker all around us. Or maybe, I was the only one who could see them. When I reached out to touch them, there was no heat, just a pure and perfect fire, protecting us both from anything that could ever hope to harm us, and as we staggered over to his bed, collapsing in a tangle of limbs, everything became crystal clear.

As long as we were together, nothing could touch us.

Chapter Twenty-Three

'It's kind of late in the season for azaleas?' Wyn remarked as we rushed back down Harris Street towards Bell House.

'I'll have to take your word for it,' I replied, staring at the bold pink and red blossoms. There were flowers everywhere, exploding in a riot of colour, all around us.

'Were they even here this morning?' he asked with a frown.

'They must've been. Flowers don't appear out of nowhere.'

Except sometimes they did. I anxiously bit my bottom lip, listening to the whispers meant just for me. The trees, the plants, the flowers, the moss. They were full of love and as happy as I was. The afternoon had passed too quickly and there was no time to worry about spontaneously blooming azaleas when I was five minutes away from being late for dinner with Catherine.

'So, I was thinking about Cole,' I said, pulling down Lydia's still damp but thankfully clean dress when it rode up my hips. It was not made for speed. 'Do you have a recent photograph of him? I won't say anything to anyone but two pairs of eyes looking out for him have to be better than one.'

'This is the last photo I have.' He pulled his phone from his pocket and handed it to me. 'It's not his best look but it is the most accurate.'

As we came to Lafayette Square, I slowed my pace, making a complete stop underneath our oak tree. The man on the screen looked much older than Wyn but the resemblance was clear. Their matching skintone, the same cheekbones. Cole's hair was wavy like Wyn's but longer and a few shades darker. In the photo, he wore a flannel shirt with ripped jeans, and even though he was undeniably handsome, the sneer on his face left me cold. He scowled into the camera with a middle-finger salute.

'Not exactly North Carolina's most charming gentleman,' Wyn said as I zoomed in on his brother's face. The colours in his eyes were just as complex as Wyn's, maybe a little more golden than grey.

'He looks so angry,' I said, aching with sympathy as Wyn tucked his phone away in his pocket. 'What happened to make him so mad?'

'No idea, he's always been that way. Doesn't mean I'm not worried about him though.'

'We'll find him,' I promised, smoothing away the anguish on his perfect face. 'And if we can't do it on our own, we can always draft in Lydia and swear her to secrecy. She's like a one-woman FBI.'

My palm buzzed against Wyn's skin and I could almost see his worries drift away, replaced by the same marshmallow puff of happiness that filled me all the way up. He leaned down as I reached up and the kiss that followed was different to all the others we'd shared that afternoon. They were hungry, exploratory, insatiable. This kiss was sure and slow, our passion building until I stumbled backwards, out of breath.

'No,' I muttered, holding my arms out in front of me as I fell to my knees hard, flesh scraping against dirt.

This was the kiss. The kiss I'd seen on my first night in Savannah. A strand of Spanish moss slid off a low branch and curled around my wrist before the world went black and a thousand confusing images flashed through my mind, all in the same moment.

'It's fine, I'm fine,' I insisted, Wyn's worried hands clutching at my shoulders before I even knew what had happened. 'I tripped is all.'

'You're sure?' he asked, unconvinced.

I nodded and he bent down to kiss me again. I let him, curling readily into his chest and the warmth of his arms. Only this time I kept my eyes open, too afraid of what I might see. Of what I had already seen.

Bonaventure cemetery. A full moon. Catherine screaming in the night and a huge, bloody, fearsome wolf lunging straight for my throat.

Lydia hadn't lied. The Olde Pink House was exactly that, big, pink and old.

'This particular mansion has a long history,' Catherine said, a daredevil squirrel sprinting across our path as we passed through Reynolds Square on our way to dinner. 'It was built in 1789 as a private house for the Habersham family.'

'It's even older than Bell House?' I replied, eyeing the Pepto Bismol pink exterior.

'It is. But unlike Bell House, it has been a bank, an attorney's office, a bookstore, a tearoom and finally a restaurant. A fate our home will never suffer.'

'Because you would never sell it,' I said as though the answer was obvious.

'Because Bell House would never allow it,' she corrected. 'Even if I tried.'

*

Inside the restaurant, there was even more colour, each room painted a different shade from floor to ceiling: deep navy, hunter green, powder-puff blue, all of them accented with gold: chairs, candlesticks, picture frames. All antique everything. But Catherine and I weren't eating in one of the colourful rooms. After an extremely effusive welcome from the manager, a server in a white shirt and pink tie took us downstairs, shaking every step of the way.

'We're eating in here?' I asked when he waved us into a tiny space with old brick walls and rafters on the ceiling and only one table, set for two. An unwelcoming deer's head peered down at me, giving me the same kind of look I'd seen on Catherine when I bolted into Bell House with one minute to spare before my curfew.

'The Olde Pink House was a bank at one time. This was once the vault. We always eat in here,' Catherine said. 'It's been a part of my life for as long as I can remember. My grandmother and I would dine here every month.'

'Can I get y'all something to drink?' Sweat was already beading on the server's forehead. It wasn't hot in the air-conditioned restaurant so I figured he'd tangled with my grandmother before.

'Two sweet teas, thank you kindly,' she replied curtly. 'And we'll take the fried green tomatoes and the artichoke fritters to start.'

'And can we get the jalapeño poppers?' I added.

'No,' Catherine said before he had the chance to reply. 'We can't.'

The server fumbled in his pocket for an order pad but her glare sent him staggering backwards out of the vault before pen could touch paper.

'How was your afternoon?' she asked, turning all sweetness and light. 'You haven't said a word about it.'

'It was great,' I said. Not a lie. 'I'm sorry I wasn't back

earlier, we were having so much fun, um, helping the community that I lost track of the time then I slipped and fell and—'

'And the Junior League?'

'We – we didn't really spend a lot of time with them.'

'Oh?' Catherine raised an inquisitive eyebrow.

'Or any time at all.'

Another server entered to fill our water glasses and my grandmother nodded with satisfaction. 'Thank you for telling the truth. Lydia Powell is not a good liar and, I'm pleased to say, neither are you.'

Better than you know, I thought shamefully, my lips still chapped from Wyn's kisses.

'The Powells are a good family but they've never been beyond testing the limits of proper behaviour,' Catherine added. 'Even Virginia could be a handful in her day. I don't doubt that Lydia will grow up to be a fine young woman but I am quite as certain she'll get into some scrapes along the way.'

She sipped her water while casting warm looks around the vault. One way in, one way out. I pulled at the collar of the oversized white cotton shirt I'd thrown over Lydia's dress, suddenly claustrophobic. Catherine turned her head towards the candles that lined the ledge behind me and in the blink of an eye, they flickered with golden flames.

'Shit,' I exclaimed before covering my mouth.

'Ladies don't curse,' she replied sternly as the candle on our table also came alive.

'Literally or figuratively?'

'Both.' She smiled and the small, unfriendly room seemed to open up a little. 'It is so nice to continue a true Bell family tradition with you, Emily. This is where my grandmother taught me most everything I needed to know.'

'About your magic?' I asked, surprised, one eye on the open doorway.

Catherine laughed loud enough to gutter one of the candles. 'Oh, honey, no. This is where I learned how to be a lady, so elbows off the table, if you please.'

I yanked my arms off the table entirely and placed my hands in my lap. Which subject did I know the least about: relationships, magic, or etiquette? It didn't seem fair to be so clueless about all three.

'But it is safe for us to talk openly here,' she said. 'This room is spelled. Anyone who is not a member of our family will forget every word they hear the moment they walk out the door. Aside from our orders, that is.'

'Acacia, adder's tongue, hickory, and lavender,' I murmured, gazing at a painting of the ocean hanging behind her head. 'They're hidden inside the frame. It's a memory charm?'

'That's right,' she confirmed, eyes bright. 'The Olde Pink House has been around almost as long as the Bell family and it has always been a safe space for us. It survived both great fires of Savannah in 1796 and 1820, along with Bell House and only a handful of other buildings. We couldn't save everything but there's something special about this place. We take care of it, it takes care of us.'

I drank my water and said nothing. It wasn't just buildings that burned down in those fires, people had died. If Bell witches could save lives but only some, how did we decide who was worthy and who wasn't? Catherine said she didn't like the word power but choosing who died and who didn't certainly seemed like power to me.

The door to the dining room opened slowly and our server reappeared carrying two teas and several plates, definitely more items than we had ordered.

'Compliments of the chef,' he said, rattling them onto the table. I couldn't help but notice my grandmother's flicker of irritation when he set the jalapeño poppers in front of me. 'Would you like to order your entrees?'

'We will both have my usual.'

Catherine did not alter her impassive expression, but when he made eye contact, he started sweating bullets. As soon as he crossed the threshold, his shoulders straightened and he strolled off down the hallway with a swagger in his step, any trace of apprehension having evaporated.

'If we eat all this there won't be room for any entrees,' she muttered as if she was mad at the food. I could not relate. I was ravenous, they couldn't bring us enough free jalapeño poppers as far as I was concerned. 'Now, where should we begin this evening?'

'The visions,' I replied quickly, before stuffing a pepper in my mouth. 'If they're going to keep happening, I need to understand them.'

Catherine looked displeased.

'Etiquette lesson number one. Ladies don't speak with their mouths full.'

I held a hand over my mouth until I'd chewed and swallowed. She nodded approvingly and motioned for me to speak.

'Sorry,' I said, clearing my throat with a sip of water. 'I'd like to know more about the visions. How far back will they go? Can I only see into my own past?'

'I believe so,' Catherine answered. 'At least for the time being. That could change as your magic grows.'

'And the visions of the future. Am I seeing events that are set in stone or is there still a chance we can change things?'

'Why? Have you seen something you believe needs to change?'

The cemetery. The wolf. My grandmother, bloody and screaming. Rather than answer right away, I stabbed several pieces of fried green tomato with my fork and dumped them on my plate.

'Emily, do try to save some room, you're not starving to death.' She pulled the plate of tomatoes out of my reach before placing one single slice on her plate. 'I wish I could be of more help with your visions but I have never experienced one for myself. It's a very rare gift.'

'Doesn't feel like a gift,' I said, my whole body deflating. 'If it was, I would return it.'

Catherine's gaze softened then she placed another slice of tomato on my plate.

'Discovering your magic should be a wonderful thing. I'm sorry this is so hard on you. We should be celebrating, not panicking. With all your magic expressing itself at once, it might be difficult to fully understand your gifts until after the Becoming.'

I took several nervous gulps of water and emptied the glass.

'Which is the other thing I wanted to talk about,' I replied. 'You said it's a ceremony that takes place on my birthday, like a coming of age thing?'

'That's correct. Very straightforward, very simple,' Catherine said, moving food around on her plate without ever taking a bite. 'We'll go through the details closer to the day, but there is something else I would like to talk over with you this evening. Something we haven't discussed yet.'

'Today's the day for it,' I said quietly, reluctantly switching my empty water glass for the sweet tea. So help me, it didn't even taste that sweet anymore. I was already getting used to it.

Catherine selected a small piece of cornbread and slathered it with butter before taking the tiniest possible nibble.

'How do you feel about the word prophecy?'

'That depends,' I replied warily. 'Who is the prophecy about?'

'We've never been entirely sure.'

She paused our conversation as our server returned with a large glass of red wine.

'Your Château Lafite. Please enjoy.'

He was gone before she could say thank you.

'I don't remember you ordering wine,' I said as she swirled it around in the glass.

'Nor will you find it on the menu. Another perk of our relationship with the owners.' She took a deep drink, savoured the wine then returned her attention to me. 'Let's start over. I would like to tell you a story instead, one that's been passed down through Bell family witches for as long as we've been in Savannah. It is a story about a very special witch and all the wonderful things she will do in the world.'

'Like run the New York marathon and win *American Idol*?'

'Entirely possible but the finer details of her life are missing from our version of the story. What we do know is this witch will do three things: revive the dormant powers of her sisters, protect our magic from its greatest enemies, and . . .'

'And?' I prompted. 'I've read a lot of books about prophecies and they hardly ever end in "then she spent the night bingeing *Friends* on the sofa and lived happily ever after".'

Catherine put down her glass and nodded. 'The prophecy says she will be strong and gifted, the most intuitive witch in centuries, and she will be able to access all the magic of her ancestors rather than connect to just one ability.'

So far so yikes.

'That's it?' I croaked. 'Apart from the greatest enemies bit, that doesn't sound too bad.'

'The final part of the prophecy says this witch will either save the world or end it.'

I stared into my grandmother's eyes, the exact same shape and shade as my own, and searched for a single shred of

231

uncertainty. Nothing. Whether the story was true or not, she believed it.

'Save the world or end it?' I repeated. 'Why would anyone want to end the world?'

'Why does anyone do anything?'

Just what this moment needed, answering a question with another question.

'There will come a time,' Catherine continued. 'We do not know when, but when it comes, this witch will be faced with a choice. Only she will be able to make the decision and act upon it. The choice will be hers and hers alone.'

'If I'm honest, I'm not loving the plot twist,' I said as Catherine reached for her wine again, the look on my face driving her to drink. 'Any idea who this witch might be?'

She gave me a look and I felt the last shred of denial slip through my fingers.

'The witch will come from Emma Catherine Bell's line, born and Become under a full moon, and on both days, the tides will rise to meet her. The day you were born, Savannah experienced a King Tide eleven feet high. You're already expressing multiple abilities, finding your way to magic I couldn't even conceive of. Emily, it's you.'

'No pressure then.' I pushed away my plate, appetite disappearing altogether. Even for the jalapeño poppers.

'I don't mean to scare you,' Catherine said. 'But it is my duty to prepare you.'

'Assuming you're right,' I replied, quietly reeling. 'What happens next? Is there a handbook or an instructional video? An instruction video would be so great.'

She said nothing but I was sure I saw her imperceptibly shaking her head.

'There are a lot of different ways to interpret saving the

world,' I added. 'I could encourage people to recycle, maybe convince some celebrities to give up their private jets.'

'I think your sisters might need a little more from you than that,' she said as I let my head loll backwards with frustration. 'I know this is a lot to take in—'

'And everything would have been easier if my dad hadn't taken me away.'

I finished the sentence before she could because as much as I might not like it, she was right, about both things. If I'd grown up learning about our magic, it might not seem so overwhelming now.

'Prophecies are hard to interpret,' Catherine said as I rolled my head back around to look at her. She was so hard to read, there was sympathy in her voice but her expression was pure exhilaration. 'Especially one passed down through generations; words change, their meanings are altered—'

As she was speaking, something occurred to me.

'If your prophecy girl is supposed to revive her sisters,' I interrupted, using a jalapeño popper as a pointer, 'there must be other witches out there?'

'Dormant ones, yes.'

'And if there are witches, there must be other supernatural creatures?'

'Yes.'

I could tell she wasn't happy about making the admission.

'But we're all quite rare and do not encounter each other often,' she said.

Excitement rolled through me and I held the jalapeño popper a little too tightly, squirting cream cheese across the table. 'What, exactly, don't we encounter often?'

My grandmother exhaled heavily, a combination of frustration and defeat carving deep lines around her mouth. 'Emily, let's talk more after we eat. This wonderful food is going cold and I would hate to waste it.'

'When we were in the garden, you showed me the aconite,' I said quickly, the facts coming together in a way I really did not care for. 'The wolfsbane. Catherine, are werewolves real?'

She put her knife and fork down and as the silverware touched the table, our server was back to clear away the barely eaten food. I closed my mouth, sitting still as a statue as he took my plate, his eyes glazed over with a milky glow.

'We witches are protected by the fact history has a bad habit of underestimating women,' Catherine replied while he stacked the plates. 'People buy crystals and burn sage and they think we're benign because they play at being witches too. But Weres are different. People do not like different. So they demonize them in books and films, then choose to pretend they don't exist in real life.'

'But they do exist.'

She smoothed a hand over her shining hair, securing one rogue strand behind her ear.

'Some of the more reliable histories suggest they originated in Scandinavia, and there are an awful lot of Were stories in Norse mythology. The Romans claimed them also. I suspect there is no one singular origin point for them or for us. We simply are.'

I looked at my grandmother, the beautiful, elegant pillar of the community, sipping red wine in a beautiful restaurant and chatting away about werewolves as though it was the most normal thing in the world.

'Is their magic inherited like ours?' I guessed.

'Not quite. Witches are born, wolves are chosen. The gift *is* passed down the bloodline but a family must select its protector. If they decide not to initiate a wolf in the next generation, their magic dies out and cannot return while ours lies dormant.

Fewer and fewer families choose to subject their children to such a life in these modern times. It's a difficult magic to live with, painful, isolating. A tough secret to keep in today's world, I would imagine. Some Weres hide it even from their own family. The only people who know the truth are the members of their pack, who they might only meet with once or twice in their lifetime.'

'Sounds lonely,' I replied, unexpectedly grateful not to be alone in my magic. 'I can see why they would choose to let it go rather than put their kids through something like that.'

'The right thing to do is rarely the easiest,' Catherine said with polite disagreement. 'I've no doubt it is a hard life but it's also a matter of legacy, and heritage. Their magic is their purpose, as it is ours.'

'What else can you tell me about them?' I asked, hungry for as much knowledge as she could give me. One thing I'd learned from my academic father, facts are more powerful than fear.

She touched her pointer finger to her aquamarine ring and twisted it from side to side, looking almost lost in thought. 'Most Weres are male because, as I understand, the families used to initiate their eldest male as a matter of tradition. No one chose a female unless there were no males to continue the line. Absurd really, female Weres are much stronger than the males but their society is as susceptible as the rest of the world when it comes to believing what a woman should and shouldn't do.' She paused to take a drink, slyly toasting us both. 'Female Weres are able to retain more of themselves after the change while the males are lost to the animal. Males must turn during the full moon. Females can choose whether or not to go wolf. We women have had eons of experience in managing our bodies once a month, after all.'

'If the men in Were families freak out like my dad when I got my first period, I can sympathize,' I muttered. 'Sorry, not ladylike.'

235

'First we'll deal with the magic, then we'll work on the art of conversation,' Catherine replied with a frown. She straightened out her napkin as our server returned with our entrees, two huge pork chops with sides of macaroni cheese and collard greens. It looked delicious but I knew I wouldn't be able to take even a bite.

'Weres are physically strong and not only during the full moon,' she carried on talking while he refilled my water glass, completely placid this time. The lavender added to the memory charm was doing its job. 'They're creative, perceptive and usually extraordinarily smart. I would love to know who started the rumour that werewolves are blunt instruments because it has served them well. If only we had thought to spread the same misinformation about witches, more of us might have survived. Less pleasingly, many years ago, they appointed themselves to the role of supernatural peacekeeper, playing judge, jury, and executioner in the magical world, mostly because they wish to remain hidden. As you might imagine, that has put Weres and witches at odds in the past. I wouldn't call them our friends.'

'But they're not our enemy?' I asked, full of false hope. 'They wouldn't try to hurt us and we wouldn't hurt them.'

'It's a little late to worry about that, don't you think?' Catherine replied lightly. 'You've already killed one, after all.'

It hit me like a punch to the gut.

'What do you mean?' I asked, my mouth dry.

'The wolf at Bonaventure,' she said, slicing into her pork chop. 'Honey, surely you'd worked that out for yourself by now.'

I was shaking, not trembling, but physically shaking so violently my water glass shuffled closer and closer to the edge of the table. My fingertips tingled, just for a second, before the palms of my hands started to burn. Catherine looked up with dismay as every candle in the vault flamed all the way up

236

to the wooden rafters. It wasn't just me who was shaking, it was the whole restaurant.

'Emily,' she hissed. 'Stop it. Stop it right now.'

'I can't stop it because I don't know how I'm doing it,' I replied, every word catching in my throat.

Outside, I heard raised voices and panicked exclamations. While the room around us rattled, the other diners scrambled for the exits. Our server blankly observed the destruction as glasses and plates crashed to the floor inside the vault but made no move to leave, even when one of the heavy gold candlesticks leapt from the wall, smacking into his shoulder on its way down. When the painting above the fireplace began to shake, Catherine leaned across the table and slapped me, hard, across the face.

The tremors stopped at once.

'Go,' Catherine ordered the server and he ambled away, blinking in confusion at the debris outside the vault and rubbing his mysteriously injured shoulder.

'I'm sorry, Emily, I didn't know what else to do.' She picked chunks of ice out of her tea and wrapped them in her napkin before pressing it to my face. 'How do you feel?'

'Like I killed someone,' I whispered, me and the restaurant both shivering with an aftershock.

She was already pale but in the dim light of the dining room, Catherine's skin was almost ghostly. The set of her mouth was grim and determined. Defiant or defensive, I wasn't sure which.

'You killed some*thing*,' she corrected. 'A wolf. A vicious, violent animal that hunted and attacked us. If you hadn't acted, we would both be dead and, believe me, that creature would have shown no remorse.'

'Maybe my dad was right to keep me away,' I said in a broken voice. 'I don't want to hurt people, I can't cope with any of this.'

My face was already streaked with tears and my eyes red and sore but my grandmother looked like a warrior, her calm elegance bolstered by the same fierceness I'd seen in Bonaventure.

'You are a Bell witch. You will not cope, you will thrive,' she declared. 'Do you realize you just now caused an earthquake without even trying? That kind of strength hasn't been seen in a single witch for centuries. Your magic is one of a kind but we cannot allow anything like this to happen again, do you hear me?'

The thrill in her eyes was more terrifying than the earthquake and the wolf combined. I gulped down my own panic, pushing it down, down, down, as far as it would go.

'Yes, I hear you.'

'Good,' Catherine said. 'You must stay calm, avoid heightened emotions and you must learn to take control of your magic, before your magic takes control of you.'

Chapter Twenty-Four

I felt him before I saw him. When I opened my eyes the next morning, I was huddled in the corner of my window seat, my legs numb from spending so long in such an awkward position. After we got home from dinner, I was too wound up to lie in bed, alone with my thoughts, and so I'd moved to the window seat and counted the stars instead. Now the stars had vanished and the sky was pale pink with dawn light when I looked out the window to find Wyn standing in our garden at the foot of the magnolia tree. His face turned up towards me like a flower searching for the sun.

'Hey,' he called quietly when I raised my window and stepped out onto the balcony.

'Hi,' I called back, the cool morning air soft and soothing. Was he really there? Was I dreaming? 'What are you doing here?'

'Something's happened,' he answered shakily. 'I have to go back home. Now.'

The last traces of my dreamless sleep were washed away by the unwelcome rush of reality.

'I'm coming down,' I said. 'Don't move.'

*

Bell House was silent as I crept downstairs, muffling my footsteps and hushing the front door as it clicked open and closed. Outside, I found Wyn lingering under the pink flowers of a crape myrtle tree. He had his backpack over one shoulder and his hands in his pockets. The look on his face was agony and the short distance between us was too far. I closed it first, stepping into him and wrapping my arms around his waist. He smelled like he'd just got out of bed, a mix of hastily applied deodorant, laundry detergent and warm skin. We stood in the corner of the garden, holding on to each other without a word. He didn't need to say anything, I could feel the conflict in him. Wyn's hands travelled up and down my back as though he was trying to prove to himself I was definitely there.

'My mom called,' he said, murmuring into my hair. 'It's Cole.'

'Is he OK?'

No answer.

'Do you know when you'll be back?'

'I do not.'

His arms tensed around me, a soft, unbreakable cage. He was leaving. He was really leaving. There were so many things I wanted to say but all my words swirled around inside me with the right ones always just beyond my reach, so I held on to his flannel shirt instead, like I could physically hold him here, stop him from going anywhere, ever.

'Please don't leave,' I begged but even as the words left my lips, I knew they were the wrong ones.

'When my mom tells you to do something, you do it,' Wyn reminded me. 'I have to go. Unless you want to run away with me instead?'

I forced a smile and nodded. 'Where are we going?'

'I'd go anywhere with you.'

But he didn't mean it, not really. His body language was already saying goodbye even if he couldn't bring himself to speak the words out loud, the slope of his shoulders, the tilt of his head, the downturned corners of his green-grey eyes. I pulled back to take a mental picture but the dawn was too serene for the situation. I wanted anger, I wanted red, I wanted this isn't fair, and why is it happening.

'I'll be back soon, as soon as possible,' he promised as I breathed in and out, trying to calm myself as my fingertips bypassed a tingle and began to buzz. 'And I'll call every day until then.'

'And send me photos of cool dogs,' I replied, trying desperately to calm myself before I caused another earthquake. 'I heard that's what cell phones are for.'

Wyn smiled sadly and heaved his overpacked backpack off his shoulder, dropping it on the ground with a heavy thud before pulling out one of his sketch pads and a pen.

'You have my number. This is everything else. Use any of them, all of them, whatever works. All day every day, I'll be waiting to hear from you.'

Shaking his head in disbelief, he scribbled down an email address, street address, and a username, then tore out the page, pressing it into my hand before running his forefinger over my cheekbone to wipe away a tear I hadn't felt fall. Then, placing his hands on my shoulders, he straightened out his arms, extending the distance between us.

'Look at how beautiful you are,' he said, staring at me with wonder, like I was some kind of impossible prize.

But I didn't feel beautiful. I felt like someone who was about to lose the only thing in her life that made sense.

'You'll come back,' I said, meaning my words to be soft and gentle but instead barking them out like an order. 'You promise you'll come back?'

'There's nothing that could keep me from coming back to you, Em.' He paused and took a deep breath in. 'This is meant to be. I love you.'

'I love you too,' I replied, melting with the words. 'I love you, Wyn Evans.'

It was easy to say because it was true. I wanted to say it to his face every day, the two of us laughing and smiling under the stars, not holding on to each other in the thin morning light with tears streaming down both our faces. I drew him down to me, pressing my lips to his and sealing in the words forever. No matter what else happened, nothing could take them away from us.

'I have to go now,' Wyn whispered, still so close to me I felt the words before I heard them. Even though every part of me told me to stop him, I didn't try. I didn't dare. After what happened at The Olde Pink House, I was almost afraid to breathe in case I accidentally summoned a tornado and tossed his pickup truck into the sky.

'I'll call you as soon as I know what's happening,' he swore and I followed him to the gate, one magnet drawn to another.

'Get home safe,' I told him, one of those empty things you say when you don't know what else to say. He climbed into the truck, tossing his backpack in first, and above him clouds began to gather in the sky. When he gunned the engine, they turned black.

'Drive safe,' I said with a shaky voice. 'Looks like there's going to be a storm.'

'Looks like,' Wyn Evans agreed over the twin rumbles of engine and thunder. 'I love you, Emily James. Nothing is ever going to change that.'

I stood in front of Bell House and watched him go, so strong but completely powerless. The bright red of his truck stood out against the muted colour palette of Lafayette Square and when it finally passed out of view, I sank down to the ground, keeping myself together until I felt him cross the bridge, leaving me and Savannah behind.

Only then did I let it rain.

Chapter Twenty-Five

'There are a million good reasons why he ghosted you,' Lydia declared, six days, seven hours and forty-three minutes after Wyn left Savannah. She was stretched out on a sun lounger in the back garden of Bell House, lemonade in one hand, a chocolate chip cookie in the other, having invited herself over when I failed to respond to her last three texts.

'Not that he has definitely for sure ghosted you,' she added when she saw my scowl. 'Maybe he broke his arm and can't hold his phone, or maybe he's in a cute little coma and he's going to wake up any second, yelling your name.'

'A cute little coma?' I replied, unimpressed. 'Lydia, no.'

Ever since Wyn disappeared, time had dragged. The first day was a black hole. Catherine left me alone, under the assumption I was coming to terms with everything I'd learned at supper. She wasn't wrong, none of that helped, but the biggest knife in my heart was Wyn's absence. He said he would call but he didn't. For the first couple of days I let myself believe he was busy with family stuff, maybe something really awful had happened to his brother and he would get in touch with me when he could. By the fourth day, my patience ran out and

I sent him a text. He didn't answer. The next day I called but he didn't pick up. I even had Lydia DM him on every possible platform but there was no reply, no read receipt, and no updates on his page.

As far as anyone could tell, Wyn Evans had vanished off the face of the earth.

'All I'm saying is, there has to be a reason,' Lydia stated. 'He is super into you, Em, he didn't have to come say goodbye. If he really wanted to ghost, he'd have left without saying anything. You said he had family stuff to deal with, right? Family stuff, as you and I both know, can be tough.'

She didn't even know how right she was.

'I think I made it perfectly clear that if he hurt you, I would end his life, and running off to North Carolina can't stop me from making good on that threat,' she added. 'All I need to hunt a man down is half a name and his hair colour. This fool gave you his number, his email address, his mailing address, and his username. It's almost too easy, there's no sport in it.'

'Maybe we should go to Asheville,' I mused for the thousandth time that day. 'We wouldn't have to go in his house or anything, I just want to know he's OK.'

'Like I said fifteen minutes ago, fantastic idea. Your grandmother wouldn't completely flip out and we wouldn't both get grounded until the end of time. Did you want to steal a car, book a flight or take a ten-hour-round-trip Uber?'

'Uber?' I replied feebly. 'Point taken.'

Lydia dusted off her hands as though she'd finished the dirty work and smiled. 'I know you're heartbroken now but there's no point sitting here sulking. Wasting the summer isn't going to bring him back any faster and your birthday is right around the corner. We have party planning to do.'

My birthday. I would be seventeen in two weeks but a

party was the last thing on my mind. When I wasn't worrying about Wyn, I was busy learning everything I could about my magic and preparing for Catherine's prophecy. Mornings were almost always spent in the garden, exploring the properties of different herbs and how they could be combined to heal and protect. In the afternoons, I studied the history of the city alongside the long lineage of the Bell family, and after supper, Catherine and I explored my rapidly expanding array of abilities. I was able to harness the elements now, not as well as my grandmother, but I could light a candle on command and put it out without it exploding in my face (like it did the first five times), and I could sense the people around me. I knew Lydia was on her way over to visit before she even left her house; her energy was as bright and bold as she was, telegraphing her intentions across several blocks without even trying. Jackson was easy to see too but I did my best to block him out. Sensing him felt a little too close to spying.

On the downside, no matter how hard I tried, I couldn't force a vision and I hadn't seen another ghost since my visit to Tybee Island. If only I knew where Wyn was, why he hadn't been in touch, I was certain I'd be able to concentrate better, find more control. But, on the upside, I hadn't conjured any earthquakes or flash floods like the one I'd inadvertently brought about when he left. No one was hurt. Only me.

My other hobby was one Catherine did not care for. Scouring our library for information on Weres. It turned out she was right. According to the few books that covered the topic, if the Were we'd faced in Bonaventure was a male, it would have killed us given half the chance. But knowing that didn't stop me from waking up in the middle of the night, every night, hollowed out by the fact I'd taken a life. He was only a wolf one day out of the month. Who was he the rest of the time?

246

Did he have a family? People who loved him? Not anymore. Now he was at the bottom of a river and they would never even know what happened to him, while I sat at home with my best friend, planning a party.

'Love that the b-day falls on a weekend,' Lydia said, chugging the lavender lemonade I'd made myself that morning. I didn't need Ashley drugging my only real friend for the fun of it. 'My birthday falls on a Wednesday. How lame is that? No one wants to party on a Wednesday, but a Friday, yes please. What's the plan?'

'There isn't one,' I said before she could get carried away.

At least there wasn't a plan I could share with Lydia. June twenty-first crept ever closer but Catherine still hadn't told me exactly what would happen during the Becoming cere-mony. Every time I asked about it, she dismissed my questions, withholding the information like it was some kind of fun surprise, but I already knew from her taste in incred-ibly boring movies we had very different ideas when it came to fun.

'I think my grandmother wants to do a family thing,' I added. 'Some sort of traditional celebration.'

Not a complete lie.

'If you can't hang Friday night, you have to let me throw you a party on Saturday,' Lydia insisted, cutting off my protests before they began. 'Virginia is going out of town to visit my mom that weekend so we'll have the whole house to ourselves. Nothing crazy, just me, you, Jackson, maybe a handful of carefully curated guests to add to the ambience. Very chill, very low-key, lots of gifts. It will be a dream party.'

A single butterfly fluttered across the garden to land on a rose bush, its wings flickering softly. No obligations, nowhere to go and no one to be. It must be nice.

'Not that I'm not grateful but I don't think I'm going to be in the mood for a big celebration,' I said when the butterfly lifted up into the sky and flew away. 'Whatever I do, it's going to be a strange birthday.'

'Because Wyn left or because your dad died or because you had to move to Savannah and live with Miss Catherine and your weird aunt?'

I shot her a look.

'Gotcha, all of the above,' she replied, firing back at me with her trademark finger guns. 'Speaking of your dad, have you hacked that computer yet?'

'No,' I admitted, running my mom's locket up and down on its chain. 'It's driving me crazy. I have my dad's laptop and my mom's locket and I can't open either.'

Without asking, Lydia reached across my chest and grabbed the golden orb from out of my hand. 'What do you mean, you can't open it?'

'It's broken.' I unfastened the clasp and handed the whole thing over before she strangled me with it. 'Dad said it was a locket when he gave it to me but there's no visible hinge or anything. Maybe he was wrong, maybe it's just a pendant.'

'Nuh-uh, it's definitely a locket.' She shook her head, rolling it between her fingers. 'My mom has one just like this only hers is silver. It is tricky though, it doesn't open outwards like a book, the two sides kinda slide apart.'

She pressed the top and bottom at the same time and pushed each side in opposite directions.

'I swear I'm not going to break it but like, if I do?'

'I thought it already was broken,' I replied, folding my legs underneath me, jittery with excitement. 'Go for it.'

With a scrunched-up face, Lydia pinched the gold bauble and pressed harder. I held my breath, then I heard the quietest possible click and the two sides of the locket slid away from each other with ease.

'Ta-da!' She handed it back to me with look of victory. 'One open locket.'

'I don't believe it,' I uttered. 'Thank you, Lyds.'

I held it to the light to see better. Inside were two tiny photographs, one of them was of my mom but the other was of someone I'd never seen before.

'Em,' Lydia said my name as she snatched the locket back out of my hand, 'why would *your* mom have a photo of *my* mom inside her locket?'

'That's your mother?' I squinted at the minuscule photo of a happy brunette, laughing at the camera.

'Yes, ma'am. I knew they knew each other but I had no idea they were friendship-necklace besties.'

'Does your mom have a picture of my mom inside her locket?' I asked.

She shrugged, still bubbling over with the happy surprise. 'I can't say for sure, I haven't looked at it in years. I'll check when I get home.'

I clutched the locket in my hand, careful not to close it completely again, just in case it got stuck. My mom had a locket with photos of herself and Alex Powell inside. Interesting.

'That's one mystery solved,' Lydia said, sliding her sunglasses down as she lay back on her lounger. 'For my next trick, I predict you will figure out your dad's password, get a text from a non-comatose Wyn Evans and have the most incredible seventeenth birthday ever because I'm throwing you a party whether you like it or not.'

'I figured as much,' I said, happily defeated. No one other than my dad had ever thrown me a birthday party before. More importantly, no one had ever wanted to. 'But just a small party.'

'The smallest,' she agreed, pinching her thumb and forefinger together until they were almost touching. 'So tiny, you'll barely notice it.'

I looked over at my friend, a walking, talking ray of light.

'OK,' I said as she whooped with joy. 'And I hope you're right about the rest of it.'

'Bestie, I'm never wrong,' Lydia replied, already madly tapping away at her phone. 'Trust me.'

I lay back down on my sunbed, sliding the locket open and closed, open and closed. What other choice did I have?

Chapter Twenty-Six

'This place is a shit heap.'

As usual, Ashley let herself into my room without knocking, giving me just enough time to close my dad's laptop and cover it with a blanket. I really did not want to discuss anything of his with her. After Lydia left, I'd gone straight upstairs and doubled down on my efforts to figure out the password. Days had passed since I'd even looked at the laptop, too caught up in everything else, and I hoped fresh eyes might help.

'Can I help you with something?' I asked as Ashley surveyed the room. Shit heap was harsh but even I had to admit, it was kind of a mess.

'You might want to clean this place up before my mother sees it.' She picked up a long-sleeved shirt from a pile of clean laundry on the floor and folded it over her arm. 'Catherine will flip.'

'I'll add it to my to-do list,' I assured her in a voice that promised I'd do anything but. 'What's wrong, what do you want?'

'An aunt can't visit her only niece without having an agenda?'

I stared at her from the window seat.

'Yeah, even I'm not buying that,' she admitted, tossing the folded shirt back onto the pile of clothes. 'You've been too quiet. I came to make sure you didn't sneak out again because the last time that happened, I was in a world of trouble I don't care to revisit. But here you are.'

'So you can leave,' I pointed out, gesturing to the door.

'Could,' she confirmed without moving. 'Not gonna.'

'Fine.' I slid my laptop all the way under the blanket and gave her my full attention. 'What would you like to talk about?'

'You excited about your birthday?' she replied, her eyes flashing dangerously. 'The big Becoming?'

'How much do you know about that?' I asked. 'Catherine really hasn't told me any of the details.'

She picked up an empty soda can and dropped it in the trash bin under my desk.

'No idea.'

'None at all?' I pushed. 'You don't know anything about what happens at a Becoming ceremony?'

'If I say I don't know, I don't know,' Ashley snapped. 'Clearly I was not here when Catherine had hers and I didn't even get a sweet sixteen, let alone a big ol' ritual ceremony. Once again, I am forced to remind you, you can thank your asshole daddy for all of this.'

I picked up the blanket-wrapped laptop and held it close, the warmth of it radiating through the densely knitted fabric like a hug. Knowing why she was so mad at him didn't make it any easier to listen to her vitriol.

'Don't you have any good memories of him?' I asked as she flicked through my bag of hair clips and ties.

'Not really. I've told you, he was too busy with his buddies to worry much about me.'

'Was one of those buddies Alexandra Powell?' I clutched my locket as she sat down on the edge of my bed.

'You could say that,' she replied with a smirk. 'I never could understand how come they all stayed such good friends. Alex had been in love with Paul since they were little kids, but then your mom came around and all three of them were as thick as thieves. What's got you asking all these questions?'

'Just something Lydia said.' I tapped my fingers against the bundled-up computer. 'She wants to throw me a birthday party.'

'Must be nice.'

'I could throw you a party,' I offered. 'But I don't even know when your birthday is.'

'Born bright and early on the morning of ninth of November 1996,' my aunt replied. 'What else do you want to know, my blood type? My social security number?'

She didn't wait for a response before standing up and storming out, leaving the door wide open. A variation on a classic Ashley combo. At least she didn't slam it this time. Only when I was certain she wasn't coming back, I unwrapped my laptop and brought up the lock screen. It had to be worth a go, I'd tried everything else.

11091996. His little sister's date of birth.

The screen flashed blue and then all of my dad's files and folders appeared, neatly organized on the desktop. I stared at the array of icons in total shock. It worked. My dad, who had never once in my life mentioned his little sister, used her birthday as his computer password. Ashley was so convinced he never even thought about her but he had typed that specific date into his laptop every single day of his life.

'Nice work, Dad,' I muttered, scanning the confusing stack of icons. 'Super helpful filing system you've got here.'

There were dozens of folders filled with hundreds of files, all labelled with a numerical system that made no sense. Little blue icons lined up in neat columns and rows, and when I clicked on one at random, a window opened containing an endless scroll of documents, images, and spreadsheets. I opened the first document in the first folder. No better place to start than at the beginning.

It was a Word doc, full of rough notes about some historical event in France in the nineteenth century and no use to me whatsoever, but seeing his words, following his cadence, I could hear him reading aloud in my head. It was like he was right there with me.

I kept clicking through, searching for his journals. Dad had spent years digitizing them as part of his ongoing quest to get rid of unnecessary physical objects, and I knew they had to be on here somewhere. He had a theory that the more stuff you owned, the more stuff you could lose, and when you lost things you cared about, the more it hurt. It was only now I realized he wasn't really talking about journals.

Twenty minutes later, I was no closer to finding the journals. There were just so many files. He'd kept digital copies of everything; bills, receipts, invoices. I would never find them at this rate. Closing another Word doc, I swirled my finger around in circles on the touchpad when a spark of inspiration hit. I flicked the cursor over the View tab and reordered the folders by date created. Every single icon switched places, sliding across the screen like they were part of a card trick. I opened the most recent document.

When we moved to Wales, he told me we were going there to research people from local communities who moved to America in the eighteenth century but according to this, he wasn't telling me the whole truth. It was a list of historical events in England and Wales blamed on supernatural occurrences; floods, crop failures, solar and lunar eclipses, and an equally long corresponding list of people who had been blamed for them. Almost all women, almost all of them executed. But according to his notes, one woman managed to escape and smuggle herself across the country, ending up in a place called Gravesend where she met and married a man who took her with him to the New World. The next document was a scan of something so old it was almost illegible and if I hadn't already known what I was looking for, I wouldn't have been able to work it out at all. A passenger manifest. A list of names of everyone who travelled from Gravesend to Savannah on the good ship *Anne* in 1732.

Dad wasn't researching random families that emigrated to the US.

He was researching the first Emma Catherine Bell.

Chapter Twenty-Seven

'Emily? Are you awake?'

I wasn't.

My room was dark when I opened my eyes, the only light coming from the open bedroom door, Catherine carved out in silhouette.

'What's wrong?' I asked, rubbing the sleep from my eyes. 'Is it Ashley?'

'Nothing's wrong, honey.'

She pulled back my quilt and handed me a pile of clothes. 'We have somewhere we need to be.'

Ever since I cracked the password, I'd spent as much time as possible in my room, ploughing through Dad's research. It had been a long, frustrating forty-eight hours. For the first time in days, sleep got the better of me almost as soon as I'd eaten my supper on Thursday night and I was dozy and bleary-eyed when Catherine helped me to my feet.

'It feels late,' I said as the room came into focus.

'It is, which means we don't have much time. Quickly now, I'll meet you downstairs. Barnett is waiting.'

'Barnett . . . we're driving someplace?' I mumbled in a thick voice.

'Quickly,' she said again. 'We don't want to lose the moon.'

I did as I was told.

Twenty minutes later, Barnett was as expressionless as ever when Catherine ordered him to pull over and let us out of the car.

'Thank you, Barnett,' she said, when he did exactly what she asked without a word. Lifting the hem of her long but simple shift off the ground, she climbed out, barefoot. 'Please wait here until we return.'

My outfit was almost identical to Catherine's, long and loose, only my dress was sleeveless where hers had long, bell-shaped sleeves. Both were made from some scratchy ivory fabric that skimmed over my body. I wouldn't have said either were particularly her style. Even though it was still warm outside, I felt exposed. Something wasn't right.

'Emily, leave your shoes behind, you won't need them,' Catherine instructed. 'This will go better if you have full contact with the earth.'

'Go better?' I repeated, stressing the words in different places. 'What will go better?'

'I'll tell you once we're on our way,' she replied, looking up to the sky. 'We need to move now.'

'But I'd be faster in my sneakers.'

She replied without words and I immediately shucked off my shoes. Barnett stared straight ahead through the windscreen, his face completely impassive.

'Is Barnett OK?' I asked when I realized he wasn't even blinking.

'He's exceptionally well,' my grandmother said with a chuckle. 'His family is under, what shall we call it? An NDA.

257

Nothing harmful, a little herbal mix that helps him forget the more stressful parts of his job. I reckon he's the best-paid driver in the entire state of Georgia. There's nothing for you to worry about.'

'Does he know?'

She raised one eyebrow. 'He knows enough.'

The night was pitch black, no stars, and the moon had been reduced to its smallest sliver, curving in the sky like the stain left behind by a coffee cup.

'The Wilcuma ritual takes place under the new moon before a witch's Weorden,' Catherine explained as we set off down the road, away from the car. I moved cautiously, expecting to step on something sharp any second, but the ground was strangely spongy, even though we were walking on what looked like concrete. 'Weorden means "becoming", Wilcuma means "welcome guest". From tonight, your connection to our magic will grow with the waxing moon until your birthday, when the moon is full. Then you will be welcomed fully into the sisterhood.'

I followed her blindly through the trees, the fabric of my dress catching on their branches. 'You could've mentioned this before now,' I said. 'I might have taken a nap this afternoon.'

'None of us knows about the Wilcuma until the night of the ritual, it must be a surprise. It only feels like yesterday that I was in your shoes.' She looked down at my bare feet and smiled. 'So to speak.'

Finally we emerged from the woods at the side of a tiny cottage with a covered porch and two white wooden rocking chairs outside. The whole area in total darkness, the only thing I could make out aside from the cottage itself was an American flag, rippling in the night air.

258

'This is where we're performing a ritual?' I was almost disappointed. As far as locations went, it was kind of a let-down. If nothing else, I'd expected at least a dozen or so candles in a circle, maybe some kind of altar.

'Not here.' Catherine took my hand and pointed off to the left. 'Down there.'

Beyond the cottage I saw what looked like an endless driveway, lined with live oaks, all of them bending towards each other and their branches reaching out like skeletal fingers. Each and every bough was weighed down with Spanish moss and it hung like sepia-toned tinsel, but unlike the flag, not a single leaf on the tree or frond of moss moved. Everything was frozen, everything was silent. This was more than dramatic enough.

'Wormsloe State Historic Site,' Catherine said in a voice that implied something about the name was faintly ridiculous. 'It's been in the same family since it was founded by a group of British settlers. They also came over on the *Anne*. Our families have known each other for centuries.'

'So they won't mind us borrowing their back garden,' I said, staring up at the moss. The way it hung, frozen in mid-air, was unnerving. 'If they're old friends.'

Something like a snort only much more ladylike huffed out the back of Catherine's throat.

'I didn't say that. But don't worry, the trees won't tell them we're here.'

I held back as she started down the driveway, more uncomfortable than ever. There wasn't a single sound, not a crack of a twig or rustle of leaves, but I was so certain someone was watching us. Catherine marched on, her long red hair loose and streaming out behind her.

'What is a state historic site?' I asked, chasing after her when I realized she wasn't going to wait.

'Wormsloe was a plantation,' she replied, still striding onwards. 'Do you know what that means?'

'Dad made sure I knew my history,' I answered. 'Why do we have to do this here?'

She turned to face me, her pale skin almost fully translucent in the black night.

'Because magic is not good or bad, it's the truth. Our connection to the blessing is strongest in places with history, where lives have been lived, happy and sad. Aside from Bonaventure, Wormsloe is one of the strongest magical sites in all of Savannah.'

'It doesn't feel right.' I clutched my arms around myself even though it was anything but cold. 'Could we not do this at Bonaventure?'

It was something I never thought I'd ask. Please, Catherine, can we go to the cemetery instead of the plantation because that is somehow less creepy and inappropriate? This was all wrong, the stillness, the surprise, my bare feet and arms. I was too vulnerable, we both were.

'We are not ignorant of the terrible things that happened here but we also know that without Wormsloe, it's very possible Savannah might have failed as a city,' my grandmother said. 'The crops grown on these lands fed thousands of people and created trade, allowing the settling families to thrive, including ours. None of that would have been possible without the enslaved people brought here and forced to live and work on the plantation. We can't go back in time and change things but we can ensure no one is forgotten, that what happened here is acknowledged. That is part of our job.'

'As witches?'

'As human beings,' Catherine replied. 'Although I fear these days we are fighting an uphill battle.'

We stayed on the path and the sultry heat of the day faded away. I didn't notice how much the temperature had dropped until there were goosebumps on my arms. The night was now cold and quiet, and full of invisible eyes, watching.

'I've been reading some of my dad's research,' I said, filling the unnerving silence with the sound of my voice without giving away too much information. If she didn't ask how I had it, I wouldn't tell her. 'It's really interesting.'

'Is that right?' she replied as cool as the evening.

'I thought he was working on a book about early settlers in the US but it was more specific than that,' I said, nodding into the night. 'I found a passenger manifest for the *Anne*. He was researching the first Emma Catherine Bell.'

Catherine gave no response for a moment and when she did speak, I wasn't sure if she'd heard me.

'This avenue of oaks was planted in the 1890s,' she said. 'They feel ancient, don't they? You'd think they were so much older.'

Not exactly what I was expecting her to say.

'Sometimes things aren't exactly as they seem. Perhaps the same could be said about your father's research,' she added, stopping to place her hands on my shoulders. 'Emily, I know it must be difficult, wondering what other lies Paul might've told you, but please always remember how much he loved you.'

'I know he loved me,' I replied, suddenly stung. 'Why would you say that? What else do you think he lied about?'

'I think there might be a lot of things he didn't tell you. But he did love you. Always hold on to that.'

And she resumed her steady march into the darkness.

*

261

The avenue of oaks went on forever and I was lost, not only in this strange place but in my own thoughts. I wanted Catherine to be wrong but I was very afraid she might be right. My own half-truths pressed down on my soul, guilt scraping at my edges. I was planning to tell Catherine about Wyn eventually. Would my dad have shared the truth with me one day? The question churned around inside me, my answers changing as quick as the breeze.

My grandmother, on the other hand, had never looked more at ease, slinking over the uneven ground like a lioness on the hunt and where my white sack dress was big and baggy, hers draped over the sharp angles of her body. Ritual attire but make it fashion. When we finally came to the end of the oaks, she directed me straight ahead, away from a squat, square building on our left and a clearing that looked very much like an empty parking lot on the right.

'You made us walk all this way when there's a parking lot right there?' I grumbled as we left it behind.

'The walk through the oaks was part of the ritual.' Catherine took my hand and pulled me off the path and into the woods. 'If our sisters deemed you unworthy, we wouldn't have made it this far.'

I didn't bother to ask what would have happened in that scenario. I didn't want to know.

The woods grew denser with every step we took, trees growing closer together, knitting their branches into a tangled mess, naturally designed to keep people out. But witches, it seemed, were welcome. Every time we faced an impasse, the snarl pulled apart to let us through. Magic pricked the tips of my fingers and the ebb and flow of warm energy washed over me as we moved closer to our destination. Whatever was going to happen tonight had already begun. There was no backing out now.

'This is the place,' Catherine said, her voice firm and strong. No point in lowering it out here. There wasn't as much as a squirrel to disturb. It was just us. The woods, the earth and the sky. But what a sky. I tilted my head back and gasped. When we climbed out of the car, there hadn't been a single visible star. Now the black night was studded with sparkling diamonds, just like the third-floor ceiling of Bell House. Directly above us, the new moon shone bright, a pure slice of light, a promise of what was to come.

'A new moon represents new beginnings,' my grandmother intoned, circling me slowly with unknown intent. 'A new moon allows us to set our intentions. A new moon welcomes you, Emma Catherine Bell. Wilcuma.'

It took a moment to realize she was talking to me, I was too busy staring at the trees. Their boughs groaned with the strain of transformation as they wove themselves into a sacred circle, building a wall around me and my grandmother until all that was visible to us was the night sky.

'All of those who came before and all of those to come,' Catherine recited. 'We ask you to acknowledge us.'

'I feel like I'm in a play and I don't know my lines,' I whispered when she came towards me to take hold of my wrist. She sank to her knees and I did the same. 'What am I supposed to do?'

'Just listen,' she replied, pulling a long, pointed dagger from her sleeve and placing it on the ground between us. 'Just be.'

But it was hard to listen when you were afraid and I was petrified. Why did we need a knife? Why had she hidden it from me until now? The stars burned brighter and the sensation in my hands intensified, building and spreading through my body until I was afraid I would come apart at the seams.

'Catherine, I'm scared,' I said, gagging on my own voice as

263

the warm waves turned into burning walls of fire that crashed into me. 'What's happening?'

She didn't reply this time. Her eyes turned black as I cried out, the pain turning into agony, growing more unbearable with every second. Collapsing to the ground, my limbs spasmed in the dirt until I was thrashing around wildly, clawing at my grandmother and pleading silently for her help. Instead, she held me in place and, with her eyes boring into mine, she plunged my hand into the dirt.

'Earth,' she said, my fingers sliding into the soil like a hot knife through butter.

'Water.'

Rain poured out of the cloudless sky, hard and heavy, soaking my dress and turning the ground to mud.

'Fire.'

The flames appeared out of nowhere. Scorching hot, they singed my eyebrows and eyelashes and burned the back of my throat. I writhed around in the mud, desperate to break Catherine's wristlock but she was too powerful, too strong.

'Air.'

This time, when she spoke, the flames disappeared and the rain stopped. I tried to take a breath to steady myself but it was impossible. The fire burned out because there was no oxygen to feed it. Our sacred circle had become a vacuum. Panicking, my lungs seized up, shrivelling in my chest. I fought against Catherine's grip, but it was pointless, she held me down as easily as if I were a rag doll. Without taking her obsidian eyes off me, she reached for the dagger and held it aloft.

'Blood.'

'Catherine, no!'

I screamed as she plunged it downwards, waiting for the stabbing pain. But pain didn't come. Instead, something hot gushed over the back of my hand, merging with the mud. Her grip on my wrist loosened and I looked up to see the point of the dagger sticking out of the back of my grandmother's hand, hilt pushed all the way up to her palm. Catherine slumped over, before falling face first into the dirt. I scrambled forward to turn her over and held her lifeless body to mine, too broken to do anything other than sob. It was only then that I saw the other woman inside the sacred circle with us.

Tall and pale with long white hair.

'*Breathe,*' she said.

'I can't,' I choked. 'There's no air.'

She pressed her hands against my chest and my lungs filled with something pure and bright, something electric. In that moment, a doorway opened, allowing me a glimpse at the lives of a hundred women who had lived before me. I saw them all at the same time, watched their whole lives in one heartbeat, and felt all of their knowledge and strength in me. Then I exhaled, the door closed and it was gone.

'*The blessing welcomes you,*' the woman whispered before turning to walk out through the trees.

Catherine spluttered loudly, a deep, gurgling sound, then jerked backwards to cough up mouthfuls of dark earth. She looked up at me, her green eyes her own again but violently bloodshot, rubies and emeralds staring out of a porcelain face streaked with dirt and tears.

And then she smiled.

'Do you feel it?' she asked, wrenching the dagger out of her hand in one decisive move, barely wincing as she flexed her fingers. I watched in horror as the wound began to close of its own accord. 'Do you feel the blessing?'

'I feel a lot of things.' My hand was still covered in her blood and my white dress stained red and black. The sound of the fire and the rain and the memory of all those lives echoed so loudly inside my head, I could hardly hear myself think.

'I feel it. We draw strength from each other, and Emily, you have so much strength to give. Enough to wake our sleeping sisters.'

She wiped the dagger on her thigh and snatched in a shallow breath as it slipped from her fingers, falling to the ground almost in slow motion. We both reached for it at the same time, our fingers crashing together as the blade sank into the earth and the world flashed a blinding white before it was all cast in black.

'Catherine?' I yelled, desperately groping around for something, anything to ground me. The darkness was all-consuming, every speck of light and life extinguished, deep and heavy and suffocating.

Then the vision came into view. White-hot, pitch-black flames, tearing through a city so fast, the people they consumed didn't even have time to scream. Buildings were incinerated, cars and trucks disintegrated on contact and the sky burned an ugly, unnatural green. Only the trees still stood, the black fire travelling along their branches, swinging from tree to tree. It was the moss. The Spanish moss and the black flames were one and the same, delivering devastation to Savannah and razing it to the ground. As the flames passed through, I saw waves as tall as skyscrapers, washing away the carnage as though the city had never even existed. I saw it all. Felt it, smelled it, tasted it. And at the very centre of the apocalyptic horror, two bodies stood in front of a stone archway under a blinding full moon, preparing to do battle in the ashes of what was once Savannah. One crouched down low, ready to attack, the other stood back, unmoved by the threat and surrounded by a halo of black fire. The physical manifestation of all this death. As I moved closer, the figures became clearer.

The Bell Witches

A woman and a wolf.
The wolf we thought we'd killed in Bonaventure.
And the woman wielding this terrible weapon, was me.

Chapter Twenty-Eight

When I came to, the trees had pulled back, the water had dried up, and everything was as it was. Catherine sat by my side, watching over me as the world flickered back into view.

'What just happened?' I murmured as she helped me to my feet.

'I don't know but it was not part of the Wilcuma.' She lifted my chin to check for injuries. 'Calling on the elements, asking our ancestors to acknowledge you, that was all part of the ritual. But afterwards . . .'

'You saw it too,' I said. 'You saw the same thing I did.'
She nodded.

'After the blood offering, we should've been released.' Catherine pulled me close to her, and I heard her heart thud. 'But instead the ancestors gifted us with a vision.'

She stepped out of the hug to gaze at me with starry eyes. She was covered in the same blood and dirt as me, but while I felt like despair personified, Catherine radiated joy.

'The vision confirmed the prophecy,' she said. 'You are the witch we've been waiting for.'

'OK, we did not see the same thing,' I replied, bending

down to scoop up the shining silver dagger from the ground. 'What I saw was terrifying. If that's what's going to happen after my Becoming, I don't know if this life is something I want.'

She held her hand out for the dagger and I paused, testing the weight of it in my hand before I passed it over. 'How do you feel now?'

'Stronger,' I admitted, exploring the changes in myself. 'Closer to the magic.'

I held out my hand and a flame sparked into life in my palm. Catherine let out a happy laugh. Just a glimpse through that open door had given me so much strength. What would happen when I stepped through it? I closed my hand and the fire disappeared. It wasn't extinguished, only gone from view. The fire was inside me.

'I saw you saving the city,' Catherine said. 'You were holding back the flames.'

'No,' I disagreed, the heat moving through my veins. 'I *was* the flames.'

She tilted her head to one side, considering my version, then picked up the hem of her dress as she walked away.

'You're wrong,' she called. 'You'll see.'

And this time, I very much hoped she was right.

When I climbed out of my bedroom window the next morning at dawn, I didn't know where I was going but the city did.

Barnett had delivered us home only a couple of hours earlier, bloody and broken, although Catherine's hand was completely healed by the time we crossed the threshold of Bell House. Neither of us said very much but when she hugged me at the top of the staircase, I knew we weren't carrying the same fear in our hearts. We might have seen the same vision but the two of us had interpreted it very differently. For what seemed like an eternity, I stood under a scalding hot shower until the water ran cold, my skin red raw and sore to the touch, but it was nothing compared to the heat of the flames I had wrought in my vision. Those all-consuming, white-hot, black flames.

Sleep was never going to come and as soon as the first rays of light were in the sky, I was out in the streets, the soft comfort of Savannah all around me. This early in the day, there was no one to share it with but the songbirds.

My dad and I had lived in a lot of wonderful places; towns and villages with centuries of stories and generations of families who welcomed us with open arms. I'd been happy in all of them, but Savannah was different. Without even realizing, I'd fallen in love with the city. Slowly at first then all at once. That's what they said, wasn't it? I loved the townhouses and mansions and every single staircase that ran up from the street to meet a red front door. I loved all remaining twenty-two squares, the oaks, the palmettos, beeches, maples, and the magnolias. I loved the dappled light that danced up Jones Street, the steep death-trap steps that led down to River Street and even the tourist-laden trolleys both Catherine Bell and Lydia Powell had declared the bane of their existence, possibly the only thing they agreed on in this world. I loved the fresh biscuits, the fried chicken, the pralines, the sausage gravy and, so help me, I was even starting to love the sweet tea. I didn't want to lose this place. I couldn't be the cause of its destruction.

As the beautiful morning flourished around me, I turned, walking south until I came to Forsyth Park. I hadn't been near it since the day of the storm but I easily found my way back to the tree with the heart, following the same path I'd taken with Lydia and Jackson. The fallen limb had been removed but no one could take away the scar it left behind. Huge strips of bark had been torn away and the exposed wood shifted from pale beige to golden brown as nature healed itself. I looped slowly around the tree, searching for the carving. It was higher up than I remembered, a fist-sized heart pierced by an arrow with a feathered flight and inside, just the insinuation of two initials. If you didn't know what they were, you wouldn't be able to read them. But I knew. P+A. Paul and Angelica.

'Emily?'

My heart all but leapt out of my mouth when I turned and saw Jackson waving at me from the footpath. He jogged on the spot, shirtless and covered in sweat. His body glistened. I'd never seen so many muscles on one human being outside of a superhero movie.

'Hi! Jackson! Hello!'

I threw both arms straight up in the air at the same time before remembering that wasn't a normal greeting in any culture. No matter what else might be happening in the world, Jackson Powell was still forget-how-to-be-a-human handsome.

'Come to check on our arch nemesis?'

'You know what they say,' I replied with a very serious glance back at the tree. 'Know your enemy. How's your leg?'

He looked down and rotated his ankle a few times, his calf muscles popping as he flexed.

'Stronger than ever. I thought it was broken but it can't have been that bad if a few herbs could cure it.'

'Herbs?' I repeated, the word cracking in my throat.

'Your grandmother gave me this crazy salve she said would help with the swelling,' he explained. 'Burned hotter than blue blazes when I put it on, but the next day my leg was as good as new. She should sell that stuff, it's magic.'

'Yeah.' I held onto the tree with both hands. 'It is.'

'How come you're out so early?' He took a second look at my outfit. 'In your . . . pyjamas?'

I glanced down at my matching cotton shorts and shirt, pale

blue with navy piping and my updated initials, ECJB, mono-grammed on the front pocket.

'Couldn't sleep.' I was aiming for breezy but came up some-where closer to hysterical. 'Trying to clear my head. In my pyjamas.'

'In your *cute* pyjamas,' Jackson corrected and I smiled. He really couldn't help himself.

'Lydia told me she's planning your birthday party,' he added, leaving the footpath to join me underneath the tree. A balled-up white tank hung from the back of his shorts, bouncing over his butt as he walked. 'According to my sister, it's going to be the hottest party Savannah has ever seen. I hope you know what you're letting yourself in for.'

'She swore she would keep it small,' I said with a groan. 'She lied, didn't she?'

'Maybe just a little.' He raised one arm and knocked on the trunk of the tree before leaning against it oh-so casually. 'She also kind of mentioned you were seeing some guy but he left town or something?'

Thank you, Lydia, I thought, straining to keep the polite smile on my face.

'Right,' I said through gritted teeth.

'Right,' he echoed. 'I wanted to offer my services as your date for the party.'

'You're joking?'

I didn't mean to sound quite so horrified by his proposal.

He pulled the tank out from his waistband and yanked it over his head. 'Should I take that as a thanks but no thanks?'

'You should take it as a thank you so much, I'm so incred-ibly flattered you would even ask,' I said right away, cringing at my lack of tact. 'What I meant was "I think you're amazing but I'm not ready to go on any dates with anyone just yet but I really would like you to be at the party". Is that better?'

'Guess I should have made my move sooner,' he replied with a self-deprecating grin. 'You know I wanted to ask you out right away but Lyds said I wasn't allowed. Being a gentleman gets you nowhere.'

'Agree to disagree. I think it gets you exactly where you ought to be,' I told him. 'When the time is right.'

'Then maybe we could rain check on that date?'

He looked so hopeful, so genuine, I didn't have it in me to say no. Hopeful and genuine with perfectly symmetrical features and eyelashes so long and lush I could have used them to sweep the streets.

'Maybe,' I replied, laughing when he jumped up to high five the tree in celebration.

'I'm going to quit while I'm ahead.' Jackson touched his fingers to his forehead in a salute then jogged back onto the path. 'Gotta finish my run before the heat starts to kick. See you soon, Em.'

I waved as he went, lingering under the tree to wonder what might have been. What if I'd stayed in the Powell house that first morning? What if he asked me out right away? How would things be different if I'd lost an afternoon making out with Jackson until my lips were raw instead of Wyn? Jackson was stupidly hot and improbably nice for someone so ripped. A month ago, I would have fallen over on the spot at the very thought of going on a date with him. But now there was just one very sticky, immovable obstacle in the way of us being together.

He wasn't Wyn.

Ten minutes of speed walking later, I found myself outside Wyn's apartment. It was empty, the shutters closed on the old carriage house and not a trace of his energy inside. But would I be able to feel him somewhere else? Quickly making sure no one was watching, I crossed the street and touched the door handle. With my eyes closed, I thought back to the last time I'd been here with him, that long afternoon spent in his bed, and searched. I cast my net wider, out through the city, all the way to the far boundaries of Forsyth Park and beyond, up to the Savannah River, over Tybee Island. Before the Wilcuma, it might have stopped there but today things were different. I focused harder, imagining a map of the United States, picturing Asheville and the little mountain town outside of it that he'd described in such loving detail.

I found him.

He was alive.

I couldn't explain, not even to myself, but I knew in my bones he was still here. He was far away, somewhere he couldn't reach me, but still alive and for now at least, knowing that was enough. Maybe it would be better if he kept his distance, I thought, dragging myself away from his apartment as the memories of my vision returned unbidden. Even if I felt like I was missing a limb or a vital organ, he would be safe.

Chapter Twenty-Nine

Catherine rushed me the moment I walked through the door, cupping my face so tightly, I was sure she would leave fingerprints on my cheekbones. She was still in her silk robe, hair down, no makeup on. I'd never seen her this way before and it didn't make me feel any better about anything.

'I came to bring you some tea but you were gone,' she said once she was satisfied I was still in one piece. 'Where were you?'

'Not burning the city to the ground if that's what you're worried about,' I replied. I carefully prised her hands away from my face and tried not to stiffen when she drew me into her arms instead.

'That wasn't my concern at all.' She brushed back my hair as she let me go. 'I only wanted to know where you'd run off to without getting a good breakfast.'

Holding my hand tightly, she led me out of the foyer and into the dining room, just in case I made another run for it.

'I couldn't sleep so I went for a walk.'

'In your pyjamas?'

'In my pyjamas,' I confirmed as though it were a perfectly normal thing to do. 'It's cooler out today.'

'Yes, we are due for a break in all that heat,' she replied, nonchalant and discussing the weather like we hadn't both seen me at the beginning of the end of the world only a few hours earlier. 'Ashley's been in the kitchen for hours cooking up a feast. What'll it be? Biscuits and gravy, grits, pancakes, eggs? Your aunt makes the most wonderful French toast. She coats the brioche in dark cocoa powder before she cooks it, cuts through the sweetness of the custard. It really is perfection.'

Through the open kitchen door, I saw a glowering Ashley, wielding her spatula like a hunting knife.

'No need to go to any trouble,' I gulped. 'I'm really not hungry.'

Catherine sat and waited for me to do the same and I pulled out the wooden chair carefully, trying not to scrape the floorboards. The dining table and its six matching chairs were impossibly heavy and, according to my grandmother, some of the oldest things in the house. I was almost as afraid of doing damage to them as I was of accidentally causing the apocalypse. Right now, only one of those things was likely to get me grounded.

'Honey, I really hope you aren't overthinking what happened last night,' she said, spreading a thick layer of honey butter on a freshly baked biscuit. 'Your Wilcuma was a resounding success. And please close your mouth, we have all this marvellous food, you don't need to catch flies for breakfast.'

'I really hope you're not underthinking it.' I helped myself to a big mug full of black coffee, astounded by her casual attitude. 'You saw the same thing I did. Fire, brimstone, end of the world.'

'What I saw was my granddaughter defending our city against an enemy.' She took a bite of her biscuit and rolled her eyes in ecstasy. 'You really shouldn't drink coffee on an empty stomach. In fact, you really shouldn't drink coffee at all, you're too young. It'll stunt your growth.'

'Buying jeans is difficult enough as it is. I don't need to be any taller.'

Still, I plucked a biscuit from the platter at the centre of the table and stared at it. The taste of ashes was still in my mouth, the heat from the flames still on my skin. How my grandmother could happily dig in to her breakfast was beyond me.

'You're looking at this all wrong,' she said, waving her butter knife around in the air. Much shorter and considerably less sharp than the one she'd been tossing around the night before. 'The vision confirmed everything we thought we knew. You are the witch who will bring the blessing back to life. You are going to reawaken your sisters. Tell me how that isn't cause for celebration.'

The bitter black coffee scalded the back of my throat as it went down.

'Because that's not what I saw.' The biscuit disintegrated in my clenched fist. 'I wasn't saving the city, I was destroying it. You said terrible things could happen if I didn't learn to control my magic. I've already killed a werewolf without meaning to, I've caused storms and earthquakes. I'm a walking natural disaster. How can you be so sure you're right?'

She looked back at me, blazing with fervent belief.

'Because I believe it. Because I have always known. The prophecy says—'

'The prophecy says the chosen witch will either end the world or save it,' I cut in. 'The prophecy that is so important no one ever thought to write it down?'

'Some things are too important to put in writing,' Catherine replied. 'Once words are written, they can be read.'

'Yes, that's literally the point of writing!' I exclaimed. 'It saves a whole bunch of confusion, you should try it.'

'Words can be read by the wrong people, interpreted in the wrong way,' she returned. 'Knowledge is power, Emily, and we never willingly give anyone power over us, so writing about the prophecy is forbidden. You're giving in to your doubts again. If you'd been here, if I'd raised you—'

'Please don't say it again,' I begged, suddenly exhausted. 'I already know.'

She exhaled through her nose and took a bite of her biscuit, chewing slowly, thoughtfully, making me wait until she had swallowed before speaking.

'The world is changing too quickly and I can't cope on my own anymore. Taking care of this city was never meant to be a one-woman job. My only desire in this life is for you to embrace your legacy and become the woman I have been waiting to meet ever since the day your daddy told me you were on the way.'

There was no point arguing with her. My birthday, my Becoming, was in two weeks. Either Catherine was correct and I was about to turn into some kind of super witch or my interpretation of the vision would be confirmed and nothing much would matter anymore. Fighting with the only other witch I knew was not going to help me any. I picked the biscuit crumbs from off the table and reassembled them on my plate.

'What should I do?' I asked, relenting. 'I'm a quick learner but I do better with a book.'

'You need to work on your control,' she replied, pleased with my response. 'A witch as strong as you must be able to open and close the door to her magic, not let anything and everything wander through at will.'

I dumped a teaspoon of sugar in my coffee and stirred. 'So you're saying right now I'm an emotional cat flap.'

'Not quite,' she replied, a smile playing on her lips in spite of herself. 'Books won't help you connect to your natural abilities. Your magic is inside you already, everything you need is inside you already. What you must find is a way to tap into that strength.'

'I'll try,' I promised, focusing on a speck of hope visible on the horizon. 'If you think I can do it.'

'I don't think, I know,' she replied smoothly. 'You are, after all, a Bell.'

Catherine might believe there was nothing useful in the books but I'd been raised to check my sources. While she was upstairs getting dressed, and Ashley was busy outside, I snuck into the library and locked myself in. It was the calmest spot in Bell House, a sanctuary, and the only room with wood-panelled walls rather than spelled wallpaper, meaning I didn't have to watch for a growing vine or flitting bird to flicker into life out the corner of my eye. In here, I felt more like a welcome presence and less like I was being watched.

I set Dad's computer down next to the creaky old desktop, the sleek matte silver casing making its beige plastic shell look even more outdated. The internet was still a no-go but at least I could compare any findings with his seemingly endless notes on the original Emma Catherine Bell. She was real, Dad was able to prove that easily enough. There was plenty of hard evidence to confirm her existence, it was only three hundred years since she was born, practically yesterday in historical terms, but there was no perfectly preserved pamphlet titled 'So You've Found Out You're A Witch' or 'Prophecies 101: Literally Never a Good Thing'. Just mountains and mountains of dry, dull research.

The library was about as well organized as my dad's files. Hardbacks sat next to paperbacks, bound manuscripts were

279

wedged in between three-ring binders full of random pieces of paper, half of them illegible and the other half too faded with age to be helpful. But it was the Bell family journals, tucked away in the back of the library, that I was most interested in. Dad taught me first-person accounts were often the most useful source, always biased but untarnished by hindsight. If Catherine's alleged prophecy was passed all the way down from our original ancestor, someone *must* have mentioned it in their diary at some point over the centuries.

After collecting as many as I could find, I lined up all the journals on my desk. Some of them were ancient-looking, thick pages sewn together by something I suspected was not vegan. Others were more modern notebooks, the kind of thing you expected to start with 'Dear diary, guess who I have a crush on?' rather than 'Dear diary, today I started Armageddon but I swear it was an accident'.

I pored over the pages, filling in some missing names and dates on my father's genealogy chart as I went and jotting down notes I thought might be useful in future; recipes for life-saving herbal concoctions, rituals to enhance abilities, spells to communicate with other witches over long distances, but there was no mention of black fire travelling along Spanish moss, no mention of one hundred foot tidal waves, and absolutely no mention of the prophecy.

Also, the journals didn't cover our family's entire history. There were conspicuous gaps, whole decades missing sometimes. Some of my ancestors only wrote a few notes while others left dozens of completed journals, as though they'd committed their entire life to paper.

Every time I came across a relatable moment, I found myself smiling. I hadn't expected it, but all these women, existing sometimes centuries apart, all wrote about the same things.

Teenage problems had been the same since the beginning of time – unrequited love, overbearing parents, a lack of freedom, and page after page of uncertainty and doubt about their place in the world. At the same time, they were living through so much hardship; recessions, depressions, war after war after war and all the pain that followed, but nevertheless, they did what they could to aid the people of Savannah.

They were all the same but different, their magics manifesting based on what was needed at the time. Healers were most common along with conduits, who could commune with the dead, and elementals like Catherine, who could manifest the elements at will. Bell women had acted as spies, healed whole communities when plague struck, they influenced powerful historical figures, and above all else they held one duty sacred above all others: Bell witches saved women when no one else cared if they lived or died.

And while there was no mention of black flames, there was plenty of talk of fire. The great fires of 1796 and 1820. The more I read, the more one thing became worryingly clear. No matter what we Bell witches did, Savannah seemed destined to burn.

Hours passed like minutes, the steady, comforting energy of the library pushing me on, lending me the strength to read one more chapter, look at one more journal. Almost the whole day passed by while I was lost in my research but I felt as though I'd only just sat down at the desk, fully sustained and content, absorbed in the lives of my ancestors. Until I came to the one book I'd been avoiding. It was easily the oldest book here, the cover made from slick animal skin that didn't feel quite like any kind of leather I'd encountered before, and any writing on the cover had long since faded away. Inside, the pages were so fragile and thin, they were almost see-through.

It fell open on a random page somewhere near the middle of the book, the title of the chapter written in ancient, elaborate script.

'A ritual for binding a Bell witch,' I read aloud.

All around me, the library shuddered.

Chapter Thirty

'Where's Catherine?'

Ashley looked up from her Saturday morning coffee and shrugged.

'Good morning to you too. Sleep well? No, me neither.'

'Where is she?' I asked again, the strange book tucked away in my backpack and throbbing against my spine. I didn't have the patience for her hot and cold attitude today. When I left the library the night before, I couldn't find my grandmother anywhere. I waited for hours, desperate to talk to her about the book I'd found, finally falling asleep on the sofa in the parlour, and when I woke up with the sunrise, she'd been back and was gone again.

'I need to find her,' I pressed. 'It's important. Why is she always gone anyway? There can't be that many meetings of the Savannah Historical Society.'

'I don't know where she went to or why she's there,' my aunt snipped. 'You think everything is important but it's not. Nothing is. You're just a cog in a wheel, honey, a part they need to keep the engine running, that's all. Get over yourself.'

'Maybe you need to work on a new tea blend, something

to sort out your mood,' I suggested, grabbing a freshly baked muffin from the counter. 'I know Catherine told you about our vision, you must see how serious it is.'

'How would you know what's serious?' She laughed, sharp and wicked. 'You're sixteen, you don't know shit.'

'Is that how you felt when you were sixteen?'

A flash of something bitter passed over Ashley's face but she composed herself and gave me a small smile instead.

'Must be a head fuck,' she said sweetly. 'All this prophecy stuff. It's Catherine's whole personality, being the grandmother of *the* witch. She's literally built her life around it. Personally, I'm more into your version, the one where you flip out and kill us all? But that's classic me, always the optimist.'

I stared at her from across the room as she chuckled to herself.

'Why do I even try talking to you?' I asked, speaking more to myself than her.

'Because you don't have any friends and no one likes you?'

Without meaning to, she gave me an idea.

'Thanks for breakfast,' I said, reaching for a second muffin and wrapping it in a napkin. 'If Catherine gets back before I do, please tell her I need to talk to her before she leaves again.'

'Will do, great chat, have a nice day,' Ashley called as I tossed the baked goods into my bag and sprinted out the front door.

The sun seared the skin on the back of my neck as I pulled up my hair into a topknot, bouncing from foot to foot on the Powells' front porch. I was about to ring the bell a third time when the door opened and a smart older woman I hadn't met yet appeared. It had to be Virginia, Lydia's grandmother. The whole time I'd been in Savannah she'd been ill with some minor malady or other, too fragile for introductions, but according to Lydia, that was standard practice. Even a splinter would see Virginia Powell take to her bed for a week.

But that didn't explain why she stared at me as though she'd seen a ghost.

'Catherine?' she breathed, clutching at the triple string of pearls fastened around her throat.

'No, Mrs Powell,' I said, glancing behind me to make sure my own grandmother hadn't followed me here. 'It's Emily, Catherine's granddaughter. Paul's daughter. I'm so pleased to meet you at last.'

Still more than a little alarmed, she recovered herself and pasted on a smile.

'No one could argue the fact you're a Bell,' she replied as she fully opened the door. 'Aren't you just as pretty as a peach? The spitting image of your grandmother when she was a girl.'

'Thank you, that's so kind of you to say. Is Lydia home?'

'I simply cannot get over how much you look like Catherine,' Virginia went on, stretching out one hand to poke my cheek and make sure I was real. 'Even your hair . . . hers was the same when she was your age, not quite all the way red.'

'Lydia's home!'

My friend thundered downstairs, ricocheting off the turn in the staircase right before leaping down the last four steps. She yanked a silk sleeping bonnet off her head and dumped it on the bench at the side of the door as her grandmother snatched her hand away from me and staggered back into the foyer.

'Em, it's criminally early to come calling,' Lydia declared, adjusting the straps of her ribbed lavender crop top and matching boy shorts. 'What's up?'

'I need to contact a friend and I need your help.'

She clapped one hand on the newel post and set one foot back on the stairs. 'You need to use my computer? No problem, let's go.'

'Not the computer,' I replied quickly with a meaningful look. This wasn't something I could explain in front of her grandmother. 'I have to go somewhere specific to send the message and I thought you might want to come with? It will be easier if there's two of us.'

'I have no idea what you're talking about,' she replied happily. 'But let me throw on some clothes, I'll be right back down.'

She raced away, leaving me alone again with her deeply distressed grandmother. Not knowing how else to break the awkward silence, I pulled a smushed up napkin from out of my bag.

'Muffin?' I offered.

'Goodness me,' Virginia mumbled, taking another step back. I double-checked the sweet treat in my hand to make sure I hadn't just offered her a baby rattlesnake by accident.

'OK, I'll take that, thank you very much,' Lydia declared as she bounced back down the stairs, still in her crop top, hair pushed back by a pink silk scarf and a pair of torn-up jeans pulled over her shorts. 'Let's go, 'bye, Grandmother, I'll be back later.'

She grabbed me by the arm, almost pulling it out the socket as she dragged me from the house.

'Is your grandmother OK?' I asked when we stopped to cross the road into Madison Square.

'The answer to that question is never yes, but that was a little more weird than usual.'

'I'm sorry,' I said, offering her the least-squished muffin. 'I didn't mean to upset her. She seemed so freaked out when she saw me.'

Lydia's sigh of response was frustrated, bordering on annoyed. 'It's not just you. My literal existence seems to scandalize her these days. How are things between you and Catherine?'

'Fine?' I said without any certainty. 'She's so happy to have me here, but sometimes I think I'm letting her down, like she expects me to be someone I'm not when I'm not even sure I know who I am, so how am I supposed to be the person she wants me to be?'

'Welcome to the world of socialite southern grandmothers,' she replied. 'We'll never be exactly who they want us to be because we'll never be them. They want clones, not granddaughters. One day, they're going to wake up and realize it's the twenty-first century and it's going to be the shock of a lifetime.'

'Does Virginia treat Jackson the same way?' I asked.

'What do you think?'

I offered her a supportive smile. 'Catherine already played the "it's different for boys" card with me.'

'Then you understand,' she said. 'Jackson is the golden child. He can do whatever he wants, go wherever he wants, see whoever he likes. He's always been the more acceptable twin, tall, handsome, charming, loves sports, does well in school. The perfect little man. Then Virginia says all the same things about me like they're bad things. I can't win. He's the good one, I'm the weird one.'

'Weird is good,' I stated as she inhaled half of Ashley's muffin in one bite. 'Brilliant in fact, because I'm about to ask you to do something extremely weird.'

'OK, but only on the condition we stop for coffee first because these muffins are delicious but they are dry,' she replied. 'And there's no such thing as too weird where I'm concerned.'

'Let's get you that coffee,' I suggested, steering her along Bull Street. 'Then you can decide for yourself.'

*

'You want to do *what* now?'

Lydia hung back by the gates to the Colonial Park cemetery, eyes almost as wide as her grandmother's had been half an hour earlier.

'It's nothing really,' I lied, shaking the ice in my triple mocha Frappuccino. 'Just this cool thing I saw online.'

And not at all a ritual to invoke a spirit that I found in my dead great-great-great-great-grandmother's journal in the spooky library of my grandmother's magic house.

'I won't lie, it's giving Satan.' She loudly sucked up her white chocolate macadamia cream cold brew through a green straw. 'I wouldn't have pegged you as a witchcraft girlie, you haven't shown any of the usual signs.'

'There are signs?'

'You know, chipped black nail polish, heavy eyeliner, one of those piercings that leaves a giant gross hole in your ear.' She screwed up her face at the thought. 'What exactly are we trying to do? Run it by me again.'

'I want to contact the spirit of one of my ancestors,' I said with a forced smile. 'I thought it might be . . . fun?'

Lydia didn't look so sure. 'So this is like a Ouija board thing? We're just asking questions?'

'That's right,' I agreed. 'We're just asking questions.'

And I had a lot of them. But I also had a plan. The book I found in the library didn't have any useful information about the prophecy or how I could learn to control my magic but it did have an entire chapter on how I could bind it. The details were vague, a recurring bad Bell habit, but according to the author, our abilities could be tied up and the blessing bound within its host. It didn't say how, it didn't say what would happen afterwards, but it was something. A possible solution to my very real problem.

The ritual to invoke a spirit, on the other hand, looked pretty straightforward. Despite Catherine's warnings about connecting to the other side, I knew who I wanted to speak to, and I had something of hers as well as everything else noted in the journal. It had to be worth a try. If I could connect to the Emma Catherine who wrote the journal, I might have a better shot at managing my magic and saving Savannah.

'I would like to go on record as saying this feels not great,' Lydia declared, but she still willingly followed me through the gates.

'I never used to like cemeteries,' I agreed, walking directly towards the moss-less magnolia tree. 'They always made me think of horror movies and I hate horror movies.'

Lydia clucked her tongue as I knelt on the ground then flopped down at my side.

'But you still think it would be cute to summon the dead.'

'No one said anything about it being cute,' I replied before laying out the items I'd swiped from the pantry the night before: salt, bay laurel leaves, an apple, and three small pieces of cedar. Nothing especially weird, nothing that might put Lydia off her cold brew.

Almost all the rituals in the Emma Catherine journals called for a second witch but I couldn't wait around for my grandmother to come home. I shook the salt out into a circle while Lydia slurped her coffee, saying nothing. Catherine said the Powells had had magic in their blood once. Maybe there was still enough there for this to work.

'This looks super professional,' she said as I crossed my legs and pulled out a box of matches. 'And that ain't a compliment. You sure you haven't done this before?'

'Definitely haven't,' I replied, striking a match. 'I don't know if this makes it better or worse but I really have no idea what I'm doing.'

I lit the three pieces of cedar and the wood burned, white smoke drifting up into the branches of the tree, then took a bite of the apple and spat it out. Lydia made a quiet retching sound.

'Gross,' she whispered loudly.

Next came the bay laurel leaf. I tore it in half and added it to my tiny bonfire.

'Shouldn't we be doing this at night?' Lydia asked through a very loud yawn, stretching both her arms over her head until the bottom of her crop top started to roll up her ribs. 'Communing with the dead feels more like a stroke of midnight thing than not-even-nine-thirty on a Saturday morning.'

Before I could answer, the flame of the burning cedar turned black. My fingertips began to prickle and the heat took over my body, pumping magic through my heart, scorching me from the inside out. Everything happened faster this time, so fast I didn't have time to warn Lydia before we were plunged into darkness. I heard her calling my name but I couldn't see her. I couldn't see anything. I was back in the nowhere space, held in black velvet nothingness, waiting.

The vision was the same but different. I was there, and so was the wolf, the same one from Bonaventure, I was sure of it. But this time, we were in a tight, dark space, lit with black candles. Outside, I heard water rushing as the flames roared, an apocalyptic contradiction. Inside, the wolf was bleeding, tangled up in wires, and behind it I saw two people. One sprawled on the floor in front of a marble altar, covered in cuts and gashes. Catherine. The other was the pale woman with the white hair.

'This isn't what I was looking for,' I said, clawing at the ground. 'That isn't what I wanted to know.'

But what I wanted didn't matter. The woman flew at me with inhuman speed, faster and faster until I felt her slam into my body, my essence matched by hers, and together we let out an agonizing scream. I fell backwards and the chaos around me disappeared, replaced by the bright blue summer sky.

'What the hell was that?'

Pushing myself upright, I saw Lydia kicking at the salt circle, her cheeks stained with tears.

'It's OK,' I said, crawling towards her, weak and empty. 'You're OK.'

'No, I am not! I am so fucking far from OK,' she yelled. 'Did you put something in my coffee? Am I tripping?'

'You saw it?'

Lydia Powell, descendant of a dormant witch had shared my vision.

She jumped to her feet and knocked over the ashes of my offering, stamping it out with her sneaker. 'I will try anything once but that was not just anything. I thought cedar repelled moths, not made you trip balls and hallucinate giant freaking wolves. Is it even cedar? Oh my god, what did we burn? What have I been breathing in?'

'Lyds, please, I'm sorry,' I insisted, pleading for her to sit back down. She might have seen the vision but I felt like I had lived it, and my insides crawled with the sensation of the ghost passing through me. I wasn't strong enough to stand and if she ran, I wouldn't be able to chase after her.

'I should never have asked you to do this. I'm so, so sorry.'

She didn't move. Instead she stared at me for a second then stamped on the bonfire once more for good measure.

'You shouldn't have asked me to do it without telling me exactly what "it" was,' she replied as she knelt back down beside me. 'You look awful, by the way. Super dehydrated.'

'I feel awful,' I replied, relieved and beyond grateful that she was still by my side. 'I really am so sorry, I truly didn't know that was going to happen.'

'Then why did we do it?'

The cemetery was empty, nothing but trees and headstones, green grass and blue sky. No white-haired woman, no red-haired grandmother. No wolf.

'I just wanted to ask a question,' I said, struggling to get the words out. 'I'm so confused about everything.'

Lydia stroked my back, a wash of compassion filling her brown eyes.

'You were trying to contact your dad,' she guessed. 'Your birthday is coming up and you miss him. I get it, Em, I really do. I pretend not to care about my father but I search for him all the time, although I mostly use the internet instead of the dark arts. It's less traumatic, but only a little.'

'It's not my dad,' I replied in a thick voice, determined not to cry. It wouldn't help the situation now. 'There's no way to contact him.'

'Wyn then?'

One perfectly round tear slid down my cheek at the sound of his name and landed in the ashes of the cedar.

Lydia took it to be a yes.

'I don't want to have to say this, Em, but you need to wake up. Sometimes people you love, the ones who are supposed to love you back, they leave and you never really understand why,' she said, her words measured, detached. 'My dad left. My mom left. Even my own twin can't wait to start college to get away from me. Sometimes the reason people aren't with you is because they don't want to be.'

'Lyds, that's just not true.' It killed me to know she was hurting and I hated myself for not seeing it before now. Lydia Powell was a walking ray of sunshine but even the brightest days had to deal with dark clouds sometimes.

'Your dad didn't leave you, he didn't even know your mom was pregnant. Jackson loves you, and your mom didn't leave,

292

she just moved. She wants you in Charleston with her, doesn't she?'

'Charleston,' she groaned, almost more upset about my suggestion than the ritual. 'You don't have to try to sugarcoat anything for me, Em. I'm old enough to know how things are. People lie and people leave. The only person I can truly rely on is myself.'

'You're definitely wrong about that,' I said, reaching for her arm. 'You can rely on me.'

Her eyes skirted the disrupted circle of salt.

'Starting now,' I amended. 'You can rely on me starting now.'

'Promise there will be no more creepy witch shit in the cemetery?'

I nodded.

There would be no more creepy witch shit in the cemetery. At least not for her.

'Good.' She hugged herself tightly and cocked her head towards the gates. 'Let's get out of here, I would like to forget everything I saw as soon as possible.'

I reached down for my bag, tucking my hair behind my ears, when something in the pile of ashes caught my eye. Poking a finger in the remains of my failed experiment, I scooped out a small black gem, faceted and sparkling.

'What is that?' Lydia asked as she plucked it from my fingers. Her eyes glazed over for a second as she stared into the shifting rainbow at its heart. Then she shrugged and dropped it back into the palm of my hand. 'Cool crystal. Anyway, sorry your little witchy trick didn't work, whatever you were trying to do. You wanna get another coffee?'

'Little witchy trick?' I repeated slowly.

She slapped her bare midriff and stretched her arms high above her head. 'Let's get something to eat. Witchcraft makes me mad hungry. Who knew?'

Her smile was too happy, her posture too relaxed. No one could get over something so terrifying so quickly, I knew I hadn't.

'You don't remember,' I murmured, the black stone pulsating in my hand.

'Remember what?'

I tucked the crystal away in the smallest pocket of my jeans, keeping my hand pressed against it for a long moment. 'Nothing. You're right, it didn't work.'

'Don't cry about it, Em,' she said kindly as she slid her arm back through mine. 'We could try again after we eat, or are we done for the day?'

Under the tree, I saw the white-haired woman standing over the pile of ashes, wearing the same dark expression I'd seen in my vision.

'We're done for the day,' I confirmed as I pulled Lydia away towards the cemetery gates. 'We're definitely done.'

Chapter Thirty-One

'Emily James, you look like you've been rode hard and put away wet,' Catherine declared when I rolled back into Bell House, still emotionally and physically spent from the invocation ritual gone wrong. 'Whatever is the matter?'

'What's a binding spell?' I asked, not bothering with niceties.

My grandmother straightened the collar of her silk shirt, the planes of her face never changing.

'Might I ask where you came across that term?' she replied as she glided into the parlour where a half-drunk cup of hot tea was waiting for her.

'In a book. In the library.'

'I will assume you do not mean the Chatham County public library.' She sat and folded her hands in her lap. 'Come, sit down, you're fit to drop.'

My legs were already wobbling underneath me. Sharing the vision with Catherine had been an even split of labour but this time, with Lydia, I felt broken and drained.

'Binding might sound simple and straightforward,' my grandmother said, handing me her napkin and confirming what I already knew. I was a mess. 'I have seen how they love to use it in the movies, it's a neat little plot device. Convenient. The reality is very different. You can't put your magic in a box and save it for later like leftover lasagne.'

'But binding rituals do exist?' I asked, the honey and lemon scent of her tea wafting towards me and soothing my smoke-ravaged throat. 'It is something we could do?'

'It's something *I* could do. But I can't imagine for a second why I would.'

The door opened on silent hinges and in came Ashley, wordless but patently furious, to replace Catherine's lukewarm white teapot with a piping hot blue one and set out two clean teacups.

'If she doesn't have any magic, she must be psychic,' I whispered as she left the room, stony-faced as ever.

'Just well trained,' Catherine said, leaning forward to pour. 'You're not exactly stealth personified when you come and go.'

I chewed on my bottom lip, thinking of all the times I'd proved her wrong on that front, but said nothing. The tea tasted as good as it smelled, easing my sore throat and calming my ragged nerves. The steel cage that had replaced my ribs began to loosen and I forced myself to breathe in, full and deep. Catherine sat back, hot cup of tea in her hand, a cool expression on her face.

'The binding rituals I know of are very unpredictable. Yes, it is possible to limit a witch's abilities but there's no guarantee she would ever get them back again. That can't happen with you, Emily.'

'Because I'm the prophecy girl,' I said with more attitude than I expected to get away with.

'Because you are the future of the Bell line. If I lost you, our whole legacy would be gone forever.'

'What about Ashley?' I said, glancing over towards the door. 'If she had a daughter, the line would continue.'

'Ashley isn't able to have children. A common problem with second children in our family.'

Catherine raised her teacup to her lips and the door I hadn't realized was still open clicked shut.

'I didn't know,' I said, struck by a pang of sympathy I wasn't prepared for. 'That must be difficult for her.'

'It's difficult for all of us,' Catherine agreed. 'And it means there will be no binding. The magic is too unpredictable. Losing your abilities would be the best-case scenario.'

My ears pricked up at her choice of words.

'If there's a best case, that means there's a worst. There's more you're not telling me.'

She did not respond.

'Catherine, please,' I begged, a crack in my voice as the memory of her bloody and broken body flashed in front of my eyes. 'I'm going to find out eventually, right? It's all part of my heritage, the good and the bad. If something happened to one of our ancestors during a binding ritual, I need to know.'

The painted birds on the parlour walls began to flit from branch to branch as she pinched the bridge of her nose, aware that she was defeated. Pale blue paint against soft white silk, the birds chirped daintily as the moss began to sway.

'It was a long time ago,' she said, her silken voice blending in with the stories on the walls. 'Things were very different then. Her magic manifested late and fast and she was unable to control it.'

'Like me,' I murmured, watching a young woman walk out from behind the trees.

'Nothing like you,' Catherine replied. 'It was 1820, we'd been in the New World less than a hundred years. Because she came from a wealthy family, not ours, I might add, her name was Elizabeth Howell, she was labelled eccentric rather than insane. But the girl was unwell and no one knew how to help her.'

'1820?' The date rang a miserable bell. 'The year of the second great fire?'

She nodded. 'They say it began in the stables of a house on Franklin Square. But why would someone have a lantern burning in the stables at one o'clock in the morning? No visitors were expected. And doesn't it seem peculiar for the city to see no rain all winter? Not a drop for weeks, months, prior to the fire?'

My teacup rattled against its saucer as the birds in the trees made way for more images forming on the wall. An older woman, silver yarn, a familiar dagger.

'If there hadn't been quite so much gunpowder stored illegally in the market square, we might not have lost quite so many lives. Savannah burned for exactly twelve hours, from Bay to Broughton, Montgomery to Abercorn. Four hundred and sixty-three buildings destroyed. I won't tell you how many lives lost.'

I didn't know I was biting my lip until I tasted blood. Two hundred years ago, that kind of fire in downtown Savannah was a tragedy. If the same thing happened today, it would be a massacre.

'It was the day of her Becoming ceremony,' Catherine's voice narrated as the scene unfolded around us. 'But Elizabeth wasn't ready to accept the blessing. She was too unstable and angry at the world, but the elders weren't prepared to cut off the line by refusing her initiation, so they left the decision to the ancestors. The Wilcuma went off without a hitch, she was acknowledged and accepted. After that the elders were sure everything would be fine once she had full control of her abilities.'

'But it wasn't,' I said, watching the women assemble on the opposite wall. 'She started the fire and they had to bind her.'

'No. She lost control during her Becoming ceremony and accidentally killed her grandmother. Thankfully we had more sisters back then, there were more families still in touch with their magic, and she was contained before she could destroy every witch in Savannah. Not that she didn't try. She wasn't bound because she started the fire. She started the fire *because* they tried to bind her.'

On the wall, I saw the two women struggling over the same dagger Catherine had stabbed through her own hand at my Wilcuma. They jostled back and forth until the older one seized up and collapsed to the ground, silhouettes of flames surrounding them and rolling around the room, obliterating everything in their path.

'So, I can see why you might have some resistance to the general binding concept,' I said, swallowing hard as the flames faded away, the original pattern of trees and branches covering the ugly scene. 'But you're not forcing this on me, I'm asking you to do it. I'm not going to hurt you.'

'You don't know what you're going to do,' Catherine replied darkly. 'It's complex magic, more dangerous than you realize. It goes against nature. A witch cannot be bound until after her Becoming ceremony and once you are in full control, you won't want to give up your magic. Today, you're a housecat; after the ritual, you'll be a lion. Do you think a lion would surrender so easily?'

'I don't know,' I answered honestly. 'Maybe. If it was the only way to save the ones it loved.'

'How many times must we go through this.' She closed her eyes and sighed. 'You're not going to end the world.'

The little black gem in the pocket of my jeans hummed.

'That's not how it felt this morning.'

Catherine's eyes snapped open and her teacup slipped out of her hands, falling to the rug.

'What happened this morning? Did you have another vision?'

I nodded but said nothing.

'I know you're afraid,' she whispered, stating the obvious. 'We can't change what's meant to be but forewarned is fore-armed, don't forget that.'

'Will you promise me something?' I asked, reaching forward to pick up her fallen teacup. She reached down at the same time and touched the damp patch on the rug, drying it in an instant.

'Anything, honey.'

'Will you research the binding rituals, just in case? I need to know there's a plan B if the worst does happen.'

'My brave, beautiful girl,' Catherine said with a sigh. 'I've waited so long to have you here where you belong, I'm not going to lose you now. Yes, I promise I will do whatever it takes to keep you and our magic safe.'

'Even if that means saving me from myself?' I pressed. 'If I lose control, you'll have a way to stop me?'

A small flame flickered out from her fingertips and set fire to the rug. She slapped it out with a scowl on her face.

'Emily, I swear it. If you lose control, I will stop you from hurting yourself.'

'Thank you,' I said, eyeing the scorch mark.

It was the first time I'd ever seen Catherine lose control of her magic. I very much hoped it would be the last.

Chapter Thirty-Two

At first, when Wyn left, the days dragged but as my birthday approached, they passed like minutes and a week whistled by in an instant. In what felt like no time at all, there were only two days left until the full moon.

I sat alone in the dining room, eating breakfast. As usual, Ashley was out back and I had no idea where Catherine might be. She was absent more often than ever, disappearing and reappearing in strange places at strange hours, often retreating straight to her room without speaking to either of us. I kept myself busy, studying my ancestors' journals, learning all I could about my magic and reading through Dad's endless, mostly useless research, before closing out each day the same way. Laid out on my balcony, imagining Wyn was beside me. It took a while but I'd stopped checking my phone every five minutes of the day. There was never anything from him, just an endless stream of texts from Lydia, who had no memory of our shared vision. Eventually, all the fear and hurt went numb. Half my heart turned to stone, perhaps forever.

301

'Emily, hurry up and get dressed, I'm taking you out.'

I looked up with a silver spoon of cereal frozen halfway to my mouth to see Catherine beaming at me from the doorway. She hadn't been at breakfast in days.

'I am dressed,' I replied, tugging at my shirt. 'These are clothes.'

She eyed my massive cotton button-down and bare legs, a look inspired by my fashion icon, Lydia.

'Emily, hurry up and get changed,' Catherine amended cheerily. 'I'm taking you out.'

'Out where?' I asked, setting down my spoon and looking longingly at the leftover cereal milk. There would be no picking up the bowl to drink it in front of my grandmother, even if it was the best part.

There was a tiny smile on her lips but the tell-tale dark shadows under her eyes told a different story.

'It's a surprise. Quickly now.'

'We don't have a great batting average when it comes to surprises,' I reminded her as I pushed my chair back to leave the table. 'You can't give me a hint?'

'No hints. You're going to love it,' she said. 'Trust me.'

It was my least favourite thing to hear her say.

'Now, look in the mirror.'

The slip of silk Catherine had used as a blindfold fell from my eyes and I blinked with surprise at the girl I saw reflected in front of me. Pinned to her body, my body, was an utterly gorgeous white gown. I'd never seen anything so exquisite in my life. I raised one hand to lightly touch the shoulder straps that curved down around my collarbone in a tasteful V neckline, before turning to admire how the bodice relaxed under the bust, flowing out in a rippling river of fabric. It was light as a feather, moving when I moved, breathing when I breathed. Not that I was breathing, I was too shocked. I'd never seen myself this way before. Grown up, composed . . .

'Beautiful,' Catherine purred. 'Just beautiful.'

'She's as pretty as a picture,' agreed the dressmaker, a pink tape measure draped over her shoulders and a shiny, spiky pin cushion in her hand. 'The measurements you gave me were perfect. Is this for her coming out?'

'More of a family tradition,' she replied. 'But it's something like that.'

The mirror had three angled panes and I twisted and turned to take in every possible view of the gown. It dropped lower in the back and I could see my shoulder blades moving under my skin as I craned my neck to appreciate the way the skirt fell all the way past my feet, covering half the raised dais and spilling onto the floor. When we arrived at a random home, a couple of blocks away from Bell House, I had no idea what Catherine was up to. Ever a fan of the dramatic, she'd insisted I wear the blindfold as the fabric was draped over my body, calling out alteration instructions while I silently wished I'd bothered to dig out matching underwear. But she was right, it was a surprise and I did love it.

'Might we have a moment?' my grandmother said to the dressmaker who nodded, her face filled with the pleasure of a job well done as she excused herself.

'Emily, what do you think?'

'I think it's gorgeous,' I replied, unable to tear my eyes off my reflection. The soft white sheen of the fabric gave my skin a luminosity I was not used to and just for a second, I completely forgot about all the darkness. The only thing I wanted in the world was to truly be the girl I saw in the mirror.

'It's for your Becoming ceremony.'

Catherine joined me on the dais, examining the dress more closely. 'I wanted you to have something very special. A gown befitting of your destiny.'

'My destiny,' I said with a chuckle. 'Two months ago, the only thing I was destined for on my seventeenth birthday was a learner's permit.'

'Things change,' she muttered, pulling the fabric in at the waist.

'I know, I have a driver now.' I took a breath in as she removed a few pins from the bodice then tightened it around my ribs. 'You still haven't actually told me what happens during the ceremony. We don't have to sacrifice a goat or anything, do we?'

'No, ritual sacrifice has never been part of our magic. We draw from nature, nature is life. Ending what nature saw fit to begin can only weaken a witch. Besides, I like goats.'

'What kind of monster doesn't?' I replied. 'So, living sacrifices aren't real? They only happen in the movies?'

Her eyes met mine in the mirror and my hope dissolved.

'Back to the Becoming.' I moved the subject quickly on as she fussed with the length of my skirt. 'You said you'd tell me exactly what happens when we got closer. We can't get much closer now.'

'The ceremony itself is very simple, hasn't changed much over the years.' She looked up at me from the floor, her eyes misty with a dangerous combination of pride and nostalgia. 'It takes place somewhere we can see the moon, somewhere we can connect to the earth and the ancestors. In the beginning, we used Bonaventure but since it was built, Bell family Becoming ceremonies mostly occurred in the garden of Bell House. There's something special about coming into your magic at home, don't you think?'

'Special *and* convenient,' I answered with a smile. 'Close to clean, indoor bathrooms. Is that where yours took place?'

Her expression turned bitter and she shook her head.

'My grandmother chose to hold my ceremony at Wormsloe. She was very friendly with the family. Through her husband, my grandfather. Trouble almost always comes through the husband.'

'You never talk about your husband,' I said as she disappeared behind my skirt again. 'I'd love to know more about my grandfather. I don't even know his name.'

Catherine grabbed a handful of fabric at my waist and cinched it tightly, making me suck in a sharp breath.

'I thought you wanted to know about the ceremony?'

'I do,' I replied, sucking in my stomach. 'I'd also like to be able to breathe while I'm wearing this. That's a little tight.'

Her hand relaxed and my lungs expanded, her sorry face reappearing in the mirror.

'I apologize,' she said with a sniff. 'It's still hard for me to talk about him. He was nothing like my grandfather, nothing like any man I ever met. I'll tell you all about him another day, I promise.' She returned to altering my dress, pinching the fabric here, opening up a seam there. 'As I said, the ceremony is simple. Once we are in sight of the full moon, the granddaughter must willingly walk under an arch, a symbol of her choice to leave her old life behind and accept her magic.'

I kept my face as impassive as possible but my mind quickly flashed back to the things I had seen in my visions. The flames, the stone altar, a prone, bloody Catherine, and behind me: a tall stone archway.

'Then I will ask if you accept the blessing, you confirm that you will, and you and I exchange blood. After that, the ritual is complete.'

I turned too quickly, hitting her in the face with the bottom half of my dress.

'Exchange blood?' I repeated as she frowned up at me. 'How much blood?'

'Really, Emily,' she said, picking her hair out of her lipstick. 'It's symbolic, a pricking of the thumbs. The archway, the dress, all these things are traditions built up around the ritual. All that really matters is you're here in Savannah, with me, under the full moon. Now turn around and let me finish pinning you. Jennifer might be the best dressmaker in town but her French seams would see your great-grandmother spinning in her grave.'

I stood as still as possible, arms held out in front of me like a ballerina as she made her alterations.

'Catherine,' I said calmly. 'The things we saw in the vision. What if it happens during my Becoming?'

A sharp stabbing sensation in my leg made me cry out and behind me I heard my grandmother curse for the very first time.

'What makes you say that?' She slid her freshly pressed cotton handkerchief between my flesh and the fabric, her sweet features soured with concentration.

'The things you just described,' I answered, instinctively reaching for the wound only for Catherine to tap my hand away. 'The full moon, the archway. I saw those things.'

'There's a full moon every twenty-eight days, honey, and Savannah has more than its fair share of archways.'

Her arguments were sound and for the briefest of seconds, I let myself relax.

'I never should have told you about Elizabeth Howell,' she said, silently admonishing herself. 'I can see it's taken root in the worst way. What we saw was something far off in the future. If it was your Becoming, wouldn't you be wearing this dress? Wouldn't you be in the gardens of Bell House? Wouldn't *I* be there?'

I watched my face change in the mirror, the hope I'd dared to entertain shifting into something else. Catherine hadn't seen herself in the vision. She didn't know she was there and I couldn't bring myself to tell her.

'It's going to be a wonderful occasion, Emily, don't ruin it by telling yourself these terrible things. The only reason you don't share my faith is because you're afraid, and the only reason you're afraid is—'

'Because I didn't grow up here.'

Catherine smiled like I'd finished the lyrics of her favourite song.

'Fear has such power over us but only because we allow it,' she said. 'I know your birthday will be a celebration. But if anything at all should go wrong, I believe I have a solution.'

'You found out how to bind me?' I asked, that dangerous hope coming alive once more.

'Not quite. I don't have a complete grasp on it yet but I will before we see the full moon.'

Gazing back at the dress, I watched as a tiny dot of red appeared on the white, my own blood marring the pristine gown. Catherine stood up, smiling at our reflections in the mirror, and once we were side by side, I was shocked at the similarity.

'Don't worry, that stain will come right out,' she said, brushing my red-brown hair back as the speck of blood blossomed. 'Nothing is going to ruin your Becoming.'

When Catherine left me outside the dressmaker's house, muttering under her breath about some local council meeting and the idiots in charge, I told her I was headed straight home, but as soon as she was gone, I changed direction. Everything in my visions pointed towards my Becoming ceremony: the archway, the full moon, Catherine's body, broken and bloody. My magic was temperamental and unpredictable, I was a ticking timebomb in a pretty dress and I couldn't help but worry that in two days' time, we would find out the hard way whether or not I was going to explode. I might not be able to evacuate the whole city but I could get the people I loved out of town.

There was no need to use magic to know whether or not Lydia was home when I arrived at the Powell house. One of the upstairs windows was thrown open and the whole square vibrated with classic rock. Her singing carried over the music, loud and passionate and totally off-key. One hundred per cent pure Lydia Powell.

'Hey!' An ecstatic grin broke out on her face when she opened the door, immediately pulling me in for a hug, no questions asked. 'If it ain't the stranger herself.'

'I'm sorry,' I replied with an apologetic grimace. 'I didn't mean to ignore you but the last few days have been a lot, my grandmother has all these plans and—'

'No need to apologize but I did try to warn you.'

She pulled me into the house and I kicked off my sneakers to follow as she padded back upstairs barefoot. 'What did I say about the whole debutante debacle? Your life is over.'

My stomach twisted into an ugly knot.

'Hopefully not,' I muttered to myself.

Lydia's room was so perfectly Lydia, it was impossible to imagine anyone else could ever live in it. What had once been a very traditional girl's bedroom, canopy bed, pretty white furniture, pale pink walls, had been transformed by a riot of clashing colour and mixed mediums. The original canopy had been removed and replaced with what looked like tactical netting, the kind they made soldiers crawl underneath during training montages in movies, and while the walls were still technically pink, she'd covered them with a collage of neon fabric, cut in all different shapes and sizes, and stapled into the plaster. I could only imagine how her grandmother had taken that.

'What can I get you to drink?' she asked, opening a mini fridge next to her bed. Ever the rebel but she still knew her manners. 'I'm glad you stopped by, there are a million things we need to confirm before the big day.'

I accepted a freezing cold can of Sprite, offering a slightly blank stare in return.

'Your birthday party?' Lydia prompted. 'Saturday night? Three days from now?'

'The party,' I said on an exhale. 'Right.'

The pop and fizz of Lydia opening her Coke punctuated her disbelief. 'Don't tell me you forgot your own birthday party? Emily James, what is going on with you?'

'Nothing, only I was thinking. Are you sure you wouldn't rather go with your grandmother to visit your mom for the weekend?' I suggested, fully aware that she would not.

'No, because I'm throwing my girl the greatest birthday party Savannah has ever seen and before you question that statement, do not ask me if I've rented a bounce house for the backyard, because I've totally rented a bounce house for the backyard. They are *wasted* on little kids.' She threw a fierce glare across the room when I opened my mouth to argue and I shut it immediately. 'The deposit was non-refundable so unless you're about to tell me the world is ending between now and Saturday, this party is happening.'

Condensation ran down the side of my Sprite and dripped onto the bedroom floor.

'Lydia, the world is ending between now and Saturday.'

She crossed her arms and glared.

'Non. Refundable. Deposit.'

'Lydia, please.' I began again, urgency creeping into my words even though I was doing my best to stay calm. 'You have to leave town. You and Jackson and anyone else you can convince to take a trip out of the city limits. It's not going to be safe.'

'Why are you freaking out? It's just a party.' She crashed back on the bed and sipped her soda. 'And why are you so pale and sweaty? Bestie, you have to get a better setting spray, you look like you've seen a ghost.'

'I haven't actually, not in the last few days anyway.'

'Shut up, you can see ghosts,' she laughed at my not-joke. 'You've been spending too much time on WiccaTok. Hate to break it to you but you're not a witch. You're the one who told me they aren't real, remember?'

'I am though,' I replied through gritted teeth.

'Em, I am all for self-expression,' Lydia said, lying down on her side and stretching out her legs along her bed, 'but you're officially taking this TikTok stuff way too seriously. The ritual in the park, claiming you can see ghosts, that's totally OK but end of the world? Come on.'

'It's not TikTok stuff, and maybe it's not the end of the world but it could be,' I said. 'Lyds, you have to believe me, I'm a witch.'

She pulled her knees up to her chest and I sensed a flicker of doubt creeping over her. I could feel her mood and she wasn't impressed.

'OK, this is starting to get weird. You can quit it now.'

'You don't remember what really happened in the cemetery,' I said, desperate for her to believe me now. 'If you did, we wouldn't be having this conversation. I don't fully understand why you forgot, but I think it had something to do with the black crystal I found in the ashes of the cedar wood. I am a witch, I'm descended from a family of witches, and I'm telling

310

you this because you're my best friend, Savannah isn't a safe place to be this weekend.'

At first she didn't move. Lying on her side on the bed, soda can in her hand, she stared at me. I didn't move, I didn't blink.

'You're a witch?' she said.

'Yes.'

'Is Catherine a witch?'

I paused then nodded.

'What about Ashley?'

'No.'

'But you are?'

Another nod.

She thought for a moment then smiled, chin raised in a challenge. 'Prove it. Do some witchy shit.'

'I'd rather not,' I replied, looking around her chaotic room. 'My magic is pretty unpredictable and I don't want to hurt you.'

'This is classic.'

Her eyes rolled like wagon wheels and she threw up her hands to make bunny ear air quotes. '"I'm breaking up with you because I don't want to hurt you", "I can't hang out with you because my family doesn't approve", "I haven't been returning your texts because I'm a witch".'

'You hear that one a lot?' I asked.

'Maybe not the witch one but I'm fluent in excuses to ditch the weird queer mixed-race girl with the hot dude twin.' Her tone was bruised and cold, another rare flash of the vulnerable version of herself that she kept so well hidden. 'Whatever, Emily, you don't need to lie. I'm sure you found more suitable friends your grandmother approves of and that's cool with me.'

'Lyds, no, that's not it at all,' I said, throwing myself down to my knees beside her bed. 'This isn't me ditching you, this is me trying to protect you. I really am a witch and there's this ceremony thing I have to do on my birthday and I'm genuinely afraid something bad is going to happen. I don't want you to get caught in the fall-out.'

Her expression changed, the defensive sneer turning curious, two little lines appearing between her eyebrows as she concentrated.

'You really think you're a witch,' she said, her curiosity evolving into intrigue. 'You really believe what you're saying to me.'

'I really do,' I confirmed.

'Sorry but I am going to have to see some proof.'

'Pass me that candle.' I pointed at a glass jar by the side of her bed, the wax already half melted away. Bouncing across the mattress and spilling her soda as she went, Lydia grabbed the jar and tossed it to me before resuming her position, eyes locked on the wick.

'Don't try any sneaky shit,' she warned. 'If you tell me to look over there then pull out a book of matches, I'll kick your ass.'

'You already owe me an ass-kicking,' I assured her as I held the candle in my hands and focused on my inhale, holding the air in my lungs, then letting it out slowly. All I had to do was concentrate. A bright pink flame sparked into life, flaring almost up to the ceiling, then settled back down to dance around the wick.

'Holy moly, you're a witch!' Lydia shrieked, jumping up off the bed. 'What else can you do? Can we hex people? Can we turn them into toads? Or is it mostly pyro powers, because that is still very cool if it's all you have.'

The weight of the last few weeks lifted just enough for me to find a smile. Of course Lydia was going to be amazing about this. Lydia was amazing.

'I'm still figuring it all out,' I told her as she waved a hand over the pink flame, dancing with delight. 'I only just found out and it's a very long story—'

'And you're not going to leave a single word of it out. I have nothing else to do today.'

'Eventually,' I promised. 'But right now I need you to swear to me that you and Jackson will get out of town Friday night. Or at the very least, be on the other side of the river by the time the full moon rises.'

'Because of your weird witchy ceremony?'

'Because there's a really solid chance I might set the entire city on fire.'

'It's not like I haven't considered that myself,' Lydia said with a little too much enthusiasm. 'But they'd catch me buying all the matches and gasoline. That's how they get everyone, I saw it on YouTube. You're lucky you have the natural resources. What can I do to help?'

'You can leave,' I insisted, reaching for her hand. 'I'm serious, I couldn't live with myself if anything happened to you or Jackson because of me.'

'But I don't want to go,' she replied with equal intensity. 'I want to help you.'

The calm quiet of her room was suddenly shattered by the sound of the front door slamming and Jackson yelling out that he was home. At once, every candle in Lydia's room roared into life with pink flames soaring up to the ceiling, one of them catching on the netting above her bed. Before I could react, she yanked it down and stamped out the fledgling fire. All the candles burned out at the same time, the wicks, wax and glass vessels dissolving into shiny, solid puddles.

'Remind me,' she said, still grinding the canopy under her foot. 'What time do we need to leave?'

'The ceremony is set for eight thirty,' I replied. 'Better to be long gone by then.'

'For the record, I do not believe you're going to burn this place down,' Lydia declared, hands on her hips as she surveyed the damage. 'But we'll be out of here by seven. Just to be safe.'

'Seven sounds good,' I agreed, biting my lip at the shiny discs of glass and wax all around the room. 'Just to be safe.'

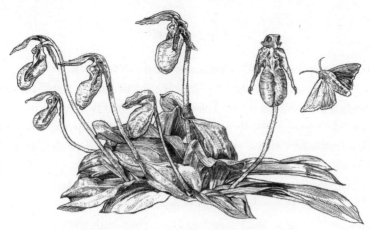

Chapter Thirty-Three

'Good morning,' Catherine said, already at the table when I came down to breakfast the next day. 'How are you feeling today?'

'Amazing actually,' I told her, taking my seat. 'Better than ever.'

There was only one more moonrise between me and my Becoming and my body was all too aware. When I woke up, I could feel every thread in the fabric of my sheets and see each individual brushstroke on my wallpaper. Without moving from my bed, I knew Ashley was getting ready to put biscuits in the oven and preparing a pot of lavender, rose and lemon balm tea, and when I closed my eyes and searched across town for the Powells, I could tell Lydia was still in bed while Jackson was completing his run. It was as easy as changing the channel on the TV, all the information right there in front of me. I didn't even have to try.

'What time is everyone else getting here?' I asked, staring at the absurd amount of food on the table. There was easily enough to feed twenty people or more. As well as the tea I could smell from my room, there was coffee, orange juice, milk, freshly cut fruit, cinnamon buns, pancakes, toast, grits, sausage, bacon, scrambled eggs, hash browns, fried chicken and waffles, and of course, biscuits and gravy.

'I woke up early,' Ashley said by way of explanation as she walked in carrying a platter of her famous French toast. 'If you don't want any of this, I've got scones, pound cake, yoghurt and granola back there. Or I could make you a frittata?'

'No, thank you, this is more than enough.'

My teeth sank into a cinnamon roll and the sweet icing exploded on my tongue. With my heightened senses, the pastry felt soft and pillowy in my mouth, the cinnamon filling melted, smooth and warm. Suddenly, I wanted to devour everything on the table.

'Ashley, do you feel OK?' I asked, covering my mouth with my hand as I chewed. 'You're not getting sick, are you?'

The cinnamon roll was the best thing I'd ever tasted but Ashley looked the worst I'd ever seen her. There were black circles under her eyes, her already pale skin was a sickly greyish-white, and her usually glossy brunette braid was dull and uneven, wisps of hair coming loose around her face and at her crown.

'I haven't been sleeping well,' she replied, pouring herself a cup of black coffee before retreating back into the kitchen without further explanation.

'Please tell me she hasn't gone to get more food,' I said to Catherine.

'It's your last day as a sixteen-year-old,' my grandmother replied as the door swung back and forth in Ashley's wake. She didn't appear to be the least bit alarmed by the state of her daughter. 'Every bit as important to celebrate an end as the beginning, we wanted to do something special for you.'

'We?' I felt for Ashley, slumped over the kitchen table with her head in her arms. 'Ashley doesn't look like she's in the mood to celebrate.'

Catherine waved her fork in the air, totally unbothered. 'Her seventeenth birthday wasn't the best. She was nursing some sad little crush that broke her heart. Inevitable, I'm afraid, but unfortunate it had to happen on her birthday.'

I chewed slowly, remembering my aunt's version of events. She hadn't mentioned it happened on her birthday.

'It would be best if you stayed home today,' Catherine added, a mild but clear warning. 'This close to the big day, everything is in flux, and we don't want any accidents. I'm sure you can feel the change already, I've had gooseflesh all morning but there is still a lot to do. I will be gone for most of the day.'

'You're leaving again?' I said, aware of the whine that stretched out my words.

'Nothing about the next twenty-four hours should be taken lightly, honey. I need to be completely prepared for every eventuality. There is still work to be done.'

The binding, I thought. She's talking about the binding.

'Don't waste the day worrying,' she advised. 'You're as prepared as it's possible to be, heck, you've spent a whole lot more time studying than I ever did. You are going to do me proud, little witch, I just know it. Promise me you'll stay home and stay safe.'

'Stay home, stay safe,' I recited, letting my eyes wander around the dining room. 'Guess I can't get into too much trouble around here.'

'Exactly,' Catherine agreed. 'Bell House is the safest place for you today.'

But we both should've known if trouble was looking, trouble would find me.

True to her word, Catherine disappeared as soon as she'd eaten, and when the front door closed, Bell House trembled to let me know we were alone. Ashley was in the garden, sweating out

317

her anger on the plants and herbs. I watched her through the kitchen window for a moment, still grey, still miserable and felt another swell of sympathy. If I was her, I might enjoy bashing things with a shovel too.

I went to my room and pulled out my laptop from underneath the bed. Things had been so hectic over the last few days, I hadn't spent as much time as I'd have liked going through Dad's files, but I needed to feel his calming influence. It helped to know he'd spent so many years here, walking on the same floorboards, sleeping in the same bed. Maybe reading his words would help settle my nerves.

Tucked away in the window seat, I opened, skimmed then closed endless documents. More notes, more research, nothing helpful. Even though I'd watched him digitizing his journals with my own two eyes, I couldn't find them anywhere. Not that his research into eighteenth-century agricultural practices wasn't fascinating (to someone other than me) but it wasn't especially helpful.

I was halfway through a file full of documents from our first year in Wales when I heard it, a low hum coming from downstairs. I closed the laptop and concentrated. Was it something I could hear or something I could feel? Maybe both. With the computer tucked under my arm, I tiptoed downstairs, running my fingers over the wallpaper, the vines and leaves and happy birds following as I went. The house had never responded to me like this before. I felt like Snow White with all of the woods around me as I searched for the source of the humming. I tried all the downstairs doors, the parlour, the dining room, the library, even the locked garden level guest rooms, but there was nothing. A tiny rabbit, no bigger than my palm, hopped along the skirting board, twitching its nose at me.

'Hello,' I said as it brushed its ears and blinked. It bounded into the next panel of wallpaper then waited.

'You want me to follow you?' I asked, dropping my voice as it hopped onto the next one, then the next, then the next. When the rabbit stopped, there was only one door left to try. Catherine's craft room.

The rabbit pulled back, trembling, as the painted vines wrapped themselves in an arch around the door, leaving a very definite gap between themselves and the sky-blue door. This was the source of the humming and Bell House wanted me to know it. I'd promised Catherine I wouldn't go in. It was her private, personal space. But that promise was made before I knew the truth. Lots of people had a craft room, somewhere they could concentrate on their hobbies, sewing, quilting, knitting. I suspected Catherine wasn't doing much needlework in hers. My hand hovered over the brass doorknob. Why would Bell House guide me to this specific room if I wasn't supposed to go inside? Shaking my head, I grasped the handle and screamed.

Black flames tore up the door, the wallpaper shredded, a cacophonous roar coming from all the animals and birds that lived within, and right beside me I saw Ashley, a walking pile of ash and bone. The moment I let go of the door handle, it all disappeared, and by my foot, I saw the rabbit with its ears pulled down, shaking as it shuffled away.

Laptop still in my arms, I backed away from Catherine's craft room, picking up pace until I was out the front door and running, as fast as I could, away from Bell House.

It was busy on the waterfront, it always was. A bunch of big hotels lined the banks of the Savannah River and tourists congregated around the souvenir shops and riverside restaurants with their beautiful water views and, according to every Savannahian I knew, overpriced and overrated food. Busier was better, I decided, huddling up into the smallest possible bundle on the corner of a bench. I wanted to see people; happy, smiling, laughing people, drinking from paper cups, eating treats and strolling along, their only concern how many free praline samples they could get from River Street Sweets before someone got wise and cut them off.

I hadn't spent a lot of time this close to the river. Bell House was like a beacon, always pulling me back whenever I drifted too far away, and there was something about the way the light found its way through the trees and the moss that always kept me close to home. The energy here was different, washing my panic and fear away downstream. I liked it. The ocean's tides pushed and pulled at my magic but the Savannah River flowed in one direction, always driving forward. It was exactly what I needed to help drown the dark memory of the deathly flames.

A black bird with a red and yellow patch on its wing skipped along the ground, flicking its head this way and that, one beady eye fixed on me. It glowed, like the stone I'd found in the ashes of my failed invocation, the one currently hidden in my bedside table alongside Catherine's silver pin.

'You must see so much,' I said as it hopped back and forth. 'So many things that we all miss.'

It took a few stilted steps towards me, pecking at the air with its sharp little beak.

'Not much of a talker, are you?' I smiled.

Strangely enough, it didn't reply. I anchored my too-long hair behind my ears, the waves falling over my shoulders, way down past my collarbone. When was the last time I got a haircut? Months ago. In another life, that was the kind of thing I'd be doing today, a visit to the salon, maybe a manicure, some new makeup. I'd been dreaming about turning seventeen forever, that's when I was sure my life would really start. There was so much I was going to do, my dad and I had made so many plans together. But not nearly as many as he'd made without me.

The bird flapped its wings twice, just enough to lift it up onto the bench beside me. It lurched forward and pecked at my laptop, fast and ferocious.

'Easy!' I exclaimed as it hopped backwards to glare at me with its dark diamond eyes. 'I only have one of these and I don't think you can afford to replace it.'

With what looked suspiciously like a disappointed shake of its head, it took off, flying into the bony branches of a nearby tree, right in front of the paddle-wheel riverboat and its long line of tourists. It continued to glare at me until I opened the laptop.

'Perfectly normal stuff,' I mumbled as I tapped in Ashley's date of birth and opened my dad's files. 'A black bird telling me to do my homework.'

Without touching the trackpad, I watched the cursor dance in circles around the screen, flickering over the stacks of folders until it landed on an image file, a close-up photograph of a camellia. I'd looked at it before but hadn't paid much attention. It was just a flower, pretty enough but nothing special. In the tree, the bird cawed loudly.

'OK, OK,' I murmured. 'I'll take another look.'

I zoomed in on the camellia. A tiny grey dot appeared, hidden in the shadow of the petals. One click and the cursor blinked. I clicked again, twice in quick succession, and a password box appeared. I tried Ashley's date of birth but the box shuddered its refusal and a message appeared, one I hadn't seen before. 'Password attempt one of three. Three or more incorrect attempts will delete all files.' I must have tried a hundred different password combinations to get into the laptop and it never locked me out. Nothing else was protected with this level of security. I tapped in my mom's birthday but it declined again and the warning came back, this time in red. 'Password attempt two of three.'

There were infinite possibilities, dates of birth, addresses, pets' names, favourite songs, bands, movies, books, foods, dates of historical events; how was I supposed to guess? I let my hands hover over the laptop then rested my fingers lightly on the keys as I stared out over the water. The sounds of the river, the rustling of the trees and across the way, the soft encouraging caw of a black bird with a red and yellow patch on its wing. The last time I'd been down by the river was with Wyn, right before I spilled chocolate ice cream on Lydia's dress. I smiled at the memory and the tender sense of calm that came with it. When I looked back at the laptop, my date of birth with the numbers reversed filled the password box.

All I had to do was press enter.

Immediately, hundreds, thousands of new files filled the screen. I'd found my dad's journals. My breath caught in my throat as I clicked through the dated entries, some were short, some were long, but every single one began the same way.

Dear Angelica.

It wasn't just a diary. Every day for sixteen years, my dad had written a letter to my mom. A letter about me. I opened a file at random and began to read.

Dear Angelica,

Today we found out Em is allergic to orange face paint. Wish I'd known that before I let Giorgio paint her up like Nemo at the carnival this afternoon. She looked more like a blowfish than clownfish but I sure did feel like a clown. Now she's OK, I can admit it was kind of funny but I don't think Em would agree.

'No, she wouldn't,' I muttered, remembering my itchy skin and sobbing on the floor of the pharmacy while my dad tried to figure out how to ask for Benadryl in Italian.

I scrolled back to some older entries, searching anything that might explain why we left Savannah in his own words instead of Ashley's or Catherine's.

Dear Angelica,

It's a big day in the James household, we have officially said goodbye to diapers. Damn good thing too, those things were about to bankrupt me. Why is everything kids need so expensive? To be honest with you, everything in New Zealand is expensive but at least it's safe. So far, so good, at least. I know we won't be able to stay here forever but for now, the ocean is enough. There's no way Catherine could travel all this way to spread her poison. I'm looking at Em right now. How can this tiny person be expected to carry so much on her shoulders? Imagine trying to grow up normal and healthy with someone telling you you're destined to save the world or end it one day. She's our daughter, not a prophecy. I haven't forgotten my promise. I'll keep her safe, whatever it takes.

Smearing tears across my face, I pressed my lips together to control my crying when strangers started sneaking uncomfortable glances my way. I scrolled forward, searching for something specific. My sixteenth birthday.

Dear Angelica,

Here we are, Em's sweet sixteen. Not that it's so sweet. I feel like shit, not being able to give her the celebration she deserves, but I have to keep reminding myself it's for the greater good. I wish you could see her today. She's such a good kid, smart, polite, conscientious, and there's something else bubbling away under the surface. She's getting more curious by the day and I don't know how much longer she's going to accept her old dad's version of the world. Wales is working out for now, the farm is far enough away from everything, there's no public transport to speak of, and I keep her busy with her studies.

But I remember being sixteen. She's already mastered the eyeroll and every day she's making plans for the future.

Alex emailed to say happy birthday from her and the twins, but there's still no update on Ashley, she hasn't seen her in months and she says Bell House is a mess. The whole thing breaks my heart but my hands are tied. What can I do? I'd get Ash out of there in a heartbeat if I could but there's no way of contacting her without Catherine finding out where we are and that is not an option. Not now, not when we're so close.

There are days when I question it all. What if I'm wrong? What if my mother is languishing in the ruins of my home, frail and failing because of me? Then I look at Em and it all comes back. Catherine never wanted a granddaughter, she wanted a Bell witch. That's the cold, hard truth.

Things will become more difficult as Em gets closer to her seventeenth. Sometimes I think her magic is manifesting already, the way she looks out the window right before it starts to rain. Maybe I'm imagining it. She killed the Chia Pet I gave her for Christmas, hardly an indication of a natural witch. All my research says she'll be fine, the world will be fine, as long as I keep her away from Savannah and away from my mother.

I looked up and stared out across the river. Alex and the twins? Did he mean Alexandra Powell? It couldn't be anyone else. Swallowing hard, I thought back to those days in Wales, trying to remember if I'd ever felt even a hint of my magic. There was nothing concrete I could recall; it rained all the time, if everyone who looked out of a window right before it started to rain in Wales was a witch, they'd have to burn the whole population. I closed the journal entry and scrolled ahead to the last file.

Dear Angelica,

We have to move. I thought we'd be safe here until her

birthday but my gut says something's wrong. I know if you were here, you'd tell me not to be so superstitious but you're not, are you? No one is here for me. Sorry, that's not fair but I'm scared. God, I wish you were here to help me, I wish you could see her. She asks about you and our family all the time but I'm keeping my promise; no stories, no photographs. She just has the one picture of you and I, by our tree. Some days that's the hardest part, not being able to tell her about you, the thought that if you were around, she would most likely walk past you on the street like you were a stranger.

As soon as I've decided where we're going, I'll book the flights. Somewhere remote, somewhere in the middle of the ocean. I'll tell Em it's a graduation gift, one last stop on our journey until her birthday. She might not be happy but at least she'll be safe. At least she'll get to live a normal life.

It was the last entry.

The next day, my dad was dead.

Chapter Thirty-Four

I let Bell House guide me home. My eyes were open but I was only vaguely aware of cars and crosswalks, and before I knew it, I was in Lafayette Square. Was I imagining it or did the house look fresher? Were the windows shinier than they were when I left? Too dazed to sneak back inside, I opened the front door and let it swing all the way into the wall, Dad's words ringing through my head and silencing all other thoughts.

Catherine doesn't want a granddaughter, she wants a Bell witch.

'Goddamn it, Emily, do I have to put a goddamn tracker on you?'

I was still numb when Ashley flew downstairs to meet me in the foyer. She didn't look any better than she had that morning. Her hair was fixed but there wasn't much she could do about her sickly pallor. There wasn't a blush and highlighter combination on this earth that could perk her up.

'Catherine is going to spit when she finds out you left the house.' She hustled me into the kitchen and pushed me down onto a stool. 'When I say she'll be madder than a wet hen,

326

you'd better believe me. You ever seen a wet hen, Emily James? I'm telling you she's going to be pissed.'

'I found my dad's diaries,' I said, gazing blankly around the light-filled kitchen. The beautiful painted cabinets, the shining copper pots and pans. 'He took me away from Savannah to keep me safe.'

'No, he took you away because he didn't want to spend the rest of his life as your servant,' she replied. 'And left that thrilling task to yours truly instead.'

'That's not it at all,' I murmured, not really registering anything Ashley said. 'He believed in the blessing, our magic, the prophecy, but he didn't want it for me. Neither did my mom. They wanted me to have a regular life.'

Ashley opened the refrigerator door and took out a jug of iced water, pouring two tall glasses. In no rush at all, she put the jug back and returned to where I stood. Then, right in front of me, my aunt raised one of the glasses and quick as a flash, threw the water in my face.

'Normal?' she yelled as I stared at her in shock, ice-cold water snapping me back to my senses. 'He wanted you to be normal? News just in, sweetie, you're not normal. You're a witch. Wherever you go, whatever you do, you'll always be a witch. Your daddy didn't hide you away to save you, he stole you out from under our noses because he didn't understand his place, and even after everything that's happened since you got here, neither do you.'

'He did understand,' I choked, wiping the water from my face. 'He was trying to help.'

'Help himself,' she replied, stone cold. 'Paul resented your magic, he didn't want to be the powerless one. He hated witches.'

'That's not true!' I exclaimed. 'He loved me. How can you say he hated women when he was protecting us.'

Ashley scoffed and threatened me with the second glass. 'That's rich. Paul didn't give a fig about me.'

'Then why is your birthday the password to his computer?' I volleyed back. 'Why does his diary say he would get you out of here if he could but there was no way of contacting you without it getting back to Catherine?'

Her arm wavered and she leaned back against the kitchen counter.

'How do you know that?' she asked, spilling the second glass of water all over the marble surface as she shakily set it down.

'Because I have his laptop and I found his journals,' I replied. 'My dad was afraid of what would happen if I stayed in Savannah, just like I'm afraid. Catherine loves to tell me I'd feel different if I'd grown up here but he grew up here, he heard all the stories and he still didn't have her blind faith. What if she's wrong and I'm right? What if I *can't* control my magic?'

'People believe what they want to believe.'

Ashley was still visibly mad but there was less conviction in her voice. She opened a drawer, pulled out a tea towel, mindlessly dabbing at the spilled water as it dripped onto the floor.

'In the eyes of the blessing, your father was no one,' she said. 'Nothing more than a packet of seeds. You know what you do when you've planted the seeds, Emily? You throw the packet away. As soon as you arrived, Paul went from being Catherine's favourite to completely expendable and he did not like that one little bit.'

'He loved me,' I said again. 'He loved you too.'

'If you say so,' she replied. 'You really believe he ran away, abandoned me, gave up this privileged life and hid you for all these years, just to keep you safe?'

'That's what parents do,' I told her as she came closer, holding up the towel to wipe the iced water from my face. 'They make sacrifices for their children.'

Eye to eye, she paused and shook her head.

'Not all parents,' she replied before handing me the towel and stalking out the door.

Ashley didn't bother me again and Catherine still wasn't home by the time I fell asleep on my bed hours later, head on my hands, laptop open in front of me. When my eyes fluttered open, my room was pitch black, darker than it should've been with the almost full moon casting slivers of milky light through the gaps in the shutters. But something was on the balcony, blocking those gaps.

Not something, someone.

'Wyn!' I exclaimed as I vaulted out of bed to throw the window open.

He was only halfway inside but his arms were already wrapped around me so tightly I could barely breathe. My hands travelled up and down his back, his shoulders, his hair, his face. It was really him, he was really here.

'You're real,' he said, holding my face in his hands and shaking his head like he was the one who couldn't believe it. 'I didn't dream you up, you're real.'

With one finger pressed to his lips, I pulled him the rest of the way inside and closed the window behind us.

'We have to be quiet, my aunt is in the next room,' I said softly. 'I can't believe you're here.'

He pushed his hair back from his face with both hands and stared at me. It was only a month since I last saw him but he already looked so much older. There was a shadow of stubble across his jaw, the threat of a beard I'd never seen before, and dark hollows under his eyes that made me want to pull him back into my arms and hold him there. But something about the grim set of his mouth and unreadable mixture of emotions in his green-grey eyes held me back.

'I promised I'd come back.' His voice was worn and dry. 'Sorry it took a while.'

'Kind of thought you'd forgotten about me,' I said, lacing my words with an attempt at self-deprecating laughter. The attempt was a failure. Wyn looked at me as though I'd just said the sun was green and the moon was red.

'Emily James, I've spent every second since I left trying to get back to you.'

'Where were you?' I asked, quickly but quietly positioning a chair underneath the handle of my bedroom door. 'It's been weeks. I tried to text and call, I sent DMs—'

'You wouldn't believe me if I told you.' He paced up and down in front of the window, occasionally throwing anxious glances at the closed shutters, as though someone might be watching, waiting. 'I shouldn't be here. All this crazy shit is going on and you're the only damn thing I can think about. I shouldn't *be* here.'

He closed his red-rimmed eyes tightly then opened them again, almost surprised to see me still standing in front of him. 'I don't know what's real anymore, Em. I don't know what to believe or who to trust. I had to break out of my own home to get here, hitched all the way to Savannah. They're already hunting me down, I know it.'

'Who is they?' I asked, confused, as he prowled around the room, his steps as soft as snowfall. 'Wyn, look at me, tell me who's looking for you? What happened?'

'You won't believe me,' he said again. 'I don't believe me.'

'You'd be surprised at what I might believe,' I replied. 'Remember what we said before? You can tell me anything, you can trust me.'

I felt a tremor in my fingertips and a swirling sensation in my belly as he rubbed a hand along his jaw, both feelings unexpected and neither completely within my control.

'I guess it doesn't matter, right?' Wyn muttered, more to himself than to me. 'Either I tell you and you send me away or I say nothing, my family finds me, and you never see me again anyway. Better to get it out.'

'Would it help if I told you something crazy?' I asked, suddenly desperate to close the distances between us, literal and metaphorical. 'Because whatever you have to say, I know I have something even more bizarre to tell you.'

'I don't think that's possible, Em.' He raised his chin and looked me square in the eye. 'Not unless you're planning to tell me you're a werewolf too.'

Thankfully, when I staggered backwards, my bed was close enough to catch me.

'I told you,' he said as my heart stuttered in my chest, pausing for far too long between each beat. 'I said you wouldn't believe me.'

My room suddenly felt too small, too dangerous. We both sank down to the floor, kneeling side by side on my rug. Wyn's eyes were wide open, his forehead creased with anguish. There was no need to use my magic to search for the truth, it shone out from his whole being. Werewolves were real, Wyn was a werewolf. And he was right. He shouldn't be here. Not because it put me in danger but because he wasn't safe.

'I do believe you,' I said, choking out the words and silently begging the house to keep them safe in my room. 'I wish I didn't but I do.'

He pulled up the leg of his pants to show me the long silvery scar.

'My scar. It was Cole. When a Were shifts, he doesn't know who he is anymore. Thank God my grandpa got to me before he could do any real damage. I blocked the whole thing out, forgot what happened, but I remember now.'

'Your family knew,' I said, rubbing my hand against the plush carpet fibres and trying to ground myself. My mind was swirling but I could not afford to lose control. 'But they didn't tell you.'

'They knew, they didn't tell me,' Wyn confirmed. 'You really believe me?'

I nodded. 'Tell me everything.'

He let his head fall back and scowled up at my ceiling, his Adam's apple bobbing up and down as he swallowed. 'Short version, according to my mom, this thing, this curse, has been in our family since forever. If Cole had never gone missing, I would never have known. She says she didn't want to burden me with the secret, she reckons some people don't cope with it so well, mentally I mean.'

I exhaled something like a laugh and pressed my fingers deeper into the rug.

'They do say keeping secrets isn't healthy.'

'Right?'

His mouth crept up into a crooked smile, just for a second, before incredulity overcame his expression. 'Growing up, my parents told me Cole had anger issues and I shouldn't be around him unless someone else was there. That wasn't hard, he didn't want to be around me anyways, but I don't know if the wolf made him angry or he's angry because they made him a wolf. All I do know is my parents did this to us and we didn't have any choice in the matter.'

'Wyn, I'm so sorry,' I said, aching with sympathy. 'Did you find out why they sent him to Savannah?'

He nodded but frustration made the muscle in his jaw tick.

'He was supposed to find out what was happening here then

come right back home. He shouldn't have been here when he phased.'

'But he was. He was here during the last full moon.' The sour feeling in my stomach spread. With one hand I reached for my locket, with the other, I reached for him. Slowly, too slowly, I was able to put the story together and I did not like where the ending was headed. 'What does your family think is happening here that's so bad they had to send Cole?'

Wyn rolled off his knees and crossed his legs underneath him. Cast in moonlit greys, the stubble and dark shadows disappeared and the extra years the last few weeks had added washed away. He looked much younger than seventeen.

'Something bad.' There was so much fear in his voice. 'I don't know what exactly but it's strong and dark, and a lot of people are in danger. My mom felt it all the way away in Asheville, Cole too. According to them, we're talking end of the world type of stuff. He was supposed to find out as much as he could then report to my mom so the pack could figure out what to do next. Together.'

All at once, my mouth felt very dry. I stood up, grabbed an empty mug from the nightstand and went to the bathroom, running the tap until it was icy cold. I took a long, cool drink, closing my eyes to avoid the guilty expression of the girl in the mirror, refilled the mug and took it back to Wyn. He drank it back right away, rivulets of water running over his jaw and down his throat.

'That's all they know?' I asked, taking the empty mug back to refill it.

'That's all I know. Mom says our intuition is stronger near the full moon but even then we're not psychic. Weres can sense imbalance in nature and whatever this is, it didn't just unbalance the scale, it blew it up. The pack is convinced they have to stop it.'

'The pack?' I repeated softly, blanching at the thought.

'My mom, my grandpa on her side. My uncle on my dad's side, he's from a Were family too, and there are cousins I haven't met yet. They'll be here soon enough. Probably here already. Everyone knew where I was headed.'

I looked down at the rug, the sound of the individual fibres bristling against my ears every time he moved.

'Wyn,' I said, fighting against the bitter taste in the back of my throat. 'What happened to you in Asheville? Why did you have to escape?'

Tears filled his eyes and I wanted to die.

'Because the pack believes Cole is dead.'

'No,' I whispered in complete denial.

'They demanded another new Were and they got one,' he went on with bleak determination. 'Tomorrow night, I'm going to phase. When the full moon rises, I will become a wolf.'

We sat on the floor in silence as his statement settled around us. Wyn nursed the mug of water while I concentrated on breathing in and out without burning the house down. Downstairs, the grandfather clock chimed midnight, officially my birthday. There would be no running from it now.

'I know it's a lot to ask,' he said, looking at me with so much pain and fear, I felt tears well up instantly, 'but will you be with me tomorrow night? They said it would happen when the moon was at its peak, around eight thirty, I think.'

Of course. The same time as my ceremony.

'I'll find a way to keep you safe, I swear,' Wyn added. 'But I don't want to be alone when it happens.'

'You won't be on your own,' I answered fiercely and without hesitation. 'You'll never be on your own again. I love you, Wyn.'

'I love you too,' he whispered, the sound of the words clearing away all that was dark and dreadful. 'They chained me up and locked me away but I still found my way back to you, and I swear I always will.'

He pulled me into his arms, tucking my head under his chin, and I heard what I knew he must be able to feel. His heart was beating faster than a normal man's, filling his muscles with blood, strengthening his organs and softening his bones as they prepared themselves for what was only hours away.

'It might not even happen,' he said. A hope, a dream. 'The initiation was such a blur, I don't recollect all that occurred but no one seemed sure that it worked. My mom could be wrong about all of it, even Cole. He's taken off so many times in the past, there's every chance he's hiding out someplace, still alive and if he's alive, I won't turn.'

'Every chance,' I made myself say, even though I knew it wasn't the truth.

Wyn might not know for sure but I did.

Cole was dead.

He'd been dead since he attacked me and Catherine in Bonaventure on the last full moon, and if that wasn't bad enough, it meant Cole wasn't the wolf I'd seen, snarling over Catherine's bloody body.

The wolf in my vision was Wyn.

Chapter Thirty-Five

He stayed in my room until the milky moonlight traded places with the hazy dawn, his body wrapped around mine. While he slept, I stared at the windows, wide awake the whole night. I couldn't tell him the truth. Whatever I said, however I pitched it, the fact was I'd killed his brother. How would he ever be able to look at me again once he knew? There were other reasons, I told myself. He needed to concentrate on the change. I needed to keep my focus on the Becoming. If we got distracted, either of us, there was no telling how badly things might end. But they were excuses and I knew it.

Wyn stirred in my arms and outside the window, the birds began to sing.

'We'll figure this out,' he promised as he crept out of my room, lingering on the balcony for too long, exposed by the early sun. 'We'll find someplace safe where my family won't find me.'

'What about Lydia's house?' I suggested, pulling my phone out of the backpack under my bed. 'Her place has a bunch of outhouses they don't use, old stables, I think.'

'You wouldn't have to explain why you need it?' he asked and I shook my head.

'She's not the kind of friend who needs an explanation,' I replied. 'Let me talk to her. If you can stay hidden for a while, I'll text you the address and meet you there later.'

He caught my wrists in his hands and leaned forward, his lips touching sweetly, softly to mine.

'I love you,' he said, his ever-changing eyes tearing me apart.

'I love you too,' I said, because it was true and I wanted him to hear me say it.

Because after he found out what I'd done, he wouldn't want to hear me say anything ever again.

'Happy birthday, Emily!'

When I finally found my way downstairs, Catherine was waiting for me. She looked beautiful, her hair was glossy and her skin shone, making her vivid green eyes leap out even more than usual. The coffee table in the parlour was covered in extravagantly wrapped gifts but I barely even noticed them.

'Everything is ready for tonight,' she said, clapping her hands together as I took in the scene. 'It's all prepared. Your dress is being delivered this afternoon, I've had the most beautiful archway crafted by a local artisan, that should be here very soon, and whatever could be so wrong to mess up that perfect face with such a sad expression? Honey, what's wrong?'

'Where's Ashley?' I asked. I couldn't sit down, I couldn't stay still.

'Ashley is outside. Emily, really, whatever is the matter?'

There was no time left to lie. I didn't know what to believe anymore, my dad's version of the truth or Catherine's, but it didn't matter much now. Dad wasn't here and my grandmother was.

'I need your help,' I said, my bottom lip quaking. 'Do you remember my first day here, when I left the Powell house? I met someone. You met him too, the boy in the square.'

'Can't say I recall,' Catherine replied. 'That was a while ago. I've had a lot on my mind lately, you know.'

It was a fair point.

'His name was Wyn,' I reminded her, clutching her hand and trying to let her know how serious this was. 'You said no dating until after my birthday so I didn't tell you that we saw each other again. As friends.'

'Friends? Is that right?'

She looked about as impressed as any grandmother who had just found out her sixteen-year-old granddaughter had been sneaking around with a boy against her wishes.

'Maybe more than friends,' I confessed. 'But he's so wonderful, Catherine, you would love him. I know keeping it a secret was wrong but he's in a lot of trouble and you're the only person who can help us.'

'What kind of trouble?'

I bit my lip and cast my eyes downward.

'Wyn is a Were.'

Catherine looked as though she might faint.

'You couldn't have fallen for something as straightforward as a petty criminal,' she muttered. 'No, that would've been too easy.'

'I didn't know, *he* didn't even know.' The words were falling out of my mouth so fast I could hardly keep up with myself. 'He's been gone but now he's back and he's going to phase for the first time tonight and I don't know what to do.'

'You send him away.' Her order boomed around the room, all the happy birthday excitement gone from her eyes. 'Emily, this is the most important night of our lives, yours *and* mine, and you brought a Were into this house?'

She looked at the door as though she was expecting to see him standing right there and I shook my head so hard my vision blurred.

'He's not here, I sent him to the Powell house. Virginia is out of town for the weekend and I asked Lydia if he could hide in their old stables.'

Spurred into action, Catherine rose to her feet. 'Those buildings won't be able to contain a first-phase Were. You need to bring him back here.'

'Here?' I repeated. 'But you just said—'

'I know what I said and I was wrong,' she interrupted, squeezing my shoulders. It should have been reassuring but I was sure I heard my bones crack. 'There's a woodshed in the garden, old but well built. We can't stop the phase but there are some herbs, some rituals that will help keep him calm if we can get to him before he changes. Once he is a wolf, he will not know you and we will not be able to help him.'

'His family will be looking for him.' My voice dropped away into almost nothing at all. 'And for me. The wolf I killed in Bonaventure—'

'Was part of his pack,' she finished, breathing in as she planted her hands on her hips. 'Oh, Emily, this just gets better and better. You couldn't have gone and messed around with the Powell boy?'

'If we could control who we fell in love with, life would be a lot easier,' I reminded her and she laughed bitterly.

'Touché, honey. That sure is true.'

She clapped her hands then pressed them together in a prayer. 'Hiding the boy from his pack will be easy enough but if they sense your ceremony, they'll find us in a jiffy and I doubt they'll be so understanding about the fact you killed one of their own in self-defence. We can't have your wolf here and perform the Becoming ceremony at the same time. We need a plan B.'

My mind spun with possibilities, almost all of them ending in black flames and green skies. All except for one.

'What if we leave?' I suggested. 'If we're apart and I'm off Savannah soil, my magic won't manifest. If I leave for the airport right now, I could be two oceans away before the full moon rises.'

My grandmother stared at me in abject horror.

'You would do that?' She was as white as a sheet. 'You would abandon your Becoming, give up your magic?'

'To save Wyn? In a heartbeat.'

If she didn't understand me before, she did now. I needed her to take me seriously and I knew there was nothing she took more seriously than our magic.

'You would let it all go.' Catherine forced out the words as though she was in physical pain, both palms pressed to her stomach to stop her from doubling over. 'Your heritage, your legacy, all the witches you're destined to awaken. You would sever our connection to the blessing, all to save a wolf?'

My entire being pulsed with conviction.

'At least we'll still be here tomorrow,' I said, 'even if we're not witches anymore. Wyn's life is more important than my magic. Catherine, I love him.'

'I can see that,' she replied, softer now, more considerate. 'You've got the same look on your face your daddy had when he came to tell me about Angelica. Nothing he wouldn't have done for her. Nothing you won't do for him.'

'It's not just that.' I fished through all the things Wyn had told me, trying to remember the exact words. 'He said his pack felt a darkness rising, something really bad. It has to be me. If I'm so dangerous Weres can feel it from hundreds of miles away, we shouldn't go through with the ceremony. If you're sure you can keep Wyn safe, I have to leave.'

Catherine moved and blocked my path to the door as though I might make a run for it right away. 'That won't help now. The full moon is on its way, the Becoming has already started,

I know you can feel it. If we don't complete the ritual, the chances of you losing control are increased tenfold. Our only hope is to secure your boy and keep his pack away until after your ceremony. Once the full moon is out of their system, perhaps they'll listen to reason.'

'And if they don't?'

'After your Becoming, you'll be strong enough to make them.' She kissed me on top of the head then pulled away with a determined smile. 'My brave, selfless girl. Ready to give up everything to save someone she loves.'

'Just like my dad,' I whispered, searching for the same determination he had shown.

'You are your father's daughter,' she agreed. Her smile only wavered for a second. 'Now, I want you to go clear out the woodshed and let me take care of everything else. We're all going to get through this just fine, do not worry.'

But as she drew me into her embrace, there was a look in her eyes I'd never seen before.

Catherine was afraid.

Chapter Thirty-Six

Emptying the woodshed was exactly what I needed. Hours of exhausting physical labour that gave me no time to think. Even though it killed me to be away from him, we all agreed Wyn would stay with Lydia until Catherine had everything figured out. This would surely be the first place his pack would look for him and while Bell House would do all it could to keep us safe, we didn't want a fight knocking on our door if it could be helped. While Catherine worked on a way to keep Wyn safe, I worked on clearing out decades of junk; broken lawn-mowers, old bicycles and pogo sticks, and a mountain of unlabelled boxes, the yellowed tape that had once held them closed disintegrating the moment I touched it. It was almost shocking to see so much useless clutter in the vicinity of Bell House. Inside, even a fly wouldn't land where it wasn't welcome and I couldn't imagine why Catherine hadn't thrown all this stuff away years ago.

Even though it wasn't visible yet, I could feel the moon as it moved along its orbit. One second I was too weak to pick up a suitcase, the next I was sure I could lift the whole house. I squatted to pick up a box labelled 'Christmas decorations' and I staggered sideways under the unexpected weight. This was one of the weaker moments.

'You need some help?'

A pair of hands grabbed the other end of the box right before my knees buckled, and helped me carry it out into the garden.

'Why does that say Christmas decorations when the damn thing is clearly full of bowling balls,' Ashley asked, pressing her hand into her lower back after we let it fall to the floor with a jingling thud. She looked around her garden, scowling. 'This is a mess.'

'I know, it's endless,' I agreed. 'Most of it looks like junk, we could probably toss it all out.'

She turned back to me, pushing the sleeves of her old denim shirt up to her elbows.

'I wasn't talking about the shed.'

I couldn't really argue with her.

'So, is he worth it?' she asked. 'This wolf?'

'His name is Wyn and he's not a wolf.' I disappeared back inside the shed and came back carrying an ancient typewriter with more than half its keys missing.

'At least that's not all he is,' I added. 'And I know you're going to say I'm dumb and too young and I'm throwing my life away for someone I just met but, yes, I think he's worth it.'

'I'm the last person who could call you dumb. Well, at least about this,' she replied, laughing unexpectedly. 'I was only sixteen when I fell in love.'

I dropped the typewriter on the wrought-iron table, a cloud of dust blowing up in my face.

'Ellie,' I said and she nodded.

'When we were together, nothing in the world could touch me.'

Ashley sat at the table and tapped absently at the typewriter.

'I knew right away, the second I saw her. She took my breath away. Most beautiful woman I've ever seen.'

'Will you tell me what happened?' I asked, slowly sinking down to sit on one of the boxes. 'What *really* happened?'

The edges of her mouth twitched like she wanted to smile but her feelings were in conflict with her face.

'Catherine happened.'

A strand of hair escaped from my topknot and fell in front of my face. I blew it out the way and even the air rushing over my lips felt like it was intruding on the moment.

'Ellie had only just moved here when we met but strangely enough, she left town with her family one month later. On my birthday. Her dad got some high-class job in New York, the offer came completely out the blue, and I never saw her again. Don't forget, my mother's influence doesn't start and end with magic. She can accomplish just as much with one phone call as she can by summoning a storm.'

Ashley flipped the top of a random box back and forth a few times then shook her head. 'Catherine located her for me a couple of years ago. She was living in New Jersey, married to an extremely average man, couple of kids running around. So I guess my mother did me a favour in the end. Would've broken me in two to find out I was just a phase.'

'When you say Catherine located her for you, you're not saying she hired a detective?' I guessed.

'Location spells are easy for her if the person she's looking for is on the same continent. All you have to do is ask the elements for help and you can find most anyone.'

She stood up, wiping away tears she didn't want me to see and headed back into the shed, reappearing with two ancient suitcases in her arms, stacked high so I couldn't see her face.

'Maybe I'm being stupid,' I said as she opened the latches on the cases, testing the rusted hinges. 'But I don't understand

344

why Catherine interfered? Was she upset because Ellie was a woman?'

'No. She was upset because Ellie existed,' my aunt replied, clipped and precise. 'Taking care of the Bell line is a full-time job and even thinking about her took up too much of my day. What if Ellie wanted to leave town someday? Or have kids? Who would tend to Catherine and Bell House if I was off living my life with a family of my own?'

'She's been so understanding about Wyn,' I said, watching my aunt sort through the contents of the first suitcase, picking up various pieces of old clothing, shaking them out, then putting them back down again. 'Did you tell her you were in love?'

Ashley laughed, cold and harsh.

'I did. Catherine told me love makes fools of us all. It made a fool of her twice. Once when she met my daddy and again when Paul met your mom. You're not going to end up with your wolf any more than I'm going to end up with Ellie. Not while my mother can still draw breath.' Her green eyes flashed a warning. 'Don't let love make a fool out of you, Emily.'

She rummaged through the clothes, shoulders pinched tight with anger, two red spots on her cheeks. It didn't make sense. We were literally clearing out space to give Wyn somewhere safe to hide. Catherine was inside right now working on spells to protect him. Ashley had to be wrong. Maybe Catherine had changed or, as much as I hated to think it, the rules for witches might be different to the rules for caretakers. A breeze shook the leaves of the magnolia tree and a swell of energy passed over me. I looked at Ashley but she hadn't noticed. The rules might be different because we were different.

'I'm about parched to death,' she announced eventually. 'You want some tea?'

'Thank you,' I replied, uncomfortable again and too polite. 'That would be nice.'

'Such a little lady,' she muttered as she marched away into the kitchen.

Even if I'd had the best night's sleep ever, clearing all this junk would have been exhausting. I was worn out but I had to keep going, there wasn't time to stop and worry about Ashley or anything else right now. First, I had to make sure Wyn was safe, and second, I needed to get through this evening without torching the whole damn city. Maybe after that we could work on her love life.

Wiping my dirty hands on my slightly less dirty jeans, I poked around in the open suitcase Ashley had left on the table. It was full of clothes, mostly women's. Dresses and shirts, some floaty tops, skinny scarves and weirdly wide belts. They smelled musty, like the vintage stores I'd sometimes poked around in back in Wales. I pulled out a cool pair of low-rise, bootcut jeans that looked like they might fit and tossed them to one side before digging back in with renewed interest. Lydia would love this stuff. At the very bottom of the case, I found two matching sweatshirts, black with gold lettering. I pulled out one and then the other, a medium and an extra-large. Two SCAD sweaters for two SCAD students. My mom and my dad.

The realization hit hard. These were my mom's clothes.

I emptied everything out in a heap on the table, my heart in my mouth. My mom's shirts and dresses and weirdly wide belts, left in a suitcase out in a shed to go mouldy when they should have been inside the house with me. I grabbed hold of a pink floral dress. It was a different style to the rest of her things and as I wrapped my fingers around it, breathing in the scent of the nearby rosemary bush, the garden disappeared and everything went black for just a second before I was nestled against the same soft fabric, tired and confused, tiny hands grabbing at I didn't know what. Two faces looked down at me, both so full of love and awe, as though they'd never seen anything quite so magical.

It was the dress my mother was wearing the day I was born.

'No,' I whimpered as the image faded away and the garden returned. 'Please stay.'

But they were gone. I was back in Savannah, in the present day, all alone and so confused. Afraid of what might happen if I let my emotions overwhelm me, I reached out to search for Catherine as calmly as possible but she wasn't inside Bell House. Reluctantly letting go of my mother's dress, I cast my net wider but I couldn't sense her anywhere. Ashley was on her way back from the kitchen, Lydia was in her bedroom, Jackson playing basketball in Forsyth Park. But my grandmother was nowhere to be found. And she wasn't the only one. Wyn's vibrant energy was completely absent from the city of Savannah. He wasn't at Lydia's house and he wasn't on his way here. There was no other glaring Were energy within the city limits so his family couldn't have got to him already, I would've felt that. Unless a person with much more power than me had decided I shouldn't. Something was very, very wrong. Something had happened to them. Panic overtook rational thinking and self-control was no longer an option. The prickling of my fingertips escalated into a searing burn before I could even take a breath and when I fell to my knees, the ground shook.

Then all I heard was screaming.

Chapter Thirty-Seven

With all the yelling and car alarms going off in the square, it took too long to realize the loudest screams were coming from behind me.

The woodshed was smashed to pieces and a deep chasm ran along the ground, wide enough to swallow up half of what we'd cleared out. In the middle of it all, Ashley's motionless body lay under one of the heavy wooden beams that used to hold up the shed's roof. I grabbed boxes and bricks, heaving them out of the way, yelling for Catherine at the top of my lungs but there was no reply. By the time I got to my aunt, her eyes were open but her lips were blue and gasping, the beam that pinned her to the ground crushing her legs like soda cans.

'Stay awake,' I ordered, blanching at the pool of red that was spreading underneath her. 'I'm going to find Catherine.'

'She's not here,' Ashley croaked. 'She's already gone.'

'Gone where?'

She grimaced and convulsed, more blood seeping out further and further.

'Doesn't matter,' I said, patting myself down for my phone. 'I'll call an ambulance.'

'No time.'

She reached out a hand, stretching up towards my face and wincing in pain with every minuscule movement. Her fingers found my hair, tangling up in the ends like a toddler. 'You have to help me.'

'But I don't know what to do,' I replied, burning with guilt and fear. Where was my so-called strength now?

'Anything,' she gurgled, flecks of red appearing at the side of her mouth. 'Do anything.'

When I was thirteen, my dad made me take a first aid class 'just in case' but this wasn't a cut or a scrape. Ashley hadn't burned herself on a pot, she was bleeding out in front of me. A deathly groan rattled out of her deflating lungs. I prised her fingers out of my hair, and tried to focus.

In the centre of the chaos I had created, I searched for stillness, begging for help from any source that might be able to give it. Inside the deafening silence, I heard a gentle whisper, an acknowledgement that felt familiar but brand new at the same time. My request was granted. Strands of Spanish moss crept down from the trees to wrap themselves around my arms like gauntlets. They breathed through me, lending me the strength of the live oaks, enough to lift the beam off Ashley's legs before wrapping itself around her limbs. I reached for more vines, wadding them together and pressing them to the bloody mess. Her eyes rolled back in her head and she went silent but I could see her chest rising and falling erratically. She was still with me. I thought back to the orchid in the parlour, how Catherine and I had knitted its stem back together with the tip of her finger. Gritting my teeth, I held out my hands. Ashley was not an orchid but I had to try.

The first pulse that came up from the earth knocked me off balance. I steadied myself, cool hands on the hot stickiness of my aunt's wounds, and concentrated. Ashley cried out, a hollow wail, as another pulse ebbed up from the ground, through my body and into hers before returning to the earth, a repeating cycle, a bargain I didn't yet know the cost of.

All the vines in the garden crept towards us, winding around Ashley's feet, binding her legs together and holding the Spanish moss bandages in place. The sweet-smelling honeysuckle and jasmine, the pretty purple wisteria, and the ivy she lovingly tended to every day, trailed down the side of the house and snaked along the ground to help, sealing the other vines in place and carrying the healing energy to where it was needed, her damaged internal organs, cracked ribs, crushed pelvis. Just like in Bonaventure, Ashley's blood seeped into the ground and disappeared too quickly, and that was when I understood. This was how we paid for the help we'd been given. One way or another, we paid in blood.

By the time her breathing was calm and even, the panic outside Bell House had died down too. Hesitantly, I stood, my knees cracking from being in one position for too long, and went to check on my damage. One of the oak trees in Lafayette Square had dropped a heavy limb on the front end of a bright blue truck, completely crushing the cabin. Anyone who had been inside was surely dead. My stomach turned and I doubled over, retching into the flowerbed, but there was nothing in me to bring up. I was completely depleted. I made myself look again, panting heavily and pushing up on my tiptoes to get a better view. Two men in matching polo shirts, one sat at the side of the road with tears streaming down his face and the other pacing up and down on the phone. It was their truck, they had escaped alive and unscathed. They would be fine but I couldn't say the same for myself. Once again, I'd lost control and almost killed entirely innocent people, people who were probably on the phone with the insurance company right now, trying to explain what had happened. An earthquake, a freak accident, just like the lightning bolt that almost broke Jackson's leg and the storm that killed my dad.

Unless they weren't accidents at all . . .

'Was it me?' I yelled, storming back to find Ashley already sitting upright and staring at the red welts on her legs, all that was left of her injuries. 'Did I kill my dad?'

'What are you talking about?' Her pupils were pinpricks and her head rolled around on her shoulders like it wasn't properly fastened on.

'Did I summon the storm that killed my dad?' I demanded, blood still boiling with the possibility.

'No,' she sighed. 'Of course, you didn't.'

'How can you be so sure?' I demanded. 'Look what I just did to you?'

Ashley smiled as a clutch of purple flowers from the wisteria sprang into life around her thighs. She wasn't just healing, she was high.

'I know it wasn't you,' she replied dreamily. 'Because Catherine killed your father.'

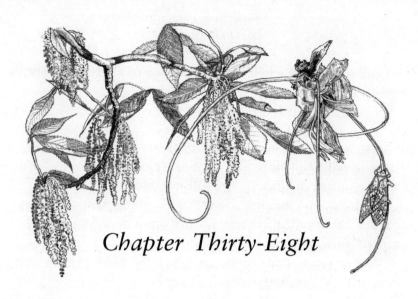

Chapter Thirty-Eight

She was still delirious when I carried her into the parlour and laid her down on the chaise longue. All the birds on the walls began to call and cry, the trees swaying in a terrible wind I could not feel. I couldn't feel anything.

Catherine killed my father.

'Don't move,' I ordered unnecessarily, the words still ricocheting around my mind. 'I'll get you something for the pain.'

'What pain?'

Ashley's words were as light as air and when I looked up, the ceiling was covered with threatening grey clouds.

'Oh, she's going to be so mad at me,' she muttered, flinging one arm above her head and almost hitting herself in the face. 'I was not supposed to tell you about your dad. I didn't think I could. Very interesting.'

Catherine killed my father. I wanted to crawl under a blanket, pull it over my head and pretend none of this was happening but there could be no hiding now.

'Why wouldn't you be able to tell me?' I asked, sifting through feelings and searching for facts, something solid I could hold on to. 'Why did she kill my dad?'

'Until a new Bell witch rises, I'm linked to Catherine,' Ashley replied, only answering the first question and overenunciating every word. 'The caretaker thing? It's not a voluntary position. She knows where I am, she hears what I say. She tied my life to the house on my seventeenth birthday. I literally cannot leave.'

'But you left when you came to collect me?'

She winced, sucking the air in through her teeth. 'Because she let me and it was still agony. Even though Catherine willed it, every mile I travelled away from Savannah was like another knife in my heart. You can take all the herbs you like but they can't do a damn thing for that kind of pain.'

On the opposite side of the room, the brushstrokes on the wallpaper rearranged themselves and a new picture took shape. The storm dissipated and a narrow country road came into view, a clear blue sky, my dad's car travelling at a sensible speed. I watched the little blue Ford making its familiar journey as the skies darkened and the rain came.

'She sent the storm,' I said, incredulous.

'Almost killed her too,' Ashley confirmed. 'Catherine's magic ain't meant to travel so far but she really wanted you home, her special little witch.'

On the walls, the terrible tableau played on. The windshield wipers wouldn't work, the headlights wouldn't come on, and when he hit the brakes, his car sped up, racing to meet the tree as it fell.

'At least he didn't suffer,' she breathed. 'Not like we will.'

The scene faded away and everything was idyllic again, powder blue skies, unmoving birds, willowy trees, but I was forever changed. Nothing could go back to the way it was.

'No point blaming yourself,' Ashley said. 'Paul knew she'd be coming sooner or later. If he didn't want her to have you, he should have killed her and don't look at me like that, you know it's the truth.'

'What kind of person kills their own son?' I sank down to the ground, shivering in the non-existent cold. Magic buzzed over me, no longer a tingle or prickling sensation, but a constant vibration, coating my whole body like a second skin.

'People will do all kinds of things when they're desperate,' Ashley said with enthusiasm. It sounded like she was enjoying her new freedom, every word bubbling out of her. 'And she was desperate.'

'To keep her magic,' I replied. 'She doesn't care about me or the prophecy. She didn't want to lose her magic.'

'Two things can be true at the same time. Her magic may be the most important thing but don't underestimate my mother's pride. She really does believe in the prophecy and she wanted her witch back.'

'I'm not hers, she doesn't own me,' I said, replaying my conversation with Wyn.

We're not our families, we belong to ourselves. And each other.

'Might want to tell her that,' Ashley clucked. 'For a real long time she believed he'd bring you back, didn't think Paul would be able to cope on his own with a new baby. She waited as long as she could but as time wore on, her patience ran out. Her regular magic couldn't locate you, she spent half her fortune trying to track you down the human way, private detectives, that kind of thing, but Paul must have spent just as much hiding you. Did you know your mom was rich?'

My head jerked up, not sure I'd heard her right.

'Oh yeah, Angelica was a very wealthy woman, but money only works for so long. Once Catherine accepted there was only one way to find you, she went all in. You wouldn't believe the darkness she channelled, and that was just to put a pin in a map. Then we went through weeks of how to bring you home. The original plan was to have you abducted and keep you sedated until the Becoming but that wouldn't work because you'd fail the Wilcuma. Had to be your choice to be here. And what better way to accomplish that than to take away all your other choices?'

'So she conjured the storm, made it look like an accident. She used magic to take a life.'

Ashley flinched with pain as she turned her head to look at me, still shaking by the bay windows.

'Catherine's blood brought Paul into this world,' she replied, all her enthusiasm gone now. 'It took her blood to take him out. Almost all of it. I sat at her bedside round the clock for days. Eventually she came around. I didn't even know if the spell had worked until she woke up.'

'That's a neat way to say she murdered her eldest child.'

Ashley didn't correct me.

'It took all those weeks between the storm and the day I came to get you for her to get right again,' she said. 'She's still struggling. All those meetings and appointments? Most of the time she never even leaves the house. She's hiding away in her craft room, doing everything she can to restore her magic.'

I felt sick. I felt hot and cold and shaky and furious. I felt everything and nothing. All this time, she was in the house? Every time I'd wished she was home to help me, she was right here, behind that little blue door? The image of Catherine bleeding out, Ashley sitting beside her while the ground swallowed up her offering, made me nauseous. Across the room, my aunt huffed out a violent sigh, beads of sweat forming on her forehead.

'There were so many times when I thought she might not make it,' Ashley said. 'But she pulled through in the end, she always does. If she hadn't, you and I would both be free now. Imagine that.'

'She didn't need to kill him,' I said, spinning through my

355

emotions like a ball on a roulette wheel, no idea where I would land. 'If she'd sat him down and explained everything, explained how we would lose all connection to the magic if I wasn't here on my birthday, he might have understood.'

Ashley scoffed with disappointment.

'When I told you not to be a fool for love, I wasn't only talking about the wolf,' she grunted, the glassiness in her eyes starting to clear. 'Why don't you get it? I tried to tell you, Paul was surplus to requirements. She only needs you.'

'And I need her,' I admitted, my teeth grinding with my great reluctance. 'I can't go through the Becoming in this state. It'll be 1820 all over again. I need her to bind me.'

'You don't know what really happened in 1820.'

Pain etched itself deeply into Ashley's face as the moss and vines that had wrapped around her legs began to wither and crack. Crawling over to her, I held my hands over the plants and tried to bring them back but it was too late. They were already gone, all their healing power spent.

'Then tell me what did,' I said as she clenched her teeth against the growing agony.

'First I need you to do something,' she croaked. 'Go to Catherine's craft room. Inside, you'll find a sunflower. Bring it out here.'

I didn't argue. I ran out the room and down the hall, Ashley's moans echoing louder once I was gone. Skidding to a halt in front of the sky-blue door, I reached for the handle ready for the burn but today it wasn't even hot. Today it sang, filling me with light as I turned it and entered the room.

The whole space thrummed with energy and as I crossed the threshold, a dozen candles sparked into life. No wonder I couldn't sense Catherine when she was in here, the room was spelled with more charms and curses than I could name. But there was no time to investigate properly, that would have to wait. Instead I scanned the shelves and tables for Ashley's sunflower, forcing myself not to reach for every fascinating thing; journals, spell books, crushed herbs, dozens of different crystals and gems of every possible shape and size. Tucked away in one corner was a narrow bed, a thin mattress studded with herbs, feathers and more crystals. I picked up one of the feathers and held it to the light. Black with red and yellow patches, with rusty stains on the shaft. I dropped it right away. These weren't feathers Catherine had found on the ground.

The sunflower sat on a high shelf above the door, the last place anyone would look, its petals withered and pale from too many days locked away in this dark place. Clambering up onto the nearest desk, I strained to reach it, stretching as far as I dared until my fingertips brushed the terracotta pot. As I made one more push to get a proper hold on it, the sunflower began to bloom and one of the brackets that held up its shelf fell away from the wall. The flower slid down, straight into my arms.

'Thank you,' I said as I climbed back down to the floor, picked up the bracket and placed it on the desk before backing slowly out of the room. It was the first time I'd gone inside. It wouldn't be the last.

'You found it,' Ashley said, unable to hide her surprise when I returned. 'The room let you in.'

'Did you think it might not?' I asked as I pressed the sad sunflower into her open arms.

'Honestly, kind of thought it might unalive you. But yay.'

I glared at my aunt as she turned the pot around in her hands, the petals and leaves of the sunflower growing stronger and brighter every second it was with her.

'Bell House is not a regular house,' she explained as if that wasn't already very obvious. 'If it let you into Catherine's secret

357

little room, well, that changes things. You are part of the house and it is part of you. When the Bell witches are strong, Bell House is strong, when the line is weakened, things begin to fall apart. Literally. That's why you can't go up to the third floor. I'd bet my bottom dollar it'll be as safe as the day is long if your Becoming goes off without a hitch.'

She paused to give me a look. 'Which it won't.'

'What about the sunflower?' I asked, my hand reaching out for the wall without even realizing. She was right. The house was buzzing with energy and urgently calling my name. We were both running out of time.

'This sunflower is me,' she said lightly. 'This is what ties me to Catherine.'

Without taking a single second to explain further, she raised the plant above her head and hurled it at the ground. The terracotta pot smashed into a million tiny pieces, damp black earth soiling the pale wool rug, and the sunflower lay limp in the debris.

'And now that tie is broken.'

'How do you feel?' I asked as we watched it wither and decay in front of us, shrivelling away until it was just dust.

'Like I got crushed by a beam and had my bones and organs put back together by magic. Thanks for that, by the way.'

'You're welcome?'

She picked up a piece of the terracotta pot and smiled, another year of misery rolling away with each heartbeat.

'We don't have much time,' I said, looking first at the clock and then at the fading light that streamed in through the window. 'I don't want to hurt anyone. You have to tell me what really happened in 1820.'

'Every Bell witch is connected, you all draw from those who came before you,' my aunt replied. There was something new in her voice, something I hadn't heard before. It sounded dangerously like hope. 'After you Become, you'll be able to access all the strength and knowledge of our ancestors, dead and alive, but that's not all. Should you choose, you will be able to drain Catherine of her magic. That's what happened in 1820.'

'Catherine said that witch was crazy and her sisters had to bind her.'

Ashley grunted out a laugh.

'Angry woman gets called insane? Wow, what a plot twist. Elizabeth Howell wasn't crazy, she was furious. Witches used to tie the younger generation to their home as a matter of course, to protect them until they came of age, and this girl took offence. Tying isn't the same as binding, it doesn't change a person, just restricts them, like one of those invisible fences they put up to keep dogs in? For me, it means I can't leave the vicinity of Bell House. For others, it might limit their magic, who they can speak to or what they can say. Elizabeth didn't want to be a witch or treated like a dog. She didn't want to live a tethered life. Once her Becoming ceremony was complete, she drained her grandmother and tried to escape but it was too much, she couldn't control all that magic and it overwhelmed her. She killed her grandmother, then set fire to the city and herself. There was no binding, they didn't even get a chance to try it. It's a miracle Emma Catherine, her one so-called friend, survived to continue our line. You and I shouldn't even be here, our family line should have ended that day like the rest of the witch families who died in the fire.'

There was no need to fact check, we had both run out of reasons to lie.

'I don't know what Catherine's planning but I do know she's not going to let you take her magic away. She is not happy with you at all. There's no telling how far she'll go now.'

'But she won't hurt me,' I reasoned. 'She can't risk losing her magic if I die.'

'If she kills you, the magic is gone, but she can bind you, just like you've been begging her to,' Ashley reminded me. 'It's not what you think, binding. You can't tuck magic away for a rainy day and walk around living an ordinary life. You *are* your magic. If Catherine binds your abilities, you'll be living half a life. It'll be agony. Learn the lesson your father didn't. There's only one way to escape her control, you must take control yourself.'

'I'll run.' I was thinking out loud as I circled the room, formulating a plan. 'If we leave now, me and Wyn can be in the middle of nowhere before nightfall.'

'With what money? With what passport? And how are you planning to travel with a phasing wolf? I don't think they allow those in an Uber.'

She flexed her legs, testing the movement before dragging herself into a sitting position. She was getting stronger by the second.

'Catherine would be on you before you'd even crossed state lines. You didn't even go through the Becoming yet and your magic is already lighting up the sky like a flare gun. Why do you think your wolf is so in love with you? Even if he wasn't fully initiated into his pack, he still had magic in his blood when you met.'

'Magic might have drawn us together but that's not why he loves me,' I said, urgent and true and sure of my heart. 'What we have is real.'

'Don't matter much. We're all three of us going to be dead by dawn,' Ashley said as she carefully lowered her feet to the ground. 'Scenario one, your boy phases and kills you. Scenario two, his pack finds you, figures out you killed his brother and they kill you. Scenario three, Catherine kills him, kills me, binds you and you wish you were dead, or best-case scenario number four, you drain Catherine, lose control, set the world on fire and we all die.'

She staggered over to the bar cart in the corner of the room. 'Do you drink? I think we should toast your birthday while we still can.'

The way she laid it out made everything look hopeless. Too many threats, too many ways this could end in nothing but death. That's what happened last time. But I wasn't Elizabeth Howell. As my grandmother so often liked to remind me, I was a Bell.

'She won't kill me and she won't let anyone else kill me either,' I said again, running through Ashley's scenarios in my head, searching for a light in all the darkness. 'It's not just the magic that's important to her, it's the whole Bell line. If I'm gone, it's all gone.'

Ashley paused, listening as she poured.

'Go on.'

'There is one possibility,' I said as she raised a tumbler filled with whiskey in a toast. 'Catherine really believes I'm the witch from the prophecy. What if I am?'

'Oh good,' Ashley cheered. 'You've chosen option four, everybody dies.'

'Maybe,' I admitted. 'But until now, everything has happened to me or around me or because of me. You're right, I need to take control of the situation. She won't kill me and she can't bind me until after the Becoming. All I have to do is fight her and win.'

My aunt yelped out a laugh. 'That's all? Great! I'll make a reservation at Husk for supper since you've got this in the bag. I heard their oysters are to die for.'

'The house let me into her craft room,' I went on, ignoring her very obvious sarcasm. 'You shouldn't be able to tell me

361

any of this but you can because I'm getting stronger. I'm more powerful than she is.'

Ashley stared at me over the rim of her very full glass.

'You know she hates that word,' she said.

'You know she's going to kill you,' I replied.

With one hand still on the bottle, she burst out laughing.

'Emily James, that was pretty good. I'll be sure to think on your heroic speech when my mother comes back here and rips my lungs out of my body.'

Before I could respond, my cell phone buzzed in my back pocket. Lydia's name flashed insistently on the screen and I tapped accept.

'Lyds?' I said as my aunt topped off her drink. 'Please tell me you're calling from somewhere far away?'

'Em, it's Jackson.' The panic in his voice crackled down the line, a bright red energy blaring all the way across town. 'There's something wrong with Lydia. She's awake and breathing but she's not moving or talking, she's just kind of staring at nothing. And I swear I just saw your grandmother out back and it looked like she was carrying a body? Do you have any idea what is going on?'

'I'll be right there,' I told him, glancing over to where Ashley was downing another drink. 'Don't panic, it'll be all right.'

'I'm going to call an ambulance,' Jackson said.

'No, don't, that will only make it worse,' I replied, cutting off his protestations. 'I know it sounds stupid but please just trust me, I'm on my way right now.'

'You've got ten minutes then I'm calling the ambulance,' he said after a moment's consideration. 'I hope I don't regret this.'

I ended the call as the patterns of the wallpaper started to shift again, trees pulling back and birds circling overhead, making way for a new addition. Two tall stone columns I'd seen once before, each topped with a sad-looking figure, both with their heads bowed. A tall, red-haired woman passed through them with the body of a teenage boy slung over her shoulder.

'Well now, ain't that interesting,' Ashley said, still holding the bottle of whiskey as the gates to Bonaventure cemetery swung shut behind them. 'Looks like the house has chosen a side. At least we know where they are. Unless it's a trap.'

'It probably is,' I admitted. 'I still have to go after them.'

She reached over and placed her hand on my shoulder, a warm smile I'd never seen before on her face. 'Whatever happens, I want you to know you're not alone in this.'

A jolt of gratitude shot through me and I returned her smile.

'Because she's going to kill us both.'

'Thanks for the vote of confidence,' I muttered, smile melting away.

'Any time,' she replied with a thumbs up. 'Let's do this.'

Things were worse than Jackson realized. By the time we tumbled into the Powells' parlour, Lydia was catatonic. Sitting upright on the sofa, she stared straight ahead, her brown eyes completely blank. I crouched down in front of her, searching for her bold energy but came up with nothing. Her body was with us but Lydia was somewhere else entirely.

'I can't believe I'm out of the house,' Ashley said, staring around the parlour with wonder. 'And I can't believe Catherine would do this again.'

She pushed me out the way and took hold of Lydia's hands.

'You know what this is? She's done it before?' I replied. 'When?'

Ashley looked back at me like she had terrible news she did not care to deliver.

'*She was awake, her eyes were open, but she simply wasn't there.*'

'My mom.' I exhaled, all the air knocked out of me. 'This is what she did to my mom.'

'Who did what?' Jackson demanded to know. 'What are you talking about?'

'I think I can help.' Ashley spoke to me as though he wasn't even there. 'I've been working on a cure, just in case she ever decided I was too much trouble but, thankfully, I haven't been able to test it out. But you need to stop Catherine. If the herbs don't work, taking her out might be the only way to get Lydia back.'

'Will someone please tell me what is going on?' Jackson yelled, his face bright red and full of fury.

I turned towards him, desperately trying to calm the energy in the room and only halfway succeeding.

'We're going to help Lydia,' I promised. 'I know it's confusing and we're asking you to take a lot on trust but I don't have time to explain it all right now.'

'Emily is a super mega witch and she's maybe going to blow up the whole city tonight but fingers crossed she won't,' Ashley said. 'My mother, also a witch, is planning to bind Emily's magic to stop her ending the family line but she needs her to go through this whole ceremony thing first so she, Catherine that is, has cursed your sister and kidnapped Wyn the werewolf to get Emily where she wants her. That pretty much brings you up to speed. Any questions?'

'Emily?' Jackson said my name weakly, turning to me for verification.

'She covered it pretty well,' I replied, forcing my mouth into the world's least convincing smile.

'Wyn is the guy you were dating?' he said.

I nodded.

'He's a werewolf?'

'Probably.'

'And you're a witch?'

'Definitely.'

He sank down on the sofa next to his sister, a similar blank look on his face.

'Before we lose you too,' I said, squatting down in front of him, 'is this a terrible time to ask for a ride?'

He wiped a hand over his face. 'It's not great.'

'Then you'll never get your sister back.' Ashley dumped out a backpack full of herbs and crystals she'd grabbed on the way out of Bell House, onto the floor. 'Emily is Lydia's best chance. Help her and you're helping your sister.'

'I need to get to Catherine,' I agreed, squeezing his hand. 'It's the only way to put a stop to all of this. I know you must have a million more questions but—'

'Em, we should be in the car already,' Jackson said decisively, pulling a set of car keys out of his pocket and striding straight to the door. 'You can explain the rest on the way.'

Chapter Thirty-Nine

'Here we are. Happy birthday, Emily.'

Bonaventure looked just like I remembered but it didn't feel the same. I didn't feel the same. Overhead, the peach-pink sunset sky promised this would all be over soon. The moon moved closer with every passing second and I felt my magic growing, covering my body like armour.

'You're sure this is a good idea?' Jackson looked extremely perturbed. 'You don't even know where you're going. I could come with you.'

'I couldn't let you,' I replied, warmed by the knowledge that he really meant it. 'Don't worry about me, she'll be easy enough to find. I have to go the rest of the way on my own.'

He rested his hand on my shoulder, eyebrows drawn together.

'But you don't have to.'

'I know.' I opened the passenger-side door of his Audi and climbed out. 'Thank you. You're a really good brother and a really great friend.'

'Walking straight into the jaws of certain doom and she still had time to friendzone me,' he said with a chuckle. 'I know this is the wrong time for it but really, Em? You threw me over for a werewolf?'

'Wasn't intentional.' I smiled, tying my hair up and back in a tight ponytail. 'And I am sorry. Anyone would be lucky to date you, Jackson.'

'Well, you still owe me that rain check. Don't think I won't hold you to it.'

He put the car in reverse and backed up a couple of feet. 'You're sure you don't want me to wait?'

Looking over at Catherine's car, parked up in front of the church, a blank Barnett in the driver's seat, I shook my head.

'If everything works out, I'll have a ride,' I told him. 'As soon as you get back, I need you and Ashley to put Lyds in the car and get as far out of town as possible. Promise me.'

'I will,' he said solemnly and I felt his fear and anger before it showed up on his face. 'Em?'

'Yes?'

'Kick her ass.'

I waited right where I was and watched him drive away, not moving until the tail lights disappeared. I couldn't promise any of them would be safe after this but at least he had a head start.

The first time Catherine brought me to Bonaventure, it was to meet our dead relatives. This time, I passed through the cemetery hoping not to join them. I moved swiftly past the graves as night fell, following whispers in the moss that guided me over and across and around, running faster than I might have guessed towards my own possible end. There was no point in delaying the inevitable. She made sure I would come, she almost certainly knew I was here. I could feel her and Wyn, their very different energies both calling to me across the cemetery. Out-of-season azaleas burst into life to draw me through the maze, leading me along the banks of the Wilmington River. The carefree flowers didn't know the danger they were in, only that a new Bell witch was about to Become and as far as they were concerned, that was cause for celebration. But the sleeping residents of Bonaventure had heard differently. The statues turned and hung their heads sadly, glowing under the full moon, and I offered them a sympathetic smile as I passed. This night should have been shrouded in darkness, not blessed by the beautiful, milky moonlight. They'd earned their eternal rest, they shouldn't have to see this.

'She's waiting for you.'

A tiny voice, sweet and high and clear as a bell, rang out from the darkness. It was a little girl, no more than five or six, with long hair and bangs framing her pretty face. Her shoes had a row of pearl buttons up one side and her dress was pristine, despite the fact she was happily sitting in the dirt. Above her, I saw a statue on top of a grave. The same hair. The same shoes. The same dress. The same little girl.

'Do you know where my grandmother is?' I asked softly. She inclined her head to one side and smiled.

'Don't you?'

'The Bell monument,' I guessed and she nodded.

'Could you open the gate for me?' the little girl asked, tiny hands wrapped around the tall railings that surrounded her grave. 'I haven't been out to play for such a long time.'

No harm could come to her now. I held the padlock that kept her inside in my hand. It was made of steel. Steel was made of iron, iron came from the earth. A flurry of vines swooped down from the closest tree, smothering the lock, squeezing it tighter and tighter until I heard it pop. The gate swung open and the little girl skipped towards me.

'People leave me presents sometimes,' she said, kneeling down to pick through a pile of trinkets that sat outside the grave. 'I can't reach them through the fence. They put it up to keep me safe but they didn't know it would trap me inside. They thought they were helping.'

'People do that sometimes,' I told her as she held her gifts up to the moon to inspect them more clearly, smiling with delight at each one. 'They mean well.'

'Yes, they do.' A deliberative expression overcame her innocent face then she giggled, listening to something I could not hear. 'Your father loves you so much,' she said happily. 'He didn't mean for any of this to happen.'

Shaken, I blew a long, slow stream of air out of pursed lips while she carried on sorting through her treasures, unmoved.

'This is for you.'

She held out a shiny glass marble, shot through with shades of green and grey and brown, the same colours as Wyn's eyes. 'Happy birthday, Emily.'

'Thank you,' I replied, slipping the marble into my pocket and rubbing my sleeve across my wet cheeks. 'Take care.'

'Goodbye!' she called as I returned to the path. 'Come play with me again soon!'

'Hopefully not too soon,' I murmured as I ran.

With clear direction, I pushed onwards, only glancing over my shoulder when I heard a rushing sound at my back. The river had burst its banks. A king tide, just like the one on the night I was born. Water swept into the cemetery and washed away my footsteps, swallowing up all the concrete footpaths so no one could follow. But who would want to?

Soon, too soon, I arrived at the Bell family monument. The sombre grey block of marble was still topped by the angelic statue but the flat slab of concrete in front of it had been replaced by a stone staircase, descending into pitch-black nothingness. The grotto chapel.

'Oh, Emily.' Catherine's voice echoed, disapproving, through the dark. 'You didn't wear your gown.'

'I'm sorry.' I looked down at my dirty jeans and blood-stained shirt. 'There wasn't time to change.'

She stepped out from behind a neighbouring crypt, one that was much flashier than ours, adorned with crosses and bells and urns. Whoever was inside had done everything they could to buy salvation but I couldn't help but think they were trying too hard. The same could hardly be said for Catherine. She looked spectacular, wearing a white silk gown similar to the one she'd had made for me, her long hair shining scarlet.

'Is Ashley still alive?' she asked.

'Ashley is doing great,' I confirmed. 'Getting out of the house has done her a world of good.'

The corner of her eye twitched and I took a bold step forward.

'I'm not going to complete the Becoming, so if you're going to kill me, you might as well do it now.'

'What makes you think I want to kill you?' She looked completely horrified at the thought. 'Honey, the only thing I want in this world is for you to Become. I've dedicated the last seventeen years to this moment, killing you is the last thing I want to do.'

'But you were happy to kill my dad,' I countered. 'And my mom.'

Her eyes and the silver ceremonial dagger I saw in her hand both flashed with the same threat of violence.

'I wouldn't say "happy" but I did what had to be done. It was all for you.'

Circling away from the staircase, I kept my distance from

the monument and stayed close to the trees, their reassuring voices rushing around me.

'You're sure about that? I think you might be doing it for yourself.'

Catherine weighed my question for a moment then shrugged. 'I guess it's a little of both.'

Just like Ashley said, two things can be true.

'I'm still not going through with the ceremony,' I declared. 'I don't want to be a witch. I want to be normal.'

'There's that heinous word again,' she sneered. 'Normal. As if you've ever been normal, ever could be normal. Refusing to go through with the ceremony won't save you from anything, Emily, only destroy who you really are. Is that what you want? To kill a part of yourself?'

'I don't know, I haven't had as much experience with killing as you have,' I replied. 'But if it saves someone I love, then I'm OK with it.'

'And what about the things I've done to save what I love?' she bellowed and the trees trembled. 'The sacrifices I have made to protect you and this family? You will complete the ceremony, albeit in that ugly ensemble. Truly, I don't know why I tried so hard with you. The ugly accent, the lack of style, like trying to make a silk purse out of a sow's ear.'

'You can't make me do it,' I told her, the moss creeping up from the floor and wrapping around my ankles, not holding me down but lifting me up, giving me strength. 'Without me, the magic dies, right? And you're just a regular old woman.'

She gasped. 'Old? How dare you?'

Slowly but purposefully, she moved towards me. I could tell she didn't believe me. It wasn't conceivable to her, the idea that I would willingly surrender my connection to magic. Not when she was prepared to sacrifice her own son to secure it.

'You've put us both in quite the predicament, honey.' Her

voice was a musical sigh. 'You *could* leave but if you don't complete the ceremony, you won't be able to save your friend or your wolf.'

'Lydia is your best friend's granddaughter, how could you do this to her?' I asked, trying to distract her while I searched for Wyn's energy. He was somewhere nearby but I couldn't see exactly where. Something was blocking me. Wherever she had him hidden, he was in pain and his pulse was getting weaker.

'It's amazing what you're capable of after you sacrifice the life of your beloved firstborn son,' Catherine replied, testing the tip of the knife with her pointer finger. 'Ginny should thank me. That girl will be a lot less trouble now.'

'You're not a witch, you're a monster.'

'Speaking of monsters,' she replied with a wink, 'it really was very helpful of you to have your wolf in the house last night so I could smarten up my Were-taming spell. Usually I don't allow dogs up on the furniture but we'll make an exception in his case.'

'You knew he was in the house?' I was instantly angry at myself for sounding so surprised.

'Emily, honey, I'm your grandmother and I'm a witch. A fly can't hiccup in my house without me knowing about it. Did you really think you could sneak around with a boy from a Were family and I wouldn't notice?' Catherine laughed but it wasn't a pleasant sound. 'I've known since the very beginning. I didn't see any harm in letting it play out for a while. Your romantic walks, the trip to the beach. I almost drew a line at your sleepover but thankfully, you've got yourself a little gentleman there. At least he was raised right. Well, as much as a wolf can be.'

Around us, the trees began to creak and bend just as they had at Wormsloe, binding together in an impenetrable wall around me, Catherine, and the Bell monument, blocking out the rest of Bonaventure and keeping me in. Keeping her in with me.

Behind my grandmother was a towering stone archway. The one from my vision. I couldn't tell if the vines that decorated it from top to bottom were alive or carved into stone. Everything pulsed with the same dark energy, dead and alive. 'He doesn't have a lot of time. If he phases while he's under my spell, well, let's just say it won't be pretty and it would be a shame to mess up that handsome face. With that in mind, shall we get this show on the road?'

Catherine stood firm, framed by the arch with the moon high above her, arms outstretched. 'Emily Caroline James, do you accept the blessing as the blessing accepts you?'

Somewhere in the cemetery, I heard Wyn howl.

This was it, this was the moment. Leave and risk Wyn and Lydia's lives, Ashley would never be safe, or Jackson. Even without magic, Catherine would still be incredibly powerful, a rich, influential woman, and what would I be? A lonely orphan with nothing and no one. She would retain her place in the world but no one would miss me if I were to mysteriously disappear. Or I could stay and Become. Complete the ceremony, accept my magic and play Catherine at her own game.

I made my choice.

'That's not my name,' I said, calmly stepping forward. 'If we're going to do this, let's do it properly.'

'I knew you wouldn't walk away,' Catherine whispered, glowing with victory. 'Emma Catherine Bell, do you accept the blessing as the blessing accepts you?'

Breathing in, I stepped up to the arch and the sky filled with clouds. The rain came suddenly, pouring down from the sky, and when the lightning struck, it was so close, I could smell the singed grass. Once I passed through the archway, there would be no turning back.

'I do,' I declared.

For Wyn, for Ashley, Lydia, Jackson, my mom and my dad. But most of all, for myself.

'As the full moon represents wholeness and completion, we ask those who came before us to complete the Becoming and make our daughter whole,' Catherine intoned, dagger held high. 'We ask those who came before us to bring her into the blessing. We ask those who came before us to offer her their strength and wisdom, and show her the path she must follow.'

The sound of the wind and the rain disappeared, engulfed by the dozens of voices that called to me, a siren song promising everything I'd ever wanted if I would just pass under the arch. I took one step, then another. On the threshold of the archway, I paused. On the other side, I saw Bonaventure not as it was now but how it used to be. Quieter and more beautiful, with fewer graves and more open space, birds and butterflies fluttering happily in the sky. The sun shone like it was the middle of the day and a tall, elegant woman with long red hair stepped into view, holding up a hand to beckon me forward. I couldn't see her face but I knew who she was.

It was me. Not as I was now but as I could be.

As I would be.

My future in Savannah's past.

I took the final step through the archway and the lightning stopped, the rain ended, the sky was clear again and every inch of my being was set aflame.

The Becoming had truly begun.

'OK then!' my grandmother exclaimed with delight as I stepped down from the arch, stumbling back into the present day, already reeling with the new magic that flowed through my veins. 'Now it's time for the fun part.'

Light hides the lies; truth lives in the dark.

I remembered my first warning as I followed Catherine down the stone staircase at the base of the Bell monument and into the grotto chapel, running my hands along the crumbling dry walls and feeling out each uneven step with the toe of my shoe before planting it down. It made sense now. All the lies I'd been told in the cold light of day while Catherine hid the truth in the dark of her craft room and down here, in the underground chapel. The way everything went black before I experienced a vision. Truth lives in the dark. The blessing had tried to tell me.

Every vine and flower in Bonaventure wanted to be close to me as my magic grew, and they followed me down, down, down until I reached the bottom of the stairs where they stopped dead, shrinking back from the darkness. I didn't blame them, I didn't want to be there either. Nothing could thrive down here, there was no chance of life, only reminders of death.

'So, what do you think of the place?' Catherine asked, waving a proud hand around the chapel as she moved comfortably through the space. 'As final resting places go, it's pretty swell.'

When she first described it, I'd pictured a small, claustrophobic space, packed full of decaying coffins, but this was one of the most magnificent things I'd ever seen. The chapel was lit by black-flamed candles and torches, and casket-sized spaces had been carved into the walls so our ancestors could rest comfortably in their polished coffins. There were two rows of wooden pews on the marble floor for living guests and small square cushions for more comfortable kneeling. At the far end of the short aisle, I saw an altar I recognized from my visions.

And in front of it stood my grandmother.

'It really is something,' I said, one hand on the back of a pew to keep me upright as the change in me intensified. 'Incredibly creepy vibes. It's giving ritualistic sacrifice. Not sure it sets the right tone for a birthday party.'

Catherine clucked her tongue.

'I did try to spruce it up a little but you know how it is, there's only so much you can do with an underground chapel.'

'Must be tough to schedule a cleaner,' I agreed, the blood in my veins burning. She had to know the pain was excruciating but I couldn't let her see my agony. 'If only you'd let me know, I could have brought the vacuum with me.'

Apparently she wasn't in the mood for anyone's jokes but her own. The black flames of the candles guttered as Catherine turned back to the altar, lightly tapping the items she had up there, the same way my dad used to check for his phone, wallet, and car keys every time he left the house. A gold cup, a pile of herbs, some sparkling twine, the dagger from Wormsloe and her silver pin.

The same one I thought was safely hidden in my nightstand drawer.

The fire inside me continued to rage and I didn't know how much longer I could contain it. I was starting to doubt my decision. How could I overpower Catherine if I could barely stay up on my own two feet?

'Are you ready, honey?' she asked, her voice soft and inviting.

'Ready for what?' I replied, maintaining a safe distance between us as best I could. 'Binding, Becoming or death?'

She laughed and shook her head. 'No one is going to die, Emily. Well, the wolf might not make it but as I believe I mentioned once before, no one mourns a wolf.'

Her green eyes flicked to the front pew and a muted howling filled the chapel. At once the veil lifted and I felt him in the same moment I heard him. Ignoring my own pain, I rushed

376

down the aisle, skidding to a stop where Wyn lay on the floor, writhing against the sharp, thin wire I'd seen on the altar. His skin was pasty and clammy, his ashy hair a dull rusty red and his sweat- and blood-soaked clothes clung to his body.

'Whatever you're doing to him, make it stop,' I demanded, my trembling hands trying and failing to soothe his agony. 'I'm here now, you've got what you wanted, you have to let him go.'

'No, I don't think I will.' Catherine took a seat on a golden chair at the head of the altar and crossed her legs at the ankles. 'It's not always easy, you know, doing the right thing. There are casualties, consequences. Not everyone will understand. For years I did my best to keep people happy, tried to be a good witch for my grandmother, a good wife, a good mother to Paul and Ashley, and look where that got me? Woman to woman, trying so hard all the time is exhausting.'

'At least help me take off the barbed wire,' I begged, not even slightly interested in her reasoning. 'It's killing him.'

'That's because it's silver. Soaked in aconite. He must be in an unbelievable amount of pain,' she said with a heavy sigh. 'Collecting wolfie here was the only fun part of my day. Took him a while to get wise, for a moment there I thought he might just walk himself right here. He's a good dog, very obedient, but what was it my mother used to say? Don't fight unless you have to but when you do, fight like you're the third monkey on the ramp to Noah's ark and it's starting to sprinkle. That boy felt it sprinkling just a little too late. I haven't had a good fight in years but he sure gave me one.'

'I'm so sorry,' I murmured into Wyn's ear but I couldn't tell if he could hear me. Holding my hands against his heart, I could feel his pain but he didn't even have the strength left to scream. Every time he moved, the silver barbs cut into his bloodless skin, pushing the aconite she'd laced it with deeper and deeper, torturing him from within.

'I do see the attraction, Emily, he loves you very much. If it weren't for the fact he's wrapped in silver wire and dosed up with enough aconite to put down a bull elephant, that boy would still be fighting for you, I guarantee it.' She picked up the silver pin and pressed the point into the tip of her finger. 'Since you took his brother out with this so very easily, I brought it along just in case he gave us any trouble, but I don't think we'll need it, do you?'

I reached into my pocket, the little girl's glass marble still there, and pulled out a pouch of herbs Ashley had pressed into my hand on my way out the Powell house. Yarrow, mugwort, and rue. Courage, protection, and self-belief. I opened the pouch and emptied it into Wyn's palm, rubbing the dried flowers into his hands. He needed them more than I did.

'If we removed the silver and allowed him to phase, he would heal right away,' I heard Catherine say. 'The only drawback to that plan is that he wouldn't recognize you once he was a wolf, most likely he'd rip your throat out. You should keep hold of the pin, just in case.'

She held it out but I didn't take it.

'You're sure? An ounce of prevention is worth a pound of the cure. Not that there is a cure for having your throat ripped out.'

'You must love to see people suffer,' I said, ignoring my own pain as Wyn convulsed beside me. 'This is inhuman.'

'Says the girl who is in love with a wolf,' Catherine snapped back.

Wyn groaned and a worrying wet gurgle emerged from the back of his throat. The dried herbs weren't going to be enough, I needed something more, something alive, but nothing could grow down here in the dark, dank chapel.

378

'You were the one, Emily. You were destined to bring back our sisters, dig the blessing out of the dark, but I see it now. You can't be trusted. Our family, *my family*, has protected this magic for centuries and I'm expected to hand it over to a girl who is perfectly happy to set that legacy on fire for an animal? After all the sacrifices I made to bring you here? I don't think so, honey.'

'You didn't sacrifice anything,' I yelled back, turning to face her with fierce eyes. 'My parents are the ones who paid with their lives.'

'I loved my son,' she roared, full of pain and rage. 'Paul left me no choice. Losing him *was* my sacrifice, taking his life almost killed me in more ways than one. I almost died to bring you here.'

I forced out a cruel laugh.

'And that would have been a real shame.'

'The mouth on you. Just like your mother,' Catherine said scornfully as I pushed my hair away from my face, my hastily tied ponytail coming loose. 'If you weren't in Savannah right this very second, your magic would have passed, taking mine along with it. Your father should have been proud to call you a witch but instead he hid you away, denying who and what you are. What was I supposed to do, betray our ancestors? Let the line die?'

'Yes,' I replied, scouring the chapel floor for something that might help Wyn. He was fading fast and I didn't dare leave his side. 'Nothing lasts forever, maybe it was time. Maybe our magic was supposed to end.'

'And that's how I know you do not deserve it.'

Catherine rose from her chair and raised her arms. At the other end of the aisle, a sheet of rock slammed down from the ceiling, sealing us all inside. 'You don't understand. Selfish, just like the rest of your generation. No concept of making a sacrifice for the greater good.'

Above us, I felt the moon rise to its highest peak and fire scorched every cell in my body from the inside out. My limbs seized up and I collapsed on the floor beside Wyn.

'I should have told you this part can sting,' Catherine said, her words far away, crackling through a different channel than the one I was tuned in to. 'After a witch passes through the archway and the moon is at its peak, she is more vulnerable until the exchange of blood. As I recall, it burns a little. Mostly the exchange occurs right away but I thought this might do you some good. Spare the rod, spoil the child as they say. Try not to fight, it'll be over soon and you won't feel anything much at all.'

Not even the marble floor of the chapel could cool me. I'd never known pain like it, the heat scalding my skin like I'd been tossed in a pot of boiling oil, and melting my insides at the same time.

'Once we exchange blood, the Becoming will be complete and I will be forced to resolve this issue. I wish things had been different, Emily, I really do. Today should've been a celebration.'

Helpless and overwhelmed, I was only able to keep my eyes open for a second but a second was enough. There was a crack in the wall, then the smallest possible split in the stone, and a single tendril of Spanish moss pushed its way through and crept along the ground towards me.

'What happens next?' I forced the words out of my bone dry throat, fighting off the excruciating pain one agonizing breath at a time. The moss was moving at such a slow pace, I had to give it a chance. I needed more time. 'If you try to bind me, I'll drain you.'

'No, you won't. Not unless you want me to end your boy's suffering right now,' Catherine said. 'I can end Lydia's life also, if you would prefer.'

Focusing only on the moss and not the horror of her threats, I said nothing.

'It won't be enough to simply bind you. You're already so strong, I can't begin to imagine what strength you'll have after the ritual is complete. Too much for anything so basic. Luckily, I found something else inspired by our friend Elizabeth Howell. When her sisters tried to bind her, she was too strong to be contained, but I believe, if I combine the binding and draining spells, things will go just fine. For me, anyway. How does that sound?'

'Not great,' I answered with a grunt.

'No, I suspect it won't be.' She stood to set the pin back on the altar. 'You can't return to Bell House, it would never approve of what I'm about to do, so I'll keep you down here where you'll be safe – not dead but it's no real life – and drain your magic back into me over time rather than all at once. Kind of a slow drip, nice and steady. That should avoid any combustible side effects. Perhaps one day, a long time from now, we'll revisit our arrangement. I can't say for sure what impact draining your magic will have on your mental capacity but I imagine you'll be more, shall we say, compliant?'

I reached one more time but the moss was still beyond my grasp. With a sob of despair, I twisted around onto my back and looked up. In my delirium, I could see through the stone ceiling and up into the sky. The moon shone brighter than any sun and I felt its cool, soothing power against my scalding skin. Then, something soft and feathery brushed against my fingers and the furnace inside me flared again. The Spanish moss.

'Catherine, I'm sorry,' I said, fighting for time as Wyn's breathing made a sharp and erratic shift. The moss wound itself around my hand, circling my wrist and creeping up my arm. A shot of adrenaline cut straight through my pain, sharp as steel. 'You were right, I was wrong. The magic is the only thing that matters, I get it now. Don't you think I've learned my lesson?'

'Don't you think I've learned mine?' she snapped. 'Actions speak louder than words, young lady, and yours cannot be trusted. This is the only way.'

As she busied herself at the altar, I forced myself to move, shuffling around to the other side of Wyn's broken body. Vines snaked around me, reviving and renewing, lending me their resilience. Above ground, the full moon set Bonaventure alight, but not with the black flames I'd foreseen. Every leaf on every tree curled in my direction and all the Spanish moss in Savannah burned with a brilliant white light, and all of that light poured into this chapel, through my body and into Wyn.

'I'd love to say it won't hurt,' Catherine said with her back to me, full of regret as she took inventory of her supplies. 'But that would be a lie. The herbs alone aren't exactly friendly. Belladonna, snap dragon, fly agaric . . .'

Wyn's screams tore through the chapel as I touched one finger to the silver that bound him. The vines knew what to do. They wended their way over to him, slipping between the wire and his wounds, creating space for him to breathe. I pulled at the loosened barbs, shredding the skin on my hands and silently screaming with this new agony. Wyn's screams were not so quiet. As soon as the last silver barb was removed, the phase began. I turned away, unable to bear the pain in his face. When I looked back, the pain was gone and so was Wyn.

All that remained was the wolf.

'I added a little lily of the valley to the spell to help put you to sleep,' Catherine called as his new mouth stretched into a snarl. 'But I don't know what good it will do. Didn't seem to help your boy any.'

'I don't know,' I replied, crawling backwards down the aisle. 'I think he's doing better.'

The wolf let out a howl vicious enough to tear the fabric of my reality in two.

Before and after.

'You little fool,' Catherine hissed, stumbling in her rush to get behind the altar. 'You've trapped us in here with a male Were in its first phase? That's not your boy anymore, it's an animal! It doesn't recognize you, all it knows is how badly it wants to kill you.'

'Better him than you.' I held my hands out in front of me, the moss that had freed Wyn wrapping around my body. 'If he kills me, at least this is all over.'

Wyn the wolf reared back, his claws scuffling against the smooth marble, struggling to gain purchase. His fur was golden but his eyes were the same, green and grey, the same colour as the Spanish moss. He might not recognize me but I would have known him anywhere. My Wyn was still in there.

Hiding behind the altar, Catherine scrabbled for something to defend herself with but Wyn wasn't concerned with her. He stood facing me, his lip curled up to reveal the threat of his razor-sharp teeth as he deliberated his next move.

'Wyn,' I said, clear but kind. 'It's me, Em.'

He replied with uncertain growls, still getting to grips with his transformation, feeling his way around his new body.

'You're not going to hurt me,' I told him, taking one very small and careful step closer. 'And I'm going to get you out of here.'

'No,' Catherine said, suddenly right behind him. 'You're not.'

Everything that happened next was a blur.

I saw the dagger in her hand but there wasn't enough time to react. The blade came down fast, sinking into Wyn's shoulder, right up to the hilt. He howled, a soul-splitting sound, and reared back on his hind legs, knocking me to the ground with his left front paw and giving my grandmother the opportunity she needed.

'Catherine, no!'

I screamed as she lunged at him, holding the silver pin in her other hand and driving it deep into his chest. He careened backwards, howling with fear and confusion, then crashed into the row of pews, leaving nothing more than splinters. Then he was still. Breathing, just barely, but completely still. I tried to go to him but I couldn't move, my strength ebbing away somehow. I looked down to see the front of my shirt sliced open, a strange new feeling pulsing through my body, hot then cold. It wasn't just Ashley's blood that stained my shirt anymore. Four clean gashes opened up my belly and painted me ruby red.

'Emily,' Catherine gasped, lurching towards me with absolute terror in her eyes. 'Emily, no.'

'He didn't mean to,' I said, woozy and lightheaded as I grasped my mom's locket.

'We've got to stop the bleeding,' my grandmother rambled as my eyes fluttered open and closed. 'You cannot die. Let me think, stay with me, just let me think.'

But it was difficult to make promises as the edges of my vision began to blur, my blood almost black against the white marble of the floor. Catherine scurried around, gathering piles of moss from the ground to staunch the blood flowing from my stomach, but as soon as it registered her touch, the moss withered away to dust. In a daze, I watched her scuttle back to the altar, searching through the objects and herbs, tears pouring down her face, while she searched for something that might help.

'We can do it together if we concentrate,' she said, nodding her head as she gathered the supplies. 'You did it for Ashley, we can do it for you.'

'This isn't the same, you can't stop it.' My words were losing shape as the light dimmed. I thought it would take longer to bleed out. I was wrong.

'Not alone but we can together. You are a Bell witch, Emily, and you are too strong to be killed by some wolf.'

'A knife can be a weapon or a tool,' I croaked with Catherine back by my side. 'You thought Wyn was a tool but you made him a weapon.'

She carried on regardless, tearing strips of fabric from the bottom of her dress and wrapping them tightly around my middle. 'Not like this, it's not going to end like this,' she muttered, holding my chin in her hand and forcing me to look at her. 'There is one last thing we can try. Whatever it takes to keep the blessing alive.'

Leaving my side just long enough to crawl over to Wyn, she reached across his trembling, prone wolf-form. Her pin had already dislodged itself, sparkling on the floor in a pool of his blood, and the sound he made when she wrenched the dagger out of his shoulder cracked a hole in the marble at the entrance of the chapel.

'Taking someone's life is easier when you don't have to look them in the eye,' she confessed, returning to me with the dagger in her hand. 'Maybe if I give you mine, you'll be able to forgive me someday.'

'Catherine, don't,' I begged, understanding what she meant only when it was too late.

'We ask those who came before us to bring her into the blessing,' screamed my grandmother, demanding the attention of our ancestors. 'As whole as the moon, she will Become.'

She wiped the silver blade on her skirt then held it out in front of me, determination on her face as she slashed her own palm with only the slightest intake of breath, and when she pressed her hand to my stomach, mixing her blood with mine,

I felt the fire reignite inside me. The final step in the ceremony. The sudden spark caught onto every fibre of my being and ignited. All the things I'd glimpsed through the open door at my Wilcuma poured into me, all the knowledge, all the history, all the magic. Every Bell witch who had ever lived, everything they'd ever experienced, now existed in me.

The Becoming was complete.

But Catherine wasn't done.

'Take from me,' she ordered, making another deeper cut in her hand. This time I could tell that it hurt. 'What is needed is offered freely. Take from me. *Drēahnian.*'

My blood ran white hot, lava flowing through me like I was the earth's core, molten metal made flesh, but it was too much, too strong. The dried Spanish moss on the floor of the chapel began to smoulder before bursting into black flames with white hearts. The fire raced along the ground, searching for an escape. I looked around, Catherine broken and bloody, the wolf, the black candles. This was it. The beginning of the end.

'You have to stop, you have to let me go,' I commanded, the fire spreading through the chapel with supernatural speed. 'I can't control it.'

Catherine shook her head. She collapsed to the ground at the side of me, no strength left to fight.

'Then let it burn.'

'If we burn, everything burns,' I argued as the flames danced around us. I felt stronger but not strong enough. 'If we don't do something, it will destroy the city.'

'Maybe it's time.' Catherine touched her bloody hand to my heart, staring into my eyes. 'I've done terrible things to keep this magic alive and at what cost? Every time I think I've done enough, sacrificed enough, I have to give more. Your mother and father's lives, Ashley's freedom, my own blood, and now you? I can't do this anymore. You were right, all things must end.'

386

'But not yet.'

Another voice. Another person. Over Catherine's shoulder, I saw the white-haired woman who had haunted me since I arrived in Savannah, only her hair wasn't white anymore, it was bright red, and her eyes shone like emeralds. Behind her, a dozen or more women, all red-haired, all green-eyed, looked down at me with love.

'It is time for a change but not an ending,' the very first Emma Catherine Bell told my grandmother, pulling her from me as my bleeding slowed then stopped altogether. 'You can let go. She is stronger than any of us.'

I pushed the makeshift bandages away from my stomach and saw the flesh knitting itself back together, just like the orchid. Choking on the rising smoke from the black fire as it raged on, I stared up at my ancestor.

'Are you doing this?' I asked. 'Or am I?'

'We do everything as one,' she replied and the other women bowed their heads. 'What's more important is what you do next. What will you decide, Emily?'

The altar had already disappeared behind a cloud of smoke and my eyes were stinging, lungs screaming out for oxygen I could not find.

'It's not my decision if I don't know how to stop it,' I told her. 'But I don't want this.'

'All you have to do is make the choice. Stop trying and know it is done.' She paused and touched her hand to my face. 'Find your peace.'

I knew what I had to do.

Rolling over, I winced as I crawled through the fire, the flames licking at me but leaving me unharmed as I made my way across the chapel floor. Wyn lay helpless, a heaving mound of blood and fur. I picked up one of his paws and brought it to my lips, the horror of the things I'd seen in my visions snapping at the edges of my consciousness. All of the destruction and decay, me at the heart of it, Wyn and Catherine in the flames. But I didn't have to accept someone else's version of my destiny. Blind faith made Catherine equally strong and dangerous. I would not follow a path that no longer served us simply because someone who died centuries before I was born said I should. Wrapping my hand around wolf-Wyn's sharp claws, I closed my eyes and slowed my breathing, relaxing into the peace only he could give me.

Everything went quiet as I fell away into the nowhere space.

This time the vision was different. I was still surrounded by black flames on every side, Catherine was still bleeding on the altar. But this time, the wolf stood by my side and behind us there were dozens of other women, all of them vibrant with magic. What we were facing wasn't clear yet but the message was that when the time came, I wouldn't be alone.

Something soft and cold fluttered onto my face, bringing me back from the vision as it smothered the flames. Snow. It was snowing inside the chapel. As the wolf's paw shifted back into Wyn's hand, his fingers curled around mine and at once, the black fires burned out.

'We weren't able to speak freely before your Becoming,' Emma Catherine Bell said as I fell on Wyn, pressing my lips to his forehead as he moaned, still not entirely conscious. 'It will be easier now we're connected.'

'My visions,' I replied, almost oblivious to the miracle falling from the ceiling, too busy watching Wyn. 'All those things I saw. They could still happen?'

'The prophecy has not come to pass,' my ancestor confirmed. 'Perhaps, at one time, what you saw could have been your Becoming but you changed that. You made a choice that set us on another path.'

'A better one?' I asked with hope.

'A different one,' she offered. 'You will not be able to turn back from it now but we will be with you. Our actions are entwined, everything you do and everything we ever did now lives in you.'

All of her descendants stepped forward to surround Catherine as she turned her attention to my stunned and silent grandmother. 'And it is with great sadness that we do this.'

They swarmed around Catherine until she was completely hidden from my view and the ground beneath us quaked with her fear. The scream that filled the chapel was as agonizing as anything that happened before or after. Then all her panic faded away. I couldn't feel her anymore. When the spirits pulled away, my grandmother's body lay on the floor, eyes closed and smiling.

'Is she . . . gone?' I asked the first Bell witch as the others moved to line the walls of the chapel, each standing sentry by their own casket.

Emma Catherine Bell ran her hands over my hair. My breath hitched in my throat as I saw it turn from reddish-brown to scarlet, her ancient magic passing through me. I was truly whole, truly who I was meant to be.

'Catherine isn't dead,' she said. 'Your grandmother has her own choice to make.'

Holding on to the rough stone wall, I staggered over to where she lay. She looked more peaceful than I had ever seen her. Serene. She was still there but too far away for me to reach.

'For a long time, she truly believed she was doing the right thing,' Emma Catherine told me, standing by my side. 'We can tell ourselves the most powerful lies when we're afraid of the truth but no good will come of it. Don't let the same thing happen to you. Live in the truth, Emily.'

I followed her gaze over to Wyn, returned to human form and panting in the wreckage of the pews.

'It's not that I want to lie,' I said, fresh tears dampening my smoke-dry eyes. 'But I'm afraid of what will happen when I tell him the truth.'

Her face was sorrowful but unrepentant. 'Betraying someone to protect them never ends well. You know that already.'

She looked over to the stairs that led out of the chapel and up to the cemetery, all the rubble and fallen marble disappeared. 'You need to go. Bell House will help heal you, both of you. Your friend, Lydia, too. Do you still have the black crystal you found in Colonial Park?'

'Yes,' I nodded, wiping away my tears with the backs of my wrists. 'Is that what made her forget the vision?'

'Arfvedstonite, yes. That's why I gave it to you,' she replied. 'Keep it close, you'll need it again someday soon.'

Every Bell witch that ever was watched on as I helped a dazed Wyn up the staircase, out the chapel. The cemetery was achingly beautiful, refreshed by the king tide that ebbed slowly back to the river, back where it belonged. Even though it was still hours until the dawn, every bird sang its sweetest song, backed by the rhythm of the cicadas, while the butterflies and moths danced in silhouette against a glorious full moon. Every tree and flower and plant was in full bloom. I stood for a moment and let it all sink in. Fire still burned inside me but now it was tempered by the soothing moonlight, light and dark. A balance.

I stumbled back down into the chapel, stooping to pick up my grandmother's pin when it flashed at me from the floor and slipped it back into my pocket. Then I froze. All the damage, the crushed pews, the cracked marble floor, it had all been restored. The herbs on the altar, a bundle of blood-stained silver wire, and the ceremonial dagger lying in the middle of the aisle the only evidence we'd ever been here. There was no other trace of anyone, living or dead, having set foot in this chapel this evening.

390

'Catherine?' I called into the empty space as the candles extinguished themselves one by one. 'Emma?'

My grandmother, and all the ghosts, were gone.

After

Chapter Forty

When the sun rose outside my bedroom, it was just another day. I stared out through the window, people walked their dogs, ran laps around Lafayette Square, went to work. None of them had any idea what had happened in Bonaventure cemetery only a few hours ago and for that, I was grateful.

Despite the sticky summer heat, Wyn shivered under the mountain of blankets Ashley had dug out from the closet and piled on top of my bed. I lifted my gaze to the fireplace and orange and red flames sparked into life to lick at the logs.

'Em?'

The sound of my name on his lips was the sweetest thing I had ever heard. In an instant, I was perched on the edge of the bed, right by his side. He opened his eyes, pupils expanding and contracting until they settled on me. Then he smiled.

'You're here.' His words were dry and raw and when he instinctively rubbed his sore throat, I saw the painful-looking scar on his shoulder. At least it was only a scar now, all but healed.

'I'm here,' I confirmed, reaching for a mug of arnica tea on the nightstand. The nightstand that held the silver pin, the arfvedstonite crystal and my birthday gift, a green-grey marble. 'I promised I would be.'

I held the cooled tea to his lips and watched every muscle relax as he drank. I'd added calendula, feverfew, and yarrow to speed up his recovery. He was going to be just fine, physically at least. This next part wasn't going to be easy for either of us.

'Do you remember any of what happened in the chapel?' I asked. 'Catherine said you wouldn't have any control after you phased but I can't trust anything she said.'

'That's what they told me too but I do remember, all of it.' He pressed his fingers along his shoulder, wincing slightly when he found his scar. 'I knew you. I wasn't completely in control but I was still there. How is that possible?'

'I honestly don't know,' I admitted. 'It shouldn't be that way.'

'Maybe it's just the fact I could never forget you. Wolf or not, you're part of me.'

The invisible connection that tied me to him shone brighter than any razor-sharp silver wire. It bound us tighter, closer than ever, but I knew there was still a chance the truth could slice it clean in two.

'There are some things I have to tell you and I don't know if you're going to feel the same way afterwards,' I said as I handed him the mug, wishing I didn't have to do this.

Wyn closed his eyes, shaking his head in disbelief.

'I think I already know,' he replied. 'Your grandmother told me you killed Cole. She said he was hunting you, so you killed him.'

It would have been so easy to say she was lying. He would have believed me because he wanted to and we could have wrapped a sad but tidy bow around the whole thing. Neither

Cole nor Catherine were here to contradict my version of events. But I couldn't do it. Too many lives had been ruined by lies in this house already.

'It happened on my second night in Savannah,' I began, pressing my palms together, nails bitten all the way down to the quick. 'I didn't know the wolf was a Were, I didn't even know I was a witch. I thought it was a wild animal attacking my grandmother.'

'But Catherine knew,' Wyn guessed.

'She knew *what* he was, even if she didn't know *who* he was.'

My words settled on him and he stared blankly up at the pressed tin ceiling, his features pinched, beautiful chameleon eyes glassy with tears.

'You didn't know,' he said. 'If Cole only saw you after he phased, he would have killed you if you hadn't . . .' He couldn't bring himself to finish the sentence.

'If there was a way for me to change things, I would,' I told him, guilt still eating me up.

'Is there?' The hope in his voice didn't help.

I shook my head. 'No. I can't bring people back when they're gone.'

Wyn moved under the covers, small, exploratory movements, testing each limb to make sure it was still attached and back where it belonged on a human man. He was all in one piece, I'd made sure of it when Ashley and I put him to bed, bandaging the worst injuries, tending to the cuts and scratches with herbal compresses, staying by his side all night to make sure his chest continued to rise and fall.

The logs crackled in the fireplace and he pushed back some of his blankets, the colour returning to his cheeks. Without even turning around to look at it, I extinguished the fire. Wyn's eyebrows lifted and I bit my lip.

'The power your family saw in Savannah,' I said in the softest voice possible, 'it's in me. I didn't think I'd be able to control it but now I know I can. It's nothing to be afraid of, I swear.'

He looked around the room, his eyes moving over everything like he was trying to memorize it for a test and I was terrified he was getting ready to say goodbye.

'You're a witch,' he replied, struggling over the word. 'And I'm a wolf.'

'I'm not just a witch,' I said, determined not to cry. 'Any more than you're just a wolf. Remember what we said? We don't belong to our families, only to ourselves.'

'And to each other.'

His gaze finally settled on me and my heart soared. Even now, with all of the truth laid bare between us, it was still there. The same wonder I saw in his eyes the first time we met. I loved him and he loved me. Nothing had ever been so certain. But I had no idea if it was enough.

'Your hair,' Wyn said, reaching for one scarlet lock. 'It suits you.'

He wound it around his finger the same way he'd touched the moss on the day we met and flames rose inside me again, white, not black, and when he let it fall back against my shoulder, they simmered in my belly.

'You have to go home,' I said, nodding for him when he opened his mouth to protest. 'You need to tell your family what happened. All of it.'

'They won't understand.' His lips pulled tight with frustration. 'My mom, she knew Cole better than most, she might listen, but it's not just her.'

'The rest of the pack will want justice,' I stated, trying not to sound too frightened. 'I guess that's something I'm going to have to figure out.'

'We have to figure it out,' Wyn corrected. 'You're not alone.'

It felt good to hear him say it even if I didn't know what one Were could possibly do to change the minds of an angry pack.

'I'll try to talk to them,' he relented. 'They never were coming here, did you know that? Your grandmother cloaked me, cast some kind of spell that made them think I'd gone to my cousin in Canada.'

Even after all she'd done, just his reference to Catherine made me catch my breath. Despite it all, I missed her. The energy of Bell House was different without her. Once upon a time, maybe before I was born, she had good intentions. They all did, Catherine, my dad, Wyn's parents. But good intentions weren't enough.

'They'll be relieved to have you back,' I said, stroking his hair, trying to memorize the silky softness.

'What happens next?' he asked. 'What do you do?'

'I don't know,' I replied honestly. 'Now there's no one around to make my decisions for me, maybe I'll finally work out what I really want. Work out who I am.'

'I know who you are,' Wyn said, his voice barely rising above a whisper when he took my hand in his, stroking the back of it with his thumb.

The pale pink buds on my wallpaper trembled when I did and their petals began to open and bloom. I paused, pulling back for just a second and they faded back into buds. Then Wyn leaned forward, wrapped his hand around the back of my neck and pressed his mouth to mine, warm and firm and full. The blooms in the wallpaper exploded into full, lush flowers.

'There has to be a way to make this work,' he whispered against my lips as he pulled me even closer. 'The werewolf and the witch.'

'There has to be,' I agreed and a shower of petals fell around us.

Maybe it was OK to lie sometimes, I told myself, sinking back into him and shutting out the world, as long as we only lied to ourselves.

'I'll call you as soon as I'm home,' Wyn said, standing on the porch of Bell House hours later. 'Before I even walk through the door, I'll be on the phone.'

'And I'll be waiting,' I replied, unable to let go of his hand as we walked down the steps, holding on to him all the way out onto the sidewalk. 'I love you.'

There had never been three words so insufficient to express the way two people felt but when he leaned his forehead against mine, I knew he understood.

'And I love you, Emily James.'

Placing one last careful kiss on my lips, Wyn untangled his fingers from mine and climbed into the passenger seat of Jackson's Audi.

'Hey!'

I looked up to the second floor to see Lydia dangling precariously out of Ashley's bedroom window.

'Jackson, can you bring my phone over on your way back?' she yelled. 'It should be charging on my nightstand.'

Lydia was feeling better.

'Lyds, it's a ten-hour round trip to from here to Asheville and you want me to add on a stop to pick up your phone?' her brother shouted back. She frowned as though it was the dumbest question she'd ever heard.

'Yes?'

'You just worry about getting wolfie home,' Ashley said, bounding out onto the sidewalk. 'I'll get her phone. You know, I can leave the house any time I like.'

'Good for you,' Jackson replied, accepting, if not quite under-standing everything that was going on.

'Thanks for this,' I told him, holding myself back from the car. If Wyn touched me again, I'd be in there with them and that wouldn't help anyone. The last thing his pack needed was an unexpected visit from the witch who murdered his brother. 'There's no one else I'd trust to get him home in one piece.'

'Get him home? I'm trying to get rid of him so we can go on that date you promised me,' Jackson joked before elbowing a still-weakened Wyn in the arm. 'You ready to go, man?'

'Not really,' Wyn replied, eyes still locked on mine as Jackson pulled away from the kerb.

He smiled sadly out the window and I watched the car go until I couldn't see it anymore. I sensed them weaving through the streets and out onto the highway and even when the Audi crossed the river, I could feel myself in his thoughts. Every time I flashed through Wyn's mind, there was a pull on the invisible string. One magnet to another. Whatever else happened, we were connected forever. He was my before and my after.

'You doing OK?' Ashley asked, draping her arm over my shoulder when we climbed back up the steps to the front porch.

'Not yet,' I said with a smile as feeble as it might be. 'But I will be.'

'Do you really think he'll come back?'

My feeble smile wavered.

'He did last time.'

She nudged me in the ribs and I winced, sucking the air in through my teeth. I was healing but not all the way healed; my magic was a gift, not a miracle.

'You need to eat. What do you want for breakfast?'

'You don't have to wait on me anymore,' I reminded her.

'You can do whatever you want, go wherever you want. *Meet* whoever you want.'

'Well, what I want right now is breakfast.' She turned around and marched back inside. 'Someone drank a lot of whiskey last night and since she lived to tell the tale, she has a hangover that needs tending to.'

'You're being so cryptic, I can't even begin to think who you're talking about,' I called as I followed her back inside.

We stood side by side, looking around the foyer, both of us searching for what was different. The house felt lighter, brighter, and when I looked up to the forbidden third floor, the constellations twinkled back down. It was mine now, Bell House, and everything that came with it. I breathed in and the sage-green wallpaper shimmered on my exhale, settling down to a soft, warm pink.

'Beats hiring decorators,' Ashley commented as the rest of the house settled itself into new shades, a fresh start. At the end of the hallway, the door to Catherine's craft door clicked open.

'Emily,' she said quietly. 'Where do you think she went?'

I glanced over at my aunt and she looked back at me, gnawing on her lower lip. She seemed so much younger than she had the day before and looked so much like my dad, I felt my heart ache and swell at the same time.

'I wish I knew. She was there when I carried Wyn out and when I went back she was gone.'

'And the chapel sealed itself back up?'

'Like we'd never stepped inside.'

She ran her hand lightly over the polished wood of the banister and let out a conflicted sigh.

'It's going to be strange around here without her. Especially when you leave.'

'Leave?' I reached for my mother's locket as I spoke, very confused. 'Why would I leave?'

'I figured you'd want to get as far away from here as possible,' Ashley said as I closed the front door on the busy morning outside and basked in the fresh, hopeful energy all around us. 'Go back home?'

'But I am home,' I replied, my gaze sweeping around Bell House. My house. 'And there has always been an Emma Catherine Bell in Savannah.'

Acknowledgements

Truly, this list should be longer than the book itself but in the interest of getting on with the sequel, I'll try to keep it brief. As ever, Rowan Lawton; agent, cheerleader and champion, thank you for your support, guidance and for raising a fine young Swiftie. Thank you to Eleanor Lawlor and all at The Soho Agency for humouring me so beautifully for all these years.

Without Natasha Bardon, this book would still be rattling around in my head, where it's been since 2009, so thank you for cracking it open and scooping it out (so to speak). You're an inspiration. Thanks to Kate Fogg for your patience and kindness and expertise, I owe you several drinks, if not the soul of my firstborn child. Thank you to Chloe Gough, Aje Roberts, and everyone else at Magpie who had their mitts on this, I appreciate you so much. As ever, to all the people who make the words into a book – design, production, sales, marketing, audio, warehouse – none of this could happen without you (as you know) and I'm beyond grateful.

I'm not sure I've ever experienced love at first sight with a cover quite like this, thank you to Teagan White, I could not adore it more.

Massive thanks to Kimberley Atkins for making this a better book, and to Kimberley Young, for all your support, and also breakfast.

I would like to thank everyone in Savannah who contributed to this story, knowingly or otherwise, with special mentions to Bellwether House, The Hamilton-Turner Inn and Marshall House for their hospitality and only being slightly haunted. Sistah Patt Gunn and Sistah Roz Rouse, Gullah Geechee truth-tellers and living legends, thank you for sharing the realities of Savannah's past with me and for the best hugs in the world. All the tour guides from the Davenport House, the Owens-Thomas House, and the Mercer-Williams House, Bonaventure Cemetery, as well as every trolley tour guide who answered one of my thousands of questions. Huge thanks to Meghan Basford (@meghanlynncontent) for her inspirational southern insults – follow her immediately. While it feels as though I did endless research for this book, any and all errors are inevitably my own. Just like Emily, I might love Savannah but getting everything right would've been easier if I'd grown up there.

Finally, endless gratitude to my husband, Jeff, and my southern family, who answered (yet more) questions about life in the south, corrected my isn'ts to ain'ts, and taught me how to make the best biscuits in all the land. Special shout out to Cole & Lydia, who inspired me with their names, as well as their generosity, kindness and a super cool great-nephew. I love y'all.